# HER DEAD BOYFRIEND

BY C. FITTON

*First published in South Africa by Kingsley Publishers, 2024*


*Kingsley Publishers*
*Pretoria,*
*South Africa*

*www.kingsleypublishers.com*

*A catalogue copy of this book will be available from the National Library of South Africa*

*Paperback ISBN: 978-1-7764468-2-7*
*eBook ISBN: 978-1-7764468-1-0*

For Karen and Jack

# *Prologue*

*Gripping the countertop with her fingertips, she pulled herself up to a standing position. Her heartbeat hammered her head like a fist; her breathing ragged. If only it was a dream – a horrible nightmare, but a dream all the same – and she could make it disappear by simply opening her eyes. She would wake up, and it would all be over.*

*But there would be no easy escape. A cold sweat prickled her skin, trickled down her back, and pooled at the base of her spine. The room tilted. Reaching out a shaking hand to steady herself, she stained the surface of the milky-white marble countertop with a bloody palm print. Her throat constricted; she was drowning under icy water. She heard a strangled cry. It seemed to come from somewhere far away. But when the same voice began to mewl like a baby, she realized, with a start, that it was coming from inside of her. Her knees buckled. The walls closed in. Her vision narrowed to a pinhole. She saw flashes of light and her world went black.*

# Chapter 1

A dull light leaked in through the purple-paned window in the foyer. It cast a sickly hue, making my hand blotchy and blue like a corpse. A year had passed since the accident, but I still clutched the doorknob with trembling fingers each time I ventured outside the walls of my Beacon Hill Brownstone. Calming my nerves with a deep breath, I turned the knob and yanked open the solid oak door. Dark-gray clouds cloaked the sky, so I pulled on a khaki rain jacket and cinched down the hood. Walking outside, I locked the door and descended the steps. Magnolia and lilac blossoms perfumed the chilly, spring air, but the thick canopy of trees spawned eerie shadows on the narrow, cobblestone lane.

I walked the few short blocks to *Jacked Up Coffee*, but when I reached the hip, industrial café, I hesitated outside. I adored my best friend, but if I detected even a hint of pity in her eyes, it would be unbearable. It had started to drizzle, and cars whizzed by on the busy street, splashing me with water, from the puddles formed. I knew that the ever-punctual Fiona Fraser would be waiting for me inside, so I drew a deep breath and wrenched open the heavy glass door.

The tin ceiling, exposed light bulbs and hardwood floors created an edgy, yet warm atmosphere inside the café. I scanned the crowded space until I spotted Fiona's familiar blond bob. Pasting on a smile, I weaved my way through the maze of rustic tables and the sea of heads, bowed over laptops and cell phone screens.

Fiona was radiant and pretty in florals and pinks. “I’m so glad you came,” she said, jumping up and throwing her arms around me. “You’ve been such a recluse, since—” She cut herself off, touching her golden hoop earrings.

Since the accident, she meant to say. Visions of blood and broken glass flooded my brain and a vice-like pain gripped my head. Pulling away from Fiona, I pressed my fingertips to my temples.

Fiona fixed her concerned cornflower-blue eyes on me.

“You’re as white as a ghost! Why don’t you sit down, and I’ll get you a glass of water?”

“No, I’m fine.” I glanced down at the foamy heart shape poured on Fiona’s latte. “I just need my caffeine fix.”

I walked up to the marble counter and placed my order. A row of freshly baked pastries caught my eye, but I forced myself to look away. Months spent alone at home with nothing to do, but grieve, meant that I’d put on a few pounds. But the sweet scent wafting in the air had weakened my resolve.

“An Americano, and one of those, please,” I said, pointing at a pinwheel-shaped cinnamon bun, smothered in cream cheese icing.

The barista ground some beans, then knocked the portafilter to even out the fresh grinds. Steam hissed from the machine; the noise rattled my nerves. I took deep breaths in and out. If I couldn’t even make it through a simple coffee date with my best friend, how would I survive an entire day at work?

My manager, Dave, at *Pemberley’s* – a popular independent bookstore – had called a week ago and asked if I was ready to come back. He said the bookstore was busy and was short-staffed; furthermore, my colleagues missed me. At first, I’d been reluctant. But when he suggested that I try a part-time schedule to start off with, I’d agreed. I was due to start tomorrow, but standing here in the coffee shop with my temples throbbing, I doubted my decision. Maybe I still wasn’t ready…

The barista placed my order on the counter, and I walked back to the table. I hung my damp jacket on the back of the wooden chair, then sat down.

“That looks yummy,” Fiona said, eyeing the sugary pastry.

“Please help yourself.” She broke off a small piece and had a tiny nibble. I peeled off a doughy layer, stuffed it into my mouth and swallowed.

A comforting warmness filled my belly. Ever since the accident, I had felt empty inside. I knew that filling my stomach was only a temporary alleviation, but it was better than nothing.

Fiona sipped some of her soy milk latte and peered at me over the rim of her cup.

"Tell me the truth. How're you doing?"

"I'm surviving."

I scooped a pill bottle out of my purse and shook a green-and-white capsule into my palm.

Fiona cocked an eyebrow. "You're still taking those?"

I nodded, popped the antidepressant in my mouth, and swallowed it with coffee.

"Just be careful." She narrowed her eyes into slits. "You don't want to become addicted."

I knew she meant well, but Fiona had no idea what it was like to be in my shoes. Shoving a piece of bun in my mouth, I almost gagged on its sickly sweetness. Then I slurped some coffee and wiped my lips using the back of my hand.

"You spilt." Fiona pointed a neatly manicured fingernail at my chest.

I looked down and brushed the crumbs off my black T-shirt.

"Have you done any writing lately?" Fiona handed me a napkin. "You don't want to let all that talent go to waste."

I shook my head. "No, I haven't felt much like writing…"

"That's too bad." Fiona pursed her lips with raised eyebrows.

I bristled. There it was—the pitying look that I'd been dreading.

"You know, Sean would want you to move on with your life."

A sliver of resentment slid under my skin. *How would Fiona know what Sean would want*?

A silence fell between us.

Finally, Fiona leaned towards me. "What about your job at the bookstore?"

"My boss called me," I said, "and I agreed to go back part-time."

"That's great news. You've been holed up all alone in your house for way too long."

I glanced over at two young girls at a neighboring table, studying their cell phones and gossiping and giggling. *Would I ever feel that carefree again?*

"How's school going?" I asked. "You must be counting the days until the summer break."

Fiona sat up in her seat. "You'll never believe what happened. One of my students brought his pet rat to class in a Tupperware® container. They were writing a test, so the room was quiet, but I could hear a strange sound. Turns out, it had gnawed a big hole through the lid." She laughed. "I told him to take the rat home, but I found out later, he just put it in his locker."

"Unbelievable." I mirrored her laugh. "By the way, how was that art show last week?"

Fiona sat up and a grin unfurled on her face. "Actually, I've been dying to tell you what happened."

"I'm all ears."

Fiona sucked in her lips. Pink circles appeared on her cheeks.

"Don't keep me in suspense." I shifted in the hardbacked wooden seat.

Fiona hesitated a moment, then placed her palms on the table. "I met someone."

A gnawing began tearing at my insides. I dropped my eyes, then tore off a piece of bun and pushed it around my plate.

"You look upset…"

"Not at all." I conjured up a smile. "I want to hear all about him."

"Well, if you're sure… His name is Mark and he came up and asked me what I thought of one of his favorite abstract paintings."

"What did you say?" I prompted her, pushing the sliver of envy to the back of my brain.

"I told him I didn't get it. He said that was the whole point, that it was supposed to spark my imagination. I said it looked like blood spatter from a crime scene—" Fiona clapped a hand over her mouth. Her cheeks reddened and the blush spread down to her throat. "Sorry, I'm an idiot."

"It's okay. I'm not going to fall apart every time someone mentions the word *blood*." I mustered a smile. "But you've just reminded me… the medical examiner finally finished her report on Sean's death."

"Oh my God." Fiona's face fell. "Did you see it? What did it say?"

"According to the ME, he died from a traumatic brain injury, when his head hit the windshield." A lump formed in my throat.

"Did the police ever figure out what made him swerve off the road?"

A nerve twitched in my temple. "They said there's no way of knowing for sure…"

"And you still can't remember what happened?"

I shook my head. "My memory's a gaping black hole."

"Why on earth wasn't he wearing a seatbelt?"

We locked eyes.

*Why was Fiona asking so many questions? Sean was my dead boyfriend, not hers.*

I swallowed another mouthful of coffee. "Why don't you tell me more about Mark?"

"Are you sure you're okay with me talking about this?" She knitted her brow. "I don't want to upset you."

"Why would it upset me?" I hunched my shoulders and stared past Fiona, at the distressed brick wall of the café. "You don't need to tiptoe around me. That just makes me feel worse." I forced the corners of my mouth in an upward direction. "So, tell me. Did Mark ask for your phone number?"

"Yes, he did. And, after an hour of drinking and flirting, I gave it to him." She beamed at me from across the table, almost levitating off her seat. "And he sent me a text the next morning!"

"That was quick. What did he say?" I twisted a lock of hair around my finger.

"He asked me out for dinner Friday night, to that five-star seafood restaurant on the waterfront. I'm counting the minutes until the weekend." Her voice crackled with excitement.

Sean and I had eaten a lobster dinner at that very same restaurant the night of the accident. My eyes thrust shut and an image of him appeared in my mind. He'd looked like a little boy, with that white plastic bib tied loosely around his neck and butter dripping down his chin. Tears pressed behind my eyelids.

"I *really* like him."

Fiona's voice jarred me out of my reverie.

"I'm so happy for you." I pressed my fingernails to my palms. "What does he do for work?"

"Mark's an emergency physician at *City Center Hospital*." Fiona twirled one of her hoop earrings. "*Doctor* Mark Rankin. Can you believe it?"

A pin pricked my heart. "What does he look like? Is he cute?"

"He's gorgeous. Tall, with dark hair, and perfect teeth. Oh, I almost forgot. We took a selfie." Fiona scrolled through her phone, then thrust the screen in my face. "Isn't he just to die for?"

I leaned forward and my breath hitched. The steel-blue eyes. The dark hair. The strong, chiseled chin. A shiver shot down my spine, as my eyes fixed on the screen.

Doctor Mark Rankin was a dead ringer for Sean—my dead boyfriend!

# Chapter 2

After the coffee date, I headed straight home. Once I was inside the house, I hung up my wet jacket, then flopped down onto the floor and my pug dog, Keeper, scrambled onto my lap. Her cocoa-brown eyes stared up at me from a wrinkled, black face. All the tension that had built up during my coffee date melted away. I scratched Keeper behind the ears, then rubbed her silky-soft belly.

"You always make me feel better, Keeps."

Mark's resemblance to Sean was probably just a trick of my grief-stricken imagination. Shoulders hunched, I let go of a long breath. I gave Keeper a final pat, then stood up, and waltzed straight to the kitchen. Whipping open the freezer, I grabbed a tub of caramel ice cream. But the cinnamon bun still sat in my stomach, making me feel full to the brim, so I shoved the container back in the freezer. The gloomy weather had chilled me to the bone, so I plopped a bag of chamomile tea into a cup and switched on the kettle.

Moving to the living room, I melted deeply into my wingback chair and placed the steaming, hot tea onto the coffee table. I brought the reading lamp to life with a switch and its golden glow illuminated the built-in bookshelves on either side of the wood-burning fireplace. After sipping a few mouthfuls of soothing herbal tea, another long breath of air seeped out of me. Listening to Fiona drone on indefinitely about her teaching career and this new guy she'd met, was the same as a hundred tiny paper cuts to my heart. Keeper nuzzled her flat, button nose against my shin. Bending and reaching down to touch her fur, I said out loud, "What do you think I should do, little one?"

Fiona's admonishing words replayed in my mind. *"Done any writing lately? You don't want to let all that talent go to waste."*

I placed the teacup on the table and took my laptop off the coffee table. But instead of searching websites for creative writing programs, I opened *Netflix*. A medical drama flashed on the screen, and Fiona's voice echoed in my mind, again: *"Mark's an emergency physician... Doctor Mark Rankin. Can you believe it?"* Jealousy coiled deep inside me, like a dangerous and venomous snake.

Exiting *Netflix*, I googled Mark's name, then clicking and selecting the images a dozen photos of Mark appeared like a movie on the screen. There he was – Doctor Mark Rankin – clothed in a white lab coat and a stethoscope snaked around his neck. Sporting a pin-striped suit, Mark was at a charity event to help the community. Mark in a red polo shirt, playing golf. Him in a tux at an opera. Mark hiking, sailing, fishing. I zoomed in, enlarging one of the pixilated images and leaned closer to the screen.

Then, I slammed the laptop shut and traipsed back to the kitchen. With a tight-fisted grip, while my mind twisted like a tornado, I gave into the comfort, dug in to ice cream and stuffed my gaping mouth.

# Chapter 3

As I walked to work the next morning, I stuffed away all thoughts of Dr. Mark Rankin. I focused on the pink, purple and white blossoms on the trees lining my route through the residential streets. I strode through the open glass doors of *Pemberley's Bookstore,* determined to make a fresh start with my life.

The store manager, Dave Perkins, was waiting for me just inside the entrance.

"It's great to have you back with us," he said, giving me a tight hug that lasted a few seconds too long.

"It's wonderful to be back at work."

"I know I said you could start part-time," he said, releasing me from his grasp, "but I really need you back full-time."

"Not yet," I shook my head. "I'm still coping with my boyfriend's death…"

"But that was a year ago."

I flinched.

"Don't you think it's time you moved on with your life?"

Did he think grief was like a dripping tap that I could simply turn off at will? But before I could respond, Dave had already shifted his attention to a young female employee who was standing on the top step of a spindly rolling ladder. She was dusting the upper shelf of the Regency-style, floor-to-ceiling, wooden bookcases. Now, Dave stood directly below her, peering up her skirt.

The young woman glanced down and caught Dave ogling her. Her face turned beet-red and she swayed on the ladder.

"Careful." I rushed over, gripping the rails to help steady her descent.

"Better get back to my office." Dave slinked away.

The young woman dismounted the last step. "Guess it wasn't the smartest idea to climb up a ladder when I'm wearing a skirt."

"Don't blame yourself." My eyebrows raised. "But watch out for Dave. He can be a bit of a sleazeball. I'm Erin, by the way."

"My name's Suzy, and thanks for the warning." Her cheeks were still flushed a beet-red.

"We, women, have to watch each other's backs," I said, shining a smile at her.

Later, on my afternoon coffee break, I headed to a café down the street with Maddie Bain, another co-worker at the bookstore. She had spikey, black hair and a green snake tattoo that curled around her wrist.

"*'I have measured out my life with coffee spoons,'*" I said, after we had placed our orders.

"I love TS Eliot," Maddie said, beaming at me. "Do you write any poetry yourself?"

The barista pressed the fresh grounds with proficiency into the portafilter.

"No, not poetry. But it's my dream to write a novel one day."

"That's amazing. I'd buy it." Maddie's eyes glowed. "And I'd come to all your readings."

"First, I need an idea. And then, the hardest part of all, I actually have to start writing," I groaned. "Ever since I won a writing prize at college, my mother's convinced I'm going to be the next Harper Lee."

"Wait. What?" Maddie's eyes widened. "You won a writing prize?"

"It wasn't the Pulitzer or anything." I laughed over the hiss of steaming milk and the gurgle of brewing coffee.

"Did you ever think about grad school?"

"I don't see the point in a second degree. What did the first one get me?"

"A job at *Pemberley's Bookstore.*" Maddie grinned, then checked the time on her phone. "Our break's almost over."

"Dave won't even notice we're gone. He's too busy stalking Suzy."

"Two coffees for Erin and Maddie," the barista called out our names over the din. "And one *pain au chocolat.*"

"My treat. To celebrate your first day back."

I started to protest, but Maddie had already handed over the money.

"You shouldn't have, but thanks." I gave her a quick hug.

We took our coffees and my pastry, then made our way through the crowded space, to the milk and sugar station.

"Speaking of Suzy and Dave," Maddie said, stirring milk and sugar into her coffee. "Guess what happened?"

I cocked an eyebrow.

"Suzy told me that he summoned her to his office and tried to kiss her."

"What?" I gasped. "Are you sure?"

"Yep. Gross, eh?" Her finger traveled into her open mouth as she pretended to gag.

"He's got to be at least twice her age."

"What a creep." I grimaced, then placed a plastic lid on my coffee. I'd only been back for one day and the drama had already started. At least it would keep my mind off myself. I took a big bite of my pastry: A dopamine fix for my first day back at work.

We walked back to the bookstore, but I paused outside the front door. I turned to face Maddie and said, "I want to share something with you. Dave had a bad habit of brushing up against me, when I first started working at *Pemberley's*."

"Since we're swapping stories," Maddie said, her face suddenly dead serious. "He used to pinch my ass whenever I walked past him in the stock room."

My eyes widened.

"I'd file a report with the police, but it would be my word against his and guess who they'd believe."

But all I heard was—*the police.*

A cracked windshield and Sean's blood-soaked skull flashed in my brain.

# Chapter 4

On Wednesday evening, I headed to my weekly appointment with the therapist. She was actually a psychiatrist, but I thought 'therapist' sounded less clinical. The office was in a nondescript, red brick building south of Boston Common, and I convulsed with anxious emotions gripping me by the throat, every time I entered the claustrophobic room with its cold, white walls.

Dr. Pritchard sat behind a glass-topped desk, a row of framed diplomas hung on the wall behind her head. She had nut-brown hair pulled back in a tight ponytail, and a string of pearls made themselves visible from the collar of her crisp, cream-colored shirt.

"How are you feeling today, Erin?" she asked, her voice chilly and flat-lined.

I melted down into the plump, beige armchair.

"Still having trouble sleeping?" The doctor's eyebrows arched.

I nodded.

"Have you tried yoga, like I suggested?"

"Yes," I lied. "But I'm still having the same nightmare."

The doctor scribbled some notes. "About the accident?"

"Yes and no." I ran my hands through my hair. My fingers snagged; I'd forgotten to brush my hair.

Dr. Pritchard swiveled her chair in my direction. "Why don't you describe it to me?"

"I see Sean lying in a coffin." I clutched the arms of the chair, with a white-knuckled grip. "All alone, buried under the earth."

Dr. Pritchard dropped her chin, as a signal for me to continue.

A splinter of sunlight snuck in through the window, casting a shadow on the wall.

"Sometimes, I'm the one in the box. It's pitch black, and I feel like I'm suffocating. Then I scream and wake up."

The doctor wrote on her notepad, then looked at me. "Why do you think you're having these dreams?"

I chewed on the corner of my lower lip. "I'm not sure. Maybe because I feel guilty…"

"What have you got to feel guilty about? The accident wasn't your fault. Unless you have survivor's guilt…"

A heavy weight of darkness pressed down on my shoulders, and I lapsed into silence.

Dr. Pritchard tapped her pen in a tempo creating a sound that emanated from her desk.

"You may be experiencing hallucinations, a side effect from the Prozac I prescribed for the depression. Maybe it's time I reduced the dosage."

I nodded. "So the pills might be causing my nightmares?"

She scribbled more notes on her pad. "It's a possibility. But recurrent distressing dreams are also a symptom of post-traumatic stress disorder."

I twisted my hands in my lap. "Is there something wrong with me? Why can't I get over it?"

"Each person's experience of trauma and grief is unique and unpredictable. There's no right or wrong way, and it's going to take time to create a new 'normal' for yourself. You need to have more self-compassion. As far as your sleep issues go, there is something we could try… but it's not for everyone."

"What is it?"

"Hypnosis. It helps some people, but only if you're open to it."

I pictured the doctor dangling a gold pocket watch from left to right in front of my eyes and a shiver made its way down my spine.

Silence stretched a distance between us.

"Would you like to give it a try?" The doctor gazed at me, with a curious, close-lipped smile.

I leaned forward. "Maybe… Would it help me remember more about the accident? My memory of the crash is a big blur."

"You might be a good candidate for hypnosis. We could give it a try. You have what's called 'functional amnesia'. When you suffer a psychological trauma, like the sudden loss of a loved one, it can cause a temporary memory loss. It's like your mind is hiding the memory, until you're ready to find it again. It's just a matter of letting go of your fear and letting your mind relax."

"I keep replaying the moments after the accident in my mind. There was blood and shattered glass everywhere. The paramedics laid Sean down onto the ground and performed CPR, but it was useless. He was gone." I picked up a small, decorative pillow and clutched it in front of my chest as if it were a baby's security blanket.

"It's common to look backwards after a loss, but try to carry more positive memories with you into the future. Why don't you tell me more about Sean and a happy time you shared together?"

"One of my favorite memories was skating on the frog pond last winter. Sean and I skated in circles, holding hands and talking about our hopes for the future. Marriage. Children." My lips quivered and my voice cracked. "Afterwards, we snuggled on a bench in the moonlight, drinking hot chocolates from the snack bar. It was extremely romantic."

The doctor's eyes crinkled and wrinkled at the corners. "That sounds lovely, Erin. And how did Sean make you feel?"

"He made me feel safe. After my father died two years ago, feeling safe was hard for me. But when Sean held me in his arms, I felt like nothing could hurt me."

She smiled and sat tight for me to speak again.

"And he made me feel like the most interesting and important woman in the world. He made me feel like I could achieve anything I wanted to, and he was always encouraging me to work on my writing. Sean really believed in me." I let out a long, deep sigh. "I know it's cliché to say this, but I feel like I've had the rug pulled out from under me. I'm stuck in limbo, as if I'm floating above the earth and looking down on everyone else, as they carry on with their lives."

"What you're feeling is a normal symptom of grief. Shock. Numbness. Disbelief. Friends can help you to feel more grounded. Go to yoga. Coffee dates. The movies. It's important not to isolate yourself, as tempting as that may be." The doctor glanced over at the clock on her desk. "I'm afraid our time is up for today. I'll see you next week and we'll give the hypnosis a try. Meanwhile, I'm going to reduce the dosage of the pills and you can let me know how you feel next time."

I conjured up a smile, but panic pulsed my insides like hot blood flowing inside me. *Reduce the dosage of my pills? Was I really ready for that?* And while part of me was intrigued by the idea of hypnosis, another part of me was terrified of what dark secrets might surface while I was under the doctor's spell.

# Chapter 5

Keeper was licking my face like it was covered in peanut butter.

"Okay, okay. I'll get up," I groaned and heaved myself out of bed the next morning. The nightmares about Sean had gotten even worse. Last night, I'd dreamt that he was standing in a nebulous corner of my bedroom and staring at me with coal-black eyes. He wanted to tell me something, but before he could, I woke up.

After dealing with Keeper's needs, I had a quick shower. As I brushed out the knots in my hair, I was appalled by the pair of bloodshot eyes staring back at me from the fogged-up mirror. I swallowed a painkiller, then threw on sweatpants and an old T-shirt, my Saturday morning comfort clothes.

I made myself a cup of peppermint tea, then settled in the wingback chair in the living room. My eyes traveled along the built-in bookshelves and my heart sank into my guts. My love of reading was another thing that had died with Sean. The thought of reading a book seemed like too much effort. I took a few sips of the soothing tea and let out a long, deep sigh.

My phone buzzed. I put down my tea and picked up the phone.

It was Fiona. "Hey. It's me. How are you feeling today?"

"Not bad. I'm just sitting here sipping a cup of tea." I didn't feel like talking about Sean and the nightmares. I'd save that for my next therapy session.

"It was so good to see you finally venturing out of your house. I'm proud of you. Maybe next time we can invite Paige and go for a drink."

"That sounds like fun. I haven't seen Paige or her kids in ages. You're a good friend, Fiona. I don't know how I would've gotten through this past year without you."

"That's what friends are for. You'd do the same for me if our circumstances were reversed."

"Enough about me. I'd much rather hear how your date went with the handsome doctor."

"Are you sure it won't upset you?" Her voice sounded concerned. "I'd understand if it did."

"No, it will help me get my mind off myself. I want to hear all about it." I forced excitement into my voice, then sank back in my chair.

"Well, if you're sure…"

"I'm sure. Honestly. Go ahead. Tell me everything." I took a sip of tea, to fortify myself.

"First of all, he's a real gentleman. He opened doors for me and pulled out my chair. I know you're a feminist and prefer to open your own doors."

"No, that sounds really nice." A throbbing, terrible ache stabbed my ribs.

"I can't remember if I mentioned it before, but Mark is a doctor."

"Yes, you did mention it. He must've had some interesting stories to tell."

"Yes, he did. You won't believe how hard he works. The emergency department sounds like the busiest place in the hospital. I don't know how he does it. All the blood and broken bones and people dying—" She gasped. "Oh my God. I can't believe I said that. I'm so sorry. What was I thinking?"

"It's okay. Don't worry about it." I took a long sip of tea to settle the roiling sea in my stomach. "Tell me more about Mark."

"He's also a really good listener and couldn't get enough of my stories about school. He loved the one about the boys planting the stink bomb in the girls' washroom. Wait 'til I tell you what happened."

I had heard the anecdote before, but listened patiently, as Fiona recounted how everything had happened.

"Mark thought it was hilarious." Fiona paused to catch her breath.

"When do you think you'll see him again?"

"Mark's having a party next weekend at his loft. I'd invite you, but I know you're not ready for bigger social events."

"Well, actually, I might—"

"Oh. Speak of the devil. Mark's calling me. Do you mind if I let you go?"

"Of course not. Talk soon."

Tossing my phone on the coffee table, I headed straight for the kitchen and scarfed handfuls of dry cereal in pursuit of filling my emotional hunger. Then, I strode straight to the bathroom and swallowed two pills.

# Chapter 6

I stood and stared at the gunmetal-gray door, handcuffed and taken prisoner by fear. The last party I'd been to was Sean's wake, almost a year ago. A cacophony of loud music and voices vibrated through the door. My nerves jangled. I turned to leave, when the steel door swung open.

"Erin! What are you doing here?" It was Fiona.

"I thought I'd surprise you."

"You sure did." She blinked at me.

A beat of time passed. Suddenly, the soft, melodic sound of a bell echoed through the corridor, signaling the arrival of the elevator…

"Aren't you going to ask me in?"

"Sorry. Yes, of course. I just can't believe you came. How did you find Mark's address?"

"I googled it, of course." She released me, and my eyes darted around, and my lips trembled as I forced a smile. "I want to meet your dreamy doctor."

"You have no idea how much this means to me." Her eyes lit up like fireworks, and she bounced on the balls of her feet with excitement. "Come on. I can't wait for you to meet him."

As her fingers intertwined with mine, she pulled me with a gentle yet determined force through the threshold, into a mysterious realm concealed by the shadows. The hallway stretched ahead, seemingly endless, its darkness enveloping us like a secret shared between lovers. A faint, flickering glow beckoned from a console table in the foyer, where a solitary tea-light bravely illuminated the gloom. Its delicate flame danced with a soft warmth, casting ethereal shadows that whispered secrets of their own. Feeling a mix of anticipation and trepidation, I held tightly onto the heart-shaped locket adorning my neck. It was a precious memento, a symbol of affection from Sean on Valentine's Day, its weight a reminder of love that once bloomed.

A tall figure strode towards us, but the air felt heavy and oppressive, as if the darkness itself was weighing down on me and his face was hidden in shadows.

"Here comes Mark." Her touch was gentle but firm, like a silent message of support. "I hope you like him."

"I'm sure I will."

The air seemed to crackle with tension as he stepped into the room, his presence filling every corner.

My breath hitched in my throat.

"Mark, this is my best friend, Erin Fitzpatrick," Fiona said, her face beaming.

"So, you're the famous Erin," Mark said, greeting me with a warm hug. "So glad you could come." The denim of his jeans was distressed, the white cotton crew neck T-shirt crisp and classic. The navy-blue blazer was trim and tailored, the pin-stripes adding a touch of sophistication to his casual outfit. "Fiona didn't mention that you're a redhead. A genetic rarity."

"Erin? Are you okay?" she asked, as a crease appeared between her eyebrows, her lips pursing together in a tight line. Her gaze flicked away for a moment, as if she was considering something before returning to me with a frown. "You look like you've seen a ghost."

"I'm fine."

"Welcome to my humble abode." Mark made a sweeping gesture and grinned. His teeth were a perfect row of tiny, ivory piano keys. His voice was strong and deep. *Just like—*

"Is that bottle for me?" His eyes were like a stormy sea, dark and turbulent, yet full of a fierce intensity that left me breathless. I felt as if I was being swept away by them, lost in their depths.

"What?" My face felt like it was on fire, the blood rushing to my cheeks in a hot, prickly wave. I could feel my pulse pounding in my temples, my eyes wide with shock. "Oh, yes." I handed him the bottle of wine that I'd brought and mentally shook myself. Maybe that extra Prozac pill I'd popped just before I left was playing tricks with my mind.

"A pinot noir from Central Otago. My favorite. My brother and I traveled to New Zealand last summer. Would you like a glass?"

My head moved up and down in a quick, jerky motion, indicating my agreement. I could feel my pulse quickening, my breath coming in short gasps.

Fiona seized my arm and guided me into the loft. My eyes took in the wide, open space of his penthouse, with its sleek steel and glass furniture. The walls were covered with large, abstract paintings.

"Erin? What do you think of Mark? Isn't he gorgeous?"

The steel-blue eyes. The dark hair. The strong, chiseled chin. "He's definitely a very good-looking man. In fact, he reminds me—"

"Shh. He's coming back." In one swift motion, Fiona swiveled around, her eyes darting around the room. I could feel the energy in the air shift, the atmosphere charged with tension.

Mark handed me a huge glass of wine. His fingers brushed mine, and I felt a spark of electricity. *Had he felt it too?*

"So Erin, tell me a little about yourself."

"I work at an independent bookstore called *Pemberley's*," I replied, taking a gulp of wine.

"But it's only temporary, until she writes a best-selling novel." Fiona's eye closed in a quick, playful wink, her expression teasing.

"***Fiona.***" I glared daggers at her.

"Erin won a prestigious writing prize in college," she said, ignoring my obvious embarrassment.

"It was nothing." I could feel the heat rising in my face, my skin prickling with embarrassment. My cheeks felt hot to the touch, as if they were on fire. "Fiona's exaggerating."

"A writer, eh?" Mark fixed me with another penetrating glance. "No wonder you seem so mysterious. You know what they say? Still waters run deep."

"Mark's cousin has just published a book." In a smooth motion, Fiona sidled up to him, her arm slipping through his. "Got a great review in *The New York Times*. Maybe he could introduce you two."

Mark's eyes cast a spell on me. "Tell me, Erin. What kind of book are you going to write? Wait. Let me guess. With those intelligent green eyes, I'd say historical fiction."

I shook my head, "A psychological thriller."

"Hmm, a thriller." Mark's eyes crinkled at the corners, a playful glint in his gaze.

I could feel my heart skip a beat, my cheeks warming with pleasure.

"I guess you're not as innocent as you look. Let me know when you get published. I'll buy a dozen copies."

My face blistered and burned under his attentive gaze.

"Erin, come with me." Fiona snatched my elbow. "There's someone else I want you to meet. He's here somewhere. Actually, I think I saw him out on the balcony. Let's go and look for him. You can check out the view of the waterfront." Fiona led me towards the sliding glass door, maintaining a firm grip on my arm.

The balcony was crowded with people, on the balmy spring night. It was a wide, L-shaped terrace, with a massive barbeque, some leafy planters, and a couple of chaise-lounges.

Fiona pulled me towards the railing. "Come and look at the incredible view."

My head was swimming with thoughts of Mark. Leaning against the glass barrier, I stared out at the night sky. The air was so thick and black, I could almost reach out and touch it.

Fiona's voice cut through the darkness. "Don't lean over too far. It's a long drop."

# Chapter 7

"Hello ladies. It's a beautiful night, isn't it?"

"Oh, just the man I was looking for. Erin, this is Oliver—Mark's brother."

"Pleased to meet you, Erin," Oliver said, sticking out his hand.

I turned my head slowly, my eyes scanning his features with curiosity. He looked like his brother – not as tall as Mark and a bit stockier – with light, brown hair and almond-shaped eyes. I could feel my mind racing, trying to piece together the similarities and differences between the two brothers.

"Erin?" Fiona whispered, directing my attention to Oliver's outstretched hand.

"Oh, sorry. It's nice to meet you, Oliver."

"Well, I'll leave you two alone," said Fiona, gleefully.

I gave her a panicked look and clutched at her elbow.

"You stay out here with his brother. Ask him about their trip to New Zealand." Fiona was in teacher-mode, barking out orders. "I have to go and help Mark."

I watched her rush away, then turned to face Oliver and forced my lips into a smile. "Mark mentioned you were in New Zealand last summer. Did you try bungee jumping?"

"Mark did. Flinging myself off a bridge and bouncing up and down on a giant elastic band didn't really appeal to me," he said as he twisted his mouth into a lopsided grin, his eyes crinkling with amusement.

I laughed and drank some wine. "Doesn't appeal to me either. Did you visit any vineyards?"

"Yes. My favorite was Amisfield Winery in Queenstown. It looks out at the Remarkables Mountains. Don't you just love that name?"

"It's quite… remarkable." I let out a burst of laughter, my body shaking with mirth.

Oliver's lips turned upwards. "I still remember the shank of lamb I ate there. The country has more sheep than people, by the way." His smile widened into a large grin.

"Where else have you and Mark been?"

"We traveled around Scotland a few years back and went to some whiskey distilleries."

"Whiskey? I tried it once and thought my throat was on fire. I couldn't stop coughing. It tasted like jet fuel."

"Mark likes it, but I'm with you. I'll leave whiskey to the men in kilts."

With a subtle movement, I covered my mouth with my hand, trying to stifle my giggles. My head was spinning, my vision blurring at the edges.

An awkward silence fell between us.

I stared out into the night sky, analyzing everything that Mark had said and done so far that evening. He was considerate. And friendly. Even self-deprecating. Fiona was lucky.

"Erin? Are you all right?"

"I'm sorry. Did you say something?" I asked, startled out of my trance.

With a subtle movement, Oliver cocked his head to the side, his eyes narrowing in puzzlement.

"If you could travel anywhere in the world, where would you go?"

I crossed my arms. "Hmm. That's a difficult question. It's hard to narrow it down to just one country, but I've always been intrigued by the Arctic. I think it'd be exciting to see a big iceberg, like the one that sank the Titanic."

"The Titanic hit one that was floating down from Greenland to the south coast of Newfoundland. Most of Greenland is covered by a thick sheet of ice, and large chunks of it break off and make their way south. The only place with more ice is Antarctica."

I arched my eyebrows. "Wow, you're very knowledgeable. I guess I'll have to go to Greenland. What about you? I know you're well-traveled, but where do you want to go to next?" I wondered where Mark was. I should've asked for a refill, so he'd come back outside.

"Iceland, which is much greener than Greenland, by the way."

"A friend of my mother's went to Iceland last winter to see the northern lights. But don't the volcanoes make you nervous?"

"No, they keep a close watch on any active volcanoes."

The lights of the city sparkled like diamonds in the distance, but my mind was elsewhere. I couldn't stop thinking about Mark, his dark hair and chiseled features etched into my mind. I could almost hear the deep timbre of his voice, soothing and reassuring.

*Just like Sean.* What was the word for it? Doppelgänger. A double.

It was nearing midnight, and I was growing tired. I decided it was time to head home, but first, I decided to pop into the powder room.

As I walked down the narrow front hallway, I passed Mark and Fiona huddled together in a corner. They were deep in conversation and didn't seem to notice me. I was lonelier in this crowd of people than I was at home by myself. When I reached the toilet, it was occupied. Defeated, I leaned against the wall and checked my phone for messages. Just one from my mom. I'd call her in the morning. My gaze slowly drifted back down the hall. Now Mark and Fiona were kissing. A jolt of jealousy hit me like a wave of electricity. *Why wasn't **I** the one he was kissing in the corner?* Then I was struck by a surge of shame. She was my best friend. What was I thinking? He was Fiona's boyfriend, not mine. *I need to get out of here.* I moved expeditiously to the door, tripping on a small throw rug. My ankle rolled. With a sudden jerk, pain shot through my body, causing me to cry out in surprise. My balance faltered, and I felt myself falling towards the ground.

A hand swooped out, saving me from a seriously genuine plummet.

"Leaving so soon?" It was Mark.

Fiona was right behind him.

"Yeah, sorry," I replied, avoiding his gaze. "I'm really tired, all of a sudden."

"It's okay. I'm just so glad you came," Fiona said, embracing me.

Then it was Mark's turn. His strong arms engulfed me in a tight bear-hug. A stream of contentment and security flowed through me. I didn't want it to ever end. A strangled, muffled cry twisted in my throat. I pulled away from him and rushed out the door.

Fiona chased after me, the steel door slamming shut behind us. She clutched at my elbow. “What’s wrong? Why did you run off like that?”

“Nothing’s wrong,” I lied then blinked back tears. “I’m just wiped out.”

The sound of the elevator’s arrival was deafening, its chime echoing through the empty building.

“Call me tomorrow?” she said.

I nodded and we waved goodbye.

The doors closed, and Fiona was gone.

My shoulders slumped and I let out a long, deep breath. I stared at the distorted image of myself in the metallic doors and whispered under my breath, “You’re in deep trouble.”

# Chapter 8

I woke up Sunday morning with a blinding headache. I fed my hungry pug then took her outside. After swallowing some painkillers, I went straight back to my cozy bed. As I hid under the covers, the events of the night before – my encounters with Mark and Oliver – were afloat in my mind. Both brothers had been charming, yet Mark dominated my thoughts. He reminded me so much of Sean. His dark hair. Deep voice. Gleaming smile.

It was almost creepy how similar they were, like the plot of Hitchcock's film *Vertigo*, in which a woman died, and her double appeared.

I grabbed my phone and googled the word 'doppelgänger'. According to *Wikipedia,* a doppelgänger is a double of a *living* person. A ghostly or paranormal phenomenon. A harbinger of bad luck. An evil twin. A shadow version of oneself. In legends, if someone came face-to-face with his or her double, it was an omen or warning of death for both. But Sean was already dead.

The weight of the world seemed to be bearing down on me, the thoughts in my head growing more and more overwhelming by the second. I groaned in frustration and threw my phone onto the bed, the sound of it hitting the mattress like a slap. I pulled the blanket over my head, hoping to escape the chaos, but the thoughts continued to churn like a stormy sea.

I heard a loud bang and nearly jumped out of my skin. *What the heck was that?* I sat up and saw a dark shape at the end of my bed.

"Oh, it's you. You startled me."

Keeper had jumped up on the bed and knocked a framed photo of Sean off the nightstand in the process.

I reached down and rescued the picture. The glass had a tiny crack in one corner, but otherwise it was fine. I held it in my hands and an idea struck me. I grabbed my phone and googled 'Dr. Mark Rankin'. His image filled the screen. I held the photo of Sean next to my phone. A surge of adrenaline rushed through my veins, my heart pounding against my ribcage like a battering ram. The resemblance was uncanny.

His hair was a messy mop of dark curls, his jawline sharp enough to cut diamonds. His eyes were a piercing blue, like lasers boring into my soul. Leaning closer and squinting, I had to admit there were a few differences. Mark had a cleft chin. Sean didn't. Sean's ears were smaller than Mark's and he had a mole on his left earlobe. But if I overlooked those tiny details, they were practically twins.

I put Sean's photo back on the nightstand, shut off my phone and flopped back onto the pillow. I stroked my pug's soft, black fur and sighed.

"What do you think, Keeper? Is Mark Sean's double?"

Thoughts about Mark continued to ricochet like a ball inside my brain. *Why had Keeper knocked the picture over at that exact moment? Was it a sign from beyond the grave? Had Sean sent Mark to make me happy, again? If only I'd gone to the art show, maybe Mark would've approached me instead of Fiona. Then he'd be my boyfriend.* But it was too late. He was dating Fiona.

I stretched my limbs, feeling the stiffness of my muscles from lying in bed for so long. The headache that had been pounding away at my temples was finally gone, leaving me feeling clear-headed and refreshed. I decided to get up and go for a walk, hoping that the fresh air and a caffeine fix would help to clear my mind.

I took an umbrella and traipsed sluggishly down the street, stepping over puddles that pooled between the Beacon Hill cobblestones.

I grabbed an espresso shot at *Jacked Up Coffee*, and was on my way back home, when my phone buzzed. Scooping and digging it out of my pocket, I stared at the number on the screen. Suddenly, I slammed straight into someone.

"Oops-a-daisy."

"Helen, I'm so sorry. I wasn't watching where I was going."

She let out a girlish giggle. "I'm fine, dear. I'm afraid it'll take more than a little bump to knock me off. I thought I'd stretch my old bones and look at all the spring blossoms. Aren't the lilacs wonderful? I can never decide if they smell like lemons or honey. What do you think, dear?"

"Um, honey, I guess." I found the scent nauseatingly sweet, but kept my opinion to myself. My phone rang, again. It was Fiona. "I'm sorry. I'd better take this call."

Helen patted the back of my hand, then shuffled off to her house next door.

"How're you feeling this morning?" Fiona asked, in a serious tone.

"Much better, thanks."

"Isn't Mark amazing? I really want you two to like each other…"

I waltzed down the street.

"…Because I really think he could be ***the one.***"

My chest tightened.

*So do I. The one for me.*

# Chapter 9

A few days later, I walked into *Joe's Garage,* a trendy new restaurant on Newbury Street. The large, rectangular opening served as the entryway to the converted garage. The paneled, metal door had been rolled up on tracks across the ceiling, revealing the spartan yet welcoming interior. Wood plank tables and mismatched, wooden, spindle chairs added a touch of warmth to the space.

"Erin. Over here."

I swiveled my head and saw Paige sitting at one of the long tables.

"This is a pleasant surprise. Fiona didn't tell me that you were coming," I said, a huge grin forming as I moved towards the table.

"The kids are at their grandparents," Paige said, munching on a piece of sourdough bread. "So when Fiona mentioned she was meeting you for lunch, I invited myself along."

"I guess you've heard all about Mark." I leaned down to give her a hug.

She smirked. "Just a bit. But you're the lucky one, who's actually met him in the flesh. Is he as great as she says he is?" Paige grabbed another slice of bread from a basket on the table.

"Hi, girls." It was Fiona. She joined us at the family-sized table and gave us each a hug. "Mark recommended this place. Isn't it cool? The gallery where Mark and I met is just across the street."

Paige and I exchanged a look.

"It's different," I replied, diplomatically.

"If I'd known we'd be eating in a garage," Paige said, "I'd have brought my car. It needs an oil change."

Fiona said, wrinkling her nose and squinting her eyes, "Very funny, Paige. Where's the waitress? Let's get some drinks, and then I'll tell you all about Mark and me. Oh, here she is. I'll order us a bottle of wine."

"Just sparkling water for me," I said.

Fiona frowned. "Don't tell me you're still on those pills…"

A knot tightened the guts in my stomach. "The lamb burger and sweet potato fries sound yummy," I said, ignoring Fiona's comment.

"I'm starving," Paige said, perusing the menu. "I'm going to get deep-fried chicken with waffles."

"A goat cheese and arugula salad for me, please," Fiona said, smiling at the waitress, who marched off to put in our order. "Now, where should I start?"

"Did you sleep with him yet?"

"Paige." My mouth hung open in astonishment.

"Listen. I'm an old, married woman," Paige said, placing her palms face down on the table. "Ever since we had kids, our sex life's been on the back burner. It's hard to make love when there are two other tiny bodies in our bed. So, spill it. What's he like?"

"Sorry. It's too private," Fiona replied, blushing.

Paige frowned at her. "Come on, Fiona. Don't be such a prude. Just give us one tidbit. Please?"

I crossed my arms.

"All right." Fiona sighed and shrugged her shoulders. "Let's just say, he's got an excellent bedside manner." A wave of red rushed up her throat and spread rapidly across her face.

"What? That's all we get?" Paige said, slathering some soft, whipped butter on another piece of bread.

"If you want to know more," Fiona said, coyly. "I'll need that wine."

Just then, the waitress arrived with a carafe.

"Perfect timing." Paige chuckled.

The waitress filled Paige's and Fiona's glasses and handed me my water.

"I'd like to make a toast." Fiona raised her glass. "To friendship. And love."

"And a brilliant bedside manner." Paige's lips curved into a playful smile as she winked at Fiona.

After we had finished eating, we ordered coffee and chatted some more.

"I've got to get going," Paige said, wiping foam from her lips. "Mark sounds awesome, Fiona. I'm so happy for you."

"Thanks." Fiona got up and gave Paige a tight squeeze.

When she was gone, I motioned the waitress for another coffee and ordered a slice of cheesecake. "Two forks, please."

"None for me, thanks," Fiona said, shaking her head. "I'm watching my weight, now that I'm dating a doctor. And speaking of Mark, he and I want you to come over for dinner this Saturday."

"Oh, Fiona, I don't know…"

"Please, say 'yes'. I really want you both to get to know each other better."

I watched the waitress pour us both steaming, hot coffee, then took a sip and winced. I scalded my tongue. "But I felt so humiliated after running from his party."

"Please, don't get mad at me."

My brow pinched and my shoulders tensed up. "What did you do?"

"As you know, Mark's a doctor…"

The cheesecake was so rich and creamy that I couldn't resist taking another bite. I closed my eyes and let the flavors wash over me, savoring the way the creamy filling melted in my mouth and the crust added a satisfying crunch.

"…So I thought you wouldn't mind…"

"Go on." I snuck in another mouthful of that delicious cheesecake.

"I told him all about Sean and the accident and that you're seeing a therapist."

"Why did you do that?" My fork clattered onto my plate and a red mist of anger swirled in front of my eyes. My hands shook with frustration as I tried to keep my voice steady, but I knew that I couldn't take it anymore.

She reached across the table and squeezed my hand. "I thought he might have some good advice. I'm just trying to help you get better. You're my best friend and it kills me to see you suffering."

I pressed my lips together into a smile, but inside, I was seething. If Fiona gave me any more of her so-called 'help', I'd reach across the table and wring my so-called best friend's slender, white neck.

# Chapter 10

"How are you feeling today, Erin?" Dr. Pritchard asked, her voice composed and abstract.

I shifted in my seat and tapped my toes on the floor. "Not bad."

"I'm glad to hear it."

I cleared my throat, indicating a desire to speak, yet the words wouldn't come.

The doctor picked a piece of lint off her neatly creased trousers.

"What about your social life? Have you been getting out of the house more?"

I smiled and sat up in my chair. "Quite a bit, actually. I had lunch with my friends, Paige and Fiona, yesterday, and last Saturday night, I went to a party."

She returned my smile. "Good for you. Were you able to relax and enjoy yourself?"

I slumped back in the overstuffed armchair. "It was an interesting night."

"Care to elaborate?"

I began bouncing my legs up and down like a jackhammer. "To be honest, Mark – the guy Fiona's seeing – reminds me a lot of Sean. When he walks into a room, everyone knows it. He's charismatic. Smart. Did I mention that he's a doctor?" I left out the part about him having Sean's steely-blue eyes. "But most importantly, he's thoughtful. At the party, he always made sure that I had a drink—"

"A drink?" Dr. Pritchard's eyebrows shot up her forehead, indicating surprise or shock.

*Oops.* "I met someone else at the party," I said, before the doctor could deliver a lecture about the dangers of mixing alcohol with meds. "His name is Oliver. He's Mark's brother. I think Fiona was trying to set us up."

"Did you like him?"

"He was nice. But I wish Fiona wouldn't interfere. I'm just not ready to date anyone right now."

A few beats of silence passed.

"Is something else on your mind?"

I blushed and kept my eyes fixed on the floor.

The doctor waited in silence, while I worked up my courage.

"At the end of the party, when Mark hugged me good night…"

Dr. Pritchard waited. Sounds of vehicles whizzing by traveled in through the open window.

"…I closed my eyes and for a brief moment, it felt like I was hugging Sean."

Somewhere outside, a car door slammed, and another car honked its horn.

I took a deep breath and lifted my gaze from the floor to the doctor. "I felt happy and safe, for the first time in months." A wave of heat rosed my neck.

"That sounds like a perfectly normal reaction to me under the circumstances. Remember, you need to practice self-compassion. You're in an emotionally vulnerable state." The doctor waited for a beat, then unfolded her hands and leaned towards me, her eyes became very serious.

"How have you been sleeping? Any improvements?"

I shook my head.

"Would you like to give hypnosis a try?"

"I'm not sure. It sounds a bit scary. Can you explain how it works?"

"Don't worry. It's nothing like you see in the movies. I'll give you some simple verbal cues to help you relax. You'll do some deep breathing, then slowly fall asleep. Why don't you give it a try? If you don't like it, you don't ever have to do it again."

"Will it help me recover my memory loss about the accident?"

"I can't guarantee that will happen. And even if you do remember some aspect of that night, it might not be a reliable memory."

I gnawed on a thumbnail, eroding its quick.

"But the relaxation techniques might help you get a more restful night's sleep."

"If it'll help me sleep, then I'm willing to try anything once."

"All right. Let's give it a shot. Lean your head back. Make yourself comfortable. Focus your eyes on an object. The doorknob or a spot on the wall."

I put a pillow behind my head, then stared at a crack in the opposite wall.

"Take a deep breath in, then slowly let it out. Your eyelids are becoming heavy. Soon they will close. Relax. Let go of your worries. Inhale. Exhale."

I took a deep breath in and closed my eyes.

The doctor's voice was soft and gentle, like a breeze. "Feel a blanket of warmth covering you from head to toe."

My arms and legs melted into the chair.

"Pretend you're descending on an escalator into a deep state of relaxation."

I descended into darkness, deeper and deeper, indicating a sense of falling or sinking.

"The escalator is taking you back in time, to a house full of memories. Each room holds a memory. Choose a room and open the door."

I saw a closed door in front of me. It looked familiar. Brown slats of wood. A brass doorknob. Light bled out from the gap at the bottom. I reached out my hand, but my fingers froze on the knob, uneasy about what lay behind it.

"Open the door and step inside the room."

I slowly twisted the knob, then pushed the door. It was heavy. I pushed harder and a sliver of light slipped through the crack. As the wave of fear hit me, I could feel my muscles tensing and my breath coming in short gasps.

"Step inside and look around. What do you see?"

I gave the door a final shove with my shoulder and it swung wide open. I took a tentative step across the threshold and froze, midstride.

*No, no, no.*

"Erin? Describe what you see."

"It's my dad's office."

"What else do you see?"

"I see my dad, standing beside his desk."

"What happens next?"

"He falls and hits his head – hard – against the corner of his desk. Now he's lying on the floor, bleeding profusely."

"What do you do?"

"I try to help him. I pull off my shirt and press it against his head. But the blood keeps pouring out. My hands are covered in it."

"It's time to leave the room now. Close the door and go back up the escalator."

I did as I was told.

"Your eyelids are feeling lighter. Soon they will open."

I heard a snapping sound and my eyes popped open, indicating a sudden and jarring awakening.

"What happened? Why did I see my dad? He died two years ago. Why didn't I find a room with Sean in it?"

"We can't control where our minds want to take us. Maybe Sean's death triggered memories of your father's passing. Would you like to talk about it?"

I rubbed my eyes, then took a sip of water. "The night my dad died, we went out for dinner, then back to his office to pick up his briefcase. He started lecturing me about my future. We argued. And the next thing I knew, he was lying on the ground. He'd hit his head on the side of his desk. There was blood everywhere. I called for an ambulance, but by the time they got there, he'd lost too much blood. He had a massive heart attack in the ambulance on the way to the hospital." I covered my face with my hands. "It was awful. And I still feel so guilty about it."

"It wasn't your fault. There's absolutely no reason to feel guilty."

"But if I hadn't fought with him…"

"Disagreeing with your parents is normal. You didn't cause his death. Don't forget—self-compassion." The doctor jotted some notes on a lined pad that was on her desk.

My hand shook, as I guzzled down more water.

"You've had two traumatic losses in a short space of time. But in both cases, you need to try and focus less on the moment of their deaths and more on the happy times you shared with them."

"I don't know how to do that."

"Think of their deaths as the final chapter of a novel. All the chapters that came before – for example, their careers, friendships, and family relationships – are what really matters. See if you can focus more on those aspects of their lives."

The burden of my dad's death was a weighted blanket that smothered me and made it hard to breathe. When I met Sean, the blanket lifted briefly, but the pain of his loss was like an intense punch to the gut. I felt like I was being dragged back down into the depths of my grief, with no hope of ever escaping. Now, with meeting Mark, the blanket had lifted again.

# Chapter 11

It was Saturday night, and I stood outside Mark's loft again. I knocked and the door swung open.

It was Oliver. He smiled warmly and motioned me inside. "Hi, Erin. Come with me. Mark and Fiona are in the kitchen."

I followed Oliver down the hallway, my heels clicked on the hardwood floor. As I passed the powder room, I flashed back to the night of the party and my heart leapt into my mouth. *Pull yourself together, Fitzpatrick.* I straightened my back, lifted my chin in the air, and pressed onwards.

"Hey, Erin."

It was him. God, those eyes.

My stomach pretzeled. "Hi Mark," I said, giving him an oafish wave. "Sorry about my quick exit the other night."

"No need to apologize." He wrapped his arms around me, and my breath hitched. In his strong arms, nothing could ever hurt me again.

"My turn." Fiona advanced forward, Mark moved out of the way, and she gave me a tight hug. "Thanks for coming," she whispered in my ear. Fiona pulled me by the hand. "Now, come and sit with me at the island. Mark picked up some oysters at the market this morning."

"Don't hurt yourself with that knife, bro," Oliver said, leaning against the kitchen counter next to us. Both brothers were dressed like twins, in jeans and polo shirts.

"The only one that's going to get hurt is you, Ollie," Mark replied, playfully thrusting the bent-tipped blade in his brother's direction.

"Now, now, boys, behave," Fiona said, in her best schoolmarm voice.

"I love oysters," I said, trying to join the conversation.

"Me, too," Fiona said, batting her eyelids at Mark.

"Did you know that an oyster can fertilize its own eggs?"

"No, Mark, we didn't know that. But thanks for sharing," Oliver said, rolling his eyes.

"I think it's fascinating," I said, flipping my 'genetically rare', red hair off my shoulders.

"Is it true oysters are an aphrodisiac or is that just a myth?" Fiona asked, tucking her blond bobbed hair behind her ears.

"They're high in zinc, which increases testosterone levels," Mark replied, smirking slightly, as he forced open another shell.

I was impressed by his knowledge and his shucking skills and watched as he inserted the short, thick blade in between the shells with a surgeon's strength and precision.

"Can I try doing that?" I asked.

"Why not?" Mark said, placing the knife in my hand. His fingers grazed mine and goosebumps rose on my arms.

"Are you sure you should?" Fiona said. "It looks tricky. You might hurt yourself…"

"Don't worry. The tip is sharp, but the knife blade is dull," Mark said, moving next to me. "Hold the oyster on this tea towel and stick the knife tip into the hinge."

I closed my fingers around the stubby black handle and pressed the tip into the crack.

"That's it," Mark said, smiling. "Now slide it back and forth to sever the muscles."

"This is harder than it looks," I said, twisting the stainless steel blade.

"You're doing a great job," Mark said as his sudden appearance behind me created tension in my muscles and caused my heart rate to increase. I could feel his breath on my neck as he peered over my shoulder, and I knew that I was being watched. My palms grew sweaty as I tried to focus on my task. I couldn't shake the feeling of being observed, but with his words of encouragement, I could do anything.

"Be careful," Oliver said, furrowing his brows.

A half-formed thought lurked like a prowler in the back of my brain, then moved to the forefront. Suddenly, I jerked the knife and the shell popped open.

"You did it," Mark said, taking the shucked oyster and laying it on a plate of ice.

"Oh my God! Look, Erin. You've cut your hand," Fiona said, pointing.

I glanced downwards. Blood spurted out of a half-inch slit in my palm.

"Hold it under the tap, while I get my medical kit." Mark paced across the loft to his bedroom and re-emerged with a black leather bag clutched in his hand. "Come and sit down over here, so I can take a closer look," he said, indicating a comfy chair in the living room.

I sat down and Mark knelt in front of me. He embraced my hand in his and inspected the wound. My skin tingled and shivered at his touch. For someone so strong, he was also very gentle. Just being in his presence made the walls protecting the scared little girl hidden inside me crumble down. Maybe Mark could heal my inner wounds too.

"How bad is it?" Fiona asked, inching next to Mark. "Will she need stitches?"

"No, it's just a superficial cut," he said, looking up and giving me a reassuring smile.

While he tended to my wound, I studied his eyes. They were more of a smoky gray than blue, with flecks of brown and gold, and rimmed with long, dark lashes. Goosebumps appeared, as he gently applied an antibiotic ointment to my wound. He was so close to me; I could smell him. His scent was a mixture of salt and brine from the oysters, with hints of citrus and antibacterial soap.

He covered my cut with gauze and put paper tape on it to hold it in place. "It should be as good as new in a few days," Mark said, snapping shut his black bag and standing up. "But if you notice any redness or swelling, see your doctor."

*I'd rather see you.*

"I can't believe I cut myself. I feel like an idiot. Thank you so much, Mark," I said, locking eyes with him. My skin got the heebie-jeebies again. A warm breath brushed my cheek. I turned my head to look, but no one was there. A thought shimmered in my mind. Was it possible that Sean's spirit was reaching out from beyond the grave to give me some kind of sign?

Mark reached out his hand and squeezed my shoulder.

My heart lurched into my throat. That was definitely a sign from Sean. He was giving his blessing. But I looked at Fiona and shuddered with shame.

# Chapter 12

Three weeks had passed since the dinner party at Mark's and the four of us had arranged to meet up again for a night of whiskey tasting. As the elevator made its steady climb towards the top floor, I paraphrased my new mantra in my mind: *Mark is Fiona's boyfriend, not mine. Mark is Fiona's boyfriend, not mine.*

The bell pinged, and the doors slid open.

"Wish me luck," I said to my reflection, then exited the elevator and shuffled down the hall.

"Come on in," Fiona greeted me at the door and threw her arms around me.

"Sorry for ruining the last dinner party," I mumbled, when Fiona released me. "Mark must think I'm so clumsy."

"You didn't ruin it and besides, Mark understands about your PTSD."

*What did my PTSD have to do with it?* I knew she meant well, so I gave a quick nod. My chest felt compact, and my stomach roiled as I tried to keep my equilibrium. The last thing I wanted was for Mark to feel sorry for me, but I couldn't help feeling defenseless and exposed.

"I miss Sean and your dad, too. They were both such gregarious and vibrant men, which makes their deaths even more shocking."

One of my lower eyelids started twitching, as if an insect was squirming under my skin. I pressed my fingernails into my lower lid to try and stop the unpleasant tic.

"First, your dad and then, Sean. You've been through a really rough time." Fiona cupped her hands around mine.

My nerves clattered. Why was Fiona going on and on about Sean and my dad?

For a brief moment I contemplated holding a blanket over Fiona's head and smothering her.

"Oh, here comes Mark."

Suddenly, Sean and my dad were forgotten. My stomach started somersaulting. The passion and apprehension were almost too much to bear, and I couldn't help feeling like I was about to burst.

*He's Fiona's boyfriend. He's Fiona's boyfriend.*

"Hey there, Erin. You look great," Mark said, pulling me into a hug.

"Oh, thanks." I blushed and my heart descended like a stone when he let me go.

"Yes, you do look nice," Fiona said. *Did her voice sound clipped?* "Is that a new leather skirt?"

"Yes, I bought it last week." *I wanted to look good for your boyfriend.* "You look nice too, Fiona. That's a gorgeous red blouse."

Fiona beamed, then linked arms with me. "Thanks pal. Come on. Oliver's waiting for us in the kitchen."

Mark opened a bottle of wine and served us a cheese plate. I nursed my glass of wine, trying to keep my anxiety at bay. Dr. Pritchard's ominous warning not to blend alcohol with my pills was still raw in my mind, and I couldn't help feeling like I was testing fate. I planned to only wet my lips with the whiskey later, too.

"I still think the ladies would prefer a night of wine tasting, instead of drinking sugared corn water," Oliver said, slapping his brother on the back.

"I'm willing to give whiskey another chance," I said. "Especially since Mark will know the better tasting brands."

Both Fiona and Oliver shot me incredulous looks.

When the bottle and cheese plate were empty, we ordered an Uber and took the elevator downstairs to wait in the lobby. The car arrived, and Fiona scooched into the back seat. Mark jumped in next to her and I followed, leaving Oliver to sit in the front with the driver. I was so close to Mark that I was afraid he'd hear my hammering and pounding heart.

After a short ride across town, we reached our destination: A hole in the wall bar called *The Old Hairdresser's*.

"It's modelled after a bar in Glasgow," Mark said, exiting the car.

"It looks charming," I said, sorry that the ride was over so quickly.

The dark interior was dotted with round tables, lit with tea-light candles, and several couples sat drinking and chatting. A Scottish flag, the white St. Andrew's Cross on a sky-blue background, hung on one wall, and a gilt-framed portrait of Robbie Burns adorned another. I gazed at the rows of whiskey bottles that were behind the bar, marveling at their golden radiance in the dim light. Each bottle seemed to catch the light in a different way, and I couldn't help feeling a sense of admiration at the craftsmanship that went into each one.

"Come on, Erin. I'm going to buy you and Fiona a flight of whiskies." Mark linked arms with both of us and led us up to the bar.

"Sounds like fun," I said, my heart thumping with elation. His enthusiasm was contagious. I'd only take a small sip of each sample, then drink lots of water. At least, that was my plan.

Oliver trailed behind.

Mark leaned over the bar – a long slab of slate – and shouted an order.

I settled on a stool, surreptitiously tugging my black, leather skirt over my knees. It was tight and uncomfortable, but if Mark liked it, then it was worth it.

A few minutes later, the bartender slid trays of snifters in front of us.

"What have you chosen for us?" Fiona asked, resting her hand on Mark's arm.

"These were all made in the Highlands," he replied, nodding his head at the row of drinks. "The first one is a twelve-year-old scotch from a distillery called Royal Lochnagar."

"Erin, you don't need to drink whiskey, if you really don't like it," Oliver said, leaning towards me. "I can order you a glass of wine, if you'd prefer."

"No, that's okay. I want to be a good sport. But maybe you could order me a bottle of water?"

"Swirl the whiskey around in the glass," Mark said, holding a tumbler up and demonstrating the motion. "Sniff its aroma and observe its color."

Fiona and I held the glasses up to our noses. I closed my eyes and inhaled. My nostrils flared. "It'll clear the sinuses," I said, with a laugh.

"Now, take a small sip and roll it around in your mouth. Slide it over your tongue, then swallow."

I lifted the shot glass to my lips, feeling the coolness of the tumbler against my fingertips. The liquid burned as it went down my throat, but I took in the sensation, eager for the rush of excitement that would follow. "It's got quite a kick."

Water was pouring out of Fiona's eyes, and she coughed uncontrollably.

"Are you okay?" Mark asked, touching her lightly on the shoulder. "You look like you're going to cry."

"I'm fine," Fiona replied. "I just need some water."

I handed her the bottle Oliver had bought for me, and Fiona guzzled it down.

"It's got quite the aftertaste," I said, constricting my jaw and straining a smile.

"The lingering finish should remind you of leather," Mark said. "Brown sugar, or coffee."

It tasted of leather, all right.

"Yes," I said, smiling. "It does taste like coffee."

"Fiona, what do you think?" Mark asked, tightening his eyes at her.

"I'm not sure. I think I can taste the brown sugar?" Fiona said, with a simpering smile, then sipped some more water.

He began to talk about the next glass. "This 'wee dram' is called Macallan Cask Strength. I think you'll both really enjoy this one. It has a sweeter finish of caramel, toffee, and vanilla."

Oliver crossed his eyes, as his brother pontificated.

"You're right. This one is much better." Fiona nodded, after taking a swig without choking. "It didn't burn my throat like the last one. I might actually finish the whole thing."

Mark patted her on the shoulder. "That's my girl. Come on, Erin. Drink up."

"Erin's not really a big drinker," Fiona said, shooting me a worried look.

But by this point, I was more concerned with impressing Mark than following the doctor's orders and I tipped the glass back, emptying it of its contents. I hoped sweeping it down with water afterwards would quell the sickness orbiting in my stomach. I gripped the seat with my fingers, as the rows of twinkling bottles tilted in front of my eyes.

Encouraged by our enthusiasm, Mark moved on to the next sample.

"The third is Glenmorangie, an eighteen-year-old scotch that's been aged in bourbon and smoky oak barrels. This one should have a fruity, floral finish. *Sláinte.* That's Scottish for 'to your health'."

"For God's sake," Oliver muttered.

I tipped my tumbler and wet my lips; I tasted coal dust blended with dirt, the abrasive composition lingering on my tongue.

"Finish it up, wee lassies," Mark said, mimicking a Scottish accent. "You don't want to waste a single drop. It took eighteen years to achieve such perfection."

I noticed him staring at me and my unfinished glass.

"As the late great Ernest Hemingway once said, *'Never delay kissing a pretty girl or opening a bottle of whiskey.'*"

*Kissing a pretty girl? Why is he looking at me like that? Is he talking about Fiona—or me?*

# Chapter 13

Mark couldn't by any means be flirting with me, not with Fiona sitting right next to him. I took a tiny sip of whiskey, then closed my eyes and fancied the idea of what it would be like to be kissed by Mark. Stars danced behind my eyelids like an angelic ballet; an influx of combustible heat crept up my neck like a serpent's embrace.

"Oh my God." It was Fiona's voice, in a hoarse whisper.

My eyes popped back open, my treacherous thoughts like a tumor in my brain.

Fiona's hand shot to her mouth, muffling a gasp as she leapt off her stool. The wooden legs scratched against the floor with a loud clatter as the stool tumbled over. She stumbled her way across the crowded pub to the ladies' room.

I darted after her. "Are you all right?"

Before I could respond, Fiona threw up into the toilet.

I entered the cubicle and gently placed a hand on my friend's back between her shoulder blades.

Eventually, Fiona was able to stand up and slink over to the sink. Leaning over, she gulped water and rinsed out her mouth.

I handed her some paper towels.

"Thanks." Fiona dabbed at the corners of her mouth. "I want to go home now."

I led her out of the restroom and back to the bar. "Mark, I think you'd better order an Uber and take her home."

"Sorry everyone." Fiona looked abashed.

"Don't be sorry, sweetheart," Mark said, rubbing her back.

My heart careened. *Sweetheart. If only...*

"It was my fault. I shouldn't have ordered so many drinks." Mark put his arm around Fiona. "Do you guys want to come with us?"

"Erin, are you up for one more drink?" Oliver asked.

Fiona locked eyes with me. "Oh yes, Erin. Please stay. It would make me feel so much better, if I knew I hadn't ruined your night."

*If you don't want to ruin my night, let Oliver take you home and I'll stay here with Mark.* But there was no chance of that happening.

I shrugged. "Sure. Why not?"

Mark and Fiona gave us quick hugs goodbye, then Oliver and I moved to a booth and ordered beers and water.

Oliver scrunched up his face. "I hope Fiona will be okay."

"I'm sure she'll be fine." Now that they were gone, I took a moment to ponder. Mark had been a tad over-enthusiastic about the whiskey tasting, but we were all grownups. She could've opted out at any time, but she stayed. And when she got sick, he took her home straight away. Mark was a man of many passions: medicine, art, travel, food, wine and whiskey. A real Renaissance man. But was he too good to be true?

"Ahem."

My head jerked up. "Did you say something, Oliver?"

"I asked if you were seeing anyone?"

I shook my head. "I thought Fiona might've told you... but my boyfriend passed away a year ago... in a car crash."

Oliver's face fell. "I'm so sorry. I had no idea."

"We met at college. His name was Sean, and he was a corporate lawyer at a private firm."

"Sounds impressive."

"He was super smart. And very driven." My voice cracked.

"You don't have to talk about it, if it's too painful..."

The whiskey seemed to have loosened my lips and lowered my inhibitions. "No, it's a relief to talk about it. Anyway, the night of the accident, Sean took me out for an expensive five-course dinner, and I was sure that he was going to pro—"

"Last call." It was the waiter. "Can I get you anything?"

Oliver and I both shook our heads, and the waiter disappeared.
"Where was I?"
"You and Sean went out for dinner…"
"Oh yeah, well, anyway, on the car ride home, we got in an accident."
Oliver took both of my hands in his. "What happened?"
"***Last call.***" The bar was closing.
"I guess we should call it a night." Oliver let go of my hands and stood up. "I'll settle our bill at the bar and be right back."
I drank some water. My head was spinning.
A minute later, he was back.
I stood up and stumbled.
Oliver encircled his arm through mine, and we walked towards the exit.
Moments later, we were in a cab, the car engine booming to life and vibrating beneath my feet as we drove away, headed in the direction of Beacon Hill. Without thinking, I rested my head on Oliver's shoulder.
"I hate whiskey," I mumbled into his chest.
"So do I."
We both burst out laughing.
Oliver tenderly caressed my head, like my mother had done when I was a little girl. It made me feel protected.
The car pulled up to the curb in front of my house, and Oliver asked the cabbie to wait for a minute.
"Can I get your number?" he asked. "I'd like to call you tomorrow to see how you're feeling."
After he'd gone, I took Keeper out, and then collapsed into bed. I closed my eyes and replayed the moment when Oliver had embraced me. But it didn't compare to being in the arms of his brother.

# Chapter 14

The next morning, my head throbbed, and my throat was as rough as an emery board. After downing some painkillers and a glass of water, I sat hunched on a wooden step out on my back deck, while Keeper sniffed around our small yard. I placed my elbows on my knees and cupped my chin in my hands. The sunlight was like needles puncturing my eyeballs, so I securely shut my lids, trying to block out the harsh rays. I pressed the heel of my hands into my eye sockets, hoping to mitigate the pain and discomfort. I wished that Keeper would hurry up and do her business, so we could go back inside where it was cool and dark. Finally, Keeper complied. I scooped her up and headed back to bed for a few more hours.

In the early afternoon, my phone pinged. It was a message from Fiona.

*How did it go with Oliver?*

*It was nice, but I'm so hungover. How're you feeling?*

*Still sick as a dog. But Mark's taking good care of me.*

*Lucky you.*

He should be here taking care of me.

My phone pinged, again, but this time, it was a text from Oliver.

*How r u doing?*

I flashed back to last night and banged my forehead with the heel of my hand. *Why had I talked so much? I'd almost told him the truth about Sean—*

*Ping.*

*Can I bring u coffee?*

I didn't feel up to having company, but coffee sounded tempting.

*Sure. That'd be great.*

When Oliver arrived an hour later, he had a coffee cup in one hand and two, small paper bags in the other.

"I won't stay long. I just wanted to make sure you're okay. And I brought you a croissant to go with the coffee."

"That's very thoughtful of you," I said, still standing in the front hallway.

He handed me the coffee and one of the bags, then turned to leave. "I don't want to intrude…"

"Wait. What's in the other paper bag?"

Oliver grinned mischievously. "I picked up a little present for you. I hope you like it."

"A present? For me?"

I watched fixedly as he reached into the bag and pulled out a flat, rectangular-shaped object. The item was wrapped in lime-green tissue paper, which crumpled softly as it was moved. It looked, suspiciously, like a book. I put my coffee and croissant down on the console table, took the present from Oliver, and carefully removed the covering. It was a brown, leather-bound journal. I ran my fingers across its dappled exterior. "It's beautiful. I love it. Thank you so much. But how did you know—"

"Mark mentioned that you're a writer and Fiona told me you're a fan of Virginia Woolf." He swallowed a smile. "I read on the internet that Woolf kept a journal."

*Mark and Fiona. Why did he have to mention their names in the same sentence?*

"Maybe it'll inspire you to write."

*Or maybe, like Woolf, I'll walk into a river with my pockets full of rocks.*

I gave him a quick hug. "It's a very thoughtful gift. Thank you."

"I'm glad you like it. I always admire a creative mind; I don't have a creative bone in my body. I'm just a science geek. Anyway, enjoy your coffee and get some rest."

I watched him walk down the path, then closed the door and let out a breath. Oliver was so nice, but I could only picture him in the friendzone. He just didn't have his brother's charisma or Sean's blue-gray eyes. And

Oliver's comment reminded me how important creativity is to me. That was a quality that had attracted me to Sean. Even though he was a lawyer, we both shared a love for the arts. He often surprised me with theater or concert tickets. In fact, for our first date, he took me to an art gallery. That's another reason why I was so intrigued by Mark, when Fiona mentioned she met him at an art show; he sounded so knowledgeable about art.

A knock at the door rattled me out of my dreaming.

Had Oliver forgotten something? But when I opened the door, my mother was standing on the stoop.

"Good morning, sweetheart. You weren't returning my calls, so I decided to drop by and see you in the flesh. You look terrible. Are you sick?" she asked, clamping a hand on my forehead. "You don't have a fever." She pushed past me and headed to the kitchen. "Why don't I make you a nice cup of tea and we can have a chat?"

"Actually, a friend just dropped off a cup of coffee and a croissant for me," I said, following in her wake. Ever since my dad's death, all my mother's attention had been focused on me and sometimes, it was suffocating. Life didn't seem fair and neither of us were handling the loss very well. Self-reproof flashed inside me for avoiding my mother, but sometimes her neediness was too overwhelming. It was hard enough handling my struggling emotions.

"You sit yourself down and relax," she said, guiding me to a chair. "I'll make myself a cup of tea and see what you have to eat in this fridge of yours. By the way, who was this nice girlfriend who dropped by with breakfast? Was it Fiona?"

I shook my head. "No, Mom. It wasn't Fiona. And the friend is a *he*, not a *she*."

My mother raised an eyebrow. "What's his name and what does he do for a living?"

I shook my head. "He's just a friend, Mom. His name is Oliver, and he is Fiona's new boyfriend's brother."

I watched as my mother investigated the contents of my fridge, like a detective searching for clues at a crime scene.

"When is the last time you went shopping for groceries? You need to take better care of yourself, Erin. I may have to drop by more often, to make sure you are eating three square meals a day."

As much as I loved my mother, I didn't want her making these unannounced visits a habit.

"Don't worry, Mom. I'm planning to go shopping after work tonight." Sometimes, little lies were necessary. I jumped up and gently moved her away from the fridge. I peered inside and found some eggs on the bottom shelf at the back. "Here, let me make you an omelet."

"That sounds lovely." She moved over to the kettle, plugged it in and busied herself with finding a teabag and sugar. "Now, tell me more about this Oliver fellow."

While I cooked the eggs, I told her about my evening with Fiona and the brothers. She asked me so many questions about Oliver, like a cop interrogating a suspect. "Where does he live? Where did he go to school? How old is he? Who are his parents? When are you going to see him again? Is he handsome?" I knew she meant well, but it was like dodging bullets.

I checked the hour and realized it was already time to leave for my afternoon shift at the bookstore. My mother gave me a goodbye hug and turned to leave, but not before I had promised to call her the next day.

A while later, I was busy reorganizing a display of Scandinavian murder mysteries and was moving on to the British psychological thrillers, when my phone pinged in my pocket. I scooped it out and saw a text from my mother.

*I'm in the hospital.*

I rang her back, in a panic, "Mom, what's wrong?"

"Now, I don't want you to worry—"

"Just tell me. Please."

"About an hour after I left your house, I got a terrible pain in my stomach. I felt dizzy. And nauseous. And I couldn't catch my breath."

"Oh my God, Mommy…"

"I was scared. So, I called a cab, and now I'm at the hospital."

"Which hospital, Mommy?"

"City Center."

*City Center. Mark's hospital.* "I'm on my way!"

# Chapter 15

I raced out of the bookstore, waved over a cab and sent a quick text to Maddie, en route.

*Family emergency, pls tell the manager. Thx.*

The cab dropped me at the emergency entrance, and I pushed through the revolving glass doors.

I arrived at the crowded waiting room, feeling overpowered by the noise and chaos around me. I searched the room, looking for my mother, and finally spotted her sitting on a bench next to a worried-looking woman. The woman's baby was crying inconsolably, and the sound echoed through the room, making it difficult to hear anything else.

"Mom! What's going on?" I asked. "Have you seen a doctor yet?"

"No, I haven't seen anyone yet. They're very busy," she replied, coughing and clutching her stomach.

My face reddened with anger. "That's unacceptable. I'll speak to someone."

"No, Erin. It's okay. It's probably just a bad case of indigestion. That's what I told the nurse." My mother winced. "Please, just have a seat. I'm sure it will be my turn soon."

I ignored my mother's pleas and advanced to the nurse's station. Three women, dressed in olive-green scrubs, sat behind a Plexiglas® enclosure that stretched right up to the ceiling. I tapped on the glass and pressed my mouth up to the gap in the glass.

"Excuse me. My mother's in pain. She needs to see a doctor right away."

"We're very busy, dear," a diminutive nurse replied.

"Page Dr. Mark Rankin. He's a friend of mine."

"A doctor will examine your mother, as soon as it's her turn," the nurse said, without lifting her eyes from the computer.

"No. No. No. You don't understand. Call Dr. Rankin. My mom needs to see him, right now!"

"What going on?" a loud, male voice boomed from behind me.

I swiveled around on my heels. It was him. He was standing before me, he had a stethoscope coiled around his neck, the shiny silver metal glistening in the light and catching my eye.

"Erin? What're you doing here? Is everything okay?"

"Mark! Thank God you're here! It's my mom," I said, pointing across the room, then clutching onto his arm like a life raft. "Something's terribly wrong with her. I'm so scared."

"Come with me." Grabbing a wheelchair, he whisked my mother away from the waiting herd to a private room. He and a nurse helped her lie down on a bed. "Mrs. Fitzpatrick, I'm Dr. Rankin, but you can call me Mark."

My mother lifted her head from the pillow and gave him a weak smile.

"Erin says you aren't feeling well," he said, taking hold of her wrist to check her pulse.

"I'm sure it's nothing."

"Do you have any pain?" he asked, with an inquiring look.

"My stomach feels like it's burning."

"Any nausea?"

My mother nodded and let out a series of short, sharp hiccups.

When Mark pressed his fingers into my mother's abdomen, she whimpered in obvious discomfort.

My body swayed and I leaned against a nearby bed.

"I'm going to run some tests on you, Mrs. Fitzpatrick. But first, I'll have the nurse help you change into a gown, check your vitals and take some blood," Mark said, reaching out and placing his hand lightly on her shoulder.

"You're in good hands with Dr. Rankin, ma'am," the nurse said, the corners of her eyes crinkling. "He's one of our best."

He left the room, and I followed.

"Mark?" I grasped onto the sleeve of his white coat.

He stopped just outside in the corridor and turned to face me.

"Is she going to be all right?"

He reached out and took my shaking hands in his. "Let me run some tests, and then I'll be able to tell you more. I'm going to take good care of her, Erin. Don't worry."

"Okay. Thanks." He let go of my hands, and I watched him walk away. Then I heard a retching sound coming from my mother's room and hurried inside.

Dark red vomit had spattered down the front of my mom's green medical gown.

I rushed to her side and gripped her hand. "Mom. Oh my God!"

The nurse pressed a red button on the side of the bed.

*

The test results revealed that my mother had salmonella poisoning; Mark prescribed a round of Imodium.

"I'm so sorry, Mom," I said, smoothly stroking her hand. "I should've checked the expiry date on those eggs."

"It's all right, dear. I'm just glad you didn't eat any."

"You're lucky to have such a caring daughter," the nurse said.

"We were lucky to have such a great doctor, weren't we, Mom?"

My mother smiled at the nurse. "I think he's wonderful. Speak of the devil," my mother said, her eyes brightening.

"Hello, ladies. Mrs. Fitzpatrick, how're you feeling?" Mark asked, moving to the end of the bed.

"Thanks to you, I'm feeling much better. And please call me Laura."

"Is there anything else she should do, aside from taking the medicine?" I asked, adjusting the pillow behind my mother's back.

"Drink plenty of fluids and take it easy for a few days."

"Sounds perfect. How can we ever thank you?" I asked, when he had signed the release papers for my mother.

"No need. I was just doing my job," he said, giving my mother a wink.

"My daughter's single, you know," she said, winking back at him.

My eyes widened and I turned bright red. "Mom, Mark is dating Fiona.

Remember? I told you all about it this morning."

My mother frowned with confusion. "This is Fiona's Mark? I didn't realize. What a coincidence."

As much as I hated hearing those words, I knew they were true. He was 'Fiona's Mark' and there wasn't anything I could do about it.

Mark took me aside. "Listen, can we talk alone for a minute?"

I followed him out into the hall.

He cupped his hands around mine, again. *I could get used to this.* "I'd like to apologize about the other night. Poor Fiona was so sick, and Oliver mentioned you weren't feeling very well either. He reminded me, that not everyone shares my passion for whiskey."

A frisson flared through my fingertips, as if Eros had struck me with one of his gold-tipped arrows.

"Forgive me?" He batted his long lashes and gave me an impish smile.

I shook my head. "There's nothing to forgive. And even if there was, you've more than made up for it."

An orderly came down the narrow hallway with a stretcher, forcing us to move apart.

"Listen, why don't you come over for dinner again, this weekend?"

*For dinner? Alone? Just the two of us? Or would Fiona be there? And Oliver.*

"You'll be doing me a favor. Cooking is my favorite way to decompress from all the stress of this place."

*He hadn't mentioned Fiona or Oliver. Could this really be happening?*

"I'm the one that owes you a dinner, after all you've done for my mother."

"No offense, but I'm not sure I'd trust your cooking…"

I laughed. "I guess I can't blame you."

"So, you'll come?"

I smiled and nodded. "It's a date."

Back at home, I felt a sudden urge to write, a compulsion that had been absent since Sean's death. But now, the creative juices flowed. I was overcome with the impulse and a sense of urgency to put my thoughts and emotions down on paper. I took out the journal Oliver had given me, found a pen and opened it to the first blank page. I was surprised to find how easily the words seemed to pour out of me, after all these months.

*I heard a strange, beeping sound in my ear. I opened my eyes, but a bright, fluorescent light blinded me, and I squeezed them shut again.*

*"You're awake," a deep, masculine voice said.*

*I peered out from under my eyelids and saw a tall man standing next to me. He wore a white cloak and a silver stethoscope hung around his neck.*

*"Where am I?"*

*"You're in the hospital, Eva," the man replied. "You had an accident, but you're fine now."*

*"Who are you?" I asked, coughing. My voice was hoarse, and my throat was as dry as gauze.*

*He held a glass of water to my lips. "I'm your doctor. But you can call me Max."*

*I took a few sips, then put the glass down on the table next to me.*

*Pressing two fingers against my wrist, he measured my pulse. The touch of his warm hand against my skin made me quiver like a violin string. Then he slid his stainless steel stethoscope inside my skimpy, hospital gown and pressed the cold, cup-shaped bell against my chest. I could hear my heart pounding in my ears like a bass drum. I could feel the heat of a blush creeping up my neck.*

*"Sounds good." He took hold of my hand and squeezed it. "You have a strong, steady heartbeat. You can go home today, Eva. But you have to remain in bed for at least a month while you recuperate. Do you have someone to look after you?"*

*I nodded. "My sister."*

*He winked at me and let go of my hand. And then it happened. A strand of hair fell across my face, blocking my vision. The doctor reached down and moved it off my face, tucking it behind an ear. Then he bent over and whispered, "Too bad you're my patient..."*

# Chapter 16

The next morning, when I glanced at what I'd written, I almost laughed out loud. The style was more romantic than literary, but it gave me a toasty-warm feeling inside. My feelings for Mark had broken the dam wall on my creative burnout and the words had gushed out in a flood of emotion. Mark was my muse. The weather outside matched my mood. The sun was glistening and warm, casting a golden gleam over everything it touched and hope flowed through me for the first time since the accident. I decided to go for a walk. Keeper was curled up on the couch, snoring contentedly, so I headed out on my own.

After about twenty minutes, I ended up, consciously or not, at the art gallery on Newbury Street, where Fiona and Mark had met. I hesitated for a minute, then shoved open the glass door and stepped inside. The gallery was empty, except for a lone bespectacled salesman seated at a desk and staring at his laptop.

"May I help you, Miss?" he asked, peering up at me over the top of his dark-framed glasses.

"I'm just looking," I replied.

He nodded and returned his attention to the computer screen.

It was a small gallery, so it didn't take me very long to find it—the painting that Fiona had so thoughtlessly described as 'blood spatter from a crime scene'. But more importantly, I remembered her saying that Mark had really liked it.

"It's such an interesting piece, isn't it?" the salesman said. "And it's a steal at only $2000. The artist is on the rise, so it's a good investment."

A worm of worry burrowed in my brain. It was way more than I could afford on my bookstore wage. It would take me ages to pay it off. But I could cut back in other areas. Eat less. Shop less.

"I'll take it," I said, smiling with excitement. It would be the perfect thank you gift for Mark and all he had done for my mother. "And I'll take that one too."

I'd spotted a print version of the same painting and thought it would look perfect hanging on the wall of my bedroom at home. It would be worth the extra cost, as long as it made me feel closer to Mark.

When Saturday night arrived, I found myself, once again, being conveyed in the elevator up to Mark's loft. The gallery owner had wrapped the painting in brown packing paper, and I clutched it awkwardly under my arm. Instead of my usual dread, I was filled with nervous anticipation.

"Tonight's going to be different," I said to the flipped version of myself reflected in the metallic doors. "This time, it's just going to be me and Mark." A tiny shred of self-disgust needled at me. Fiona was my best friend, and I was about to have a romantic dinner alone with her boyfriend. Although he was the one who had invited me and if he preferred me to her, then it wasn't my fault. The image of Fiona burst through my mind, but I pushed it away, resolved by focusing on the present moment.

I traipsed down the hall with renewed determination in my newly-purchased nude pumps. I felt a twinge in my ankle but ignored it. When I reached his door, the sound of my heartbeat filled the room, drowning out all other noise: I paused to say a silent prayer. "Please let this night go perfectly and may it be the first of many such nights to come." I took a deep breath, lifted my hand and knocked on the door.

For a few minutes, nothing happened. *Had he forgotten about our date? No, that was impossible. Maybe he'd been called to the hospital for an emergency?* I decided to knock again, this time a lot louder. Maybe my first knock had been too tentative. It was a large loft, and he might not have heard me if he was in the bathroom or out on the balcony.

A moment later, the sound of approaching footsteps resonated, then stopped suddenly, and I held my breath, anticipating what would come next. Slowly, the doorknob began to turn, and my heart lurched into my esophagus. This was it. Tonight could be the most important night of my life. My whole future's happiness could depend on it.

Finally, the door opened.

"Erin, you're here. Come on in."

I stood frozen on the threshold. My heart sank like a ship's anchor.

Fiona was standing on the other side of the door. *What the hell was she doing here?* She grabbed my arm and ushered me into the cool, air-conditioned loft. She wore baggy khaki pants and an extra-large men's blue dress shirt that she had obviously borrowed from Mark. I had chosen to wear skinny jeans and a low-cut maroon blouse that I secretly hoped would catch Mark's eye. But what an idiot I'd been. I'd obviously misunderstood his invitation. I supposed Oliver was here too.

"What on earth is that?" Fiona asked, gesturing at the painting.

"It's for Mark."

Fiona raised an eyebrow. "For Mark? Why? What is it?"

"I wanted to get him something special to thank him for saving my mom's life."

"Saving her life? I thought she had food poisoning. Besides, you really didn't need to get him anything. He was just doing his job."

"You don't understand. I thought she was going to die. I was freaking out; however, Mark took such good care of her and me. Where is Mark, anyway?" I tried to sound nonchalant.

Fiona glanced over her shoulder and down the hallway. "He's on the phone with the hospital right now. They call him at all hours, but if you're a doctor, I guess that's the sacrifice you have to make."

I was reminded of Sean, who had spent his rare nights at home, fielding a steady stream of emails from demanding clients. Casting my eyes down, a black cloak of grief enveloped me. I clutched my heart-shaped locket like a talisman.

Fiona slid back a sleeve to check the time on her watch. "He should be finished his call by now."

I followed her down the hall and when we entered the living room, I leaned the painting against a wall. I examined the room. No Oliver, after all.

"Yes. I'll take care of it first thing. Have a good night." Mark concluded his phone call and turned to face us.

I gulped for air. Those cobalt-blue eyes…

He wore jeans and a black polo shirt and stood slanting against the kitchen counter.

An influx of heat spread through my body. *Why, oh why, was Fiona here?*

"Hey, Erin. How's your mom?" He gestured for me to join him in the kitchen.

I rushed over and gave him a hug. "She's fine. Thanks, again, for everything."

"Are you okay?" Fiona asked, when I moved away from Mark. "Your face is flushed and your neck is covered in red blotches."

"Probably all the stress I've been under with my mom." *Pull yourself together.* "Speaking of my mom, I bought you a present."

Mark looked surprised. "A present? That really wasn't necessary. I was just doing my job."

"That's what I told her," Fiona said, folding her arms.

"Please, just open it." I handed him the painting.

"All right, why not? My curiosity is killing me." He tore open the paper and tossed it aside. His brow furrowed. "I don't understand… How did you know?"

Fiona gasped. "It's the horrible painting from the art show."

"You said Mark liked it."

"I ***love*** it. Thank you." Mark gave me a hug. "It was very generous of you."

I felt a fluttering sense in my stomach, like thousands of butterflies departing.

"Too generous." Fiona stared fixedly at the painting.

"I'll have to find just the right spot to hang it." He propped it against a wall, then returned to the kitchen.

Fiona trailed behind him.

"How's the book trade, Erin?" Mark asked, as he poured me some wine.

"Busy." My hand shook as he handed me the glass. *I shouldn't drink. But I need it. I'll just have one glass to calm my nerves.*

Fiona waved her hand at the vast array of food spread out on the kitchen counter.

"Mark didn't have time to cook, so we got takeouts from a French bistro."

"Fancy." I mustered a smile, but suffered a tiny stab of disappointment that Mark hadn't cooked for me – for us – but the cheese board, a seafood platter, and *foie gras* with sliced baguette, did look extremely appetizing.

"The main course is *confit de canard*, paired with pinot noir," Mark said, busily moving around in the kitchen. "I hope you like duck."

I picked up a piece of bread and smeared it with brie. "How was your week at school, Fiona?"

"You won't believe what three of my students did last weekend," she said, sauntering up to Mark.

"This is really funny," Mark said, sliding his arm around Fiona's waist.

"What did they do?" I asked, tearing off a piece of bread with my teeth, like a hungry cougar.

"They broke into the school and stole chocolate bars from the cafeteria," Fiona said, laughing and resting on Mark.

"Wish I'd thought of that when I was in school," Mark said, grinning and giving Fiona a peck on the cheek.

"You were too smart to do something like that," Fiona said, giving him a playful smack on the shoulder. "Of course, the whole thing was caught on video."

"What happens to them now?" I asked, in between bites. All the fawning and toying was starting to make me feel like a third wheel. It was going to be a long night, but I switched on a smile.

"They're all on probation and have to volunteer in the library after school every day, shelving books," Fiona replied, nibbling on a piece of cheese.

"Bet they'll love that," Mark said, smirking.

"Sounds like more of a reward than a punishment to me." I took a swig of some wine, and said a silent apology to Dr. Pritchard, but I needed alcohol to numb myself.

"Why don't you tell us about your week at the hospital?" Fiona prodded Mark's arm, then popped a shrimp into her mouth.

"I did have an interesting case yesterday. A man came in with multiple gunshot wounds…"

"Oh my God!" Fiona and I shrieked in unison.

"Let me pour you both some more wine. Then I'll tell you how I saved the life of a notorious gang member."

As midnight approached, we had consumed more wine than food. Empty bottles crowded the table. The room around me seemed to dissolve, and all I could focus on was the sensation in my legs and on the twenty-foot-high ceiling above. Mark was about to open another bottle, but Fiona announced that she wanted to go to bed.

"I should get going," I said, standing up. But my vision clouded and I collapsed back onto the chair.

"Erin, why don't you stay over?" Mark said. "You ladies can share my bed and I'll sleep on the couch."

"Oh no, I couldn't…" I said, half-heartedly.

"Come with me," Fiona said, grabbing my hand. "I'll get you one of Mark's T-shirts to sleep in."

Fiona led me to Mark's bedroom, the only room in the loft with walls and a door, other than the two bathrooms. A king-sized bed, with a black leather headboard, dominated the space. Fiona tossed me one of Mark's T-shirts, and I tugged off my clothes. As I struggled to pull the large shirt over my head, I lost my balance and tumbled over onto the giant mattress.

"This is fun. It's like a pajama party," Fiona said, flopping down beside me. She laid her head back on the pillow and yawned and a minute later she was softly snoring. I closed my eyes and tried to drift off to sleep. But the alcohol kept my mind buzzing.

A while later, the mattress concaved beneath me, as if someone had just sat down next to me and I sensed something move nearby. I opened my eyes in the dark and my breath snagged in my throat.

It was Mark.

"I'm so sorry, Erin," he whispered in the dark. "I hope I didn't wake you."

I shook my head, "It's okay. You didn't wake me up. I couldn't sleep."

"I hope you don't mind," he said, peeking at me. "My back was killing me on that couch."

"Of course, I don't mind. It's your bed." I did not dare move. He was lying so close to me that I could feel his body heat, and it was turning me on. I glanced over at Fiona, but she was still passed out. My audible heartbeat filled my ears, like the reverberating of bells in a carnival game. Another look in Fiona's direction confirmed that she was completely unconscious. I lay sandwiched between them, staring at the ceiling, with its web of exposed pipes, while ideas swirled around in my head.

A hand brushed my hip and a shiver shot through my body. I looked back at Mark, and we locked eyes. I did not know if it was Mark, or too much alcohol mixed with my pills, or all the above, but my desire for him had an intensity that I had never experienced before—even with Sean. The dusk seemed to cover Mark's profile, making him appear almost unearthly in the stillness of the night. My stomach filled with apprehension and my mind raced.

*No, I can't do this. I've got to get out of here.*

Carefully climbing to the end of the bed, I felt around on the floor for my clothes. The darkness seemed to attach to me like heavy drapings, making it difficult for me to find my whereabouts. I left the room clutching my jeans, silk blouse, undergarments, and heels to my chest.

Safely ensconced in the washroom near the front door, I pulled off Mark's T-shirt and put on my wrinkled clothes. Bathing in a wine-induced haze, I studied myself in the mirror. *What were you thinking? He obviously doesn't care about you, at least not in the way you want him to. He's Fiona's boyfriend.* I turned on a tap, splashed cold water on my face, and dried it off on a fluffy, black hand towel hanging next to the sink. I noticed the medicine cabinet and could not resist eyeballing inside. Surveying the contents, I spotted a manly cologne in the shape of a gold bar, a classic, double-edged razor, and a row of pill bottles. After swallowing a handful of painkillers, a preventative measure against another hangover, I took the cologne and read the label. The scent was a mixture of leather, wood, spices, patchouli and amber. I sprayed some onto the inside of my wrist, then held it up to my nose and inhaled. A swell of heat rolled over my body.

I heard a bang and nearly jumped out of my skin. *What was that noise? Was someone else up?* I shoved the cologne back onto the shelf and closed the cabinet. Holding my breath and listening for more sounds, I slowly opened the door to the bathroom and peeped outside. It was dark and quiet, with no one in sight. Maybe the sound had been a figment of my imagination.

Then I heard a clunk and a clank. The noise was coming from the kitchen and sounded more mechanical than human. Maybe it was the ice machine. Whatever it was, I decided it was time for me to get going, so I made my way to the door. With a hand on the doorknob, I turned and scanned Mark's loft one final time. It definitely had a masculine aura, with the distressed brick walls and the wide-open space. On a console table by the door, I noticed what looked like an ornamental fish hook that was carved out of bone, perhaps a souvenir from his trip to New Zealand. My hand scooped it up and dropped it into my purse. *I need to take a piece of Mark home with me.*

As I stood out in the hall, anxiously waiting for the elevator to arrive, a swell of disloyalty drenched me. Even though I hadn't done anything, I had come very close to betraying my best friend. I wouldn't have survived after Sean's death without Fiona's support. *And this is how I repay her? By lusting after her man? Thank goodness I got out of there, before I made a fool of myself and did something I'd regret.*

As the ping echoed through the hallway, its sharp audio cut through the air, interrupting the concentrated self-reflection that consumed my thoughts. The sound reverberated like a sudden awakening, roughly pulling me from the depths of my inner commotion. I exhaled with relief, as the doors closed behind me. I needed to get home and think everything through. As the elevator made its slow descent to the ground floor, I sniffed the spicy scent on the inside of my wrist and closed my eyes. I let my imagination run wild with thoughts of what might have been if I'd given into temptation.

*Mark kissed me, and his tongue explored my mouth. His hand moved to my hip, and something hard pressed on my leg. In a flash, he was on top of me, and I dug my nails into his back. He slipped his hand under my T-shirt – his T-shirt – and moved it towards my breasts. He caressed my nipple and a shiver launched through my body. I wrapped my arms around him and pulled him closer. And then, he was inside me.*

The elevator's cheerful chime resonated, penetrating the stillness of the corridor.

In a comeback to the sound, my eyes popped open, wide with sudden vigilance. I had reached the ground floor.

But as the doors slid apart, a small smile crept onto my face.

# Chapter 17

After a short Uber ride home, I stepped through my front door, and Keeper rushed up to greet me. I took her outside for her to relieve herself, then went straight to my bedroom and placed the fish hook I'd stolen from Mark on the table underneath the crime scene art print. As I took a step back, my gaze brushed across the room, and a mischievous smile formed on my lips. Before me, was, what I realized I'd created—a pseudo-shrine to Dr. Mark Rankin.

In bed, my mind was too wired, and sleep refused to come. I reached my hand for the light and knocked something on the floor with a loud thunk. I found the switch, and the room lit up. My new journal from Oliver lay on the ground.

I lifted it up and flipped to an empty page. With a gentle sweep, I lifted the book towards my face, bringing it closer to my nose. The inviting scent of fresh ink infused the air as I inhaled deeply, savoring the special fragrance of the blue-lined pages. A sense of eagerness washed over me, arousing a spark of creativity within. Driven by a yearning need to capture the fleeting thoughts flying through my mind, I hastily combed through the contents of my bedside table drawer. Amongst the mishmash of knickknacks and forgotten valuables, my fingertips brushed against the smooth exterior of a pen, its presence almost other-worldly in that moment. As I opened the pen, a sense of structure coursed through me. The words, like insensible threads, readily began intertwining themselves into comprehensible sentences within the depths of my mind. With each motion of the pen against the unsullied paper, the world around me faded into irrelevance, leaving only the dance of creation and the whispered words of a wayward story.

*"Eva. I'm here to take you home," a familiar, feminine voice said from the doorway of the hospital room. She smiled at me, then turned to Max and said, "Good morning, Doctor. I'm Faith. Thanks for taking such good care of my baby sister."*

*He turned around and his mouth dropped open. He stared at Faith, then swiveled his head back to me.*

*"You're twins."*

*"Yes," Faith said. "Identical."*

*"But you called her your 'baby' sister."*

*"I was born just before midnight, and she followed a few minutes afterwards," Faith replied.*

*His eyes twinkled, then he leaned over and whispered in my ear, "I guess I can take you – or at least, the other you – out for dinner, after all."*

*And in that moment, a tiny pebble of hate hardened inside my heart.*

*"You're coming to stay with me, while you recover from your accident," Faith said. "I've got the guest bedroom all ready for you in the basement."*

*"You're very lucky to have such a kind sister," he said. "And such a beautiful one, too."*

*The guest bedroom, my new home for the next month, was the size of an average jail cell. The walls were lined in a dark, wooden paneling that made it seem even smaller. A twin bed was pressed against one wall, and a desk, and a straight-backed chair sat in the opposite corner. There was no room for a closet, so I stuffed my clothes into a dilapidated dresser, its once-brown paint now chipped at the edges. A single light bulb dangled in the middle of the room, casting shadows across the walls of my claustrophobic cave at nighttime.*

*For the first few nights, the strange, shadowy forms had frightened me and kept me awake. But now, I found them oddly comforting. They were like friends, keeping me company in the long, lonely hours of my recovery.*

*Night after night, I could hear my sister and Max – my former doctor – moving around and talking in animated voices upstairs, while I rotted away in my solitary confinement below. Until, one night, heavy footsteps signaled that someone, other than my sister, was descending into my dark dungeon.*

*

I had successfully evaded all contact with Fiona on Sunday. But as I waited for my order at *Jacked Up Coffee* before work on Monday, my phone buzzed, and I answered it out of habit.

"Erin? It's Fiona. I tried calling you a few times yesterday, but it kept going straight to voicemail. I hope you weren't as hungover as I was."

"Oh, sorry." My forehead pinched. "I turned my phone off, while I was having a nap, and forgot to turn it back on."

"That's okay. I totally understand," Fiona said. "Did you have fun Saturday night?"

I forced a nervous chuckle. "Guess we all had a bit too much to drink."

Fiona echoed my laughter. "That's an understatement. I can't believe I passed out. By the way, what time did you leave? I woke up in the morning, and the bed was empty."

"Yeah, I had to go home and let Keeper out…"

"Oh, right. Anyway, Mark wanted me to call and ask you something."

"He did?" My pulse raced. I started pacing up and down the narrow space between the counter and the tables of the crowded coffee shop.

"He wants you to come up with us to his family cottage in Cape Cod."

"He has a cottage in Cape Cod?" *And he wants me to come?* Going to a cottage with Mark would be like jumping down the throat of a live volcano, but despite my best intentions to do right by Fiona, I longed to see him again.

"It's in a town called Truro, right on the beach. Mark said he has a sailboat, and I know you like sailing. He really wants you to come. And so do I. It'll be good for you and so much more fun for me if you're there." Fiona's voice crackled with excitement.

*If you knew how I feel about your boyfriend, you'd be telling me to go to hell instead of begging me to tag along with you to Cape Cod.*

"It sounds wonderful, but are you sure I wouldn't be in the way?"

"Oliver's coming, too."

My mind was in turmoil. I liked Oliver, as a friend, but I didn't want to lead him on. But if I refused to go, Fiona would wonder why. I could tell her the truth, that I wasn't into Oliver, but she would probably just blame it on my grief for Sean and start lecturing me on how I had to move on with my life. She meant well, but sometimes she treated me like a child, and I already got enough of that from my mother. Still, I decided it would be easier just to play along with it. Besides, it would give me a chance to get to know Mark better.

"Please say 'yes'. Please. Please. Please."

My willpower was weakening. The idea of spending an entire weekend with Mark was just too tempting.

"Okay, I'll go."

Fiona squealed. "Thank you so much. You're the best friend ever."

On my way to work, my mind was filled with thoughts of Mark. I popped into a drug store and roamed up and down the aisles.

"May I help you, ma'am?" a young salesclerk asked.

"Ah, yes, thanks. Where is the men's cologne?"

"Aisle two on the left," she said, pointing and smiling. "A gift for your boyfriend?"

I nodded, then walked down aisle two. He wasn't my boyfriend yet; however, it was only a matter of time. I found what I'd been looking for and paid for it, then slipped it into my purse and rushed to work. The perfume bottle lay hidden at the bottom of my purse, while I put in my shift at the bookstore.

At home that night, I took off my work clothes and showered, then spritzed the spicy-scented cologne – the same brand I'd discovered in Mark's medicine cabinet all over my body. I nestled into the soft sheets, a smile pulling at the corners of my lips.

With a gentle breath, I let my eyelids flicker shut, submitting to the sweet caress of my ideation. In my mind's eye, the whiff of salty sea air ladened my nostrils as I anticipated the peaceful cottage snuggled on the shores of Cape Cod. The sound of roaring waves toyed like a melodic tune in my ears, serenading our secret getaway. In this heavenly realm, Mark and I rejoiced in each other's company, relaxing in the delightful privacy that only true love could bring.

# Chapter 18

I nearly knocked Dr. Pritchard over, as I barreled into her office after work on Wednesday. Still wearing my black work clothes, I flopped down into my usual chair and leaned my head back on the cushion. It had been two weeks since my last appointment. I had cancelled the last one, because I had been too busy dealing with my mother's health scare.

"My life is a mess," I said, placing both hands over my face like a mask.

"Calm down. Take a deep breath, and tell me what's happened," the doctor said, in a motherly tone.

I didn't speak. Instead, I peered through the gaps in my fingers and fixed my eyes on the ceiling, as if I were examining *The Last Judgment* by Michelangelo in the Sistine Chapel.

"Did something happen to upset you?"

I removed my hands down from my face, but remained slouched in the chair.

"My mom was in the hospital and—"

"Oh, Erin. I'm so sorry. Is she all right?"

"Uh-huh. Thanks to Mark."

"Mark?" The patch of skin between the doctor's eyebrows crinkled.

"Mark is my friend Fiona's boyfriend. He works at the hospital. Anyway, I was afraid my mom was having a heart attack or something, but Mark diagnosed it as a bad case of food poisoning."

"You must've been so relieved."

"I was. Afterwards, Mark invited me over for another dinner. And I was really looking forward to it. But it didn't turn out the way that I expected..."

"Do you want to tell me what happened?"

I could feel my cheeks burning and tugged on a fistful of hair. "I'm too embarrassed."

"You know that anything you say here remains between these walls. It's a safe space, without any judgement." The doctor's voice was soft and soothing.

Maybe it would make me feel better to share my secret with someone. I took a deep breath. Lifting my head off the cushion, I pushed my body into a vertical position and looked directly at her.

"I'm attracted to Mark."

Dr. Pritchard was unresponsive.

I tried to read her expression, but she remained poker-faced. "You're shocked, aren't you?"

"Did something happen between you and Mark?"

"No, but I was tempted. The opportunity was there. And I actually considered it." My face crumpled, and I slumped in my chair. "I know what you're thinking. I'm a terrible person."

"What I think is irrelevant." The doctor took a sip of coffee, then eyeballed me over the rim of her cup. "How do *you* feel about it?"

"I feel awful. After all the support Fiona has given me since Sean died, this is how I repay her..."

"Feeling attracted to someone is normal. Why don't you start from the beginning?" She took a long gulp of her coffee, put the mug down on her desk, and gave me an encouraging grin.

I leaned forward, placing my elbows on my knees and resting my chin in my hands, like a Catholic penitent, about to make a confession to my priest, except there was no screen to hide behind. A sense of eagerness jabbed my skin as I took a deep breath, preparing myself to dispense the pieces of my tumultuous story. The doctor, with a collected manner, sat across from me, her eyes filled with silent understanding. We existed in a dangling moment, the weight of unexpressed words interlacing a tapestry of strain. The antiseptic room seemed to lie in wait, punctuated only by the soft hum of fluorescent lights. Beyond the window, the lively melody of cars coming and going merged with the speechlessness of our discussion, expanding the gravity of the beat. In this pregnant quietness, I sensed that the doctor's steadfast patience was an inspiration, welcoming me to untangle the threads of my wretched tale at my own pace. My stomach stirred with nervous energy, but I sat up and straightened my shoulders.

"We had dinner. And several bottles of wine…"

The doctor gave me a grave look. "You know mixing alcohol with your anti-depressant medication is extremely dangerous, not to mention that alcohol is a depressant. Even a small amount can make you feel worse. Overdrinking can also lead to bad decisions and acting on impulse."

I kneaded my hands. "I know. I'm sorry. I'll cut down on the drinking."

The doctor gave me a piercing look. "I strongly recommend that you cut it out—completely."

"Got it." I nodded. "Anyway, it was late, and they suggested I spend the night. Fiona and I shared a bed and Mark took the couch. Fiona passed out, but I couldn't sleep. Then Mark came in."

She raised her carefully shaped eyebrows a smidgen.

"He said the couch was hurting his back. It was a big bed, but his hand grazed my hip. I'm sure it was an accident, but I wanted more. Still, I did the right thing and got the heck out of there. Fast."

"So, you felt attracted to Mark—"

"Oh, God. I know it sounds bad." I began to hyperventilate, and my cheeks puffed in and out like bellows. I was sure my face must have been burning bright red.

The doctor's voice was subdued. "Slow down and take a deep breath. You need to focus more on the positive. You did the right thing and removed yourself from the situation."

I lowered my head between my legs and tried to calm my breathing. When my nerves finally stopped jangling, I sat back up.

"Ready to continue?" Dr. Pritchard gave me an encouraging smile.

"Ready." I clamped my hands down on the arms of the chair.

The doctor leaned forward. "Why do you think you ended up in that situation?"

"We'd all had too much to drink." I dropped my hands into my lap. "But the truth is, I've been really sad and lonely since Sean died. I isolated myself and pushed my friends away. I just couldn't risk being hurt again.

But with Mark, I feel like all my fears are beginning to crumble. Mark reminds me of Sean, and he's been so kind to me."

The doctor gave me an inscrutable look and wrote some notes on her lined pad.

I knotted my fingers together. "I know it's no excuse. But everything changed after the scare with my mom. I thought she was going to die. I was terrified. Ever since I lost my dad and Sean, a chunk of my heart's been missing. I'm not ready to lose my mom, too." I started crying, and the doctor handed me a tissue. "The scene at the hospital was total chaos. The nurses were ignoring my mother, and she was in real pain. It made me so angry; I thought my head might explode. And then Mark miraculously appeared. He took charge, and I've never been so relieved and thankful in my entire life."

"It's completely understandable that you feel grateful to Mark." Dr. Pritchard cleared her throat and gave me a closed-lipped smile. "But he's a doctor, and it's his job to help the sick."

"I know it is." I whimpered and hung my head in embarrassment. After a few minutes, I slowly lifted my head up and looked directly at the doctor. "And when I saw him with Fiona the next weekend, I felt jealous."

"Mm-hmm." She pressed her fingertips together like a church steeple.

"It was so confusing." I let out a breath that was so long it could have blown out a row of candles. "I think I just wanted to feel good, again. When Sean died, a part of me died, too. I know it's wrong, but being around Mark makes me feel alive, again." I studied the doctor's face, as if it were a road map that would point me in the right direction, but she remained unreadable.

Dr. Pritchard lowered her hands to her lap, lacing her fingers together in a neat, little bundle. "If you think your actions are related to your recent loss, is it possible that you're fixating on Mark because there's no chance of losing him—since he isn't yours to lose in the first place?"

I began pushing my fingernail cuticles back with my thumb. "I never thought of it that way."

The doctor sat back and crossed her legs. "How do you feel about your friend, Fiona?"

*Envious. Her life is perfect.* "Of course, I feel terrible. And full of regret. I almost stabbed my best friend in the back." I pinched the skin between my eyebrows with my thumb and forefinger. "But what am I going to do now?"

"What do you think you should do?" The doctor maintained a neutral expression.

*Get rid of Fiona. Obviously. What's wrong with me? Our friendship is more important than any man, even if that man is Mark.*

"Make sure I'm never caught up in that kind of compromising situation, ever again." I slapped my hands down on the arms of the chair.

"Sounds like a sensible plan. You might want to avoid Mark for a little while and just see Fiona on her own. Seeing them together seems to stir up too many mixed emotions in you right now."

*Easier said than done. The Cape Cod weekend was looming on the horizon.*

"I was going to reduce your dosage even further today, but after what you shared with me, perhaps we should leave it as is for a while longer. What do you think?"

"I agree. Let's leave it, for now. By the way, I've started writing in a journal."

She smiled with approval, "That's a wonderful idea. Is it helping?"

I nodded, but if she knew the story I was writing, she'd whip out a straitjacket.

# Chapter 19

Avoiding Mark was easier said than done. Fiona kept calling, begging me to come up with her to Mark's cottage in Cape Cod for the Fourth of July's long weekend. And then Oliver got on the case.

"It'll be so much fun with all four of us up there. Swimming. Boating. Biking. Barbequing."

I kept putting them off, until I finally ran out of excuses. Besides, it did sound like a lot of fun.

Oliver had offered to take me on the two-hour drive to the Cape, and when he pulled up at my house on Saturday morning, in a silver, two-door Tesla, I was impressed.

He jumped out and gave me a hug. He was wearing plaid, knee-length shorts, and a forest-green polo shirt.

"It's good to see you. It's been a while," he said, grabbing my bag and chucking it into the trunk. Then he opened the passenger-side door for me, and I sat down in my seat.

"Nice ride," I beamed and buckled up my seat belt.

"Thanks." Oliver smiled back at me and settled in beside me.

"I've always wondered why it's called a 'Tesla'?"

"It's named after a Serbian engineer, Nikola Tesla, who invented the induction motor and alternating current power transmission."

"Show off," I teased. "I have no idea what you just said, but it sounded very impressive."

"Sorry, I just geeked out on you." He laughed. "It just means that he invented the electric motor." Oliver tapped the touch screen, shifted into drive, pressed his foot down on the pedal and pulled away from the curb.

The car was quiet, but fast.

My heart thumped in my chest. I gripped the armrest, and my knuckles turned white.

Oliver glanced over at me and seemed to sense my anxiety.

"Sorry. The Tesla tends to accelerate faster than gas-powered cars." He moved into the slow lane and stuck to the speed limit.

I smiled at his thoughtfulness, then felt a wistful twinge in my chest. If only his brother was at the wheel.

"Does Mark have a car like this?"

"No, he drives a giant gas-guzzling Range Rover."

I wondered whether I would ever get to ride in it.

An awkward silence hung in the air.

Pivoting in my seat, I peered over at Oliver. He really did look a lot like Mark. If I squinted my eyes, I could almost imagine that he was Mark. But not quite.

"So… you and Mark travel a lot together?"

"Yep. Globetrotting's in our DNA." He kept his eyes focused on the road.

"Did you go on lots of trips when you were kids?"

"Yeah, we definitely got the travel bug from our parents. They took us all over the States and Europe." He darted his eyes in my direction. "We were lucky."

I smiled at him and fiddled with my hair. "That's so cool. You and Mark must have so many great memories." I hoped he hadn't noticed how many times I was mentioning Mark, but I couldn't help myself.

He glanced in the rearview mirror, as if the memories lay somewhere on the road behind him. "They took us to a Spanish bullfight once."

"What was that like?" I reached into my purse for my sunglasses. The glare of the early morning sunlight through the windshield was making my eyes water.

"I hated it. Blood sports are not my idea of entertainment. But Mark loved it—all the guts and glory. He was obsessed with the idea of being a matador for months afterwards."

*Mark would look sexy brandishing a sword and a red cape.*

"He's always been comfortable with the sight of blood," Oliver said. "Both our parents are in the medical field. Dad's a family doctor and Mom's a dentist."

"Wow. That's impressive." So, Mark had followed in his father's footsteps. I wanted to hear more stories about Mark, but did not want to push it. "Did you ever consider becoming a doctor?"

"Me? No way. I hate the sight of blood, unless it's oozing out of a T-bone steak." Oliver tilted his head towards me, before turning his focus back to the road.

I scrunched up my eyes, behind my tinted sunglasses. "Ha, ha."

Oliver adjusted the controls for the A/C. "Is it cool enough in here for you?"

"Yes, thanks." I glanced out the window, as we reached the outskirts of the city. I couldn't wait to get to the cottage and see Mark. "Why don't you tell me about your job?"

"I work in cybersecurity." He tapped the U-shaped steering wheel with his thumbs. "I just finished a job involving 'business email compromise'."

"What happened?" I turned to face him.

"Someone spear-phished their accounts payable—"

I cocked my head. "What's spear-phishing?"

"It's when the hacker uses social engineering to draft an authentic-looking email…"

"Social engineering?"

"Sorry, I forget people don't know all the buzzwords. When a hacker has inside knowledge about an organization, he can create an email that looks like it's from a real supplier and target specific individuals…"

"So, the hacker catches money instead of fish?" I grinned.

"Exactly." Oliver seemed delighted. "And that's where I come in. I upgrade their systems and educate the staff about spear-phishing, to prevent it from happening again."

I folded my arms. I stared straight ahead, as we merged onto the highway. "Very impressive. What's your next job?"

"I'm helping the Boston Police Department—tracking data and phone records of suspected criminals." Oliver signaled and moved into the middle lane.

I jerked my head around. "Is that even legal?"

"Only for the police." Oliver shrugged. A shadow seemed to fall across his face. "I probably shouldn't have told you that. It's supposed to be top secret."

"I promise not to tell." I pressed my index finger against my lips. I relaxed into my seat as the conversation flowed, and we got farther and farther from Boston. We drove past green farm fields and roadside signs saying, 'Fresh eggs for sale'. The sight of a grazing Palomino horse, with its golden coat and white mane, stirred memories of my girlhood riding lessons. My thoughts drifted back to the past, to the summer I had gone to a girls' riding camp—Saddleback Stables. For a range of two weeks, I determinedly cared for a horse named Gypsy, assigning myself to her nourishment, preening, and the delight of riding. As the final day of camp came, an air of electric elation swept through the scads of girls. It was time for the long-awaited show jumping contest, a performance designed to display our equestrian skills before the observant eyes of our parents. Excitement coursed through my veins as I boldly navigated Gypsy over each hurdle, my perseverance glowing in sync with her steadfast spirit. The triumphant moment arrived when a brilliant yellow ribbon was produced to me, representing my achievement. The vivid image of my mother's face, radiant with pride, carved itself solidly in my memory. Her eyes glittered with delight, imitating the illumination of the golden ribbon that was seized tightly in my hand. Yet, a nostalgic twinge tugged at my heart because my father was unavailable. He had missed the peak of my success and his absence left a vacancy, a longing for his attendance in that moment of triumph. "Where's Dad?" I had asked my mother on the drive home. "Busy building a new hotel," my mother had replied. "He has a lot of people depending on him." My heart pinched, as I remembered the disappointment.

The sound of Oliver's voice pulled me abruptly back into the present.

"Do you want to stop for a snack or a drink in the next town?" We had just passed a giant billboard on the roadside advertising, 'burgers ten miles ahead'.

"Sounds good." I shook off the emotional cobwebs.

Awhile later, he pulled over onto a gravel drive, and the tires crunched the stones underneath. There was a food truck, painted white with a bright, red roof. The signage boasted of 'Footlong Hot Dogs', 'Big Papa Burger', and 'World's Greatest Ice Cream'. Someone had carved a black bear out of wood, and it stood guard in front of the truck. A yellow rain hat sat on its head and a rod dangled from its paw. 'Gone Fishing'! There was a small playground for children off to the side, with a giant truck tire to climb on and a rickety, rusted swing set.

Oliver hopped out of his side of the car and came around to open my door.

I looked up at him and smiled. "Thanks. Do you and Mark usually stop here on your way up to the cottage?" *Mark. Mark. Mark. Could I be more obvious?*

"Yeah, Mark loves this place." He walked towards the order window. "I know it doesn't look like much, but they sell homemade pies and milkshakes made with real ice cream. What do you feel like?"

I skimmed my eyes over the menu. "I think I'll have a homemade lemonade."

"Good choice. I'll have the same."

As we waited for our drinks, my eyes drifted upwards to the expansive blanket of blue sky. I wondered what Mark would've ordered if he was here. Then my eyes drifted downwards when a blackbird, with a bloodred patch on its breast, landed at my feet. Was it a good or a bad omen?

Oliver returned with our refreshments, and we settled at a picnic table. "Any luck with your writing?"

"Yes, as a matter of fact, I've almost filled the beautiful journal you gave me. Once I started writing, I couldn't stop; it felt like my college days." I sucked some lemonade up through the straw, wincing as the sweet, tart taste touched my tongue.

"That's awesome." Oliver wiped some lemonade that had dribbled down his chin using the back of his hand. "Do I get to read it?"

"Nope. It's top secret. You'd have to kill me first." My mind drifted to my story, with the chirping of birds and passing cars filling the silence.

*"How's my patient feeling tonight?" It was Max. He was dressed in a slate-gray suit and crisp white shirt.*

*I shivered when he pressed his index and middle fingers against the carotid artery in my neck. He held them there and looked at his watch. It felt so intimate to have the blood underneath my skin pulsing against his fingertips. In the meagre half-minute it took him to measure my heart rate, time slowed and each second seemed like an hour.*

*He pulled his hand away and stuffed it down into the pocket of his jacket. How I envied that pocket. But not nearly as much as I envied my sister.*

"Erin?"

"Sorry. What?" A pink bloom arose on my throat.

"You looked like you were miles away."

I swallowed a mouthful of lemonade to cool myself down. "I was just thinking about my story. Ever since I started writing, it's like I'm living in two worlds. Sometimes, I get so caught up in the imaginary space, it feels even more real than this one."

"That's a sign of a true writer, isn't it?"

"I suppose it is; I never thought of it that way."

"And it's one of the many things that intrigues me about you."

I arched an eyebrow. *I wonder if his brother is similarly intrigued.*

"Anyway, if we want to get to the cottage before lunchtime," he said, slapping his thighs. "We'd better get back on the road."

After passing through farmland, with rolling fields of green and golden-yellow, we slowed to almost a standstill at the endless line of traffic leading to Sagamore Bridge.

Oliver frowned and drummed the yoke steering wheel with his fingers. "It's the one drawback to having a place on the peninsula."

"No worries." I was anxious to see Mark, but grateful to be sitting in the climate-controlled cocoon of the car.

After crossing the busy bridge and traveling through quaint towns, with charming names like 'Sandwich' and 'Barnstable', we finally arrived in Truro.

"Do you think Mark and Fiona are waiting for us?" I asked, as we passed a stone church, with a billboard advertising a Sunday fish fry.

"Probably. I think they left Boston even earlier than we did."

I tried to concentrate on the scene outside my window. The town center consisted of a general store, a post office, and a gas station. But as hard as I tried to stop thinking about him, Mark remained at the forefront of my mind. And despite my guilt-ridden conscience, I couldn't wait to lay my eyes on him. We left the main street, and Oliver drove along a road that ran parallel to the water.

Finally, he turned down a winding, gravel driveway through a canopy of cedars.

My heart cartwheeled when I saw a big, black Range Rover. *He's here!*

# Chapter 20

My eyes moved from the Range Rover to the house. It was a typical New England style cottage that emerged into view. Covered in dark gray shingles, its maroon-shuttered windows symmetrically framed a white front door. Dormer windows eyed us, like a pair of curious peepers from the steep gabled roof. All it needed was candy canes and lollipops, and it would be straight out of *Hansel and Gretel*. We were just steps from the Atlantic Ocean, and I could see right through the main floor windows to the sparkling water.

Oliver climbed out of his seat and came around to open my door. I got out and turned to thank him, but he was already unloading our bags. I followed him up the wooden steps and, even though he was holding our bags, he managed to open the screen door and hold it ajar for me.

Before I had time to compose myself, Mark materialized in front of me. His appearance was sudden, a revelation that left me unprepared. Without a word, he sealed the space between us, his lips descending upon my cheek. The graze was tender, heated, but as his face approached mine again, his plan became apparent. The soft compress of his second peck browsed my lips, lighting a flicker that journeyed through my whole being. It was as if electric energy ran down my spine, leaving me briefly short of breath and longing for more. In that moment, words were inessential, for the ferocity of the feeling revealed everything I needed to know.

"Welcome to the Cape, Erin. Come on in and make yourself at home," Mark said, waving me inside. He looked like a surfer in red swim trunks, a white T-shirt, and flip-flops. "It's a bit of a drive to get up here. What can I get you to drink?" He held a beer in his hand.

"A cold gin and tonic would be great," I replied, flopping down onto a large, L-shaped couch and sinking into the well-worn cushions and nautical-themed throw pillows. Through windows that stretched from the floor to the ceiling, I could see the spectacular, cobalt-blue ocean. The cottage appeared to have its own beach, littered with boats. Mark returned with my drink, and our fingers touched as he handed it over.

A tingle traveled along my arm. "Thanks. Where's Fiona?"

He waved his beer in the direction of the road. "She biked back into town. The general store has a small bakery. But she should be back any minute."

Mark sat down on the couch, so close to me that I could smell him. His scent reminded me of black coffee and pancakes: a rare Sunday morning ritual with my father. Mark made me feel both safe and sexy. I could feel the heat of his thigh and took a sip of my drink to chill myself down. Then I pressed the frosted glass against my face, hoping to ward off the deep flush that I could feel creeping up my neck and onto my face. *Behave. He's your best friend's boyfriend, not yours.* I kept flip-flopping between my feelings for Mark and my friendship with Fiona.

The screen door swung open and slammed shut, as Oliver brought in the last of his gear.

"Erin, I'll put your bag in your room," he said, disappearing down a hallway.

The screen door swung open once more, and Fiona leaped into the cottage. "Erin, you're here."

Mark immediately jumped up and grabbed the groceries out of her arms.

"Thanks, sweetie," Fiona said. "Erin, I'm so glad you came." She gave me a tight hug. "Isn't the cottage beautiful?"

"It's amazing."

"How's your mom doing?" she asked.

Mark handed her a glass of white wine.

I gulped down more gin. "She's fine. Just getting lots of rest."

"You two girls enjoy your drinks, but not too much. We're sailing this afternoon."

Fiona took a sip of wine. "Mark's an expert sailor. But so are you, Erin. It's too bad we don't have two sailboats, so you could challenge him to a race."

Mark's head swiveled in my direction; eyebrows raised in surprise.

"I'm afraid Fiona is overselling my skills," I said, shooting daggers at her with my eyes. "I did some sailing at summer camp, but I'm hardly an expert."

*

Later, after we'd eaten some lunch, and I had settled into my room and unpacked my bag, I changed into my bathing suit and joined the others on the beach.

Mark and Oliver carried the sailboat down to the water and hoisted the sail. I helped them attach the rudder and centerboard. Once the boat was fully rigged, Mark and Oliver debated who would take it out on the water first. Both seemed to want a chance to show off in front of us women. Finally, Fiona suggested that Mark let his brother take me out first. Mark tossed a couple of life jackets to Oliver, who clambered into the stern and grabbed the tiller. Then I climbed in after him and took hold of the main sheet. Mark gave the boat a strong push, and we were off.

The sailboat skimmed across the surface of the water, splashing my face as it cut through the waves. The tension in my muscles started to unknot. Being around Mark had been stressful, and it was nice to have a brief reprieve from his sexual energy. Back on the shore, Mark and Fiona waved at us. Holding the rope in one hand, I waved back at them with the other.

*I wonder if he's thinking about me.*

"You might want to trim the sail a bit, Erin. It's luffing."

"Oops. Sorry." I tightened my grip on the rope and pulled it taut.

Oliver stared straight ahead. "We're heading for that green buoy. Where did you learn to sail?"

"At summer camp in the Berkshires when I was a teenager. We used to race against the boys' camp across the lake."

"That must've been fun." He gave me a quick glance.

I basked in the brisk briny air. With my toes tucked under the foot strap and my hands gripping the main sheet, I leaned back off the side of the boat until the top of my head dipped under the water. My stomach and leg muscles strained, as I lifted myself back up.

"I forgot how much I love sailing." I laughed, as my wet hair dripped water down my back.

Oliver shot a smile in my direction.

It was nice that he was open to sharing the onboard duties. A lot of men insisted on having total control of the boat, with women acting as rail meat or bow ornaments.

As we approached the green buoy, Oliver asked, "Do you want to go about, or keep going to the red buoy further out?"

I wondered if Mark would be a risk taker, sailing close to the wind to maximize speed. I loved that style of sailing—flirting with the danger of capsizing.

"Erin?"

"Sorry. Let's go to the red buoy."

Oliver seemed pleased and pointed out a nearby island, with a red and white stone lighthouse.

"It's been taken over by thousands of seagulls."

I saw a flock of white specks floating in the wind. "It reminds me of a scene from the Daphne du Maurier story *The Birds,* when a squadron of seagulls swooped down on people's heads like kamikaze pilots."

"I saw the film, but I thought Hitchcock wrote it."

I shook my head. "Nope. Typical IT guy, watching the movie instead of reading the book."

"I read books, too." He pouted his lower lip.

But I ignored his chagrin and kept my eyes on the gulls.

"Du Maurier lived in Cornwall, right?" Oliver asked.

My head swung in his direction. "How did you know that?"

"Our Truro is named after a town in Cornwall."

"Interesting." I glanced back at the white sand and green dunes of the shoreline and was amazed at how far out we had come in such a short time. The houses looked like tiny Lego® blocks.

"There's a shipwreck called Frances, hiding under the waves out here, and sometimes, it pops out above the water when the tide is low."

"Really?" *I wonder what Mark and Fiona are up to.*

"It crashed on the rocks during a storm in 1872."

When Oliver glanced over at me, I smiled back at him, and he seemed to take it as encouragement.

"They built a replica of the ship at the museum in Sandwich. Maybe you'd like to see it?"

"Maybe."

We reached the red buoy, and I was surprised by how much larger it was than the green one. Its bell clanged loudly back and forth, rocked by rolling waves. We had to be careful to keep our distance; the buoy was as big as the boat and could inflict serious damage.

"Let's take the boat about. Okay, Erin?" Oliver checked that I'd heard him.

I nodded and tightened the main sheet.

He shoved the rudder away from his body, and the boat turned back towards shore.

Ducking as the boom glided over my head, I moved to the other side of the boat. As we sailed back in the direction of the cottage, I wondered if Mark and Fiona were lying on the beach waiting for us or whether they were swimming together in the cold water. Oliver had mentioned that the ocean did not warm up until August, but it would be refreshing on a hot day. I would have to take a dip and cool off if I got too close to Mark again.

As we neared the shore, I caught sight of Mark. He had removed his T-shirt and was wading into the water. My heart raced like a freight train, at the sight of his hard-ripped, washboard abs and I imagined running my hand along his chest. Before I had time to take the daydream any further, Mark seized hold of the painter and pulled the bow of the boat onto the shore. Oliver hopped out and gave me a hand.

"Glad to see my brother didn't drown you," Mark said, his blue eyes twinkling in the bright sunlight.

Oliver tossed his life jacket at him.

Mark laughed, as he pulled on the jacket, and beckoned Fiona to join him.

"Sorry, it's soaking wet," I said, as I gave her the one that I had been wearing.

"No worries," Fiona replied, smiling. "You two looked like you were having fun out there."

The brothers turned the boat back out towards the ocean and this time,

Oliver held the boat steady, while Mark and Fiona jumped in.

Mark turned the boat as close to the wind as he dared. It skimmed across the top of the waves and headed straight out to the red buoy at a clip. I could see the triangular, white sail off in the distance and watched, as Mark held the tiller fast, and the boat cut through the rough waves. I was Gatsby, gazing across the water at the solitary green light on the end of Daisy's dock. A black coal of resentment scorched my belly. *It should be me on that boat, not her.* Picking up a smooth, flat stone, I whipped it into the water and watched as it skipped twice before sinking. *I know it shouldn't bother me, but it does. I just can't help it.* My mind drifted to du Maurier's novel *Rebecca,* in which Maxim de Winter's first wife drowned during a sailboat accident.

# Chapter 21

"I'm going for a quick swim." Oliver handed me a beach towel, then dove into the waves and swam out towards the green buoy.

The wind had picked up. The ocean was choppy and rough. I felt a prickle of unease and scanned the horizon for a sign of Oliver amongst the foaming, white crests of water. Where was he and why had he swum out so far? I strained my eyes against the blinding sun. Finally, I spotted a tiny, black dot bobbing up and down in the water. It was Oliver and he had started to swim back toward the shore. When he emerged from the waves, his hair was plastered to his head, and water trickled from his burly body.

"You swam out so far. Weren't you afraid a great white shark might decide to eat you for lunch?" I asked, with exaggerated concern.

"I don't think a shark would find me very tasty," Oliver replied, laughing. "But I like the fact that you were worried about me."

I threw a towel at him, and he ducked. "How did you get to be such a strong swimmer?"

"I was on the swimming team in high school and played water polo in college."

"Wow. That's so cool. Did you ever dream of going to the Olympics?"

Oliver laughed. "I wasn't that good. But it's nice of you to ask."

"Maybe you could be one of those open water swimmers…"

He shook his head and laughed out loud. "Those people have a death wish. Sharks, jellyfish, ocean currents, hypothermia, hurricanes… Thanks for the suggestion, but I value my life too much. Anyway, I'm going to have a quick shower." He picked up the towel and wrapped it around his shoulders.

"I think I'll go inside and cool down a bit. I'm baking out here."

Oliver stretched out his hand and we walked towards the cottage with our fingers intertwined. It felt a bit awkward and strange, but I did not want to offend him by pulling away.

Once we were inside the cottage, he headed off to the shower, while I went to the kitchen to get a drink. My mind drifted to my story, and I began composing lines in my head.

*"Come on, Max. We'll be late for the theater," Faith said, poking her head down the basement stairwell.*

*"I'd better go," he said, patting me on the head like a puppy.*

*"Have a wonderful time." It was a strain to keep the sarcasm out of my voice. I watched, as he disappeared out my door, and listened to his footsteps clop up the stairs.*

*"Don't wait up," Faith said, her words drifting down the stairwell.*

*My nerves clanged, as I listened to my sister's high heels clicking on the floorboards above, resembling the sound of the hooves of a trotting pony. I felt a gnawing feeling in the pith of my being, as if a sharp-toothed rodent were ravenously picking at my insides. When the front door banged shut, my throat tangled. Gritting my teeth, I clutched a few strands of hair and yanked them out from the roots. The physical pain brought only momentary relief from my mental torment. I growled like a trapped animal. I glared at my reflection in the handheld mirror Faith had provided me. My pupils looked like two black pinpricks. Tipping my head back against the pillow, I closed my eyes and pictured birds pecking out Faith's eyeballs, as her corpse lay rotting in a shallow grave. The corners of my mouth twisted into a smile, and the knot in my throat unraveled. Then I slammed my palms down on the bed in frustration.*

*"I need to stop thinking about them," I muttered to myself and opened my eyes. I needed a distraction.*

*Faith had stacked half a dozen books on the tiny table next to my bed. "These should keep you entertained during the day when I'm at work," my sister had said. She had included a few of Shakespeare's plays, since both of us loved the theater. "Since you can't come and see the new* Hamlet *production on stage, with Max and me," Faith had said. "I thought I'd give you the printed version of the play to read, instead." "You're always so thoughtful," I had replied, repressing my rage.*

*I picked up the centuries-old tragedy, and as I thumbed through the pages, I felt a strange kinship with the eponymous hero, whose life was filled with death and betrayal. Claudius had taken his brother, King Hamlet's wife and crown by pouring poison in his ear while he slept in the garden. And when his nephew, Prince Hamlet, found out what he had done, Claudius poisoned him, too. I closed my eyes and imagined poisoning my sister's drink. Then I could have Max all to myself. I chose to ignore the fact that in the end, Claudius – and his beloved Gertrude – had fallen into his own trap.*

After transcribing my story ideas into my journal – before I forgot them – I decided to wander around and explore the cottage. *I can't believe I'm really here in Mark's cottage.* I had noticed some Rankin family photographs displayed on the coffee table in the living room and wanted to take a closer look. Picking up a silver-framed photo of the two brothers when they were young, I studied it closely. Mark was in the forefront, while Oliver stood slightly behind his older brother, like a shadow.

Glancing out the window, I noticed that the sailboat had changed tack and was headed back in the direction of the beach. Returning the photograph to its place on the table, I went outside to help them land the boat.

"Why don't I sail with you now?" I said to Fiona, who was seated at the bow of the boat.

"That's a great idea," Mark said, jumping out and handing me his life jacket.

I threw on the life jacket, scrambled into the stern and took hold of the tiller and main sheet.

Mark turned us around and gave the boat a big push. "Bon voyage."

"Sailing with Mark was exciting, but I felt so incompetent," Fiona said. "Maybe you should've gone out with him instead."

"I wish," I muttered under my breath.

"What did you say?"

My body stiffened like a corpse, as I realized my slip. "I said, 'I saw a fish.'"

The wind blew in gusts. The rope burned my hand and I struggled to trim the sail. I clenched the rope in my teeth, so I could stretch out my aching fingers. We were traveling at quite a fast clip and had already raced past the green buoy. Waves crashed over the bow, soaking Fiona from head to toe.

"This life jacket is sopping wet," she said, loosening the straps.

"Ready to go about?" I thrust the tiller away from my body and ducked my head. The metal boom swung across to the opposite side of the boat. I heard a loud *thwack.* The boom had struck Fiona on the head. She flew off the bow of the boat and disappeared under a giant wave. Her life jacket lay behind on the bow.

"Help! Help me!" Fiona's head materialized above the water's surface, her wild hands splashing intensely in a desperate bid for floatability.

But before I could react, she swallowed a mouthful of water and sank below the surface, again.

# Chapter 22

The bell from the red buoy tolled in the distance, rousing me to action. *What am I doing? I can't just sit here and let her drown.* Thrusting the tiller away from my chest, I moved the boat into the wind. I let go of the rope, and the sail fluttered loose. Reaching down into the surging sea, I searched for something to grab onto.

"Fiona? Where are you?"

The untethered sail whipped and cracked against the mast, and the boat rocked violently, back, and forth.

Suddenly, a hand rose out of the water and clutched my wrist like an iron grapple.

"I've got you!" I screamed. With a surge of adrenaline, I managed to hoist Fiona's leaden body partway onto the boat, where she hung, shuddering and panting.

"Come on." I heaved her the rest of the way onto the bow deck.

Fiona lay on her stomach, like a lifeless corpse, then lifted her head and puked over the gunwale.

"Hold on." I regained control of the sail and headed straight for shore.

"I thought I was going to die," Fiona sobbed from her supine position.

"You're safe now." I wrapped the rope around my hand to strengthen my grip.

When we neared the shoreline, I raised the centerboard and sailed right onto the beach. Leaping up, I grabbed the painter and dragged the boat as

far up onto the sand as I could.
Oliver ran towards us.
"Are you guys okay?" He gave Fiona his hand and helped her out of the boat.
"I almost drowned." Fiona gasped. "Erin saved my life."
The cottage door banged, and Mark strode down the beach towards us.
Fiona rushed into his arms.
"Looked like you ladies were having quite the time out there," he said, rubbing her back.
Fiona clung onto him. "I almost drowned."
"You're okay now, sweetheart. Come inside and I'll run you a hot bath and make you a warm cup of sugary tea."
Oliver, who was busy derigging the boat, lowered the boom with a loud clank.
Fiona shivered in Mark's arms. "Sounds perfect. Are you coming inside, Erin? Mark could make you a warm cup of tea, too."
"You go ahead. I'll help Oliver with the boat."
As they headed inside, I overheard Mark say to Fiona, "I thought you said she knew how to sail…"

*

For dinner that night, the brothers roasted fresh, locally grown corn on the cob and tossed some juicy, bloodred steaks on the barbeque. After devouring the food and imbibing several glasses of wine, Fiona was in good spirits and fully recovered from her near-drowning experience. We watched as the Independence Day fireworks were displayed across the water in Provincetown, and then Mark made an announcement.
"Time to toast marshmallows," he said, leading us towards the fire pit. "It's a Rankin family tradition. Every man worth his salt should be able to build a decent fire."
"Every woman too," said Fiona, following closely behind him.
"Yes, I'm sure Fiona and Erin could both build a fire," Oliver said, chiming in. "As well as you, Mark."
Settling onto a battered log, a tremble coursed through me, evidence of the twilightish chill moving in from the ocean. My intent turned to Mark, unfazed by his brother's cutting remark, immersed with the duty

at hand. He crinkled sheets of newspaper into tight balls, each clamping comfortably within his palm. Gathering fragments of driftwood he had collected from the shore, he creatively constructed a teepee-shaped tower. Stepping back, he prized his design before striking a match against the coarse surface, inflaming a creased chunk of newspaper. In a matter of minutes, the flames glowed and increased, warping into a blazing campfire that brightened our surroundings.

I moved closer and held out my hands to warm them.

Mark passed out long sticks, and Fiona opened a bag of marshmallows.

I took one and pushed it onto the pointed end of my stick. I held it over one of the smaller flames, but it caught fire and I let out a high-pitched squeal.

"Oh no. I've ruined it."

Mark blew out the flame for me, pulled the charred ashy mess off the stick and tossed it into the fire.

"Don't worry about it, Erin. I'll make you another one." When he was done, he held the evenly tanned treat up to me like a trophy. "Your masterpiece, mademoiselle," he said, grinning with pride.

Oliver rolled his eyes.

Pulling it slowly and carefully, off the stick, I popped the marshmallow into my mouth. It burned my tongue, but I chewed and swallowed it anyway. Mark had made it for me and his attention made me feel special.

"Mm. That was yummy. Thanks," I said, licking my sticky fingers.

"Can you make me one, please, babe?" asked Fiona.

I now had a bitter, metallic taste in my mouth. I stared into the fire as Mark shoved a marshmallow on the tip of his stick and thrust it into the flames. Within seconds, it was a blazing inferno and had burned to a crisp. He ripped the blackened confection off the stick, singeing his fingers. He cursed and hurled both the ruined marshmallow and his stick into the fire. The rest of the group looked on in silent amusement.

Meanwhile, Oliver had gingerly removed a roasted marshmallow from his stick and slipped it, surreptitiously to Fiona. She gave him a conspiratorial smile. Moving next to Mark on the other side of the fire, she put her arm around him and kissed him on the cheek.

"Sorry, guys," Mark said. "I kind of overreacted."

"That's okay. Why don't we call it a night?" Fiona said.

"Sure. Okay. I'm pretty wiped. Ollie, I leave you in charge of the fire,"

Mark said, slapping his brother on the shoulder. "Just make sure it's completely out when you go to bed."

"I know how to look after a fire, bro," Oliver muttered, not looking up.

"Come on, sweetie. Let's go make our own fire indoors," Mark said to Fiona, disregarding his brother. As the clichéd pet names wound off their tongues, an enraged jealousy flared within me; its severity similar to a blazing flame. In that minute, a part of me welcomed a wicked thought—I practically wished I had permitted her to submit to the depths of the water, absorbed by its embrace.

# Chapter 23

I mentally shook myself and scratched an itchy mosquito bite on my arm. But I scraped too hard and blood trickled out of the tiny, puncture mark. The chirping of crickets in the distant dunes were like a maddening chorus of ringing cellphones.

Oliver picked up a stick and poked it into the fire. Sparks crackled and shot up into the air. Dropping the stick into the fire, he turned to me.

"Mind if I join you on that log?"

"Sure. Why not?" I screwed on a smile. He was such a gentleman. "There's lots of room."

Sitting down next to me, Oliver reached into his pocket and pulled out a joint. I watched him, as he placed it between his lips and lit it with a match. The sickly, sweet smell mixed with the woody smoke of the campfire. After a few puffs, he passed it to me.

"I must say I'm pleasantly surprised." For a moment, I thought of Dr. Pritchard's warning, but marijuana wasn't alcohol. I held the tightly rolled joint in my fingertips and took a hit.

Oliver gave me a roguish grin.

I chuckled and took another toke.

We passed the joint back and forth for a while, and a comfortable silence hung between us.

My muscles relaxed, as I sucked smoke deep into my lungs and held it there until it burned. I was slowly releasing it when a bat swooped close to my head. I ducked out of the way and nearly toppled off the log.

"Whoops." I giggled like a teenager.

Oliver grabbed my free hand and pulled me back onto the log. Then he slid his arm around me and squeezed my shoulder. "Are you okay? I like seeing this playful side of you. You're a complex woman—creative, self-confident, yet vulnerable. And that vulnerability brings out my protective instincts."

Vulnerability? What he saw as a vulnerability was more like the darkness inside of me that I had boxed away, but was slowly creeping its way back out. What he didn't know was that this side of me posed more of a danger to others than to me. He was such a nice guy, but I was too obsessed with his brother to consider being with him.

"I hope you don't mind, but I think I'm going to crash." I handed him what remained of the joint and stood up.

He stared into the fire. "No problem. I understand. Have a good night's sleep."

As I walked back towards the cottage, I looked up at the night sky. Millions of stars sparkled in the vast darkness, tiny pinholes of light. Back in Boston, the artificial brightness of the city made the stars nearly invisible. I smiled with satisfaction when I spotted the Big Dipper and, for a moment, Mark was forgotten. I imagined the strange creatures that surely must exist on other planets, somewhere out there in the endless universe. The infinite sea of black above made my earthly concerns, like my desperate craving for Mark, seem paltry by comparison. Finished with stargazing, I headed to the kitchen for a glass of water and a snack. Then I went to my bedroom and shut the door behind me.

Quickly changing into my pajamas and brushing my teeth, I got into the queen-sized, sleigh bed. The ocean air cooled down considerably at night, so I pulled the fluffy duvet up to my chin and snuggled my head into the pillow. At first, the soothing whoosh of waves breaking on the shore lulled me into a trance-like state. But then the sound of muffled voices seeped in from the other side of the wall. My room neighbored Mark and Fiona's, and I was overhearing the faint sighs of love-making. The cottage walls appeared to be paper-thin.

*I suppose they'll be up all night, fucking...*

Bitterness festered inside me. Pulling a pillow over my head, I prayed it would smother out the sickening noises. I remembered how Iago had warned Othello, *"Oh, beware, my Lord, of jealousy! It is the green-eyed monster which doth mock the meat it feeds on."*

*Easier said than done.* I tossed the pillow on the floor and turned on a light. Since I could not sleep, I decided to write in my journal.

*I envisioned pressing a pillow over Faith's mouth as she slept. The lack of air might wake her up, and I pictured her arms flailing wildly, but I would hold firm until I felt my dear sister's body convulse and her legs jerk and stiffen. And then, all would be still. I would lift the pillow from her face and hold my fingers against her pale throat, just like Max had done to me. But there would be no pulse. Faith would be dead. Rigor mortis would set in. And Max would be mine.*

After writing for a while, I noticed it had grown quiet next door. I got up and slowly cracked opened my door. The only sound was the crashing of waves on the shore and my heart pounding in my ears. I crept down the hall and paused outside of Mark and Fiona's door with my hand on the doorknob. *What am I doing? Do I dare?* I twisted the knob, until the door clicked open. A sliver of light lit up the two sleeping figures. I slinked inside their bedroom, stealthily feeling my way along the wall in the dark. I stood in the back corner of the room, like a sentinel keeping watch. I could hear their rhythmic breathing in the pitch black. The big red numbers on a digital alarm clock glowed 2:13 a.m. Squinting in the dark, I studied Mark's slumbering shape. *This is madness, I should get out of here,* I thought to myself, my senses begging me to retreat from the situation.

Yet, I lingered and rooted myself in place, reluctant to disrupt the closeness between us. There was an inconceivable nearness that wrapped around me, and I hungered to relish every brief second of it.

A sliver of moonlight streamed in through a gap in the blinds.

Suddenly, Mark's eyes shot open, like two white orbs.

With a minute signal, I invited him to slip out of bed and join me in the retreat to my room. However, he stayed stationary, his face fixed with a confused expression, as if wrestling with the sudden revolve of events.

"What's going on?" Fiona said, her voice a sleepy whisper.

*Shit. Shit. Shit.* My heart jackhammered against my ribcage. *Why the hell did she have to wake up?* I wanted to take hold of the blanket and smother her with it.

"Probably just a mouse," Mark replied.

"A mouse?"

"Don't worry. I'll protect you," Mark said. "Come closer."

I held my breath and waited.

There was rustling of sheets.

Finally, the rhythmic breathing resumed.

Clasping my breath, I tiptoed along the floor near the wall. But my foot caught on a loose floorboard and I stumbled. *Shit.* I stopped and listened. Had Fiona heard me?

Seconds felt like hours. Outside the cottage, I could hear the swash of waves breaking on the beach. Finally, satisfied that both Mark and Fiona had fallen back asleep, I snuck out the door.

Back in my room, it took a few minutes to calm my breathing. Then I switched off the light and huddled under the blankets. Thoughts of Mark and Sean swirled around in my mind. But the bedroom was like a starless cave, and the undertow of sleep eventually pulled me under.

In the depths of the inky night, I rolled over and felt a warm body next to me in my bed. My heart whooshed in my ears. Mark must've snuck into my room while I was sound asleep and slithered soundlessly into my bed. His hand brushed against my thigh and I shivered with excitement.

*Swish.*

I heard a soft rustling sound on the other side of the bed and my mind clouded with confusion. What was going on? I spun my head and panic snagged all the air from my lungs. It was Oliver.

# Chapter 24

Bright sunlight streamed in through the window blinds on Sunday morning. I stretched my body and yawned. What a restless night it had been, filled with noises from next door and disturbing dreams about the brothers. At least it was better than the nightmares I'd been having about Sean in his coffin.

I decided to get up and made my way down the hallway, past Mark and Fiona's room, to the living room.

A few moments later, Fiona came in wearing a large T-shirt – presumably one of Mark's – her hair disheveled.

"I heard someone walk past our bedroom door and thought it might be you." She stretched her arms, opened her mouth and yawned. "Did you have a restful night, Erin?"

I shifted my gaze out the window.

A seagull squawked in the distance.

"I can't remember," I replied, lying. "So I guess I must've."

"It's all the fresh air and exercise." Fiona arched her back, until it cracked. "I wonder where Mark is? He got up a while ago. I thought he was going to the bathroom, but he never came back. Maybe he went for an early morning swim. We didn't get much sleep last night." Fiona smirked.

I managed a splintered smile when both brothers appeared. Mark came from the direction of the beach and Oliver, from the bedroom hallway.

"Mark, where did you disappear to? Did you go for a swim?" Fiona asked.

"I went down to the beach to do some sketching and to check out the wind for sailing," he replied.

"I think I'll skip sailing today," Fiona said. "But I'd love to see your sketches."

"You draw?" I said, my interest piqued.

"Sometimes I like to do a little scribbling with a pencil to unwind after work."

"What types of things do you draw?" I asked, gazing at him with wonder. What other hidden talents did he have? "Landscapes? Still life? Body parts?"

"This and that. I wouldn't even call them drawings. They're more like doodles."

"I think you're being too modest," I said, giving his arm a playful swat. "I bet they're good."

"Honestly, they're not. I'm afraid that you'd be very disappointed." He gave me a warm smile, then turned his attention back to Fiona. "If you don't feel up to sailing, what about kayaking?"

"I think I'll stick to the dry land today," Fiona replied, looking sheepish.

"Erin, I thought you and I might bike to the museum in Sandwich," Oliver said, piping in.

"What a snooze," Mark said. "Erin don't feel pressured into going to the museum with my brother. It's a beautiful day out, and I doubt you came all the way to beautiful Cape Cod to spend your time in a dusty museum."

"Actually, I think the museum in Sandwich sounds interesting," Fiona said. "Local museums often have unique treasures that you don't find in big city museums. Erin, what would you like to do?"

I felt conflicted. In my heart, I knew that I wanted to join Mark out on the water, but a stab of conscience was telling me that going to the museum with Fiona and Oliver was the right choice. I glanced over at Oliver, who was anxiously rocking from side to side. Then I looked over at Mark who was leaning, nonchalantly, against the kitchen counter.

"Let me know when you've made up your minds; I'm heading to the beach." Mark took one of the blueberry muffins that Fiona had picked up at the bakery the day before, and walked out the back door.

"I'm sure the museum would be interesting, but – like Mark said – it's a beautiful sunny day. I hate to waste this good weather by being inside. If you don't mind, I think I'll take him up on his offer of kayaking. I could use the exercise."

"Why would I mind?" Fiona said. "We can all meet up later for lunch."

I glanced at Oliver. He looked disappointed. I supposed the museum visit had been his plan to get me alone.

Fiona prepared the coffee percolator, then plugged it in.

I rushed back to my bedroom and quickly changed into a vibrant red bikini. I did not want to keep Mark waiting. My heartbeat thumped inside my chest like a quick-tempo metronome. Scraping my hair back into a ponytail, I examined my reflection in the mirror. All the sun and wind had turned my pale, freckled skin a reddish-brown.

Rushing to the back door of the cottage, I caught a glimpse of Fiona and Oliver eating muffins and drinking coffee in the kitchen. I was too excited to eat. A flash of shamefacedness shot through me, but I squashed it and scurried down to the beach.

Mark had already gathered the paddles and life jackets for the kayaks. He wore dark blue swim trunks, and his legs were long and muscular and covered with black hair. My gaze moved upwards, lingering on his six-pack, which also had its share of thick, dark hair. Seeing his body exposed made me ache for his touch, but my stomach swirled with fear of the forbidden fruit.

"Here's your life jacket." Mark stretched out his arm towards me. "And I put an ice-cold water bottle in your kayak."

"Thanks, that was thoughtful of you." I took the life jacket from him and grazed his fingers. A frisson flooded through my body.

Mark gestured across the waves. "We'll make our way over to that island with the lighthouse. I thought I might do some sketching while we're there. Do you want to do some writing? I can put your notebook in this waterproof plastic bag along with my sketch book, if you want."

"That sounds wonderful," I replied. "I'll just run back to my room and grab my notebook."

A few minutes later, I watched as he sealed our books together in the waterproof bag and tucked it into a cubbyhole in the front of his kayak.

"I packed a few snacks for us, too," he said, closing the cubbyhole lid.

Stepping carefully into my kayak, he established himself at the bow, balancing it in the gentle waves of the water. The nearness between us left me spent, my racing heart unable to find comfort. As I settled myself in the seat, he considerately shifted to the stern, pushing me forward with a gentle shove in the route of the distant island. Then he jumped into the other kayak and pulled up alongside of me.

"Let's see who can get there first."

"You're on."

My right hand tightened around the paddle's shaft, as I dipped a blade in the water and pulled as hard as I could. I engaged my core and shoulder muscles, as the blade caught the water, and the boat surged forward. Rotating my torso, I pushed the other blade down towards the water's surface. Soon lost in the push-pull rhythm, I was making steady progress in the direction of the island.

"Looking good, Erin. But let me know if you want me to slow down." A smile stole across his face.

It did not take long for Mark to pull ahead of me, but I did not want him to get too far away, so I used all my strength to keep up with him. At the same time, I was trying to enjoy the fresh air and the beauty of the ocean. The sun glistened off the surface of the water. I could see the green buoy in the distance to my right and I thought, briefly, of Fiona and Oliver and hoped that they were not too disappointed that I had chosen kayaking over the bike ride to the museum. Pushing the others out of my mind, I returned my focus to Mark, the Atlantic, and my task at hand.

Mark had stopped paddling and seemed to be waiting for me to catch up. "There's a section of the island where the water gets shallow and sandy enough to land your boat on the shore."

I quivered with anticipation.

"Let's land our kayaks and do a bit of exploring."

My lips stretched into a smile. "Sure. Sounds like fun."

"We have to paddle around the east side of the island and towards the back. The part where we're going to land is hidden from view, but it won't take very long to get there. Follow me."

Mark's back was tanned golden-brown and slick with sweat. My breath lodged in my throat, as I watched his shoulder muscles flex with each stroke. I looked at his hands, gripping the center of the paddle—healing hands that had saved countless lives. For a moment, I imagined those strong hands gripping me around the waist, pulling me close and touching my hair. I knew in my heart that Mark was the only one who could put all my broken pieces back together again.

"We're here!"

Our venture led us to a secret shoreline burrowed privately at the end of the island. Mark landed first, jumped out, and pulled his kayak up onto the shore. Then he waded back into the water and held the bow of my boat securely, until I had joined him. He pulled my boat up next to his and made sure that they were solidly on land.

"Ready to explore?" Mark took off his life jacket and tossed it to the ground.

I took off mine and threw it on top of his.

He stretched out his hand, interlacing my fingers with his. My heart leapt into my mouth. He led me across the small beach, through some trees, to the interior of the island. It was a very secluded and romantic spot. And I was finally alone—with Mark.

# Chapter 25

The seagulls seemed to be the only other living creatures on the island. Suddenly, the trees disappeared and in front of us was a vast field of spectacular, purple flowers.

Mark turned to me and smiled, "You'd never know that these were here, would you? This looks like a perfect spot to sit and sketch. What do you think?"

I smiled and nodded.

We stood, silently, side by side, staring at the flowers. I couldn't believe Mark was a secret artist. He really was a Renaissance man, like Leonardo da Vinci. What other talents was he hiding? Soon I'd find out that he was a concert pianist in his spare time. Or that he'd invented a new medical machine, that was going to help save millions of lives.

He found a large flat rock for us to sit on, side by side. He handed me my notebook and pen and then opened his sketchbook.

"What are you going to sketch?" I glanced down at his crisp, white paper.

"I'd love to sketch you. With your perfect bone structure and beautiful smile, you'd make a great model. But I'm hopeless at portraits. So, I'll sketch the view of the landscape. My eye is drawn to that cluster of windblown trees over there." He pointed his pencil at a spot in the distance.

"I'm sure you could draw anything, if you set your mind to it." *He wanted to sketch me? Perfect bone structure? Beautiful smile? Did he really just say that?*

"You're being too kind, Erin. But thanks for the vote of confidence." He turned towards me. "You know. I've never told this to anyone, but I feel like you would understand."

My stomach churned like the sea with anticipation. He was staring at me, with such a penetrating gaze, like he could see right through me and into my soul.

"When I was in high school, my favorite subject was art. I used to dream of being the next Picasso or Van Gogh. But my parents discouraged me. They said that if I wanted to end up a starving artist, that was my choice. But if I wanted them to pay for college, I had to study science. And here I am. Don't get me wrong. I love being a doctor. But sometimes, I wonder what my life would've been like if I'd followed my true passion." He looked off wistfully into the distance.

"Thanks for confiding in me and trusting me with your dream, Mark. And as far as being a painter goes, it's never too late. For what's it's worth, I believe in you."

"Thanks for listening, Erin. I knew you'd understand. But please don't mention any of this to Oliver or Fiona."

"It will be our secret. I promise."

He leaned over and gave me a peck on the cheek.

A rush of warmth flooded me.

"Guess we'd better start drawing and writing." He turned away from me and pressed his pencil against his lips, the same lips that had just touched my cheek.

For the next thirty minutes or so, we worked in silence. We nibbled on the cheese and crackers and salami slices he'd so thoughtfully packed for us.

But it was hard for me to concentrate on writing, with him so close to me. And after sharing his secret with me, my thoughts were racing. Besides, I was more interested in sneaking looks at what he was drawing. The sound of his pencil scratching the surface of his paper and the constant attack of the waves upon the beach made my heart flutter with a sense of peace and happiness that I hadn't felt for a long time.

"Can I have a peek?" He peered over at my notebook.

I covered the paper with an open palm. "Not on your life."

"I understand." He chuckled. "Writers are very secretive about their work. But you can't blame a guy for trying. You're an interesting woman, Erin. Well-read. Athletic. Artistic. And an amazing listener. Whoever ends up with you is going to be one lucky guy. Anyway, enough talking. Back to work."

*What was he saying? Was he hinting that* he *wanted to be the* one lucky guy? *If that was true, I wish he'd just come right out and say it.* But maybe he was afraid to make a more overt move because I was Fiona's friend. Maybe he was hoping that I'd be able to read between the lines and make the first move myself. His pencil scratched against the page. Seagulls cried above our heads. Seated side by side, our creative ventures interlacing, a deep sense of proximity surrounded me as I brawled with my writing. His sketching pursuits enflamed a strong allure within me, for there was nothing more captivating than a man who possessed an artistic awareness. I squinted at the pencil settled in his fingertips, a gush of jealousy flowing through me. Oh, the fleeting existence of that pencil, the stories it could ingrain upon the canvas of his imagination. A wistful chuckle freed from my lips as I shook my head, relishing the outlandish idea that swayed in my mind.

Mark turned his gaze towards me. "You look hot."

*Hot? Hot as in sexy or hot from the sun?* I covered my chest with my hands. My heart began to flutter against my rib cage. Suddenly, I saw stars, and then, everything went dark.

The next thing I knew, I opened my eyes, and Mark was looking down at me. His forehead was furrowed and he was holding me in his arms.

"You fainted. I guess you've had too much sun."

"I'm so embarrassed."

"No need to be embarrassed. It's my fault. I should've picked a shadier spot for us." He helped me back up into a sitting position, crouched by my side, and held a water bottle up to my lips. "Feel better?"

"Much better, thanks."

As he loomed over me, his eyes filled with distress and actual discomfit, my heart expanded with emotion. His words of concern resounded in my ears, and I could feel the heaviness of his care. Without reasoning, I moved nearer, my body naturally leaning towards his. The air amid us sizzled with eagerness, and, in that minute, time seemed to remain still.

Our eyes found each other, embracing in a wordless understanding.

It was as if the planet around us vanished away, leaving only us in that inseparable area. The defenselessness in his eyes characterized my own, and a rush of bravery coursed through me.

Closing the length between us, I bent upward, our lips uniting in a silky, delicate connection. The heat of his breath blended with mine, forging an exhilarating mixture of emotions. In that straightforward act, a ton of unexpressed feelings formulated between us. It was a kiss that voiced numbers, communicating a depth of affection that words could never seize. In that exact moment of shared inseparability, I felt his reaction. His lips responded to mine, advancing simultaneously as if led by an undetectable force. The kiss intensified, developing into a dance of passion and yearning. Our bodies compressed, every touch lighting a twinkle of urgency that increased in our veins.

No words were necessary to specify what we felt in that instant. The force of our attachment outdistanced dialect, which unrivaled any spoken declaration of love. It was a speechless melody of emotions, a quiet admission of love and need that reverberated in every strand of our beings.

And, as we withdrew, breathless and laden with a recently discovered appreciation, I knew that in that sole act, our hearts had voiced deeper than any words ever could.

# Chapter 26

*No, no, no. I can't let this happen.*

A boulder of bad conscience pressed down on my shoulders, but my backbone weakened. Part of me knew that I should turn around and run. I should jump in the kayak and paddle away from Mark – and this island – as fast as I could. But I had never felt like this before. Even with Sean. Every bone in my body was crying out for his touch.

He pulled me closer. I closed my eyes, and he explored my mouth with his tongue. We were fused together into one body. Was this really happening? I opened my eyes. Yes, it really was happening. Finally, after weeks of fantasizing, Mark and I were enmeshed in one another.

My body said, *yes, yes, yes.* But my mind told me, *no, no, no.*

I pulled away from him. "We shouldn't be doing this."

If only Mark was *my* boyfriend. *Oh, Fiona, why did you have to meet him first?*

"I don't know what came over me. I'm so sorry, Erin. This is all my fault. You looked so fragile, and I… Never mind." Mark stood up and gathered all our things. "We should head back. Fiona and Oliver will be home soon, and they'll start wondering where we are." He helped me up, and we headed off in the direction of the kayaks.

I was dying to know his thoughts, but at the same time, I was too scared to ask. Was he going to break up with Fiona? Or was this just a one-off? A mistake? I followed him in silence, until we arrived at the kayaks.

"Do you feel well enough to paddle back to shore?" Mark asked.

"I feel much better now. I'm sure I'll be fine."

Mark helped me climb into my boat, then leaned over and gently pushed me out into the water—without uttering another word.

The wind had picked up, and I was using up most of my strength just to stop from drifting backwards. I dug the blade of my paddle into the water and pulled. It was the same as stirring a giant bucket of cement.

*Left. Right. Left. Right.*

There was no time to think of anything else, except steering the kayak and struggling to keep forward momentum.

*Dip. Lift. Dip. Lift.*

The muscles in my arms burned. I kept a steady rhythm by counting in my head.

*One. Two. One. Two.*

Tiny beads of perspiration dribbled down my forehead and in between my breasts. The ocean had been fairly calm, when we had headed towards the island. But now it was churning like a washing machine on the spin cycle. The waves had swelled to white-capped mountain peaks over which my kayak climbed and dived. Water gushed over the sides of my boat, soaking my legs and forming a shallow pool around my feet.

Mark was far ahead of me, by now. He did not appear to be having any trouble navigating his way through the turbulence and seemed oblivious to my struggles. As he moved further and further away from me, a sickening feeling spun in my stomach. A quiet whimper escaped from my lips, as I pictured my kayak overturning and a great white shark chomping my legs. My shoulders ached, and both my hands had blisters forming in between the thumb and forefinger. Even the sky had grown ominous. Dark, gray clouds had appeared overhead, and I thought I heard a faint rumble of thunder. I scanned the horizon for other boats, yet I could not see any. Where had everyone gone? I knew that lightning would hit the tallest target on the water, which, at this moment, was the metallic paddle in my hands. Why were we the only idiots still out on the water?

Maybe Zeus and Poseidon had decided to punish me for my sins. And after what I'd done to Fiona, I almost deserved it. Maybe this was my destiny: I was going to drown.

# Chapter 27

Suddenly, Mark swiveled his boat back in my direction and was next to me in a matter of seconds.

"That storm came up out of nowhere. I didn't realize you were so far behind or I would've turned back sooner. Do you need some help?"

I nodded. I knew I would burst into tears if I opened my mouth, so I bit down on my quivering lip.

He unraveled a rope. "Here. I'll tie your boat to my stern and we can paddle in tandem."

Relief swamped my body, as I watched him feed the rope through a hook on my bow and tie a complicated knot. Then we started paddling through the waves.

After a while, I squinted back at the island; it had shrunk to a shimmering speck.

We landed on the beach and relief enveloped my body. Mark helped me out of my kayak, his expression inscrutable. Without exchanging any words, I handed him my life jacket, and he handed me my notebook and pen. Then I walked up to the cottage and headed straight to the shower to warm up and rinse off my body.

I took off my wet bathing suit and let it drop to the floor. Climbing into the shower, I closed my eyes and let the steaming hot water cascade over my head and down my body. Now that I was on my own, I began to analyze Mark's behavior. He was physically attracted to me. That much was obvious. But he'd said, "I'm sorry. I shouldn't have done that." And deep down, I knew that I shouldn't have done it either.

Yet despite my doubts, I'd invested too much time and energy into thinking about Mark to let go of the fantasy completely. I was like a fish, caught on his hook. My obsession had helped stop my nightmares about Sean, better than any session with Dr. Pritchard ever had. Most of all, I was afraid that if I gave up on Mark, I'd fall back down the dark, lonely hole of depression.

Turning off the water and with the towel wrapped around my body, I opened the bathroom door and made my way down the hallway towards my bedroom. I was half dreading that I would run into Mark and – I had to admit, despite all my misgivings – half-hoping, too. However, even if we wanted to, we couldn't risk another encounter now that we were back at the cottage. Fiona and Oliver could return from the museum at any instant. Safely back in my bedroom, I closed the door behind me.

My shoulders were burned bright red from the sun, so I lathered my skin with cream. Then I put on a pale, yellow sundress and a thong. The sun had dried out my lips, so I moistened them with some lip gloss. When I felt presentable, I made my way to the living room.

Mark was in the kitchen drinking an ice-cold beer; it looked refreshing.

"Do you want one?" he asked.

"Please."

He handed me a bottle, his fingers touching mine. Goosebumps sprang up on my arm. I flashed back to our island kiss and began to blush. *Had Mark noticed?* When I looked at him, he had the fridge door open and seemed to be scrounging around for something to eat.

"I'm starving," he said. "A good workout always makes me hungry."

How could he think about food when all I could think about was our make-out session? Should I seize the opportunity and talk to him about what had happened? Was he going to say anything to Fiona or was he going to act like nothing had happened?

"Mark, I was wondering—"

"Hello? Anyone there?"

The screen door at the front of the cottage opened. In walked Fiona and Oliver, arm in arm.

"How was the museum?" Mark asked, shutting the fridge door. "Not as much fun as kayaking, eh Erin?"

I bit my lip so hard; I tasted blood.

"We had a great time at the museum, didn't we Ollie?" Fiona said, giving him a kiss on the cheek. "And we went for a short walk on the dunes. Your baby brother knows how to show a girl a good time."

I looked over at the two of them. Was Oliver blushing?

"But I missed you, honey." Fiona rushed over to Mark, wrapped her arms around his neck and kissed him on the lips.

A fist tightened inside my chest. Looking away, my eyes affixed with Oliver's.

"Erin, maybe you and I can spend some time together this afternoon," Oliver said. He threw me a hopeful look, as he took a beer out of the fridge. "How about a bike ride?"

"It looks like it might rain," I said, peering out the window. His invitation had caught me off guard. My muscles ached from all the kayaking, and I wanted to be near Mark.

"It'll blow over," Oliver said.

"Typical maritime weather," Mark said, laughing and chugging back his beer.

I knew that it'd probably be best if I maintained the status quo – for the time being – and stayed away from Mark for the rest of the day.

"Sure. Let's go after lunch. I still have a bit of energy left."

"Great. We're all set for this afternoon. Now, let's eat." Mark threw a loaf of bread on the kitchen counter, while Fiona put out some condiments. Working as a team, they threw together an array of delicious sandwiches in no time. With fresh fruit – that Fiona and Oliver had picked up from a farmer's market on their way back from the museum – they carried everything out to the picnic table on the beach.

I stayed behind to make some iced tea. I found a plastic pitcher in the kitchen pantry, then dropped in two tea bags, added boiled water and some sugar. When it was sufficiently steeped, I opened the cupboard under the sink and tossed the used tea bags in the garbage. I was about to close the door when I spotted a bright yellow box with a black skull and cross bones. My hand hovered mid-air and a nerve twitched in my temple. The label said *rat poison.*

Rejoining the others outside a few minutes later, I found Fiona and Mark cuddling together on the bench opposite Oliver.

*He's touching her with the same hands that were holding me such a short time ago*. I felt sick to my stomach. My brain fizzed. An overwhelming tide of jealousy and anger threatened to engulf me. I wasn't sure if I could keep down any of the sandwich that was sitting on the plate in front of me; however, I decided to take a small bite, so nobody would start to wonder what was wrong with me. Under the picnic table, I began to dig my bare feet into the sand. I wished that I could bury my whole body in it and disappear. I forced myself to take another nibble of my sandwich, while resentment and guilt gnawed away at me.

"Oh, crap. I forgot to get a drink," Fiona said.

"I can get you a beer," Mark said.

"Thanks, sweetie. But I don't really feel like a beer right now…"

"I made sweet tea and I can add lots of ice," I said, swinging my legs out from under the picnic bench.

"Sounds perfect," Fiona said, giving me a grateful grin.

I returned a few minutes later with a glass of iced tea and placed it in front of Fiona.

"Thanks, pal." Fiona picked up the glass and pressed it against her cheek. "Mm. Nice and cool."

I watched as she took a small sip, then put the glass back down on the table.

"Tell us more about your kayaking adventure," Fiona said. "Did you go out to the island?"

I peered over at Mark. How could he look so calm? I was a churning sea of anxiety.

"Yes, we went all the way."

I blinked. *Did he really just say that?*

"In fact, we landed on the island and explored. But there are lots of gulls out there, and bones and shit, so we didn't stick around too long."

"I'd be scared of snakes," Fiona said, cuddling up to Mark. Her elbow knocked the glass of iced tea off the table.

I stared at the puddle of tea that was soaking into the sand.

# Chapter 28

Oliver and I rode our bicycles along a meandering oceanside trail. Out on the kayak, the water had appeared a deep indigo, but now, it seemed emerald-green. My eyes took in the wild grass and goldenrod that sprinkled the edges of the bike trail. An orange-and-black-veined monarch butterfly sailed around the clouds of pink milkweed.

Oliver glanced back to check on me, and I gave him a warm smile.

The bike ride turned out to be better than I had expected. As I soaked in the scenery, all the knots in my body slowly unwound. Although, when we rode past clusters of purple, trumpet-shaped flowers, my mind jumped back to the island and Mark. I allowed myself to imagine riding this trail with Mark. It would've been so romantic. We rounded a sharp curve, and I saw two cotton-white swans floating in a small, marshy bay. I sighed, as I watched the pair preen their feathers like prima ballerinas in the sheltered, half-moon of water. *Was it a sign?* I had just been thinking about Mark, and then these two lovebirds appeared.

We came to a steep hill. I rose off my seat and pumped my legs. My leg muscles burned, and Mark was momentarily forgotten. But when we reached the top, the seagull island came into view and triggered the memory of Mark's lips pressing down on mine.

Suddenly, a dark shape slithered across the path in front of me. I squealed and swerved off the trail.

Oliver stopped and turned back to check on me. "Are you okay?"

I laughed with embarrassment and relief, as the snake disappeared into the grass like a ghost.

Arriving at the end of the trail, Oliver hopped off his bike. He leaned it against one end of a bench, under a shady forest of giraffe-sized cedars. He waited for me; I'd fallen a bit behind. When I pulled up next to him, Oliver took my bike and leaned it against his. Then we both sat down on the bench and stared out at the Atlantic.

"What're you thinking about?" Oliver asked me.

"Mark." My stomach pitched and rolled. I'd blurted his name without thinking.

"Mark?" Oliver's eyebrows arched.

"Uh… um… I'm just wondering how committed he is to Fiona."

"My brother seems more serious about Fiona, than I've seen him about anyone in a long time."

I bit my bottom lip. "What's his longest relationship?"

"To be honest, most of his girlfriends don't last more than a few months. But Fiona's the complete opposite of his usual type."

"In what way is she different?" I tried to keep my voice neutral, but I was dying to learn about Mark's 'usual type'.

"Fiona's remarkable." He beamed. "She's so selfless and completely dedicated to her students…"

"It almost sounds like *you* have a crush on her." I twisted a loose strand of hair around my finger.

"No." His color took on a brilliant, reddish color. "But I do have a crush on someone."

*Oh no. Please don't say it.* The hairs on the back of my neck bristled with unease.

He fixed his eyes on me. "You must know that I like you, Erin."

I pressed my lips into a smile. "You're sweet. And I'm flattered, but—"

"I know. You're not ready. I understand."

*No, you don't understand. I'll never be ready, because I have a crush on your brother.* I liked Oliver – as a friend – but I liked Mark more. I was sure that Oliver's assessment of Mark's feelings for Fiona was totally inaccurate. If Mark was really so serious about Fiona, why had he kissed me on the island? Come to think of it, Mark and Fiona were completely wrong for each other; they were total opposites. She didn't understand his artistic side, like I did. That's why he felt comfortable sharing his secret with me, and not her.

"Erin?"

"Sorry. What?" The mist cleared from my thoughts about Mark.

"I want to know more about you. Is family important to you?" Oliver slid a few inches closer to me on the bench.

"Family is really important to me."

*I'd like to get married and have my own family—with your brother.* I just needed to be patient and wait until Mark figured out that Fiona was not the one for him and that his future lay with me.

"Do you want kids?" His voice was tentative.

"Maybe one or two." I gazed out at the ocean and imagined what my children with Mark would look like. I pictured a little girl, with auburn hair like mine, and a boy, with dark hair like Mark's.

"I can't wait to have kids." Oliver looked straight at me, shielding the sun from his eyes with his hand.

I turned to face him. "What about Mark? Does he want a family?"

Oliver gave me a puzzled look.

"I'm just asking for Fiona's sake…"

"I think that's why he's so interested in her. Ever since he turned thirty, he's been thinking about settling down. And he can picture Fiona as his future wife. He told me that he thinks she'll make a wonderful mother, since she cares so much about her students."

It was true. Fiona would make a great mother. A shimmer of shame shook me, as I realized how much my feelings for Fiona had altered. The mere interest in Mark lit a ferocious vortex of emotions within me, similar to the persistent pull of a propeller. It was energy that opposed reason, pulling at the very fabric of my being. Like a puppet tangled in its strings, I found myself powerlessly influenced by the concealed currents of my obsession.

I stood up, walked over to the edge of the trail, and stared out at the water. A pair of sailboats traversed back and forth on the waves, their sails flapping as if they were tiny flags. My gaze shifted to a swarm of squawking seagulls that were following a fishing trawler. They were like ivory kites, floating on the wind, their wingtips dipped in black ink.

Oliver got up and stood beside me. "Did you know that seagulls mate for life?"

"Really? I didn't know that."

"And it's an equal partnership. The males and females take turns incubating the eggs and feeding the chicks and protecting the nest."

"How do you know so much about them?" I turned to look at him. "My knowledge of birds is limited to their literary symbolism. You know, a raven or crow appears, then a character dies. It's made me view birds with a superstitious mind."

Oliver chuckled. "When I was a kid, I wanted to be an ornithologist when I grew up. I used to bring home injured birds and try to nurse them back to life. It drove my parents crazy."

I laughed. "I can imagine. But I think that's great."

"Cats kill the most birds, but each year, almost one billion birds die by crashing into the windows of skyscrapers."

"That's terrible."

"All the new glassy towers going up in the city is turning Boston into a real danger zone for birds."

"What can we do about it?"

"They could use gray-tinted windows instead of blue. And turn all their lights off at night."

I looked at Oliver with newfound admiration. "So, what happened to your childhood dream?"

"My parents insisted that I study something that'd offer more financial security than zoology."

Just like Mark had been pressured to study science instead of art. I'd had the same pressure from my dad. He thought my writing was a waste of time.

"Anyway, I volunteer for the Boston Bird Rescue Society, updating their website and helping them with fundraising."

"That's so cool." I looked at him and wished I felt more than just friendship.

Oliver took both my hands in his. "I really like hanging out with you."

"I enjoy your company, too." My chest was constricted with shame, for thinking so much about his brother.

"Ready to ride back to the cottage?"

We mounted our bikes and began the return journey. But we were now heading into the wind, so the ride was a bit more challenging. When we reached a fairly steep incline, we decided to dismount our bikes and walk up the hill. We laughed at ourselves and chatted away. I appreciated

Oliver's quirky sense of humor and his attentiveness. Eventually, we remounted our bikes and rode side by side the rest of the way back, pointing out birds and sailboats.

When a brown rabbit raced across the path, I let go of a handlebar and pointed: "Look, *Peter Rabbit.*"

"He forgot his blue jacket back at the farm." Oliver gave me an impish grin.

Laughing, I raced ahead with renewed energy.

When we arrived back at the cottage, we had rosy cheeks and child-like smiles on our faces.

Oliver took a cold beer from the fridge. "What can I get you?"

"I'll have one of those, too." I wiped away the beads of sweat that were dotting my forehead. I took my drink and went out the back door, where I collapsed on the hammock strung up between two trees. I'd had so much fun on the bike ride with Oliver that I was starting to feel confused. He was so knowledgeable and interesting to talk to. I could relax and be myself with him. Was it possible that I liked him after all? I needed a bit of solitude to sort out my thoughts. I slowly sipped my drink; the cold beer was refreshing after the brisk, return ride. Closing my eyes, I laid my head back in the hammock and let its gentle rocking soothe me.

The cottage door slammed, and my eyes burst open. I lifted my head to see who it was.

Fiona greeted me with a big smile. "How was the bike ride?"

"The scenery was breathtaking. But my legs are like jelly." I knew that I should ask Fiona how her afternoon had been, but I really didn't want to know. Hearing Fiona gush about her time in bed with Mark would be pure torture, and I was afraid that I wouldn't be able to hide my true feelings.

"You seem a lot happier, than I've seen you in a while." Fiona winked. "Perhaps it's because of a certain man…"

*You've got that right, but it's not the man you think.* "It's all this fresh air and exercise." I sat up and tried to swing my legs over the side of the hammock. "Can you give me a hand?"

Fiona grasped my hand and gently pulled.

My feet touched the ground and I shot up out of the hammock, barreling into Fiona and knocking her to the ground.

She shook the sand out of her hair, then shot me an odd look.

An inch more and her head would've cracked open like an egg on the trunk of the tree.

# Chapter 29

Exhausted from all the activity on Sunday, everyone slept in on the holiday Monday. Mid-morning, the four of us met up in the kitchen and ate some lunch.

"When are you guys heading back to Boston?" Oliver asked, skimming at his phone.

"Pretty soon," Mark replied. "I'm needed at the hospital, and Fiona's got her summer literacy camp."

"Let's finish packing," Fiona said, leading him back to their bedroom.

I was mentally and emotionally drained. "Oliver, do you think we could leave sooner rather than later?"

"Sure, Erin," he said, leaning on the counter. "We can leave as soon as you're ready. Just let me know and I'll load up the car."

When all four of us reappeared in the living room with our bags, the brothers loaded up the two cars. Fiona and I checked that we hadn't forgotten anything and made sure all the lights were off. Then we joined the men outside, and Mark locked the front door behind us.

Fiona hugged me and whispered in my ear, "Give Oliver a chance."

I stiffened, and she released me.

When Mark swooped in for a squeeze, a tremor traveled through my body. But he released me, like a startled fish, and strutted over to the Range Rover. Fiona – who was already perched in the passenger seat – waved goodbye. Gravel flew up in a water-like spray, as Mark gunned it out of the driveway.

My spirits sank, as I watched his black behemoth disappear down the driveway in a cloud of dust.

Traffic out of the Cape was heavy, so the return drive to Boston was slow. I struggled to stay awake; my head lolled and my eyes drooped. The frisson I'd felt during my quick hug with Mark, replayed itself over and over in my mind.

But feelings of self-reproach kept interrupting my thoughts. Throughout the years, Fiona's generosity emitted a delicate warmth that absorbed everyone fortunate enough to know her. Our connection, forged through innumerable shared moments and treasured reflections, altered us into kindred spirits who maneuvered life's expedition hand-in-hand.

How could I have stabbed her in the back, after everything she had done for me? Fiona had been there for me, through countless challenges, especially the death of my father. And what about this past year? How would I have survived the devastating grief after Sean's death, without Fiona by my side? Was Mark worth risking our friendship for?

We had been driving for an hour when I opened my eyes.

"Have a good nap?" Oliver asked.

"Yes, thanks," I replied, sitting up in my seat. I gazed out the window, as we passed a turkey farm. Then I forced myself to make conversation. "So, tell me more about the exciting world of IT."

"Well, let's see. I helped a college deal with a security breach."

"What happened?" I peeled my eyes away from the beauty of the countryside to look at Oliver.

"A hacker broke into their system, encrypted all their files, then asked for a ransom in exchange for a key to unlock all their data."

"Spear-phishing again?

"Yep, but this time they used a hyperlink to install the ransomware."

"Did the college pay the ransom?" I turned in my seat to face him.

"Not right away. They were concerned that the hacker would just ask for more." Oliver clenched the steering wheel. "But, in the end, they didn't want to risk losing years of academic research."

"Won't that just encourage other cybercriminals to give it a shot?"

He glanced over at me. "Unfortunately, yes. But it keeps me in business."

"True." The corners of my lips curled up. "I knew hackers targeted the government and celebrities, but I didn't know things like this were going on. I guess I shouldn't be surprised." A nerve fluttered in my forehead. If only I could hack into Mark's computer.

"They even attack hospitals and churches…"

"Some people have no shame." *I wonder if Mark's hospital is at risk.*

As we drove through a village, the conversation lagged, and a tumbledown, antique store caught my attention. An old, wooden rocking chair stood on the sidewalk, and an image of my baby brother – lost at such a young age – came bubbling up to the surface. I thought I'd buried all those childhood memories, so deep they'd never resurface. Maybe being around the two brothers this weekend had triggered me. Now, a vision of my mother rocking my baby brother to sleep scrolled in my mind's eye. Without realizing what I was doing, I began humming a lullaby.

"Is that *Rock-a-Bye Baby?*" Oliver asked.

"Oops." A rosy blush appeared on my cheeks.

"I always thought that was a creepy song: *'When the bough breaks, the cradle will fall.'*"

"*'Down will come baby, cradle, and all,'*" I completed the rhyme. "You're right. It is super creepy."

Our eyes interwove fleetingly. Then I looked away, and Oliver accelerated the car. I maneuvered the fragile dance between flashbacks and forgetting, cautiously balancing between protecting the reminiscences and safekeeping my fragile heart. The unsaid connection with my dearly departed baby brother stayed, its presence obvious in the quiet moments, reminding me of a bond that surpassed the physical realm. "So, what do you do for fun?" I asked, changing the subject.

"I go for long walks with my dog."

"You have a dog? What kind? Why didn't you bring him to the cottage?"

"A Jack Russell Terrier." Oliver took his eyes off the road to smile in my direction. "He's a bit hyper, and I didn't know if you and Fiona were dog lovers, so a neighbor offered to take him for the weekend."

"You should've brought him. I love dogs. What's his name?"

"Digger. What about you? Do you have any pets?"

"I've got a dog, too. A little black pug called Keeper. My mother's looking after her."

"I've never heard that name before. Is it because she's 'a keeper'?" His face broke into a grin.

"She's definitely 'a keeper', but I named her after a bull mastiff owned by the novelist, Emily Brontë. Apparently, the dog was so attached to her, it lay outside Brontë's bedroom door for days after her death. It even followed the casket down the aisle of the church at her funeral."

"Dogs are amazing, aren't they? Much nicer than most humans."

"That's for sure."

"But I can't quite picture Digger doing that for me if I died." Oliver laughed.

By the time we were back in Boston, we had agreed to meet for a dog-walking date the following Saturday.

I lugged my bag into my bedroom and got busy unpacking and sorting my clothes into piles for the laundry. Oliver was such a nice guy. The dog-walking date would be fun. Maybe I should forget about Mark and try to give his brother a chance. It would make Fiona happy. But when I picked up my red bikini, my thoughts flipped back to Mark and our encounter on the island. My knees almost buckled, as I remembered his passionate kiss.

Abandoning my laundry along with my new resolve, I collapsed on my bed in an ecstasy of daydreams. Grasping one of my duck-down pillows, I squeezed it against my body and tried to pretend that it was Mark. I slid my hand down between my legs; however, the pillow was a poor substitute. I groaned with frustration and flung the pillow across the room. I had to see Mark again, as soon as possible. How was I going to fill the endless seconds, minutes, and hours until I saw him again? The time until our next encounter would be pure torment.

Suddenly, an idea struck me. Later in the week, I'd walk by his apartment building and the hospital and see if I could 'accidentally' run into him.

# Chapter 30

My phone buzzed. "Hi, Mom. I'm home from the cottage. Sorry I didn't call. I got busy sorting my laundry."

"I was beginning to wonder where you were. Would you like me to bring Keeper over right now?"

"That would be great, Mom. I miss my little baby."

"But I do have one stipulation."

"What's that?"

"You have to tell me all about your weekend."

After I'd ended the call, another idea struck me. I googled Mark's hospital on my phone and dialed the general number. When the recording directed me to enter a surname, I typed, *R-A-N-K-I-N* and held my breath.

"You have reached Dr. Mark Rankin in the emergency department at *City Center Hospital.* If this is an emergency, dial 911. Otherwise, please leave your name and number."

In a way, it was an emergency. I needed – desperately – to see him again. But I ended the phone call without leaving a message. It was time to finish loading the laundry. My red bikini, now a memento of Mark and our island tryst, I hand-washed in the bathroom sink.

Now that I'd taken care of the laundry, I noticed the hungry ache in my stomach. I didn't have much food in the fridge, so I'd have to make do with a bowl of cereal. After adding a handful of almonds for protein, I grabbed a sharp knife to cut up some fruit. Clenching the black handle of the stainless steel blade, I sliced into the strawberries. Red juice bled onto the wooden cutting board and onto my fingers. When I was finished, I put down the knife and rubbed my hands together under the tap.

A line from Lady Macbeth flashed into my mind. *Out, damned spot! Out, I say!*

There was a knock at the front door and my heart juddered. It must be my mother delivering Keeper. I had really missed my little sidekick. When I opened the door, Keeper leapt from my mother's arms into mine. She licked my neck, tickling me and making me laugh, and I kissed her flat button nose.

"I was going to ask you for a kiss," my mother said. "But now I'm not sure that I want one, after all the licking and kissing between you and that dog."

"Oh, Mom. She's my little baby. It'd be mean if I didn't return her kisses. Anyway, thanks for looking after her. I hope she behaved herself." I put Keeper down, then leaned over and gave my mother a tight hug.

"Oh, she was no trouble, really. She spent most of the time sleeping or chasing squirrels outside at the park." My mother chuckled. "Now, enough about the dog. I want to hear all about your weekend."

I took a deep breath. "It was very nice."

My mother frowned. "I need more details than that. We had a deal, remember?"

I walked down the hall to the kitchen. I opened a cupboard door, got out two mugs and banged them down on the counter. "We did a lot of sailing and hung out on the beach."

"What's Dr. Rankin's brother like? Are you interested in him?"

"Oliver? He's very nice." I braced myself for an inquisition.

"The weekend was 'very nice'. Oliver is 'very nice'. For an English major, your vocabulary is *very* limited."

I turned away and reached for the kettle.

"Are you going to see him again?"

I filled the kettle with water and plugged it in. "Next weekend. We made plans to take our dogs to the Common. Time for some tea."

"That sounds nice, dear. I mean the tea *and* the dog walk." My mother smiled. "Pity Oliver's not a doctor, like his brother."

"Not everyone can be a doctor, Mom. It takes a special kind of person. Speaking of Mark—he and I spent some time alone together. We went kayaking and landed on an island." I stopped talking and could feel my face burning.

There was an awkward pause.

My mother gave me a quizzical look, and I feared that she could read me like a book. Her silence was more disturbing than a barrage of questions. *Has she guessed how I feel about Mark?* If my mother could gaze into the center of my spirit that easily, maybe Fiona could, too. I started scrounging in the cupboards for a package of cookies. As the kettle whistled, I unplugged it, poured the boiling water into the teapot, and added two teabags. By focusing my attention on small tasks, I could avoid my mother's penetrating gaze.

"How's Fiona doing these days?"

An uneasy energy grew through my nerves, but I attempted to answer my mother in a nonchalant manner.

"Fiona? Oh, she's fine." I placed the two cups and the pot on the table and let the tea steep. "It was nice to spend some time with her this weekend, although we didn't have much of a chance to talk away from Mark and Oliver."

"Do you think her relationship with Dr. Rankin—"

"Call him Mark, Mom."

"Is her relationship with *Mark* getting serious?"

"I don't know how well matched they are. Fiona told me she's concerned about the long hours Mark works. I'm not sure the relationship has any long-term potential."

"I see." My mother poured herself some tea.

I passed the plate to my mother. "Cookie? I hope these aren't too stale. I'm not sure how long they've been in my cupboard."

"Thank you, but I think I will decline the offer, tempting though it may be." My mother took a few sips of hot tea. "It sounds like you had a fun weekend and, while I think it's good for you to be around other people, you're still emotionally vulnerable." She paused to drink more tea, then peered at me over the rim of the cup. "Your father's and Sean's deaths have been hard on you, and I worry that you've become somewhat fragile. I guess, what I'm trying to say is—just be careful."

"Yes, Mom." I nodded and swallowed some tea.

"As much as I want to see you settled in a committed relationship," she said, looking at me pointedly, "I'd hate it to be with the wrong person."

*Wrong person? What does she mean? Am I that obvious?*

My mother picked up a cookie, held it up to her nose, then returned it to the plate.

I stared down into my teacup.

"Well, I can see that you're exhausted," she said, patting my hand. "I'll leave you alone, so you can get some rest."

I collected our empty cups and rinsed them under the tap at the kitchen sink.

My mother rose out of her chair and made her way to the front door.

"Thanks again, for looking after Keeper," I said, giving her a kiss.

"You're most welcome, dear. And next time you see Mark, please tell him that I'm feeling much better."

"I will, Mom, but I don't know when I'll be seeing him again..."

She placed her hand on my wrist and looked me straight in the eyes. "Remember what I said—just be careful."

# Chapter 31

I sublimated my obsessive desire for Mark by spending most of the night writing, in a trance-like state. It was as if my heart was pumping ink through my veins and out of my fingertips and onto the paper.

*"I'm really worried about you," Faith said, as she picked up my tray of dirty dishes after dinner one night. "It's been weeks since you came home from the hospital, and Max says you should be better by now."*

*"I know," I said. "But I just feel so weak."*

*"Well, get a good night's sleep," Faith said. "I'd better get back upstairs and clean up these dishes. Max is taking me out again tonight."*

*When my sister was gone, I took out the steak knife that I had slipped under my pillow and hid it under the mattress. And later, when I was sure that Faith had left for the night with Max, I got up out of bed and walked around upstairs. Unbeknownst to my sister and her doctor-boyfriend, I was fully recovered. But maintaining their belief in my bedridden condition was all part of my plan.*

The next morning, I woke up, ate breakfast, fed Keeper and left for work.

But instead of heading for the bookstore, I found myself walking downtown in the direction of *City Center Hospital.* It was like an invisible thread was pulling me towards Mark. Like an automaton, I texted Maddie.

*Running late. Cover for me.*

After cutting through the Public Garden, where the pedal-powered swan boats floated around the lagoon, I hopped on a passing, crosstown T-bus. Mindlessly, I stared out the window as the city scape rolled by in a blur. Before long, the hospital loomed on the horizon like a beached white whale, and I jumped off the stifling hot bus.

Stepping into the glass-paneled airlock of the hospital's revolving doors, I was momentarily suspended in time. When the chamber released me into the Leviathan's stomach, there was no turning back. *I'm here. And Mark is here, too. We're breathing the same air.*

I wandered aimlessly and lost my bearings in the labyrinth of endless hallways. *Where are you, Mark?* At least it was air conditioned. I soon started to seriously question the sanity of what I was doing. *If I do run into Mark, what on earth will I say to him?*

I rounded a corner and, suddenly, as if I had summoned him from my obsessive imaginings, there he was—his presence was brought out by the sparkle of a silver stethoscope, carefully wound around his neck like a serpent, an emblem of his devotion and skills. It gleamed in the fluorescent light, proof of the countless lives he had impacted and cured with his expert hands and benevolent heart as he leaned on the counter of the nurse's station. My thoughts careened. I stood still and tried to get control of my breathing. *What am I doing here?* A nerve twitched in the corner of my eye. *I shouldn't be here.* I slipped behind a post and secretly watched him. He was talking to a petite brunette in pale, pink scrubs. Was she a nurse or a fellow doctor? Mark said something, and the woman threw her head back and laughed. Jealousy speared me in the heart. What was so funny? The woman touched his arm and smiled up at him. *Is she flirting with him?*

Without warning, Mark turned in my direction.

I shrank back behind the post, but it was too late. He'd seen me.

"Hey. Erin, is that you? What're you doing here?"

I stepped out from my hiding spot. "Oh – uh – hi. I'm fine. Just getting some tests done."

"Nothing serious, I hope." He gave me a hug. "Got time to grab a coffee?"

*I can't believe this is happening.*

"That would be great, but I know you're busy—"

"I am always busy, but I have time for a quick coffee, especially for Fiona's best friend."

*Fiona's best friend? Is that how he sees me? Of course, it is.*

"It's really great to see you, Erin." He looped his arm in mine and led me down a long hallway. I assumed that we were headed to a *Starbucks* or a cafeteria. But he stopped at a door with a sign that said, 'Hospital Staff Only'. Mark unlocked the door and led me into a small room with a kitchenette, a comfy couch, a round table and chairs.

"Hope you don't mind, but the cafeteria is always packed with people." He put a filter and some grounds in the coffee maker and filled it with water.

I smiled, nervously, and fiddled with my hair. My heart pounded so violently against my rib cage, I was sure he would see it. Summoning all my courage, I moved towards the couch and sat down.

He handed me a coffee, then sat down next to me. "I'd ask you how your writing is going, but you probably hate being asked that question."

"That's very astute of you." I smiled, sipped some coffee, and examined him over the rim of the mug.

A look slid between us.

My body emerged with goosebumps, as if there was a sudden chill in the air. I put down my coffee on the table, and he did the same.

Then Mark put his hands on my shoulders and pulled me towards him. He kissed me, tenderly, on the lips and, slowly, moved down to my neck. Without delay, our lips connected with a hurry that withstood rationale. Our bodies close to one another, the fabric of our garments an obstacle we urgently wanted to shed. With a proficient touch, he undid the buttons of my black blouse, enabling it to charmingly fall from my shoulders. Concurrently, I witnessed the supple descent of his white medical coat, revealing the organic passion that flared between us.

Every particle of pent-up emotion that had been soundlessly brewing within me, hidden behind a front of limitation, erupted like a cyclone unleashed. It was a plethora of longing and submission, an outflow of all the unsaid thirst that had absorbed my thoughts in the time leading up to this moment. The mass of assumptions and eagerness melted away, substituted by a seductive mixture of exposure and release.

As he delicately situated himself above me, a charge of ecstasy soared through my veins, engulfing my senses. It was a magical attachment, a merging of bodies and souls that left me breathless and dangling in the realm of euphoria. In his caress, I found an ardor that outdistanced any previous experiences, which unparalleled even the core of what I had once assumed to be true with Sean.

Mark, the manifestation of my innermost yearnings and urges, became the revelation of the man who had possessed my dreams. In him, I recognized my soul's equivalent, the hidden piece that concluded the labyrinthine puzzle of my existence. His touch, dense and certain, followed the shape of my body with an artist's accuracy, stirring a powerful mix of satisfaction and restriction that endangered me and possessed me completely.

As his lips ventured lower, roaming the scenery of my torso, a rush of energy boiled through my being, eradicating responsive thought. Sensations crashed and evolved, overpowering my senses until I could no longer discern where satisfaction began and ended. The borders of my mind disintegrated, leaving only the unrefined, primal connection that unified us in this heavenly dance of intimacy.

Afterwards, I rested my head on his chest and listened to his rhythmic heartbeat. If only I could lie here forever, safe in my lover's arms. Cocooned with Mark inside this small room, made me feel like nothing could ever hurt me again.

But while my passion was sated, my mind buzzed with questions. I hoped that we could finally, discuss what was going on between us. I waited until he got up and dressed, then broached the subject.

"Mark, we need to talk."

"I know we do." He lifted his right hand and tucked a loose strand of hair behind my ear. Then he gently stroked my cheek. "And we will. I promise. But unfortunately, right now, I've got rounds. You can hang out here for a while, if you want. Help yourself to more coffee."

I stood up, and he gave me a long hug.

Then he pulled back and gave me a final kiss. "I'm so sorry, but I really have to get going."

"It's okay. I understand. Go and save some lives." I forced a smile and gave him a gentle push towards the door.

He opened the door, then turned and looked at me over his shoulder. "See you soon, beautiful."

*Beautiful. Mark thinks I'm beautiful!* My head and heart whizzed with emotions. It was overwhelming. I sat back down on the couch, hugged my knees to my chest, and let out a long sigh of frustration. I wished we could've talked. Maybe he just needed more time to figure out what to do about Fiona. And what was I going to do about Fiona? If Mark and I did end up together, I'd be sacrificing our friendship. The thought of hurting Fiona made a stone drop deep in my stomach.

But I wasn't going to solve anything by sitting here by myself, so I got up and picked my clothes up off the floor. There was a small washroom, where I tidied myself up and finger-combed my hair. I stared at my reflection in the mirror. *I got what I wanted, didn't I?* It was time to leave. I poked my head out the door.

The coast was clear, so I slinked down the hall and searched for the way out. Finally, the exit was in sight. I hurried towards the revolving doors, but a familiar female voice stopped me in my tracks.

"Erin? Is that you? What're you doing here?"

# Chapter 32

I swiveled around on my heels. It was Paige. My breath hitched in my throat.

"This is a surprise," I said, forcing a smile.

"I've got a mammogram in half an hour," Paige said, folding her arms across her chest.

My smile faded. "I hope everything's okay."

"Yep. It's just my annual checkup."

*I need to get out of here.*

"But wait. Why're you here?" Paige knitted her brows. "Are you okay? You look flushed."

I hesitated and started nibbling on a nail.

"What's going on?" Paige stood an inch from my nose and gripped me by the arm. She had never been one to respect personal space.

I gave her a blank stare. *What do I tell her?* "Sorry, Paige, but I've got to get going or I'll be late for work."

"Oh my God." Paige's eyes widened. "Is it your mom?"

"No, I mean, yes." I tripped over my words. "She's fine. I was just picking up some forms for her." *What the hell am I doing? First, I slept with Fiona's boyfriend. Now, I'm lying to Paige—about my mom.*

"That's a relief." Paige released her hold on me.

I glanced at the time on my phone. "I've really got to get to work."

Paige tugged at my shirt sleeve. "Hold on. Isn't this the hospital where

Fiona's new boyfriend works?"

My insides fizzed. *Why did I have to run into you?*

"Did you see him?" Paige's eyes darted around.

*God, get me out of this mess, and I swear I'll never sleep with Mark, ever again.*

"Wait." Paige's eyes sparkled with mischief. "Since we're both here, why don't we try and find him?"

"Find Mark?"

"I've heard so much about the fabulous Dr. Rankin, but I want to see him in the flesh. You can introduce us. It's not fair that you've met him, and I haven't." Paige stomped a foot like one of her children.

I yanked my arm away. "I'm sorry, Paige. I've really got to go. My boss is a real stickler for punctuality. Besides, I'm sure Mark is far too busy…"

"Oh, all right." Paige stuck out her lower lip like a pouting child.

"It was great running into you." I scuttled away from my friend. "Say 'hi' to Angus and give my love to the kids." As I pushed my way through the heavy, revolving doors, my panic subsided. *That was too close for comfort.* Running into Paige had been a warning. A sign. An omen. In future, I would stay far away from the hospital, unless it was a legitimate, life-or-death emergency.

After my morning escapade, the bookstore would be a sanctuary. As soon as I arrived, Maddie rushed up to me. I noticed a fluorescent, green stripe amongst her dyed black locks.

"Thanks for covering for me. I owe you one. By the way, I like your new look."

"Oh, thanks. I'm glad you like it." Maddie looked pleased and ran a hand through her hair. "Anyway, you sure picked the right morning to come in late. Dave and Suzy had a run-in, so he's been hiding in his office all morning."

"That's lucky," I replied. "For me, I mean. You'll have to tell me all about it on our coffee break." I wondered what Dave had done this time. But at least it sounded like Suzy had stood up for herself.

Maddie darted away to help a customer.

The time at work went quickly enough. There were a lot of demanding customers looking for obscure books. But forgetting about Mark was easier said than done. Daydreaming about him had become a compulsive habit. And habits were hard to break. *I wonder if he's thinking about me and our time together in the on-call room? Or is he too busy saving lives? And what are we going to do about Fiona?* When I walked through the classics section, past a shelf of Shakespeare's plays, a copy of *King Lear* caught my eye. I'd studied it in Professor Douglas's class at college. I pulled it off the shelf and flipped through the pages, reminding myself of the plot. Goneril, jealous of Edmund's love for her sister, Regan, poisoned Regan's drink. The 'green-eyed monster' rearing its ugly head. Four hundred years later, here I was, caught in its clutches. I remember the professor telling us that it was Shakespeare's understanding of human nature that made his works truly timeless.

My train of thought was interrupted by the bookstore manager, Dave, who had emerged from his office and was hovering over my shoulder.

"I'm paying you to sell books, not to stand there and read them."

"Sorry. I was just—"

"I don't care what you were doing. I need you to start setting up for the reading and book signing tonight."

"Yes, Dave. I'll get right on it." At least it would help keep my mind off Mark.

On my coffee break, I noticed that I had a text from Fiona.

"We're going out for coffee. Want to join us?" Maddie and Suzy said.

"Thanks for asking, but I'm going to stay here and catch up on my emails." I watched them leave, then stared down at my phone. I wondered what Fiona wanted, but I was afraid to open it. The moral side of me, the side that was ashamed of backstabbing my best friend, wanted to avoid any contact with Fiona for as long as possible. I reddened when I thought of my behavior that morning. I would have to reply to my friend at some point, since we texted each other regularly and failure to do so might worry Fiona or cause the very suspicion that I was trying to avoid. I would have to watch every single word that I uttered. She could never find out what had happened. It was the ultimate treachery. If only we could both be happy, but only one of us could have Mark, which meant one of us was going to be devastated in the end.

But the darker side of me was too curious about what Fiona had to say. Maybe she would mention something about Mark. *Why can't I stop obsessing about him?* After taking a deep breath, I opened Fiona's text. Curiosity had trumped trepidation.

*Let's meet 4 coffee. BTW, Mark says 'hi'.*

So, he did think about me! Just reading his name sent trembles down my spine. My promise to forget all about him, after my close call with Paige, had all but disappeared. Suddenly, I was eager to become Mark's official girlfriend rather than his secret lover, if I could even use that word. But what about Fiona? She was my friend, but also the major obstacle blocking my path to Mark and preventing me from being with him in the way that I envisioned. Fiona had always been there for me, when my dad died and then, when I lost Sean. How could I even think about double-crossing her and causing her pain? Losing her friendship would be like another death in my life. Was Mark really worth such a loss? My mind was a tangled knot and every time I tried to loosen a strand, it only got more tangled.

On my way home from work, I switched my phone back on. A red dot indicated I had missed several calls, all from Paige.

*Crap. I wonder what she wants.*

When my phone buzzed, I automatically swiped the green answer button. "Hey, Paige. What's up?"

"Listen. I need to talk to you about this morning."

"This morning?" I asked, choking on my words.

"I know you weren't picking up forms for your mother."

# Chapter 33

"We've been friends for a long time, and I can read you like a book. Pardon the cliché," Paige said. "If there's something wrong with you, I hope you know you can trust me."

There was an awkward pause. I could hear Paige's son, Lochlan, squealing in the background.

"I'm coming over," she said, then hung up the phone.

At home, I changed out of my work clothes, showered, and put on camouflage capris, a slate-gray T-shirt, and flip-flops. I took a spinach quiche out of the fridge and threw together a simple green salad.

When Paige arrived, dinner and two place settings were on the kitchen table.

"I hope you're hungry. I threw together a quick dinner, just in case."

Paige rubbed her hands together. "You know me. I'm always starving. The kids are at a friend's house for dinner, so I'm all yours."

"Great." I opened a bottle of white wine and poured two glasses. *Sorry Dr. Pritchard.* "Have you done something new with your hair?" I wanted to delay the cross examination for as long as possible. I needed to come up with a story.

"Thanks for noticing." Paige lifted the wineglass to her lips. "I needed a bit of pampering, so I decided to get a manicure and a haircut." She held out one hand and waved ten crimson-tipped fingers for my approval.

"Sexy. I bet your husband likes them."

"He won't care. These days, I don't think Angus would even notice if I dyed my hair purple." Paige chuckled, then slugged back more wine. "I switched hairdressers, and she suggested I try a more layered look."

"It suits you."

"Thanks." Paige swished her newly shorn locks from side to side. She picked up the bottle and refilled her glass.

"I might have to get your hairdresser's number." I hoped all the flattery would put Paige in a sympathetic mood.

Paige sipped more wine. "Sure. But enough about my hair. I need to know what's going on."

My nerves rang. I sucked back some wine and sat down at the kitchen table.

Paige joined me, then fixed me with a hawk-like stare.

Fortified with a half-glass of wine in my belly, I started my story. "Please don't tell anyone, but I thought I had an STD."

"Oh my God." Paige almost spat out her mouthful of wine.

"But I don't." I handed her a napkin. "So, it's all good."

Paige stared at me for a few moments, then wiped her chin. "I don't believe you."

A nerve twitched in my temple, and I shifted in my seat.

Paige gave me a steely gaze. "I can always tell when you're lying. And besides, you haven't slept with anyone since Sean… unless you've been holding out on me."

*God, why did I say I had an STD? I'm such a terrible liar.*

"Okay. Fine." I shrugged, admitting defeat. I emptied my wine glass. "I'm sorry. You're right. I made that up."

"Obviously." Paige gave me a satisfied smirk. She poured us both some more wine, then crossed her arms and waited.

I had never been able to fool Paige, in all the years that I had known her. It was as if she had psychic powers. "I guess I'd better tell you what's really going on…"

"Please do."

"But first, I need complete reassurance that you'll keep what I'm about to tell you in the strictest confidence. Most importantly, you can never tell Fiona." I got up from the table and walked over to the fridge, keeping my back to Paige.

"Oh my God." Paige put down her wine glass. "What is it?"

"Do you promise to keep my secret?" I took another chilled bottle of white out of the fridge. Maybe I could distract Paige with alcohol. With any luck, if she drank as much as she usually did when she had a night off from the kids, she might even forget this whole conversation in the morning.

"Yes, of course. I promise." Paige looked like she was going to burst a blood vessel if I didn't hurry up and explain myself.

"Okay, here goes." I sat down and drank more wine. *I know, Dr. Pritchard. I know. I'll be better tomorrow. I swear.* I took a deep breath and straightened my shoulders. "I have a crush on someone."

"Oh my God. What a relief. I thought you were going to tell me you had cancer or something. You really scared me."

"Paige, I'm so sorry. God, I never meant to scare you."

"It's okay. Just hurry up and tell me about this crush. Who is he? Wait, I bet I know. It's Mark's brother, isn't it? What's his name again? Owen? Oscar?"

"Oliver."

"That's amazing. I'm so happy for you. But wait…" Paige put down her wine glass. "Why all the need for secrecy? And you still haven't told me *why* you were at the hospital. Don't tell me Oliver's a doctor, too?"

"No, Oliver isn't a doctor. He works in IT."

"But then…why were you at the hospital?"

I had to put Paige out of her misery. There was no way out. I'd backed myself into a corner.

"I like Oliver. He's a great guy. But he's not the one I have a crush on."

"I give up." Paige raised her palms in a gesture of surrender. "If it isn't Oliver, then who on earth is it?"

My heart hammered against my ribcage like a woodpecker.

"Is your mystery man a doctor? Is that why you were at the hospital?"

I nodded.

Paige slapped her forehead. "I don't believe this. You and Fiona both fell for doctors. What's your guy's name?"

I hesitated.

"Come on. Tell me. I can't take the suspense one second longer."

"Okay. Here goes." I took a deep breath. "It's Mark."

"Mark." Paige's forehead creased. "Oh my God! Not Fiona's Mark…"

# Chapter 34

I pumped my knees up and down under the table, like I was riding a bicycle. Why had I ever gone to the hospital? And why did I have to run into Paige, of all people? Maybe it had been some kind of warning. Shaking my head, I dismissed that idea and chose, instead, to see the whole situation as an unfortunate coincidence. I picked up my wine glass and gulped down half its contents. Then I stared at the ground and wished I could disappear like a mouse behind the baseboards.

Paige slumped back into her seat and swirled wine around in her glass. She seemed, unusually, at a loss for words.

A silence lapsed between us. The fridge hummed in the background.

I picked up my glass of wine and drained it.

There was a click, a crash, and a whirring sound. We both jumped in our seats, then erupted into laughter.

"My ice machine's on the fritz. I need to get it repaired."

"It sounded like someone was trying to break in." Paige tried to tuck her hair behind her ears, but it was too short and kept falling back in front of her eyes. "I think that damn hairdresser cut too much off."

"No, I think it looks great. Maybe you could try using a hairband or some gel." I was thankful the tension had broken, but I knew I wasn't off the hook.

Paige grabbed the bottle, sloshing more wine into both our glasses. "So, tell me, how did this 'crush' develop? I know you all went up to

Cape Cod on July the Fourth weekend…"

I took a deep breath and squared my shoulders. "When I first met Mark at the party in his loft, I thought he was a nice guy. And I was happy for Fiona. I really was. But he reminded me so much of Sean. Haven't you noticed the resemblance?"

"I've only seen a photo of him, but now that you mention it, he did look a bit like Sean. But I'm sure the resemblance never occurred to Fiona. She would never want to do anything to hurt you; she loves you too much."

"I know she does, but Mark doesn't just look like Sean. He acts like him, too. He's charming and kind and thoughtful. And after he helped my mother at the hospital, I started to think of him in a different way."

"I can understand that you'd be grateful. But he was just doing his job."

"That's what my therapist said."

"Smart lady." Paige smirked, then narrowed her eyes. "Back to you and Mark."

"There is no 'me and Mark'." *Not officially, anyway.* I ogled the bottle of wine. Lying to Paige distressed me, but it was for the best. If she knew that we'd had sex – in an on-call room – she'd be horrified. After all Fiona had done for me, Paige would never understand how I could double-cross her in the worst kind of way. And it suddenly struck me, that if the truth came out, I'd lose Paige's friendship too. She'd definitely side with Fiona, and I wouldn't blame her. Neither one of them would ever trust me again. The consequences of my actions were huge. The more I thought about it, the more a big boulder of concern compressed my chest.

Paige took a long swallow of wine. "I'm still waiting for you to explain what you were doing at the hospital."

I guzzled more wine. "I went there to see Mark."

"What on earth for?" Paige arched her eyebrows.

"I don't know exactly. I thought maybe we'd grab coffee and I could confess my feelings…" It was a relief to confide in someone about Mark, even though Paige would've been my last choice for the role of confidant, since she and Fiona were also close friends. But it hadn't really been my choice; Paige had backed me into a corner.

She stared at me, shaking her head back and forth like a pendulum. "We need more wine."

I topped up our glasses.

Paige inhaled the wine, then fixed me with an ice-cold stare.

"You know this is never going to work." Then she leaned forward and her gaze softened. "This is what I think is going on: Fiona has a new man and it's brought your feelings about losing Sean bubbling back up to the surface. It's completely understandable. But Mark is not Sean, no matter how much he may look, or act like him."

I lowered my eyes and analyzed a nail, like a scientist studying an unusual specimen under a microscope.

"You have to forget about him." She squeezed my hand, but her voice was as hard as nails. "If you keep on this way, everyone will end up hurt."

"I know." But I also knew that it was easier said than done.

"And you know what they say—food on someone else's plate always looks tastier."

I nodded.

"Fine, it's settled. You'll stay away from Mark." Paige slapped her thighs. "Let's eat. All this excitement has made me famished." She cut a piece of quiche and stuffed it into her mouth.

I pushed a piece of quiche around my plate. Paige was so lucky to be done with all the dating drama. Right now, I'd give almost anything to trade places with my friend.

Paige grabbed the bottle and emptied it into my glass. Then she picked up her fork and popped another piece of quiche in her mouth.

"Please promise you won't say anything to Fiona about me liking Mark."

"I won't—as long as you promise to stay away from him."

"I'll try my best." *How can I promise to stay away from him, when I spend every waking moment thinking about him?*

"You have to do more than try. He's Fiona's boyfriend, not yours."

I lowered my eyes.

"Everyone gets crushes, Erin. It's human nature. But you cannot take it any further. Fiona's a good person, and she doesn't deserve this, especially from you of all people."

I raised my gaze, and our eyes met in an intense lock.

"I know. It's just—"

"Let me put it this way: If you hurt Fiona," Paige said, crossing her arms, "I'll kill you."

# Chapter 35

After my dinner with Paige, I had booked another appointment with Dr. Pritchard. If I was serious about staying away from Mark, I'd need the doctor's help and advice.

"You recently lost your boyfriend in a car accident and now, you're fixating on your friend's new boyfriend – who's clearly unattainable – in order to avoid getting hurt again."

I stared at a spot on the floor.

"And when you find yourself obsessing over someone, it's often because you have a low sense of self-worth," the doctor said, in a quiet voice. "The solution for that is to focus on developing your own interests. Do things that make you feel good about yourself. Exercise. Start a new hobby. Take up a musical instrument. Or try ballroom dancing. And surround yourself with friends, who make you feel special and important."

*Friends? Like Paige and Fiona? And ballroom dancing required a partner...*

"Family can also be a great support. And speaking of family, early events in our lives can often have a significant impact on our adult selves. I know that your father passed away two years ago, but I'd like you to go even further back this time, to your childhood and the loss of your brother."

The old-style clock on the doctor's desk ticked in the background.

My eyelids pulsed. "I don't know if I can handle going back there."

Dr. Pritchard leaned forward in her chair. "I really believe this will help you heal. Will you trust me?"

I clutched the arms of the chair, to steady my shaking hands. "I do wish I could remember more about him, but it was a long time ago."

"Why don't you close your eyes and relax?" Dr. Pritchard's voice was gentle and soothing. "Breathe in and out. Feel yourself going down the escalator, down through the years and back to your childhood."

The tension slowly left my body. I let my mind drift back in time, until I was my six-year-old self.

"Imagine yourself back in the house you grew up in. Find the door to your brother's room. Open it up and describe what you see."

I opened the door of my bedroom and traveled down a dark hallway to my brother's room. An image of Gordie floated into my mind.

"I see my brother. He has chubby cheeks and bright, blue eyes that shine like glass marbles."

"Very good, Erin. What else?"

"I feel something soft in my hands."

"What is it? Can you describe it?"

I squeezed my eyes tighter. "It's a blanket." I leaned over the railing of Gordie's crib and placed it over his head. *No, no, no.* That couldn't be right. My breath came in pants, like a tongue depressor stick had been inserted into my mouth.

"Your eyelids are becoming lighter. You're rising up the escalator." The doctor's voice pulled me back to the present.

I let out a long breath, like a deflating balloon. I heard a snap and my eyes popped open.

"What happened?"

"You became extremely agitated, so I brought you back. Did you see something that upset you?"

I stalled and took a sip of water, my eyes at half-mast. What could I say? That I'd smothered my baby brother to death with a blanket?

"I don't remember."

"Do your parents ever talk about him?"

Oh my God. My poor parents. It's all my fault. I killed Gordie. I caused my parents so much suffering. I flashed back to my mother's mental breakdown. My dad buried himself in his work. Was that why he had a heart attack? I needed time alone to think about all this.

"Erin? What are you thinking about?"

"My mother has a photograph of my brother on her bedside table, and my father kept one on his desk at work. My dad adored him; he was convinced that little Gordie was going to follow in his footsteps and become an architect. But we never talked about him after he died. What I do remember is the dark shroud that's hung over my family ever since. And a sense of guilt—"

"There's that word 'guilt' again. Siblings often experience survivor's guilt: 'How come this happened to my brother and not to me'? And in cases of sibling rivalry, survivors often feel guilty that they somehow caused the death by wanting to get a sibling out of the picture so they could get more attention from their parents."

Sweat prickled under my armpits. Had I said something out loud during the hypnosis? Was she going to call the police? Could I be charged with a crime I committed when I was six years old? But doctors were sworn to keep patient confidentiality, weren't they? Did it still apply in cases of homicide? I was too afraid to ask.

Suddenly, I heard myself speaking, "He was only four months old. They said he died from crib death, but I overheard my parents arguing, each blaming the other for his death."

"That must have been extremely upsetting for them—and for you."

I bit my lip. Had I sounded too defensive? "My mother was so distraught, she had to be hospitalized. Later, she self-medicated with wine."

"And your father?"

"He buried himself in his work."

"The loss of a sibling is like a double loss because you lost your parents, too, when they became wrapped up in their own grief and emotionally withdrew."

And now, I know that it was all my fault.

"That's when friendships become so important."

"I also lost most of my friends. I became known as the girl whose baby brother died. The kids in the neighborhood and school kept their distance. They acted like death was something they could catch. I felt abandoned by my friends and by my parents, so I escaped into the world of books. The characters became my companions."

The doctor nodded.

"Eventually, the memory was just too painful, so I followed my parents' lead. I locked all memories of my baby brother in a box at the back of my mind and tossed away the key." My throat was as dry as a bone, so I picked up the water glass and took a long swallow.

"It's common for surviving siblings to repress their feelings of loss, instead of processing and growing from them." Dr. Pritchard clicked the button on her ballpoint pen. "But it's always lurking, just below the surface, waiting to be reawakened under times of stress."

"After Gordie died, my dad shifted all of his attention and expectations onto me."

The doctor wrinkled her brow. "And how did that make you feel?"

"Guilty, at first. And burdened." I drained the last drop of water. "And then, I don't know, kind of good? My dad would take me on father-daughter fishing trips. He took me to museums and art galleries. He told me about his job as an architect. My dad was my hero. I wanted to make him proud. He designed award-winning buildings, and I wanted to write an award-winning novel. But who knows if that will ever happen. And even if it does, he'll never know about it now."

"It sounds like you had a close relationship."

"In some ways, we did." I paused. "But I could see a sadness in my father's eyes, and I knew it was because I wasn't Gordie."

"Often the parents try to push the surviving sibling into the role of the dead child. And the survivor either rebels or distorts her own personality to accommodate the parents. But it's impossible to live up to the idealized memory of a dead child."

I nodded and bit back the pain.

"Survivors of sibling death can develop a neurotic need for affection and approval and be extremely sensitive to rejection or criticism."

The doctor was right. I definitely had a neurotic need for affection from my father, and then, from Sean. And now, from Mark.

# Chapter 36

For the rest of the week, thoughts about my baby brother looped around in my mind. I'd close my eyes and replay what I'd seen under hypnosis. I entered his room and smothered him with a blanket. I was buried under an avalanche of guilt for all the pain I'd caused my parents. Thank God my dad would never know what I had done, and I'd have to make sure that my mother never found out. It would kill her all over again.

Was it possible that the hypnosis was faulty? Maybe the sibling guilt Dr. Pritchard talked about had caused me to imagine that I'd done away with my sibling rival. But no matter how hard I tried to retrieve another memory of that night, it remained an elusive shadow in my mind.

The only thing that took my mind off Gordie was Mark. Despite Paige's warning and the doctor's advice, I couldn't stop replaying our rendezvous at the hospital over and over in my mind. The sex had been amazing. Was he falling in love with me? It did not seem to matter whether I was at work or at home; if I wasn't thinking about Gordie, I was thinking about Mark. Every morning, I'd wake up, grab my phone and stare at the screensaver picture of Mark. Next, I'd scroll through all the other photos of him on social media. At bedtime, I'd repeat the entire procedure all over again.

*

When the weekend arrived, it was time for my dog-walking date with Oliver. But as nice as he was and as much as I liked him, I was tempted to cancel and stay home and brood about Gordie and Mark. But then, I remembered the doctor's advice about exercise and friends.

As I lathered my body in the shower that morning, I began to formulate questions to ask Oliver. I wanted to learn more about their childhood and what Mark had been like in high school. I also wanted to know more about Mark's personal life and his history with women. Oliver had told me a few things about his brother on the cottage bike ride, but I wanted more details. How many serious relationships had he had before Fiona? Had he been in love before? I had a multitude of questions, but I was not sure how I would be able to present them all to Oliver, without raising his suspicions. The bathroom was increasingly becoming like a steam room, so I turned off the taps and grabbed my towel.

I glanced at the clock next to my bed. I was going to be late for our walk if I didn't leave the house right away. I had probably done enough thinking and daydreaming for one morning and would be better off getting some exercise outdoors. Hooking Keeper's leash to her harness, we headed straight out the front door.

I tried to walk quickly, down Charles Street towards the Common and Public Garden, but Keeper did not like the fast pace. Her pink tongue hung out of her mouth, and she panted like a steam engine. I lifted her up in my arms and carried her the rest of the way. It was only a short distance, but it felt like I was carrying a sack of potatoes. As we got closer to the Public Garden, Keeper became excited and more difficult to hold, so I plopped her down. The area near the pond, with its weeping willows, was her favorite spot, and she suddenly revived and started chasing the ducks and swans. Keeper especially loved to bark at the touristy swan boat as it floated past.

I strode along the path through the park, with Keeper now tugging at the lead. When we reached the edge of the pond, I was panting and perspiring, while Keeper romped around, happy-as-could-be. I saw Oliver playing fetch with his black-white-and-tan-colored Jack Russell Terrier.

When Oliver spotted me, his face broke into an eager beam and he rushed over and gave me an exuberant embrace.

"You're here. It's so good to see you."

He sounded so relieved that I wondered if he had thought I was going to stand him up.

Keeper headed straight for Digger and sniffed his backside, but Digger was too busy investigating a burrow to notice.

Oliver bent over and patted Keeper on the head. "Don't mind Digger. It's his hunting instinct. He's always on the lookout for rats or squirrels or rabbits to chase."

"Sorry we kept you waiting," I said, releasing Keeper from my lead. "Shall we let these guys run free for a while?"

"Sounds like a plan." Oliver unhooked Digger and he raced after Keeper. Oliver cleared his throat and turned to face me. "Your hair looks beautiful, by the way."

"Oh, thanks." I smiled at his thoughtfulness. It was nice to get a compliment. Gazing in his direction, I realized that I had forgotten how handsome he was. Oliver had a more solid build than Mark, which reflected his dependable nature. His red polo shirt, knee-length white shorts and brown loafers reflected the clean-cut, Ivy League look that both brothers seemed to favor. All he needed was an argyle sweater draped around his shoulders. I found their style a tad conservative, but they were, undeniably, a pair of good-looking brothers.

A series of loud barks interrupted my thoughts. Digger and Keeper had been in hot pursuit of a squirrel, but it had scurried up a tree.

"Lucky squirrel," Oliver said. "If Digger had caught it, he would've snapped its neck."

I flinched. "Are you serious?"

"It's in his blood. Terriers are hunters. He's killed more mice and rats than I can count." Oliver shook his head and laughed. "Anyway, it's so good to see you, Erin. I'm glad we made plans to meet up after the cottage."

I nodded. "Speaking of the cottage, does Mark go up there often?" *Ugh. I couldn't even wait five minutes before uttering his name. How pathetic am I?*

Oliver arched an eyebrow and twisted Digger's leash around his hands.

"I mean, ***you and Mark.***" I chewed on my lower lip.

"No, he doesn't get up there very often, not as much as I do, anyway. It's a great place to escape. Sometimes, I go on my own, but it was nice having you up there. You should come with me next time."

"That'd be nice." I knew that if I went up there again, I would spend a lot of the time reminiscing about Mark. It was his presence and our moments alone, in the kayaks and on the island, that had made my time at the cottage so exciting. "Fiona and Mark would have to come too, of course."

"I guess we could invite them along, if you really wanted to, but like I said, Mark's usually far too busy at work to get away to the cottage very often."

A sharp, shrill bark came from a nearby thicket of bushes.

Oliver's head swiveled away from me.

Digger was down on his haunches, gnashing his teeth at something hidden in the shrub.

"It's Keeper," I said, my voice shaking. "He won't hurt her, will he?"

Oliver rushed over and scooped Digger up in his arms. "Bad boy," he said, snapping the leash back onto his harness. "Sorry about that. He tends to see anything smaller than himself as fair game."

"That's all right." I forced a smile, but inside, I was roiling with anger. If Digger had bitten my precious pug, I would've killed Oliver. I crouched down and rescued Keeper from her hiding spot. "Come here, little girl. You're okay."

"Digger's sorry he scared you." Oliver took a treat out of his pocket and popped it into Keeper's mouth.

"You know the way to her heart." I laughed, as Keeper happily chomped away on the biscuit.

Oliver rubbed Keeper's wrinkled forehead, then slipped her another treat.

The sun shone directly on his face, and I was struck by the unique hue of his irises. "What color are your eyes? I thought they were brown, but now they look green."

"Hazel."

I leaned in and looked at them more closely. "I see some tiny flecks of gold."

"You're very observant. It must be because you're a writer."

*Mark's eyes are blue-gray, but they have the same gold flecks.*

"How's your work going at the bookstore?" he asked.

"Actually, I'm really excited about an upcoming event. One of my favorite authors, Rowena George, is on a book tour and I'll be hosting a promotional event with her at our store."

"Very cool. Speaking of books, have you written anything lately?"

"Actually, I have. It's become a compulsion, again." *I scribble all night long about your brother; that's why I've got moons under my eyes.*

"If you ever need a quiet space to write," Oliver said, kicking a piece of loose dirt with the toe of his shoe, "you could go to our cottage."

"I'll keep that in mind."

"Anything to help. Who knows, you might end up winning a Pulitzer…"

"Or the Booker or Nobel." I playfully swatted Oliver's arm.

"Maybe *Netflix* will turn it into a movie." Oliver gave me a big grin.

"And the screenplay will win an Oscar."

"Why not?" Oliver's eyes crinkled. "Maybe we can go to a movie together sometime?"

"Sure. Maybe Fiona and Mark could come too." Seeing a movie with Mark by my side would definitely be better than sitting at home alone and obsessing about my baby brother. Maybe I could sit next to Mark during the movie and pretend that I was his date. The idea was starting to appeal to me, more and more, as my imagination took hold.

A little pug, nudging my shin and barking for attention, brought me back to reality.

"That's her way of reminding me that it's time for lunch."

"We'd like to walk you two ladies home, if that's okay with you?"

I nodded and the four of us headed to a path leading out of the park, but the more I tugged at the leash, the more Keeper dug her paws into the ground.

"Let me do the honors." Oliver handed me Digger's leash, then picked Keeper up into his arms. "Wow. You're heavier than you look."

"She's like a potbelly pig." I laughed.

"Or a pot roast." He ruffled her ears. "It's a good thing she's so cute."

"And she knows it." I smirked. "All this fresh air has given me an extra burst of energy. Come on, I'll race you up the hill."

"Not fair." Oliver laughed. "I've got an extra load."

I ignored him and took off up the hill, with Digger at my heels. Halfway up the incline, my shoe caught on a tree root, and I catapulted forward.

Oliver hurried over and helped me up. "It looks like you've hurt your knee."

I glanced down and saw tiny red beads of blood, but laughed it off.

"I'm fine. Just some scraped skin. No big deal." *If only Mark was here to patch me up.*

# Chapter 37

Saturday was fast-approaching, and I had texted Fiona several times to confirm her attendance at the movie. For now, I had rolled all my two-faced feelings about sleeping with Mark into a tiny little ball and tossed it into the back corner of my mind. Secretly, I crossed my fingers and hoped that Mark would be available to join us. If he couldn't make it, then Fiona wouldn't come either, and that would leave me alone on a date with Oliver. Walking our dogs together during the daylight hours had been one thing. A movie date at night was a whole different situation.

Saturday arrived, but I still hadn't heard back from Fiona. I forced myself not to check my phone for messages more than once every half hour.

By mid-afternoon, I started to get frantic. I picked up my phone in exasperation and my heart skipped a beat when I noticed a new text. It was from Fiona.

*We're coming. See you there.*

'We' meant Mark was coming, too. I tossed the phone on my bed and almost jumped in the air with joy. Flinging myself on the bed, I closed my eyes, and began to fantasize about the night ahead. I wondered what Mark would be wearing and whether he would give me a hug. *Will he try to get me alone? Will that even be possible, with both Oliver and Fiona there? How will he behave around me?* My mind whirled with thoughts and questions and possible scenarios, until Keeper's insistent barking pulled me out of my reverie. She had her paws up on the bed in an attempt to get my attention; she was far too small to jump up on the bed by herself.

I reached down and flopped her down next to me. "What do you think will happen tonight, Keeper?"

After giving my dog a good scratch behind the ears, I started to get myself ready. I only had a few hours left to shower and do my hair and apply my makeup. And on top of all that, I had yet to find the perfect outfit. A frantic search through my closet followed. Nothing seemed quite right. Eventually, I settled on skinny jeans and an off-the-shoulder pale-pink blouse by my favorite designer. My mouth turned up at the edges, as I assessed my appearance in the full-length mirror. *This should get Mark's attention.*

When I arrived at the movie theater near Boston Common that evening, Oliver was already there waiting for me. He certainly was punctual. I let him give me a quick peck on the cheek and glanced around to see if Mark and Fiona were nearby.

"Hey, there's Fiona." Perfidy pricked at me like a needle, but I ignored it and smiled and waved my arm. "We're over here." My smile faded, as Fiona rushed towards us. She was wearing the exact same off-the-shoulder top as me, but in a vibrant shade of fuchsia. A gush of blazing anger arose within me, racing through my veins like molten lava. My jaw clamped firmly, and my fists naturally tensed, searching for an outlet for the extreme emotion throbbing within, yet she threw her arms around my shoulders and gave me a giant bear hug.

"I've missed you. It seems like so long since we were all together at the cottage. You haven't been returning my texts. I was beginning to think that you were avoiding me, until you invited us to the movie." Fiona gave me a playful frown.

"I've just been really busy with work. I'm in charge of organizing a big author event. Rowena George."

"Oh, I love her books. They make the perfect beach reads."

*Beach reads? Was that an intentional slight?* A burning heat traveled up my neck.

"Actually, her writing has won a lot of prestigious awards. I was lucky enough to get an advanced reader copy of her latest thriller. And I think it's her best yet. Anyway, there's so much to organize. You know how it is. Enough about me. How have you been? I'm sure Mark has been keeping you company." I couldn't resist saying his name and fishing for information.

"To be honest, I've barely seen him since the cottage. We tried to get together a couple of times, but he always had to cancel because of some emergency at the hospital."

A small smile played on my lips, but I swallowed it.

"Mark said he was definitely going to make it tonight, but I can never really count on him, even when he promises. He's not here yet, so who knows…"

My chest pinched. *What if Mark doesn't make it?* I had spent so much time dreaming about it. I had even gone out and bought new makeup and spent, what seemed like hours, applying it. My hair had taken forever as well. And I had tried on so many different outfits that I had lost count. I had felt sexy when I left the house, and if Mark ever showed up, I hoped that he would not be able to take his eyes off me. Why did Fiona have to find some fashion sense tonight, of all nights? She looked so fresh and feminine in that fuchsia blouse. A perfect princess. I began to wonder if I'd put on too much makeup. Maybe I should steal off to the washroom and check.

"Where is he?" Fiona murmured, tapping a finger on the screen of her phone.

"I think we should head in without him," Oliver said, his voice taut.

"Maybe we should," I said, my shoulders slumping, but I could not resist turning my head towards the entrance one more time.

The three of us started to make our way to the door of the theater, when Mark arrived at last and gave us all friendly hugs. I was secretly thrilled when he awarded me with an extra squeeze. True to form, a ripple of gooseflesh trickled across my entire being, resembling a field of elevated hairs on my skin. I was glad that I had spent all that time preparing, after all. It seemed to have had the desired effect.

"Sorry, I'm so late. I almost didn't make it. We had an emergency, but another doctor's looking after it, so here I am. Wow. You ladies both look pretty in pink."

A bitter taste swirled in my mouth. *Why did he have to lump me and Fiona together in the same compliment?* I knew I was being a terrible friend, but I just couldn't help it.

"Does anyone want popcorn?" Mark asked. "Let's grab some and head into the theater. What's everyone waiting for?"

Oliver offered to get the popcorn and drinks, so the rest of us could go and grab our seats. I felt obligated to stay and help him, even though I was worried that I might not get a seat next to Mark.

When we entered the theater, I was pleased to see that a seat was free next to Mark. Oliver took the aisle seat and passed down a big bag of popcorn and some drinks to Mark and Fiona. He had bought another big bag to share with me.

The theater lights dimmed, and the previews began. Mark and Fiona were whispering furiously. I strained my ears in an attempt to hear what they were saying. It sounded like Fiona was reprimanding him for his tardiness, and that he was attempting to defend himself, but I couldn't be sure. The Dolby surround sound was simply too loud. Oliver was trying to press the bag of popcorn on me, but I was too excited to eat.

The film finally began. The latest edition in a horror movie franchise, it didn't take long for the frightening scenes to start. The first time the killer popped out, I jumped in my seat and clutched onto Mark's arm. I had done it unintentionally and my cheeks burned with embarrassment, particularly when Mark turned and laughed at me, with an amused look on his face. I scanned Oliver, but he was so absorbed in the movie that he hadn't noticed. As the movie continued, I got more caught up in the plot, but I was always aware of Mark's palpable presence next to me.

Suddenly, I felt a hand on my right leg. *Oh God, it's Oliver.* I shifted in my seat, but his hand was still there. I didn't want to offend him or cause a fuss, so I tried to ignore it and focus on the movie.

A few minutes later, I felt another hand slip onto my other leg. It was Mark's! This was just like the dream I'd had at the cottage. I pressed my eyes shut and then opened them. *Nope, not a dream this time.* My breath lodged in my throat. Unlike Oliver's immobile hand, which rested rooted in one location, Mark's hand discreetly chanced toward the inner area of my thigh. The dash of blood hammered in my ears, suffocating out the surrounding sounds, as if my pulse had reformed into an intense drumbeat. My mind tottered in disbelief at the nerve, a fierce mix of surprise and rage streaming through my veins. Every fiber of my being quietly pleaded that Oliver and Fiona stayed ignorant to the clandestine advances that were happening. The hairs on my arms bristled. I was getting shivers all over my body and, even though I was terrified of being discovered, I liked it and did not want him to stop.

Without warning, and to my complete and utter horror, the hand on my right leg was also on the move. Oliver had obviously gathered up enough courage, since I had not removed his hand, to move it in the direction of my right thigh. As his hand continued its journey, I knew that if I let this continue, the two hands were bound to meet.

I shrieked and jumped in my seat, which knocked both hands off my thighs and sent the popcorn flying. At the same time, the killer had slashed someone's throat in the movie, camouflaging my outburst.

"Are you okay?" Fiona whispered, leaning over Mark and looking at me.

I nodded and twisted my lips into a half-smile.

*That was close.* I slid down in my seat and focused on breathing. *In, out, in, out.* But it was hard to relax, with Mark sitting right next to me and a sadistic serial killer shedding human blood up on the screen.

When the film finally ended, the four of us headed out of the theater and stood together in the lobby. I studiously avoided eye contact with both brothers and Fiona.

"That movie was too violent for my taste." Fiona shuddered. "I know you two boys liked it, but what did you think, Erin? I heard you scream a few times."

"I was on the edge of my seat. Literally." *But it wasn't just the murders that were making me squirm.*

"Me too," Fiona said, hanging off Mark's arm.

*Do you have to flaunt it in my face?*

"Shall we all go out for a drink?" Oliver asked.

"Yes, that sounds great," I said, looking hopefully at Mark.

"I think we're going to call it a night," Fiona said. "Mark's pretty tired, aren't you honey?"

"Well," Mark said. "I could go for one—"

"But don't let that stop you and Oliver," Fiona said, interjecting with an impish smile.

"There's a pub just around the corner on Boylston Street," Oliver said.

"Oh well, I'm actually a bit tired too," I said, yawning. "I think that movie wore me out."

Fiona leaned over and whispered in my ear, "Do it for me? Please? Mark and I need our alone time."

Her voice was like a needle pricking my brain. *Mark and I need* ***our*** *alone time.* I just needed to figure out when and how we were going to get it. I was definitely the worst friend ever, but I was obsessed. Mark was my soulmate. My destiny. But sometimes, destiny needed a little push in the right direction.

# Chapter 38

But for now, I was destined to spend more time with Mark's brother. The pub was a cute hole in the wall, just as Oliver had said. He opened the door for me and followed me into the pub. Inside, the atmosphere was dark and intimate, and he led me to a secluded table in the back corner.

"I'll grab us some drinks and be right back."

"A cranberry soda, please." I'd decided to be responsible for once and avoid alcohol. While I waited for him to return, I noticed that the walls were decorated with prints of old ships and flashed back to the summer weekend at Cape Cod. But before I could indulge in a fantasy about Mark, Oliver was back.

He sat down and placed my drink on a coaster in front of me. Tipping back his beer, he seemed to chug half its contents. Then Oliver put down his bottle and gazed at me with the intensity of a dermatologist, examining the microscopic pores on my skin.

I shifted uncomfortably in my seat, then drank some of my soda.

"So, you enjoyed the movie?" he asked, picking at the label on his beer bottle.

"It was… entertaining."

Raucous laughter erupted from the bar behind us.

"My dad used to take Mark and me to all the superhero movies, when we were kids. Did you ever go with your parents?"

"My mom took me to see all the *Disney* movies, but my dad was too busy working to join us."

"Did your father ever take time off?"

"Once in a while, he'd take off on an exotic adventure—like fly fishing for salmon in Alaska."

"Alaska's on my bucket list."

"It's on mine, too."

"Maybe we can go there together, one day."

"Maybe." My nerves jangled like keys. His talk about future plans was flattering, but also made me feel uncomfortable. If I ever went to Alaska, it would be with Mark.

"Let's make a toast." Oliver raised his bottle of beer in the air. "'To future exotic adventures.'" We clinked glasses, then both took lengthy swallows.

"Anyway, back to fishing." Oliver put down his drink and fixed his eyes on me. "Did your dad ever take you with him?"

A lump formed in my throat, and I looked around for a waitress and waved her over.

"Two more of the same?" the waitress asked.

"Actually, I think I'll have a white wine," I replied.

"Another beer for me, please." Oliver waited until the waitress had returned with our drinks, then smiled, encouragingly. "You were about to tell me a story about your dad?"

As I swallowed some wine, a distant memory flickered in my mind. "Once, when I was about ten years old, my dad took me to the Saugus River, at Breakheart Reservation. He'd bought me a canary-red rod and had a tackle box filled with shiny, rainbow-colored lures. While we sat on the shore, waiting patiently for a bite, he asked me about school and told me about the buildings he was designing." I closed my eyes and pictured the trail through the forest of green pines and the rocky outcropping by the river, where we'd sat and cast our lines into the weedy depths.

"What a cool experience to share with your dad." Oliver rubbed my arm.

"It was." But I'd secretly suspected that my dad had spent the whole time wishing that he was there with Gordie instead. Tiny fingers pinched my chest, but the sound of Oliver's voice jerked me away from any dark thoughts.

"Did you catch any fish?" He gazed at me, as he gulped down some beer.

A smile split my face. "Of course. I'll never forget hooking my first, smallmouth bass. It was such a rush."

Oliver flopped back in his seat. "I wish I could've met your father."

When the bartender announced the last call, I looked at the time on my phone in surprise.

"Thanks for opening up tonight about your dad." Oliver cupped his chin in his hand and gazed at me from across the table. "I know it must be difficult talking about him."

"It isn't easy for me to open up, but you make me feel safe and you're a good listener." I couldn't believe how quickly time had passed and how much I had liked talking to Oliver. Unlike a lot of men, who were mainly focused on themselves, Oliver was always an attentive audience. But so was Mark.

When the bar closed, Oliver walked me the short distance home, through Boston Common. Standing outside my front door, he grasped both of my hands in his and looked me in the eyes.

"Thanks for coming to the pub with me tonight. I had a great time."

"Me too."

Oliver leaned in and kissed me on the lips.

A surprising rush of tingles spread down my neck. I closed my eyes and kissed him back, but I was picturing Mark's face in my mind.

# Chapter 39

I pushed both brothers to the back corners of my mind, as I raced to work on Monday morning. It was going to be a busy, but exciting week at the bookstore. On Thursday evening, Rowena George, the popular thriller writer, was doing a reading and book signing at *Pemberley's* to promote her new novel, *The Dead Girl.* Despite her 'international bestseller' status, George liked to support independent bookstores. I had volunteered to organize the event and the details involved were overwhelming. George was from England – the BBC had turned several of her novels into a hugely popular television series – and I had delegated the job of booking her a hotel room and car service to Maddie. I had asked Suzy to run the technology components and hoped she could cope with it. It was my job to handle publicity and order extra copies of *The Dead Girl* for the signing. On the night of the event, we would need chairs, a table, microphone, speakers and refreshments.

"All set for Thursday?" Dave asked, sidling up to me.

I jumped and took a subconscious step away from him.

"Getting there," I replied, recovering my composure.

"This is going to be a big night for the store, so I want everything to run smoothly. Okay, Erin?" Dave gripped my arm with his meaty fingers.

"Yes, Dave. Don't worry."

"All right. I'm relying on you. Don't let me down." He gave my arm a final squeeze, before letting go.

"I won't. You can count on me." But could he? The pressure was overwhelming. My mind was like a fractured pane of glass. One gentle push and it would shatter into a million pieces.

As Dave walked back to his office, I let out a deep breath. I had tried to project an air of confidence, but inside, I was stressed. There were so many details that still needed my attention, and I hoped that I had remembered everything.

*

My resolve to push Mark to the back of my mind after the movie night didn't last long. After a late shift at work on Tuesday, I had found myself wandering in the dark around the marina and right past Mark's building. I stood and looked up at all the brightly lit windows. Which one was his? How could I possibly figure it out? I tried to count the floors and then carefully moved my gaze along the windows, until I found a balcony that I thought might be Mark's. Was he home or was he at the hospital? If he was home, what was he doing? Was he alone? Or was Fiona there? The thought of them together made me cringe. Did I dare go up and knock on his door or would it seem desperate? And what if Fiona was there? No, I couldn't risk it. I started to walk away when another idea struck me.

A few minutes later, I was inside the elevator of Mark's building, but I was going down to the parking garage instead of up to his loft. The doors slid open, and I started walking up and down the rows of cars, searching for his black Range Rover. Five minutes passed, then ten, and I still hadn't found it. Suddenly, I heard the roar of an engine and a black SUV drove in my direction, illuminating me with its headlights. Was it Mark? A bloom of embarrassment swept across my cheeks, saturating them with a rosy hue. How would I explain my presence in his parking garage?

The black SUV drew closer and closer.

Blood thrummed in my ears.

It was inches away and then… it was gone.

Relief crashed through my body. It wasn't Mark's truck. I decided to give up my search and headed for the exit, when a familiar license plate caught my eye. Rustling around in my purse for a notepad and pen, I wrote a message to Mark and pinned it to his windshield. *Call me. We need to talk. Erin.*

Wednesday passed and I hadn't heard from Mark. Maybe he hadn't seen my note yet. Or maybe he'd seen it and misinterpreted my intent. I worried that the tone of my note had sounded too harsh, like I was threatening blackmail or delivering an ultimatum.

*

By Thursday, I barely had time to think about him. I had promoted the book reading on social media, and the bookstore buzzed with excitement. Chairs were filling up fast, and it would soon be standing room only. Dave had even hired a security guard, who was keeping an eye on the growing crowd. It was an impressive turnout.

I knew that George had a large following in Boston. Her latest book shot straight to the top of the bestseller list as soon as it was released. A prolific writer, she had penned over thirty thrillers, and I had read at least half of them. In my opinion, *The Dead Girl* was her best yet. Her books were all set in the south of England, which was one of the great appeals of her work. George had a talent for writing descriptive passages that were just the right length. Quaint English villages and the idyllic countryside were brought vividly to life, as if they too were characters in her books. Castles, with their requisite ghosts loitering in the passageways, often figured in her stories. There was nothing like the escapism of a well-written crime novel. I could not wait to meet George, with her bright red, bouffant hair and flamboyant clothes; I hoped that she would be as inspiring in the flesh as she was on the page.

When George arrived, Dave immediately ensconced her in his office and was busy monopolizing her attention. He would be introducing the author and conducting the post-reading interview.

Just before the reading was due to begin, I received a text. I glanced at my phone and my chest tightened. I squinted at the screen in disbelief. The message was from Mark.

*Meet me at The Old Hairdresser's.*

Blood rushed to my head. This is what I'd been waiting and hoping for. I messaged him back.

*I can meet you at ten p.m.*

The event was scheduled from eight till nine-thirty, leaving me plenty of time to get to the pub.

"Erin?" The brusque, masculine voice made me jump.

It was Dave. His thick fingers pressed into my arm.

"Is everything ready? I'm going to bring George out here in a few minutes."

"Yes, Dave." I detached myself from his clamp-like grip and moved towards the podium.

"Test, one, two, test." Suzy was doing a final mic check.

Pushing Mark to the back of my brain, I forced myself to focus on the task at hand. It was my responsibility to make sure that everything ran smoothly. I reminded myself that it was a big coup getting a writer of George's stature to read at an independent bookstore like *Pemberley's*. It was a chance to meet one of my favorite authors and tell her how much I loved her books. Maybe George could even help me get an agent, one day, if I ever finished writing the story about Max and the twins.

But try as I might, Mark kept emerging in my mind. Meeting up with him would be crossing another line. I could try to rationalize the hospital rendezvous as a one-off, a one-time mistake, never to be repeated. But if I met up with him tonight, that excuse would fly out the window. Was I really willing to risk losing Fiona by meeting Mark out in a public space, especially in an intimate setting, like a bar? Alcohol would lower our inhibitions. It would definitely be a step beyond a kiss on an isolated island or a quickie in the hospital on-call room. He would no longer be just a figment of my subversive fantasies. This would be a real date and yet another betrayal. A big one.

But no matter what I told myself, Mark's text continued to tug at my mind. If I met him at the pub, it would be the first time we had ever been on a real date – alone without Fiona and Oliver. I had been praying for just such a move on his part for so long, and this might be my only opportunity. I was desperate to meet him. Maybe he was going to confess what I had suspected all along—that he was secretly in love with me. Maybe he was finally going to break up with Fiona, so he could be with me. If I did not meet up with him tonight, I might never find out. I might lose my one and only chance with him.

# Chapter 40

I made opening remarks and welcomed everyone to the bookstore. Then I motioned Dave to the microphone, and he introduced Rowena George. The next hour flew by. She gave a riveting reading and told fascinating anecdotes about her research, including visits to the morgue. Then Dave led the Q&A. There were many thoughtful questions from the crowd, but at nine-thirty p.m., it was time to wrap things up. Rowena George was on a tight timeline. I led her to a table piled with her best-selling thrillers, where eager fans were lined up to get a signed copy of her latest book.

As much as I wanted to stay and try to chat with her afterwards about my writing, I didn't want to be late for my date with Mark. If I was going to get to the pub on time, I'd have to leave immediately.

"Um, Dave." I jogged over to him. "Can I speak to you for a second?"

"Sure, Erin. Great event tonight. Well done."

I wasn't used to him being so complimentary. "Oh, thanks so much Dave. I couldn't have done it without the help of Maddie and Suzy."

"To thank all you girls for your hard work, I thought I'd take you out for drinks afterwards. And Rowena and her agent said they'd love to join us for a quick drink."

Drinks with Rowena George and her agent? I couldn't believe I was going to miss such a once-in-a-lifetime opportunity. But Mark would be waiting for me and the pull towards him was magnetic.

"That sounds wonderful, Dave. Thanks so much. But the thing is,"

I said, chewing on my lip, "my mother just texted me." My stomach lunged, as the lie spilt from my lips. "She's not feeling well. I hate to do this to you, but I think I'd better go and check on her."

Dave's face flushed red. "Right now? Are you serious?"

My eyes widened. Even though I was lying through my teeth, Dave's total lack of empathy was appalling.

Dave cleared his throat. "Sorry, Erin. If it's an emergency, of course, you have to go." He placed a sweaty palm on my shoulder.

My duplicity jabbed at me, but I turned away and pushed through the crowd, cornering Maddie, who was packing up seats at the back of the room.

"Maddie, it's my mother. She's at the hospital, again."

"Oh my God!" Maddie covered her mouth with her hand.

A gnawing pain ate at my heart. I felt like a monster, but it was too late to change my mind. "I'm so sorry, but I've got to go. Can you handle the rest of the evening without me?" Lying to Dave was easy, but lying to Maddie troubled my conscience. I hoped I wasn't making a huge mistake.

"Of course. No worries. There's not much left to do. Go." Maddie gave me a quick hug. "Text me later."

"I will." I turned and hurried out the door. This had better be worth it. What was I saying? It's Mark. Of course it'd be worth it. For the first time in a year, I felt alive again, and it's all because of Mark. I felt so connected to him, like a string was pulling us together. We shared an artistic sensibility. And I admired how he'd committed his life to healing people. Plus, his dedication to his work reminded me of Dad. And when Mark fixed his blue eyes on me, I felt as high as Mount Everest.

I found an Uber nearby, and he arrived five minutes later. After giving the driver directions, I rummaged around in my purse, scooped up my pocket mirror, and began to reapply my mascara. I could not believe that I was on my way to meet Mark and almost had to pinch myself. Puckering my lips, I put on raspberry-red lipstick, then ran a comb through my hair. Satisfied, I sat back in the black vinyl seat, but doubts and fears churned like a hamster wheel in my head. Should I have given up the chance to talk with Rowena George and her agent? And what about Oliver and Fiona?

But when the car pulled up in front of the pub, I pushed all my doubts to the back of my brain. Then, I thanked the driver and catapulted out of the car.

It took my eyes a moment to adjust to the dark lighting inside the pub. Once I could see properly, I looked from side to side, but did not see Mark. As I made my way over to the bar, I kept glancing around the room, in case I had missed him. It was fairly crowded, but I was sure I would have caught sight of him if he were here. Maybe he had gone to the washroom. Perching on a stool, I thought back to the first time I had come to the pub with Mark and Oliver and Fiona. But tonight, it would be different. It would be just the two of us.

"What can I get you?" the bartender asked, intruding on my thoughts.

"A white wine, please," I replied.

When he placed my drink on the counter, I asked, "Have you seen a tall man with dark brown hair and blue eyes in his early thirties?"

The bartender shook his head. "Sorry, can't help you."

I gulped down some of my drink and tried to ignore the sinking feeling in my gut. *Mark, where are you?*

I checked my phone for new messages, but there were none. Maybe he had been delayed at the hospital. That had to be it. He was never on time. The man liked to make an entrance. I sighed and put my phone down on the bar. Suddenly, it started to ring. *It's got to be him.* I was about to slide a finger across the screen and answer it, when I saw who was calling and my smile faded. *Oliver. Why did he have to call me now? Why did I feel so duplicitous?* We'd only kissed once. Glancing at my watch, I had a pang of regret. I could've been having drinks with Rowena George right now.

But tonight was going to be the most important night of my life. I was sure that Mark had summoned me here to finally say the words that I had been longing to hear: *"You're the one I want, not Fiona."*

A sliver of doubt slid into my mind. If he cheated on Fiona, would he cheat on me? I shook my head. Fiona wasn't the right match for him, and I was. Soon, I would be the happiest woman alive. If everything went according to plan, it would be the official start of my relationship with Mark. Skipping ahead to the future, I pictured him proposing to me on a bended knee. We would get married at a vineyard in Sonoma. Honeymoon in Iceland. No, in Fiji. In an overwater bungalow with a glass floor. Turquoise water. White sand. And Mark, all to myself.

Lifting my glass to my lips, I tipped it up to drain the last drop and ordered another one. He would be here soon, I was sure. Doctors were notoriously late. It was nothing to be concerned about. I would not let myself check the time. It was irrelevant. I would just wait patiently, until he could manage to join me. There was no way I was going to leave without seeing Mark—even if I had to wait all night.

# Chapter 41

"Can I buy you a drink?"

I started. I turned my head so quickly, in the direction of the voice that had addressed me, that I got a kink in my neck. But it was not Mark. The man was short, bald, and pushing forty.

"No, thanks," I replied, my face falling. "I'm waiting for someone. He'll be here any minute."

"Oh, no problem. Lucky guy." The man ordered a pint of lager and moved away to another part of the bar.

I felt pathetic, sitting at the bar all alone for so long. I hoped no other men would hit on me, while I continued to wait for Mark. Every time the door of the pub swung open, my eyes darted in its direction and my hopes surged. But each time I was disappointed. The more time that passed, the less optimistic I became. Was he going to stand me up? Hope started to seep out of me like air out of a slow, leaking tire. I decided to send him a text.

*Where R U? I've been waiting over an hour.*

Negative thoughts began to cloud my previously blue-sky vision of how the night was going to progress. When he did not respond, I grew increasingly agitated and suspicious. Text messages shot out of me like bullets from an AK-47.

*Still waiting...*

*Mark?*

*Where R U?*

Four drinks later, the bartender slid a glass of water in front of me. "I don't think your date is coming, do you?" he asked, with a raised eyebrow.

My shoulders sagged. "No, I guess he's not." Finally permitting myself to look at my phone one last time, I was shocked to see that it was now well past midnight. Had I really waited that long? How dare he treat me this way! I would make him pay! But for now, I fired off more messages.

*WTF?*

*R U with Fiona?*

*Maybe I'll text her instead...*

Suddenly, my phone started ringing. My heart leapt in my throat. *He'd better have a good excuse.* But when I looked at the number, my heart sank like a ship. It was Oliver, again. Why did he keep calling me, and so late at night? But I was in no mood to talk to anyone related to Mark, so I turned off the ringer and buried the phone in my purse.

Sliding off the stool, I staggered to the ladies' room. As I entered the bathroom, I avoided looking in the mirror. I had a lump in my throat and tears burned behind my eyes. Inside the cubicle, I wiped off what was left of my lipstick with some toilet paper and flushed it down the toilet. A liquor glass was the only thing that would be touching my lips tonight. Why hadn't I stayed at the bookstore? I had been so excited about the chance to talk with Rowena George and her agent. But now, I had missed it all for nothing.

On the Uber ride home, I drifted in and out of consciousness. In my dreams, I was falling down a pitch-black, bottomless tunnel. No one heard my screams for help, as I tumbled further and further away from the pinprick of light.

"Here you are, Miss."

The driver's voice pulled me back to the surface. I shook myself awake and tapped my credit card.

As I stumbled up the path to my house, a car door slammed, and someone strode up the path behind me.

A hand clutched my elbow.

I swiveled around. My stomach dropped with disappointment. "Oliver. I thought you were—never mind. What on earth are you doing here?"

"I wanted to make sure you were okay," he said, hugging me.

"I don't understand," I said, with a puzzled look. "Why wouldn't I be okay?"

"I heard your mom was sick," he said, after giving me a kiss on the cheek.

"Who told you that?" I tried to focus on his face, but I was seeing double.

"Your boss at the bookstore."

I broke out in a cold sweat. "You were at *Pemberley's?*"

"I saw an Instagram ad about the reading." He scuffed the toe of his shoe against the step. "I thought I'd show up and surprise you." He shoved his hands in his pockets. "But I got caught up at work, and when I got to *Pemberley's*, he said you'd left. That your mom was sick."

"It was… it was a false alarm."

"Oh, you must be so relieved." His voice sounded strangely quiet.

"How long have you been waiting for me?"

"A while." Oliver clutched his cell phone. "I tried calling you."

"Really? My phone must've been turned off." How many more lies was I going to have to tell before the night was over? My throat tightened at the thought of him sitting in his car worrying about me, while I was sitting at the bar waiting for his brother. And just when I thought the night couldn't get any worse, my belly heaved, and bile rose in my throat. I turned away from him and searched in my purse for the key to the front door. My fingers found lipstick, a compact, tissues, my wallet—but no key ring.

"Is something wrong?"

"I can't find my keys. Can you do me a favor? There's a spare set hanging behind the window shutter."

Oliver reached behind the shutter, unlocked the door for me, and returned the key to its hiding place.

"Are you okay?"

"I need to lie down." *I just want to go inside my house and lie down in my bed and pull the covers over my head and pretend this night never happened.*

"Here, let me help you inside." Oliver wrapped his arm around my waist, pushed open the door, and half-carried me to my bed. He took Keeper outside, then got me a glass of water, and gave me a kiss good night.

As soon as the front door banged shut, I grabbed my phone. I sent another string of angry text messages to Mark, then passed out cold.

# Chapter 42

An early morning *ping* from my phone roused me from a disturbed sleep. A headache pounded like a sledgehammer inside my skull, as I shook myself awake. I reached for my phone, but knocked it off the table and it crashed onto the hardwood floor with a worrying thwack. I leaned over the side of the bed and retrieved the fragile device with my fingertips. Luckily, the touch screen was free of cracks. I stared at the phone, holding my breath while it unlocked. It might be a text from Mark, explaining why he had stood me up last night. Even though Oliver's concern and kindness had massaged my ego, the humiliation caused by his brother lurked inside me like an unwanted stalker. Touching the small, lime-green icon with my index finger, I scrunched my eyes and focused on the tiny words that popped up on the screen.

*How's your mom?*

My hope wilted like a flower. It was from Paige. Why was she asking about my mom?

And then I saw them. All the text messages I had sent to Mark last night. My face burned with embarrassment. I deleted them as fast as I could, even though I knew that he'd still have them blazing on his screen. While I was reeling with regret, my phone rang.

"Erin? It's Paige. Is your mom okay?"

"My mom?"

"Maybe I shouldn't have called so early, but I've been worrying all night. One of your co-workers told me you'd rushed off after the reading, so I knew it must be bad."

"Wait. You were at the reading?"

*First, Oliver, now Paige. Was the whole world at the bookstore last night?*

I swung my legs over the side of the bed and pulled myself into a sitting position. The band of a headache tightened around my brain.

"It was very last-minute. The kids fell asleep early, and Angus was home. I love Rowena George so when I saw, on Facebook, that she was coming to your bookstore, I was really excited. But by the time I got there, she'd finished and you'd left. At least I managed to get a signed copy of her book."

"Sorry I missed you." I didn't know Paige read her novels, or any novels, for that matter. I remembered her declaring that she had not opened a single book since the day her first baby was born.

"No worries. Your co-worker – I think her name was Maggie or Maddie – told me your mom was sick, again. I would've phoned last night, but I didn't want to bother you."

My double-dealing lies pressed down on my shoulders like deadweight, coupled with a sickening sense of regret. Not only had I missed my chance to have drinks with a best-selling author, but I had been let down by Mark and sent him mortifying messages. I had told a horrible lie to my boss and co-workers. Then, Oliver had shown up, forcing me to tell more lies. And now, even Paige was tangled up in the mess. Could it get any worse?

"Erin? Do you want me to call you back later?"

"No, it's fine. I mean, my mom is fine. It was a false alarm."

"What a relief. Maybe I could drop by her place with some flowers, anyway."

"No!" *Why can't Paige ever mind her own business?* "I really don't think she's feeling up for any company just now." It was as if an axe was splitting my head right down the middle.

"Are you sure? I love your mom. She's such a sweetheart. Maybe I could drop off some magazines for her to read."

"***No.***"

An awkward silence hung between us.

I pressed a knuckle between my eyes to try and stem the blinding pain. If only I could turn back the clock and ignore Mark's text. My desire for him was making my life so needlessly complicated.

"Erin, what's going on? You don't sound like yourself. Is everything okay?"

"I'm fine. I just…" *What do I say that'll get her off my case?*

"Oh my God! Your mother isn't even sick, is she? Please, please, tell me that this has nothing to do with your crush on Mark."

"Listen, Paige. I really don't want to talk about this right now."

"Oh, Erin. You promised to forget about him. He's Fiona's boyfriend."

I let out a loud groan. "Fine. If you really want to know, I was going to meet up with Mark last night. I thought it might be a chance to sort out my feelings."

"So, what happened? Did you sort everything out?"

I could hear the angry disapproval in Paige's voice. She was usually so upbeat; I was a bit frightened by her confrontational tone.

"He stood me up."

Paige laughed. "Serves you right. Maybe now, you've learned your lesson."

"I have." *Have I?*

"Fiona is my best friend, and I thought she was yours, too."

"Of course she is." I swallowed hard.

"You need to forget about him, Erin. I mean it." Her voice was like an axe chopping me up into a pile of kindling.

"I know, I know. I will. Can we drop this topic now, please?"

"Sure. I hope we never have to talk about it again. But I have to ask you one more thing before I let you go."

I squirmed on the edge of the bed, readying myself for a fatal blow.

"We've got tickets to a concert tomorrow night, and I was wondering if you'd mind looking after our kids?"

"Is that all? I mean, I'd love to." Maybe a night with Paige's kids was just what I needed to get my mind off Mark.

But as soon as I hung up the phone, I googled his name; it had become a compulsion. I was like a drug addict getting my daily fix. Despite my humiliating night at the bar, it was like he'd taken possession of my mind. When his images appeared on the screen, my anger morphed into a desperate determination to make him mine. I clicked on my favorite photo of Mark, the one of him in his white medical coat, and took a screenshot. After gazing into his steel-blue eyes for several minutes, I decided to make the picture my new screensaver. That way, his image would be there waiting for me every time I looked at my phone.

# Chapter 43

"How's your mom?" Maddie asked, her forehead creasing.

"She's okay. It was just a bad reaction to some spicy Thai food," I replied, inwardly cringing. At least my lies were getting more creative. "How did the rest of the night go?"

"It was awesome. We all went out for drinks afterwards, and Dave treated. Oh, and you'll never believe what else happened."

I braced myself, and the muscles in my neck tightened.

"I know it was nervy, but I asked Rowena George if she'd mind taking a look at one of my poems."

"I didn't know you wrote poetry, Maddie."

"I've written hundreds. I think of them more as song lyrics, but they're the same thing, really. Anyway, she was so nice, so gracious. She actually took the time to read it, and guess what she said?"

Every word that Maddie uttered hit my spirit like a wrecking ball. I should have been the one showing my writing to George. After all, I had organized the whole event. Still, I managed to squeeze out an encouraging smile.

"Tell me."

"She said, 'You have talent, young lady.' Can you believe it? The great Rowena George thinks I have talent."

"That's incredible, Maddie." I forced a smile. "I'm so happy for you."

"And she's going to pass on my poems to a contact."

A nerve twitched in my cheek.

"Can I speak to you for a minute, Erin?" Dave stood in the doorway of his office.

"Sure. Be right there." I was preoccupied with anxiety and tension. "I wonder what he wants?"

"He's been in a weird mood this morning."

"Guess I'd better not keep the big bossman waiting."

"By the way, one of your friends was here last night. And a cute guy was looking for you, too." Maddie nudged me with her elbow.

"Oliver?" I took a few steps in the direction of Dave's office.

"I didn't catch his name, but I saw him talking to Dave," Maddie said, calling after me.

"Shut the door and have a seat," Dave said, as soon as I got to his office.

I sat down in a cheap plastic chair. I noticed that he had what looked like an employee file open on his desk. Was it mine?

"So, how's your mother?" He rocked back and forth in his black leather office chair.

I avoided eye contact. "Fine, thank God. It turned out to be nothing."

Dave stared at me over the tips of his fingers, which he had pressed together like a steeple. "Interesting choice of words."

"What do you mean?"

"When you told me about your family emergency, I was very concerned." Dave fixed his eyes on me.

"I called the hospital, and then, I called your mother."

"You called my mom?" I rubbed my forehead. "But how did you get her number?"

He jabbed a finger at the file in front of him.

It was my file. I covered my face with my hands. I had listed my mother as an emergency contact.

He clasped his hands behind his head and leaned back in his chair. "Your mother had no idea what I was talking about."

"Okay, okay. I lied. I'm sorry." I threw my arms up in the air in mock surrender.

"I'm very surprised by your behavior, Erin." Dave sat up straight and crossed his arms. "You knew how important last night was. Rowena George is a big-name author, and she asked where you'd disappeared to.

When I mentioned your mother's illness, she was very concerned."

My temples throbbed and my face reddened. "I'm really sorry, Dave." I didn't want to lose my job. I needed the money, and it was the only thing keeping me grounded these days.

"Sorry doesn't cut it, Erin."

"Isn't there something I can do to make it up to you?"

He glared at me. "You've been a reliable employee up until now. But if there's one thing I cannot tolerate, it's being lied to."

I hung my head and stared at the ground.

"I'm putting you on probation. One more mistake and you're fired. Understood?"

"Thank you, Dave." I was limp with relief. "You won't regret it."

"I'd better not. Now get back to work."

Near the end of my shift, a delivery arrived for me. Maddie and Suzy peered, excitedly over my shoulder, as I lifted the lid off the long, white box.

"Oh my God," Maddie said. "They're beautiful."

I stared down at a dozen, long stem, red roses.

"Who're they from?" Suzy asked. "A secret admirer?"

I shrugged, but my heart was thumping like a rabbit. Mark must've sent them to apologize for standing me up. He must've got caught at the hospital, just like I'd suspected.

"Look," said Suzy. "There's a card."

I held my breath and opened the tiny envelope.

# Chapter 44

I paced up and down my front hall, my red heels clicking on the hardwood floor. I was dressed in a cream-colored, sleeveless sheath dress. It was Friday night, and I was waiting for Oliver to pick me up. He'd refused to tell me where we were going, but had assured me that I would not be disappointed.

I had considered cancelling our dinner date. Most women would've found a dozen roses a thoughtful and romantic gesture, but I'd been disappointed and embarrassed when I'd opened the card and seen Oliver's name and not his brother's. However, I'd decided that a night out with Oliver might help heal my bruised ego.

As usual, he arrived punctually, and after giving him a perfunctory 'thank you' for the roses, we headed off in his Tesla. We pulled up at *Komorebi,* a modern Japanese restaurant and bar, located in the business district. I had read impressive reviews about it in the local paper, but had never eaten there. Oliver parked the car and we headed inside.

*Komorebi* tended to be populated by the gray-suit business district crowd, but tonight, the atmosphere in the restaurant was dark and romantic. Oliver pulled out one of the high-backed, velvet chairs at the sushi bar and helped me make myself comfortable. The caramel-colored chairs were curved on both sides, which created the impression of being in our own private dining room.

Behind the glass countertop, two sushi chefs, dressed immaculately in white, were busy creating exquisite masterpieces. I enjoyed watching them slice the fish and roll it inside rice and seaweed.

"Komorebi means 'sunlight filtering through the leaves of trees'," Oliver said, reading the back of the menu.

"I think the interior reflects that." I glanced around the room. "The soft lighting and muted colors remind me of a forest or temple."

"You're very observant, Erin." He peered at me over the top of his menu. "That's something I admire about you, your artistic sensibility."

"I guess I've got a bit of my father in me."

"Definitely. I wish I were more creative."

*Your brother is creative. Stop it, Erin.* I'd promised myself that I wasn't going to think about him tonight.

"I'm sure you have to be imaginative to outwit those hackers." I pulled my seat closer to the counter.

"I suppose that's true." His hazel eyes twinkled at me in the dim light. "What do you want to order?" Oliver turned his gaze back to the menu. "I usually like to start with a bowl of miso soup."

"I like miso, too. I'd also like some vegetable tempura and sushi. My favorites are salmon, tuna, and eel."

"Excellent choices." Oliver nodded his head. "I would advise against ordering the blowfish—"

My eyes widened. "Isn't that poisonous?"

"Yep." Oliver grinned. "It's a thousand times more lethal than cyanide. It paralyzes your muscles, but you stay conscious until you stop breathing."

"Why would anyone risk eating it?"

"It's supposed to be a delicacy, but one I can definitely do without. Would you like to share a California roll?"

Ideas ping ponged inside my skull. *Maybe Eva could kill Faith with cyanide.*

"Erin?"

"Oh, sorry. A California roll sounds good."

"You looked like your mind was somewhere else."

"I was just thinking about the story I'm writing."

"Can I help?" Oliver put down his menu and turned to face me. "I know that you wanted to keep it a secret, but maybe if you run some of your ideas past me, I could give you another perspective."

"Maybe." I twirled a strand of hair around my finger. "Character A has to kill character B, but I can't decide how. There are too many options."

"Well, if blowfish isn't available, a knife has always been a simple, but effective, tool." Oliver stabbed into the air with a chop stick.

I laughed. "I didn't know you had a dark side."

"Everyone has a dark side."

"Not you. You're too nice… unless you've been hiding something from me."

"No, not me. I'm an open book." He grinned. "Now that we've solved your plot dilemma," he said, with a nod of satisfaction, "let's move on to the matter of beverage options."

"Yes, let's." I bobbed my head vigorously.

Oliver skimmed the list of drinks on offer. "Would you like some hot or cold sake or would you prefer white wine?"

"I'm not really into sake." I scrunched my face in disgust. "Why don't you choose a wine for us?"

Oliver rubbed his chin between his thumb and forefinger. "I think a fruity white pairs well with the sweet taste of rice and spiciness of wasabi."

*You sound just like your brother. No, I'm not going to think about him.*

Oliver ordered our wine and food. Then he moved his chair closer to mine and stared straight into my eyes.

"You look serious." I shivered with unease.

"I was just thinking—"

"Uh-oh." I fidgeted with my chopsticks.

"Relax." He placed his hand on my wrist. "I'm trying to give you a compliment."

"Oh." I put down my chopsticks and forced myself to meet his eyes.

"I was thinking about how lucky I am," he said, sliding his fingers from my wrist to my hand, "to have met such a beautiful and intelligent woman."

I averted my eyes. His remarks had caught me off guard. He was saying the words I'd wished his brother would utter.

"Please don't feel any pressure to respond." He tried to catch my eye. "I know that my feelings have been developing at a faster pace than yours and I'm fine with that."

*Feelings?* I felt obligated to say something in response, but struggled to find the perfect combination of words that would neither hurt him nor lead him on. "I like you, Oliver. You're an incredible guy and I enjoy your company…"

"Why do I feel nervous, all of a sudden?"

"But like I told you at the cottage, I'm not ready to get involved with anyone right now." I bowed my head and stared down into my lap. "I'm still dealing with Sean's death." *And I'm obsessed with your brother.* "I hope you can understand."

"How did you two meet, if you don't mind me asking?"

*Mark? No, he means Sean.* "Sean and I met in our final year of undergrad, in an American literature course. A group of us used to go out for drinks after class and have heated debates about who was the most influential American writer. Sean argued for Ernest Hemingway and JD Salinger. I was for Emily Dickinson and Harper Lee."

"My vote would go to Melville." Oliver crossed his arms and a smile tugged at the corners of his lips.

"Oh yeah, I loved *Moby-Dick*—Ahab's obsessive quest for revenge on the elusive, white whale that bit off his leg…"

"It was out of print, when he died, in 1891. But now, it's viewed as a 'Great American Novel'."

My forehead creased. "So many artists are only appreciated after they die."

"Tragic, but true." Oliver nodded. "Anyway, I'd like to hear more about you and Sean, but only if you feel comfortable."

I took a deep breath. "In spite of our different taste in literature, or maybe because of them, there was a definite spark between us, and we became inseparable."

"Like they say, 'Opposites attract'."

I dipped my chin in agreement. "He was smart and outgoing and full of energy and exciting to be around. Anyway, I started working at the bookstore, while he went through law school. He graduated top of his class and got a job at a big law firm. I was so proud of him. He was on the fast track for making partner. The night of the accident, he'd taken me out for a special dinner. I thought he was going to propose—we'd been together for more than five years…"

"Erin, are you okay?"

Suddenly, it all came rushing back like a river overflowing its banks.

# Chapter 45

"Erin? Are you okay? We can talk about something else—"

"No, I want to talk about it." But when I opened my mouth, no words came out.

Oliver reached over and took hold of my hand.

Suddenly, flashbacks from that fateful night began to resurface from the deep, dark fathoms of my mind. I took a long breath and let the memories flow out of me.

"Sean announced that he'd been offered a new job in New York, at an even bigger and more prestigious law firm. And then, he dropped an even bigger bombshell. He was going without me. 'I want a fresh start,' he said. 'And to be honest, I don't see you in my future, in New York.'" Tears bubbled behind my eyes. Oliver squeezed my hand, and I continued, "After the accident, everyone treated me like a grieving widow, and I felt like one. The accident must've deleted the break-up from the hard-drive in my mind… until tonight's conversation brought it all crashing back."

"I'm so sorry, Erin." Oliver lifted one of my hands to his lips and gently kissed it. "I cannot imagine anyone wanting to break up with you."

"That's sweet of you to say, Oliver." I pasted on a smile, but the sand had shifted under my feet and my mind was clouded with dark thoughts.

The waiter approached and presented a bottle of wine. Oliver checked the vintage and nodded his head. I was grateful for the short reprieve, as the waiter poured a little wine into Oliver's glass. He swirled it around, sniffed it, then took a small sip. He nodded his approval, and the waiter filled our glasses and departed.

I had a long slug of wine. "Why don't we change the subject? I don't want to talk or think about Sean any more."

Oliver tenderly patted my hand and nodded his head. "I know that you love reading and that you enjoy working at the bookstore and that you won a college writing award, but why leave it so long to start writing again?"

I sipped more wine, then settled back in the nest-like chair. "I don't know why. I think I just needed inspiration."

"You have such a creative mind, and are so well-read, that I'm sure you'll have no trouble writing a great story. And I want to be the first person to read it, when you're done." Oliver raised his wine glass in the air. "Let's toast to your future novel."

I coiled my fingers around my glass. I clinked it against his, gave him a sly smile – *To Max and Eva* – and took another big gulp of wine.

While we'd been talking, the chef had been busy preparing our food. We had finished our miso soup, so the waiter removed our empty bowls and placed the board full of sushi on the bar in front of us.

I poked at one with a chopstick. "They look like finger-sized Christmas presents tied with tiny bows of seaweed."

Oliver grinned. "See, you're so imaginative."

"Stop it." I laughed, and some of my sadness slowly seeped away. I lifted a piece of sushi towards my mouth, gently gripping it between the chopsticks.

"Why don't you tell me more about your parents?" He peered at me over the rim of his wine glass. "How did they meet?"

I swallowed the sushi, then took a sip of wine. "It's kind of a funny story. My mother's friend had a crush on my dad and invited her to a college dance, so she could point him out."

"Uh-oh." Oliver made a face. "I think I can guess where this is heading…"

"Unfortunately for my mother's friend, but luckily for me," I said, with an impish grin, "my dad preferred my mom."

"I knew it."

"They dated for a year, married right after graduation, and were together for over thirty years before my father passed away two years ago." I paused to catch my breath. I glanced over at Oliver to see if he was getting bored, but he appeared to be genuinely interested in hearing my parents' story.

"How did your mom cope after his death?" He leaned towards me and looked me dead in the eye.

Cupping the bowl of my wineglass, I broke eye contact and stared off into the distance. "At first, she sank into a deep depression. But I think my father's death made us both more aware of our mortality. She and I grew closer, especially after Sean's death. Seeing me settled before she 'shuffles off this mortal coil', has become her main focus in life."

"Makes sense." Oliver nodded. "That was Shakespeare, right?"

I smiled, then dropped my chin to my chest. My face clouded. Should I tell Oliver about Gordie's death—and the pall it had cast over my family ever since?

But Oliver interrupted my thoughts with another question, "By 'settled', does she mean 'married'?"

I nodded my head. "Career. Marriage. Kids. All of it."

He paused and ate a piece of sushi. "I can understand why your mother's so focused on you, since your father's death." Oliver put down his chopsticks, then picked up his wine glass and drained it. "But doesn't the added attention cause some tension between the two of you?"

"Sometimes, but mostly, I think my dad's death and Sean's have made both of us feel more apprehensive about the future." I ran my hands through my hair.

"It's only natural." Oliver poured us both some more wine.

"But I don't want to get married, just to make my mother happy. It has to be with the right person, and it has to be forever."

He stared at me like a sharpshooter. "I feel the same way."

I returned his gaze, struck by my own words. I did long for a committed, honest relationship and I knew that Mark was taken. Oliver was available and interested, but it wasn't always easy to be rational when it came to romantic relationships. Mark was just too potent a force to resist. *Ahh. Why am I thinking about him, again?*

"What about your parents? You told me what they do for a living, but tell me something else."

"What would you like to know?"

"For starters, how long have they been married?"

"They divorced when Mark and I were teenagers."

"Oh, I'm sorry." I swallowed some wine.

"It was for the best. They loved each other, but they grew apart. They're both married to their careers."

"It must've been hard on you."

"In the beginning, I felt angry. But I got over it. Most of our friends had divorced parents, too. It's more common than not, these days… unfortunately."

"How did Mark take it?" *God, why can't I stop thinking about him?*

"Pretty hard. He idealized my parents and felt like they'd let us down. I think he built up a wall to protect himself, but don't ever tell him I said that. He'd kill me."

*A wall? He sounds like me. Maybe I can be the one to finally break his walls down.* I swallowed a piece of pink, pickled ginger to cleanse my palate.

"Speaking of Mark, what was it like growing up with a brother?" My heart tightened as if a clenched fist had imprisoned it, memories gushing back to a faraway era when I had a brother. For a brief moment, I could feel his pudgy fingers clamped unto mine… but that was a lifetime ago.

"It's great having a brother when you're a kid, although we've always had a fairly competitive relationship. Mark always wanted to be the best at everything: the best athlete, the best student, the most popular, and the one with the prettiest girlfriend. I think he inherited my parents' competitive nature, and that's why I think Fiona's perfect for him."

*Fiona's perfect for Mark?* I almost gagged on the sickly-sweet ginger. "What makes you think so?"

"She's more laid-back and down-to-earth," Oliver said. "She works hard, but she seems to really care about helping people. And she puts time into her friendships. If anyone can break down his walls, it's Fiona."

The ginger in my mouth tasted like sour vinegar. I spat into my napkin and crushed it inside my fist, until it was a hardened, red ball.

# Chapter 46

Midnight came and went, and Oliver paid the bill. He stood up, pulled out my chair for me, and we left the restaurant. Oliver opened the passenger door for me. We drove away from the restaurant and headed in the direction of Beacon Hill.

We pulled up in front of my house and he turned off the car. When he leaned over to kiss me, I put up my hand to stop him. I was determined to stop leading him on.

He froze and his face crumpled. "Did I do something wrong?"

Suddenly, I changed my mind. I wasn't sure if it was the wine or the intimate conversation during dinner, but I was starting to have feelings for Oliver. It was nice to be appreciated and admired.

"Why don't you come inside?"

"I'd love to." Oliver, practically, leapt out of the car and raced around and opened my door.

"That was quick."

"I want to get inside the house, before you change your mind."

I laughed and took his hand and climbed out of the car.

Once I had let Keeper out and given her a quick cuddle, we headed straight to my bedroom. Tipsy from the wine, I staggered towards the bed, falling onto its soft surface. Oliver followed suit, lowering himself beside me. As our lips met, a rush of comfort flowed through me, compelling him to draw me closer, our kisses growing more passionate with each brief minute. His hands journeyed, exploring my body, expertly undoing the zipper of my dress, and allowing it to drop down, leaving me exposed. Surprisingly, an extreme wave of desire saturated me, catching me off guard. Clashing emotions churned within my chest, an impulsivity that I couldn't ignore. *If only it were Mark,* I thought, admonishing myself for my flawed nature. Why couldn't I gather greater fondness for Oliver? In contrast, the passion he aroused paled in comparison to the overpowering intensity that Mark produced. Even Sean, with his mere presence, induced a stronger response within me than Oliver ever could. Life, as it stood, felt unfair. While thoughts ping-ponged in my brain, Oliver pulled down my underwear and moved his head between my legs, and I lost the ability to think.

Afterwards, I lay wide awake, staring at the ceiling. Sex with Oliver had been more of a physical and emotional release than anything else. It had expunged my disturbing memories of Sean and my frustrations with Mark, rather than expressing any love for Oliver. Duplicity churned inside me like currents in the ocean.

I slipped out of bed, careful not to wake Keeper, who had curled into the crook of Oliver's neck. While I sat on the toilet, I scrolled through my text messages and noticed I had missed some that Fiona had sent the previous afternoon.

*Surprised Mark last night...*

I quickly opened the rest of the message.

*...With theater tickets & a late dinner. He was thrilled.*

I could feel my shattered ego begin to repair itself. Mark hadn't stood me up. It wasn't his fault. My anger had a new target. *Damn Fiona. Why did she have to ruin everything?* But it was too late now. I had slept with Oliver and he was asleep in my bed.

I opened the next message and stared, stonily, at the screen.

*I think it's true love.*

My nostrils flared, and I switched off my phone. I knew I would never be able to sleep now, so I made my way to the kitchen, nonchalantly placing a bag of chamomile tea leaves into a waiting cup. With the press of a button, I switched on the kettle, anticipating the soothing warmth it would soon provide.

Moving to the living room, I sat down in my wingback chair, and cupped the warm tea in my hands. I'd bought this Victorian brownstone townhouse, with the money that I inherited from my father, but I knew it wouldn't feel like home until I shared it with Mark. After sipping some tea, I opened my journal and the words spilt out onto the page.

*One night, I lured my sister downstairs to my own private hell.*

*"I don't feel right," I said, as Faith entered my room.*

*She sat down on the bed, and I pulled the knife out from under the covers.*

*"What're you doing?" Faith gasped.*

*I answered her, by slitting her throat.*

*Faith fell backwards off the bed and her head hit the floor with a thud. Blood spurted out of her neck like water from a hose.*

*"Must've hit an artery," I said, smirking to myself.*

*My sister clutched at her throat, as blood gurgled like a clogged drain. Then, her hand fell to her side, and the room went silent. Faith stared up at me, but her eyes were like marbles, glassy and lifeless.*

*I kicked the body under the bedframe. I soaked up all the blood with the sheets and shoved them under the bed with my sister's corpse. Standing up, my face cracked into a crooked smile. I brushed my palms against each other and turned away. Then I left my dungeon room and locked the door behind me.*

*That same night, after soaking in a steaming, hot bath to rid myself of my sister's blood, I slept as soundly as the dead in Faith's bed.*

*The next day, as the sun rose and streamed in through the window of the second story bedroom, I felt reborn. After dressing in my sister's clothes, I decided to chop off my hair. My long locks had been the only physical difference between us twins and a simple way for others to tell us apart. As I sliced the scissors across my scalp and washed the cuttings down the drain, I transformed myself into Faith. And when I looked in the mirror, I saw my sister's reflection beaming back at me. Max would never know.*

*

*"You look especially beautiful tonight, Faith," Max said to me the following evening, when he came to take me out for dinner.*

*It made my blood boil to be called by my sister's name. But I reminded myself that the real Faith was just a pile of bones and rotting flesh hidden down in the dungeon, and it made me chuckle inwardly.*

*"I'll just pop downstairs for a minute," he said. "To check on Eva—"*

*"Oh, didn't I tell you? She's gone away." I swallowed the smile that had stolen onto my face.*

# Chapter 47

It was Saturday night and time for my babysitting gig with Paige's children. It had been a while since I had seen them, so I bought them each a present – to assuage my guilt – a battery-operated excavator for two-year-old Lochlan, and a talking, dancing, plush *Pooh Bear* for Kyla, who was four.

Paige and Angus lived in the artsy community of Jamaica Plain in south Boston. They had managed to buy an old semi-detached, triple-decker house a few years ago, when it was a buyer's market. After taking a short train ride, I emerged from the station. I felt fairly safe, as I walked through the leafy, suburban neighborhood, but it was dusk, so I quickened my pace. I waved at some people sitting on their front stoop and sipping beer. I hoped my friends would have something for me to eat and drink. I had only had time to wolf down a pot of noodles for dinner. A few more blocks and I would be there. As I crossed the street, I thought I heard someone behind me. But when I glanced back, there was no one there.

Finally, I spotted Paige's silver minivan parked in the driveway and headed up the wooden steps of their home. The siding had been painted mint-green, while the porch and window trims were white. I knocked on the door and stood back and waited. Maybe they were upstairs getting ready. Lifting my hand to knock again, the door suddenly opened, and I stumbled into the beefy arms of Angus.

"Hiya, hen, how are ye?" he asked, holding onto my elbow, until I had recovered both my balance and my composure. "You're looking as lovely as ever."

Angus hailed from Scotland, which explained their choice of children's names. He had a burly build, a head of thick, red hair, and a gregarious nature, but sometimes I had trouble understanding his thick, Glaswegian accent.

"Oh, hi Angus. I'm fine, thanks," I replied. Had he really just called me a 'hen'?

"Cheers fur lookin' after th' weans." He released me from his firm grip. "It's dead brilliant of you."

Following him inside, I grinned, uncomfortably, while I tried to figure out what he had said. "Where are the kids? Where's Paige?"

"Erin, you're here."

"Speak o' the devil," Angus said.

"Thanks so much for doing this," Paige said, descending the stairs from the second story.

"Sure, anytime," I replied.

Paige anxiously inspected herself in the full-length mirror, which had been hung in the narrow foyer to create the illusion of a bigger space. "Do you like my outfit, Erin?" She had on jeans and a black, silk shirt, with ruching across the waist.

"You look really pretty," I replied, infusing my voice with enthusiasm. "Doesn't she, Angus?"

"Och Aye."

Was that really all he could manage? Paige could use more encouragement than a throat-clearing grunt. I would have to come to the rescue.

"Black is always slimming. No one would ever guess that you're the mother of two. By the way, I brought these for the kids," I said, handing over the toys.

"You shouldn't have," Paige said, frowning. "But thanks. I'm sure they'll love them."

"Where are the little cuties?"

"The bairns are asleep upstairs. We'd better be off, or we'll miss the opening band," Angus said, sliding his arm around his wife's waist.

Paige turned away from the mirror. "There's some food in the fridge, if you get hungry…"

"Thanks. And don't worry. We'll be fine. Relax and enjoy the concert. You deserve a night out," I said, smiling. "Now, off you go."

"Cheers," Angus said, opening the door and waving at the waiting cab.

"Text me if there's any problem," Paige said.

After grabbing a bag of chips from the kitchen pantry, I made my way to the living room and turned on the TV. I flipped channels and munched, contentedly, on the salt and vinegar chips.

Halfway through the movie, *The Secret Life of Walter Mitty,* which was filmed in Iceland, I fell into a deep sleep on the couch.

But an hour later, an ear-splitting scream from upstairs jolted me awake. I groaned and sat up. I looked around the room and suddenly remembered where I was.

*Paige's kids!*

The worn hardwood floor underneath me complained in objection as I dashed up the staircase, my heart hammering in my chest. Yet, in my hurried state, I miscalculated the last step, my foot clutching the edge, threatening to send me plummeting back down. I managed to reclaim my balance, but not without a jerk of adrenaline speeding through me. Still shaken from my near fall, a penetrating shriek punctured the air, generating from the direction of the bathroom. Perseverance fueled my movements as I reached for the doorknob, only to find it resolutely resistant, denying the turn in my grasp. Panic inching in, I slammed my shoulder against the uncompromising barrier, hoping to force it open. Alas, my efforts were in vain—the door stayed securely locked, as if guarding its secrets.

"Who's in there? Kyla, is that you?" I was answered with wailing sobs. "Can you open the door, please? It's Auntie Erin."

But the crying continued. As I rattled the doorknob in frustration, a small hand tugged at my shirtsleeve. It was Kyla.

"Auntie Erin, Lochie's locked himself in the bathroom." Kyla looked like she was about to burst into a torrent of tears.

"It's all right, sweetie. Don't cry. I'll get him out." I jiggled the door so hard it shook on its hinges. But it was no use. Kicking my feet against the flimsy, wooden barrier that stood between me and my two-year-old charge, also proved ineffective. My heart leaped with a sudden jolt as the obvious sound of gushing water found my ears, triggering a surge of panic inside me. What in the world was he doing in there? Anxiety curled securely around my chest, persuading me to act rapidly before tragedy struck. The looming possibility of a flooded bathroom swamped my mind. Realistic images of a soaked ceiling crashing down into the living room, carrying little Lochlan with it, sent shivers down my spine. The chilling insight gripped me, pushing me to the edge of despair.

Kyla started crying and yanked, vigorously, at my arm.

When I looked down, I was horrified by what I saw: two tiny pink feet stood in a puddle of yellow spreading across the floor like spilt ink. *Oh my God.*

Brother and sister were now bawling in unison.

My own eyes began to well with tears. Maybe this was fate's way of punishing me for duplicitous behavior towards Fiona. *If I get Lochlan out, safe and sound, I promise to forget about Mark—forever.*

Picking up Kyla, I raced to her bedroom and stripped off her soaking wet pajamas. After quickly rummaging through a chest-of-drawers, I located a clean, princess-themed nightie and tossed it over her strawberry-blond head. The blubbering continued, but at least Kyla was dry.

Rushing back to Lochlan and the imminent tidal wave, I wondered whether I should call Paige or run next door to the neighbors, or even call 911. If I did not get into the bathroom soon, it would really be an emergency.

But first, I decided to try and get Lochlan to unlock the door.

"Push the button in the middle of the knob with your finger." With my ear pressed against the door, I strained for any sign of movement, but all I could hear was gurgling water and hiccupping howls. "Or turn the doorknob, until the button pops out like a jack-in-the-box. Please, Lochlan. You can do it." But my efforts were in vain, and his ululations continued.

"I want my mommy!" Kyla squealed.

I grabbed my hair with both fists and pulled. "***Ahhhh!***"

I was nearing the end of my mental tether with the trumpeting toddlers, when I heard the door downstairs bang open.

Who was there? It couldn't be Paige and Angus. They were at the concert. Slinking to the top of the stairs, I stood listening to the strange sounds coming from below. I could hear someone moving around. Was it a burglar? A rapist? An axe-murderer?

I grappled with my phone. It was time to call 911. My hands shook, and I dropped my phone on the floor and bent down to pick it up, when I heard footsteps coming up the stairs. It was too late to call the police. I swiveled my head from side to side, searching desperately for something to use as a weapon. But all I saw was a stuffed teddy bear. A scream rose in my throat.

# Chapter 48

“Oh my God, it’s you. I thought you were a burglar. What are you doing home?”

“The concert was shite,” Angus said. “The music was too loud. And Paige got a headache.”

“And we missed the kids,” Paige said, reaching the top of the stairs.

“Mommy, Mommy!” Kyla raced down the hall and wrapped her arms around Paige’s legs. “Lochie drowned in the bathroom.”

“What’s she talking about?” Paige asked, gazing directly into my eyes.

“Lochie’s fine,” I said, with a weak smile. “But he’s locked himself in the bathroom.”

“Grab me a screwdriver from the kitchen,” Angus said to Paige, rattling the bathroom door. “Lochie, Daddy’s here.”

I blinked back tears.

Moments later, Paige raced up the stairs, with a screwdriver clutched in her hand. She knelt by the bathroom door. “Lochie, sweetheart, can you hear me? It’s Mommy. Stand back from the door, honey. We’ll have you out of there in a few minutes.”

Angus started unscrewing the doorknob. He slid the inner mechanism back and opened the door.

Paige squeezed past him in a hurry to turn off the taps. The water had flowed over the lip of the sink, soaking the cotton bathmat, but the flood was abated. She turned her attention to Lochlan and folded him into her chest, then carried him into his room.

I watched from the doorway, as Paige lowered him onto his *Thomas-the-Train* bed, murmuring reassurances, "It's okay, now, Lochie. You were very brave."

After wiping his tear-stained, freckled cheeks and runny nose, Paige tucked him under the covers and lay down next to him.

"How's the wee laddie?" Angus asked me, as he kneeled on the ground and screwed the doorknob back in.

"He's fine, thanks to you," I replied, holding the door steady for him, as he twisted the tiny screws back into place.

"It's not that hard, if you ken what to do." He smiled and stood up. "Why don't I drive you home?"

I nodded and followed him down the stairs, that cracked like an old man's knuckles.

Twenty minutes later, Angus pulled his minivan up in front of my house.

"Sorry, again, about tonight. I feel like I let you guys down." I chewed the corner of my lip.

"Don't be daft." Angus nudged me with his elbow. "At least the wee ankle-biter didn't lock himself in the van."

I tipped my head back and laughed, then reached for the door handle.

"Before you go," he said, placing a hand on my arm. "Paige told me that you're dating Oliver Rankin."

"I'm not sure if dating is the right word…"

"Oh, well, anyway, my company hired him last year, to update our security system, but I didnae get a good vibe from the bloke."

I raised an eyebrow. "Really? That surprises me."

"There was a rumor going around, that he cyber-stalked a young intern."

"Rumors aren't always true. He's been nothing, but a gentleman with me."

"Just promise me you'll be careful."

"I promise. But you don't need to worry. I can look after myself." I leaned over and planted a kiss on his cheek, leaving a smudge of red lipstick on his collar. "Oops. I've made a mess." I tried to rub it off with my fingers, but I just made it worse. "You're a good guy, Angus. Paige is a lucky woman."

As I walked up my front stoop, his warning words about Oliver rang in my ears. *Didnae get a good vibe. Cyber-stalked a young intern. Promise me you'll be careful.*

# Chapter 49

The following afternoon, I put in a long, exhausting shift at the bookstore. But at least being busy had helped to keep my mind off the babysitting fiasco and Angus's worrisome warning about Oliver.

On my way home, I had the eerie feeling that I was being followed. But no matter how many times I checked over my shoulder, I didn't see anyone suspicious. *Must be my mind playing tricks on me, again.*

Back at home, I was about to eat a bowl of cereal and climb into bed, when I received an unexpected text. I tapped the green message icon and my eyes bulged.

*What's your address? Can I come over? I'll bring dinner.*

My breath lodged in my throat. I squinted my eyes and held the screen up close to my face. No, my eyes had not deceived me. The text was from Mark. And he wanted to come over to my place. And bring dinner. For a brief moment, I wondered what Fiona was doing tonight. But I pushed the thought to the back corner of my mind and tapped open the text box, with a shaking fingertip. I hesitated. The cursor pulsed. *Am I really going to do this?* His timing was unbelievable. Only two days ago, I'd gone out for dinner with Oliver, and we had, finally, slept together. But now, Angus had planted a seed of doubt in my mind about Oliver. And I'd been waiting for a chance like this with Mark for so long.

I typed out my address. My finger hovered over the little blue arrow that would send my response out into the ether. I inhaled sharply, then stabbed the arrow with my finger.

Shifting from neutral to fourth gear in a matter of seconds, I ran around my house, tidying up. I lit a fire in the living room, remembering the campfire Mark had built at the cottage in Truro. Did I have time for a quick shower? I decided to chance it.

Afterwards, I searched, frantically, through my closet and decided on skinny jeans and a red cashmere sweater with a deep V-neck.

Half an hour later, there was a loud knock at my front door. Keeper raced down the hall, barking and howling.

I stood with my hand on the doorknob and tried to calm myself. Then I opened the door and there he was – Mark – on *my* doorstep. My eyes traveled up and down his body, as he stood there clutching a brown paper bag in his hand. He wore jeans, a navy-blue turtleneck, and a black bomber jacket.

"Can I come in?"

"Sorry, yes, come in." I moved aside and waved him across my threshold.

He stepped inside and gave me a quick, one-armed hug.

I inhaled his scent, detecting a mixture of leather, soap, and a woody cologne.

He let go and said, "You look nice."

I reddened like a ripe cherry under his gaze. "Thanks. Let's head to the kitchen. Follow me."

"Sorry about standing you up the other night." He gave me a sheepish look.

"It's okay. I understand."

"I brought some Chinese takeout and a bottle of white wine." Mark put the bag on the counter and reached down to pet Keeper. "Cute dog."

*Mark's here, in my house, in my kitchen. It's just the two of us. No Fiona. No Oliver. We're all alone.*

He uncorked a bottle of white wine and filled two glasses.

I laid out two plates, and he doled out the noodles, rice, sweet-and-sour pork, and chicken chow mein.

"So, to what do I owe this pleasure?"

His face crumpled. "I lost a patient today—a sixteen-year-old boy."

"Oh Mark, that's terrible. Why don't we move to the living room, and you can tell me what happened?"

We settled on the couch and ate in silence. I waited for Mark to open up and pushed the food around on my plate with my chop sticks.

Mark drained his glass, then started to talk. "I guess he reminded me of myself at that age."

I waited for him to continue.

"He was holding onto the back of a friend's car, when he lost control of his skateboard and fell onto the road. He wasn't wearing a helmet and died of severe head injuries." There was a tremor in his voice. "I tried everything, but I couldn't save him." His head drooped, and I reached over and rubbed his arm.

I loved this sensitive side of Mark, the one Fiona always talked about. *No, I'm not going to think about her right now. He's at my house, not hers. He called me. He wants to be with me.* I was touched by his desire to be open and his ability to share his sadness. My heart swelled like a windswept wave and I stifled the urge to smother him with kisses.

When we had finished eating, Mark got up and jabbed at the fire with the poker. I took our plates out to the kitchen, rinsed them off, and stacked them in the sink. I paused to look out the purple-pained window at the flickering light from a vintage gas lamp. Every second I spent in Mark's company was like a vignette I'd carry with me and replay, over and over, in my mind. My home felt different with him in it. The air was charged, the colors more vibrant. It was time to rejoin Mark, but I decided to make a quick stop in the powder room to freshen up.

Addressing my image in the mirror, I said, "What happens next will determine your whole future. Good luck."

But when I came back to the living room, my heart drooped with disappointment. He had fallen asleep. I listened to his rhythmic breathing, then reached down and lightly touched his tousled hair with my fingertips, just to make sure he was real. Then I covered him with a blanket.

His eyes flicked open.

"Oh, sorry," I said. "I didn't mean to wake you…"

"Thanks for being here and listening to me tonight."

My face flushed. "Of course…"

"I didn't want to be alone…" He shut his eyes and fell back to sleep.

I stomped over to the fireplace, snatched the poker, and stabbed at the dying embers. *Now, all I had to fix was Fiona.*

# Chapter 50

A few days later, Fiona called and asked me out for coffee. We arranged to meet at an Italian pastry shop, near the school where she was running a summer literacy camp.

When I arrived at *Paolo's Pastry,* Fiona was already seated at a table waiting for me. She stood up and trapped me in a tight hug.

"It's so good to see you, Erin. I can't believe the summer's almost over and the cool weather's already here."

I noted Fiona's crisp white dress-shirt, black leather pencil skirt and black high-heels. She'd really stepped up her game since meeting Mark.

"Nice outfit," I said, grinning through gritted teeth.

"Thanks. Mark likes it, too."

"Are you growing your hair?" I asked.

"Yes, I am. Mark likes it longer."

*Mark likes it. Mark likes it.* Her fawning made me feel nauseous. She reminded me of a Stepford-wife, as if she were rehearsing for her future role as 'Mrs. Mark Rankin, doctor's wife'.

A sudden sparkle of light caught my eye, pulling me back to the present.

Fiona had pulled her hair back behind her ears, exposing two large, diamond earrings. "What do you think?"

"Where did you get those?" I asked, with a dead-eyed stare.

Fiona beamed from ear to ear, twirling one of the diamonds round and round. "They were a gift from Mark. They must've cost him a fortune.

Isn't he wonderful? I think it's a sign that he's taking our relationship very seriously."

*A gift from Mark.* My head spun with confusion. *Why would he do that? Why would he come to my house and cry on my shoulder, but give Fiona diamonds?* It didn't make sense. Maybe he was feeling guilty, or he was stalling, until he built up the nerve to break up with her. Sometimes, when a man gave a woman an expensive piece of jewelry, it was a way of signaling that he had something to hide. Mark was clearly overcompensating.

Now that I'd rationalized it in my mind, I pasted a smile on my face and forced a compliment from my lips. "They're stunning."

"Stunning is the perfect word for them. I couldn't wait to show you. Anyway, we've so much to catch up on. I need to talk to you about Mark and I want you to tell me all about Oliver. I still can't believe we're dating brothers. Isn't it amazing? But first, you should grab a coffee. They make a really good latte here. I hope you don't mind, but I already got one for myself."

I walked up to the counter and waited for a barista to notice me. Why did everyone assume that Oliver and I were dating? And after Angus's warning, I didn't know if I could trust Oliver anyway.

"Next customer?"

"A latte and a chocolate-dipped, ricotta-filled cannoli, please." Ever since I'd slept with Mark, I was ravenous. While I waited for my order, I started speculating about what Fiona wanted to tell me about Mark. Whatever it was, I would have to perform my 'friend' role to perfection, listening and nodding when required while false-hearted feelings frothed inside me.

When the barista called my name, I picked up my coffee and cannoli, and a packet of sugar on my way back to the table. As I sat down, I ripped open the packet and poured it into the latte. I stirred the sugar into the hot liquid to speed up its absorption.

Fiona drooled over the decadent treat. "That looks yummy." It was covered in dark-chocolate sauce, which was coagulating into a messy pool on the small white plate. "I wish I'd ordered one."

"We can share mine." I pushed the plate across the table.

"Oh, no." Fiona slid the plate back. "Remember, I'm watching my weight."

I rolled my eyes, picked up the cannoli, and bit into it with gusto. Sauce dribbled down my chin and all over my fingers, and as soon as I had swallowed the first mouthful, I took another bite. But I could not delay the inevitable forever.

"So, how's it going with Mark?" That wasn't so hard. Maybe I should be an actor instead of a writer.

"Good… I mean, great." Fiona reached across the table and dipped a finger into the chocolate sauce. "Mm," she said, after sticking it in her mouth. "Even though we've only been seeing each other for such a short time, things are starting to get serious."

"I'm so happy for you." I stuffed the last piece of cannoli into my mouth, while my mind plummeted off a cliff. *Fiona must be exaggerating, surely.*

She handed me a napkin.

Someone's cell phone started blaring a *Star Wars*-themed ring tone.

I laughed, but Fiona knitted her brow. Her smile had disappeared.

"Is something wrong?"

"It's probably nothing…"

I held my breath.

"It's just that Mark's been very moody, lately. Either he's been too exhausted to come over or when he does, all he wants to do is watch movies on *Netflix*. But I'm not worried. I'm sure it's just all the stress from working in an emergency room."

"I'm sure you're right."

"Sometimes, I worry about being a doctor's wife. I think it could get lonely after a while, if he's never home."

"Don't get ahead of yourself." My mind was a blur, but I tried to focus on what Fiona was saying. "You haven't been seeing him very long."

"I know, but I can't help thinking about the future. You know I've always wanted lots of children, but I wonder how much time he'll have for being a father. What do you think? Am I overreacting? Maybe you're right and I'm getting too far ahead of myself. I really value your opinion, so please don't hold back." Fiona finally paused to catch her breath.

I bounced my legs up and down under the table. Listening to Fiona's extended monologue had really tested my patience. If she knew the truth, she would be shocked. I did not think Mark was Fiona's potential future husband, because he was mine. But a sliver of doubt worked its way into my brain. Could Mark ever be faithful to just one woman? Another disturbing thought crept into my mind. Why was he so moody and exhausted? Had Mark been sleeping with other women besides Fiona and me? The image of his female colleague I'd seen chatting and laughing with him that day at the hospital flashed into my mind. But I quickly dismissed such paranoid thoughts. He was a doctor. Being exhausted came along with the job. How could he possibly find the time to fool around more than he already was?

"If you really want me to be upfront with you…"

"I do." Fiona leaned forward, fiddling with one of her new earrings.

"…I think it's far too soon to be contemplating marriage and kids. Give it more time. I mean, how well do you really know him?"

"I know, I know. But my heart is telling me that Mark's the one."

I sipped my latte and another thought struck me: *What if Mark had decided to mend his ways after losing that young patient? What if he had given Fiona the diamonds as a way of making up for his transgressions? Maybe Oliver was right, and Mark really did love Fiona.*

"I know he isn't perfect, but he's perfect for me. I just can't help it. I'm head-over-heels in love with him. He's just so irresistible, don't you think?"

I choked on my mouthful of coffee, and some of it went down my windpipe. I coughed into a closed fist.

"Are you okay?"

"I'm fine." I wiped my teary eyes with a napkin.

"Now, tell me all about Oliver. I've been totally monopolizing the conversation and I really want to hear about you two."

"We've been spending a lot of time together—"

"And he obviously adores you." Fiona jumped in. "But how do you feel about him?" The skin creased between her brows, as she waited for my response.

"I'm fond of him. He's a sweet guy. And considerate. And an excellent listener."

"It sounds as if you do like him, but you're just not admitting it to yourself. Don't play hard to get too long, Erin. You don't want to lose him." Fiona gave me a warning look.

Her condescending, teacher-tone grated on my nerves.

"Men like Oliver don't come along very often."

*You can have him, and I'll take Mark.*

"I wish you could be as happy with Oliver, as I am with Mark."

*Mark is mine.* Fiona's delusional faith in Mark seemed both patronizing and pathetic. On the other hand, I realized, it was possible that I was the one deluding myself. The next time I saw her, she might be wearing a diamond on her finger.

Fiona glanced at the time on her phone. "Unfortunately, I need to get back to work." She quickly finished her coffee and stood up. "We have so much to talk about these days. Maybe the four of us could go out sometime soon?"

"Sure, that'd be fun." I stood up and walked out with her onto the busy street. We stood facing each other on the sidewalk, as cars and trucks whizzed by. "I guess we're headed in opposite directions."

Fiona leaned over and hugged me. "Call me soon, okay?"

When I let her go, Fiona stumbled backwards off the curb and directly into the path of an oncoming T-bus.

The driver screeched his brakes and stopped just in time.

"Yikes, that was close," I said. "Are you okay?"

"Look at me. I'm shaking like a leaf." Fiona stepped back onto the pavement, then fixed her eyes on me. "It almost seemed like—"

"You need to be more careful. I'd be devastated if anything happened to you—and so would Mark."

# Chapter 51

The intimate Italian restaurant, on Hanover Street in North End, Boston, consisted of a long, narrow space with high ceilings. We were sitting at a table in the corner, and the waiter had just opened the bottle of wine Oliver ordered for us.

"Just a small glass for me." I didn't want to end up in bed with him again, especially after Angus's warning. I wanted to keep my wits about me.

Oliver lifted his glass and smiled across the table at me. "I'd like to make a toast: To a wonderful evening with a wonderful woman."

I reddened, but clinked my glass with his. "To a wonderful evening." I took a small sip, then put my glass down and scanned the menu. "It's going to be hard to choose. Everything sounds so delicious." I was trying to decide between butternut squash ravioli or gnocchi with braised rabbit, when a petite, attractive blond approached our table.

"Oliver. I can't believe it's really you," she said, in what seemed an overly flirtatious manner.

"Rachel. It's so good to see you." He stood up, placed his hands on her shoulders, and kissed her on one cheek and then the other. "This is my girlfriend," he said, turning and pointing at me.

*Did he really just call me his girlfriend?*

"Rachel and I knew each other at university."

"Knew each other?" Rachel raised her eyebrows and poked her elbow into Oliver's ribs. "That's an understatement if I ever heard one. You always were too modest. I had a massive crush on Oliver during our last year of university," she said, glancing at me. "But he was too busy studying to even notice me."

Sipping some wine, I gave Rachel a curious look over the rim of my glass.

Rachel swung her eyes back to Oliver. "I always wondered what you were up to. I'd love to catch up with you sometime, if Erin doesn't mind?"

"It's fine with me," I said, shrugging.

"Can I get your number?" Rachel asked, passing him her phone.

Oliver obediently entered his number into her list of contacts. She waved goodbye and sashayed over to the bar to rejoin her group of girlfriends.

"Sorry about that," he said, sheepishly. "I haven't seen Rachel in so long; she caught me by surprise."

"Don't worry about it." I smiled and shrugged. "You should definitely call her and meet up for a coffee or a drink or even dinner, if you want to."

Oliver drank some wine and glanced over at the bar, where Rachel was laughing with her friends. The waiter arrived to take our orders, and we both became temporarily distracted by the dinner menu. When we had made our selections, the waiter departed to give the kitchen the order. An awkward silence fell between us and was only broken by the arrival of our appetizer. Since we both loved fish, Oliver had ordered a grilled seafood salad for us to share.

"How's life at the bookstore?" he asked, stabbing his fork into a scallop.

"Maddie got a new tattoo."

"Oh yeah? What did she get?"

"A Chinese dragon on her left shoulder blade." I bit a shrimp in half.

"The girl with the dragon tattoo."

"Ha, ha. Very funny. She says it's a symbol of good luck." I picked up a crab leg. "Maybe I should get one."

"Don't you dare." Oliver almost choked on a mouthful of food.

"Relax. I'm just teasing."

Eventually, the waiter cleared our plates and delivered the main course shortly afterwards.

"How's your work with the police force going?"

"I helped them install spyware."

"Spyware?" I ate some gnocchi with rabbit.

"They can use it to track someone's movements," Oliver said, pouring us both more wine. "Using cell phone GPS."

"Someone… as in a suspect?"

"Yep. In this case, they used it to track drug dealers."

I tapped a fingernail on my wineglass. Angus's story about Oliver cyber-stalking an intern flashed into my mind.

A while later, our plates were empty. "All done?" Oliver threw his napkin on the table.

"Yep." I patted my stomach. "It was delicious, but I'm full."

"I'll get the bill." He summoned the waiter.

We walked outside into the cool autumn air. When I shuddered from the cold, Oliver put his arm around me. It had been a pleasant evening, but I wanted to get home and do some writing, which had become as much of a compulsion as thinking about Mark.

"I know it's the weekend, but if you don't mind, I think I'll call it a night."

He gave me a hangdog look. "I hope all my work talk didn't tire you out."

"No, it was really interesting." I smiled up at him. "It's just been a long day."

Pulling me into his arms, he whispered in my ear, "I don't want to let you go."

My back stiffened.

"Are you sure you're not upset about Rachel?" Oliver took a step back and looked down into my eyes. "I don't have to see her, if it bothers you."

On the contrary, I was all for it. If Oliver started seeing Rachel, he'd be less hurt when Mark and I ended up together. I shook my head, then stretched out my arms and yawned.

"Well, as long as you're sure—"

"I'm sure."

"Do you want me to get you a taxi?" He was still holding onto my hand.

I nodded.

Reluctantly, he released my hand and moved to the curb. After hailing me a cab, he gave me one more hug and a kiss. "You're sure I can't come over?"

"Not tonight. But thanks for dinner." I walked towards the waiting car.

As the cab pulled away from the curb, I saw Rachel emerge from the pub and pounce on Oliver like a hungry hyena.

# Chapter 52

I got into bed and opened the drawer of my bedside table. *That's strange. I could've sworn that I left my journal in the drawer.* I always hid it away when I finished a writing session. The last thing I wanted was for anyone to find it and read it. I yanked out the drawer and tipped the contents upside down on the bed. But it wasn't there. I raced around the room, examining every surface. Where was it? And then I saw it, sitting on the top of the dresser. But I had no memory of putting it there. *God, I really need to get more sleep.* I grabbed a pen, then cozied up with Keeper on the bed and started writing.

*I started to make plans for my – or rather Faith's – wedding. Max had not proposed yet, but I knew he would soon. I began sketching designs for my bridal gown. Using a graphite pencil on thick, fibrous paper, I drew off-the-shoulder gowns with long, luxurious trains. The rough, toothy surface of the paper allowed me to create areas of light and shadow, giving my drawings an aura of romanticism.*

*But my sweet dreams were marred by the pungent smell of my sister's rotting corpse. The stench permeated the walls of the house; it seeped up through the floorboards and out of the wallpaper.*

*And sometimes, during the night, I thought I heard Faith whispering to me, "Help me, help me." And other times, I heard her ask, "Why did you hurt me?" But I was not going to allow the tiny twinges of guilt about my sister's murder, ruin my future happiness with Max.*

*"What's that horrible odor?" Max asked, when he came over to visit one night.*

*"I think there's a dead rat decomposing behind the walls," I replied. "I'll have to get it fumigated."*

*"That's a good idea," he said. "But it'll have to wait until you get back."*

*"Get back from where?"*

*He handed me a pair of plane tickets. "I'm taking you to Iceland."*

*My mouth hung open, as I stared at the tickets in my hand.*

*

*As the plane prepared to take-off from the Boston airport, I took a deep breath and looked out the window. I lifted my hand to fiddle with my hair, forgetting that I had cut it all off. Instead, I jiggled my legs to relieve my restlessness. I was not exactly afraid of flying, but the idea that my life, and the lives of all my fellow passengers, were in the hands of unknown pilots did give me pause. Strapped into the rear fuselage, a claustrophobic tin can, I took a few moments to take stock:* If I died on this flight, would I have any regrets?

*Suddenly, I was jolted out of my morbid ruminations when a strong hand grabbed hold of mine.*

*"Are you okay, Faith?" Max asked. "You seem tense."*

*I glanced over at Max and smiled. "I'll be fine, as long as you're next to me."*

*

*"Can you believe it? We're here!" Max said, like an excited school-boy.*

*I smiled back at him, but my body shivered as we waited in line for our rental car. I was glad that I had brought one of my sister's light, winter jackets, as the temperature was quite cool, despite the warm Gulf stream. From the window of the airplane, I'd caught a glimpse of the Atlantic Ocean and a snow-covered peninsula just before we landed.*

*Our first destination was a visit to a geothermal spa. On the way, we drove past endless miles of black, moss-covered, lava rocks.*

*"The landscape has such a bleak beauty," I said.*

*It seemed almost post-apocalyptic. Iceland was a remote island, where people still believed in ancient magic. I had read on the internet that strange, invisible elves hid in the cliffs and rocks. Trolls lived in dark, underground caves carved out by lava and these vengeful monsters turned into stone if exposed to the sun.*

*When Max and I arrived at the Blue Lagoon, I was amazed by the milky-blue water and the fog-like steam rising from the sulfuric pool. We were greeted warmly at the entrance and given towels and directions to the change rooms. Max and I parted, briefly, going into our separate change rooms, before meeting up at the pool.*

*We slowly descended into the hot water together, hand-in-hand.*

*"Did you miss me, darling?" Max asked.*

*"Of course, I did." I was excited to be at the spa and immediately covered my face with the silvery-gray silt, that was said to rejuvenate the skin.*

*"How do I look? Do you see any improvement?"*

*"If it's possible, you look even younger and more beautiful than ever." Max playfully splashed some water in my direction.*

*I beamed at his flattery. Even though I knew he was teasing me, I did wonder if the clay really had any effect. Sipping on the pint of Gull ale Max had bought, I felt myself begin to relax from the combination of warm water and the alcohol. Max snuck in a few kisses, and we held hands under the warm water.*

*

I had been up half the night writing and was just about to drift off to sleep, late Sunday morning, when my phone pinged with a text from Fiona.

*Hey, are you busy? Can you come over? It's important.*

I wondered what was up. I had just seen Fiona a few days ago.

*Sure. I'll be there in an hour.*

Reluctantly, I slid out of bed, then turned and grabbed my journal, which lay beside the pillow. I opened the drawer of the bedside table, dropped the journal inside and slid the drawer shut. After taking care of Keeper's needs, it was time to shower and get dressed. I went to the bathroom and sat on the toilet, then stood up and stared down into the bowl. My mind reeled. Insomnia was no longer my biggest problem.

My period was late. And if it didn't start soon, I'd have to take a pregnancy test. What if I peed on the stick and a blue line appeared? Mark had worn a condom, and I was on the pill. I googled birth control stats and discovered that condoms had a typical failure rate of 15%, but the pill was 99% effective. Granted, I'd forgotten to take it a few times. Still, the odds were against it. There was no way that I was pregnant. I decided to postpone the test for a few more weeks.

# Chapter 53

"I brought you sunflowers."

"They're beautiful. Thanks. You're always so thoughtful," Fiona said, taking them from me after we had exchanged a light embrace. "But you don't have to bring gifts every time you visit. Come on into the kitchen. I just made a fresh pot of coffee."

We headed down the narrow, windowless hallway to the tiny kitchen. The floors were slanted and groaned with every step. The dreary one-bedroom apartment on Boylston Street had been built in the 1920s. The fresh flowers I'd brought would help brighten the place up.

"Hey, Erin." Mark got up and gave me a quick hug.

My pulse thumped in my ears. Why hadn't Fiona warned me that Mark would be here, too? My thoughts tangled, as I sat down at the Ikea kitchen table and tugged a hand through my hair.

A vase with white orchids sat on the kitchen countertop.

"Mark brought those," Fiona said, pointing at the vase. "It was so sweet of him, wasn't it?" She cut the sunflower stems with a pair of scissors, then plunked them in a mason jar and placed them next to the orchids. I noticed a heart-shaped box of Belgian chocolates lying on the table. Flowers and fancy chocolates? He was really overdoing it. Then again, I had brought my own guilt gift.

"I'm afraid I'll have to leave you two ladies. I've got to head to the hospital."

My chest tightened like a tourniquet, as I watched Mark and Fiona kiss.

"I'll text you later, Fiona. It was nice to see you, Erin," he said, flashing his blue-gray eyes at me.

I raised up out of my seat, but he was gone. No hug this time.

Fiona handed me a cup of coffee, then sat down opposite me.

"So, what's this all about?" I had a lengthy drink of coffee, then waited for her to explain what was so important.

"Oliver popped by for breakfast today, and he was very upset."

My gut clenched.

"He said that he ran into an old friend from college last night, and that you'd encouraged them to go out together."

I crossed my arms. "That's right. I did."

"He said that your response really confused him." Fiona, nervously, twisted one of her diamond earrings.

I tilted my head. Why was Fiona getting so involved?

"He'd actually been hoping that you'd discourage him from seeing her."

Who did Fiona think she was? My mother?

"And he said you took a cab home right after dinner."

I swallowed more coffee.

"If it were anyone else, I'd mind my own business." Fiona kept her eyes fastened on me like a sniper. "But you're my best friend, so I'm going to be upfront with you."

I chewed on my thumb and waited for the lecture to begin.

"Oliver's a great guy."

"I know he is."

"Let me finish." Fiona placed her palms on the table.

The tendons in my neck tautened like a rope.

"I don't think he's interested in this Rachel person, but she's already sent him several texts. I'm afraid that if you don't make up your mind, one way or the other, you may lose him—and you'll regret it."

"Do you have any sugar?" My nerves jangled, like an untuned guitar.

Fiona passed me a bowl, with some hardened sugar.

I scraped some out and stirred it into my coffee, rattling the spoon against the sides of the cup.

"I don't think you'll find anyone better than Oliver." Fiona arched her eyebrows. "I just want you to be happy, like me and Mark."

*You mean like Mark and me, especially if it turns out that I'm carrying his baby.*

# Chapter 54

Monday morning, I woke up and raced to the bathroom. I stood up and peered into the bowl. My stomach sank. My period had started. I would not be having Mark's baby. My head told me that I should be relieved. But a fist clenched around my heart, and I swallowed a sob. I opened the medicine cabinet, took out the small orange bottle with the Prozac and shook a green-and-white capsule into my palm. Then I placed it on my tongue and washed it down with tap water.

Menstrual cramps and the accompanying nausea had set in, so I decided to stay home from work and spend the day in bed. As I cuddled up with Keeper, Fiona's scolding replayed in my mind. Maybe I should call Oliver.

But by midday, I was under such a dark cloud, that I decided to postpone calling Oliver and phoned my mother instead.

Later that afternoon, my mother arrived with a giant pot of homemade chicken noodle soup and a pile of fashion magazines.

"Thanks, Mommy," I said, my voice feeble and child-like.

"I'll warm this up for you," she said, waltzing her way to the kitchen. "And I'm going to make sure you finish every drop."

I watched her pour the soup into a bowl and place it in the microwave.

"Why don't you give Oliver a call? Maybe he could come over after work and cheer you up." My mother placed the steaming bowl down onto the table.

I slurped some soup.

She sat down. "He's such a sweet young man."

I dropped my spoon, and it clattered against the bowl. "What did you just say?"

"I said, 'He's a sweet—'"

"I know what you said." I arched my back. "But how do you know that he's 'sweet'?"

"Well…" She dropped her eyes. "He didn't want me to tell you—"

"Tell me what?"

"He took me out for tea."

I clapped my hands to my forehead. "He what?"

"He got my number from Fiona, and called me up yesterday morning," she said, the corners of her mouth curling up. "And invited me out for afternoon tea at the *Courtyard Restaurant*."

"At the *Public Library?*"

She nodded and smiled. "He even brought me the most beautiful flowers."

"Oh my God." I scraped my chair back and stood up, with legs akimbo and my hands on my hips.

"Now, sweetheart, please don't be angry."

My mouth hung open, as I waited for my mother to explain.

"He really cares about you."

My eyebrows shot up my forehead.

"He's worried that Sean's death has made you put up emotional walls."

I paced and panted. "I don't believe this."

"Try to calm down, dear. You're hyperventilating."

The walls started to press in on me and sweat streamed down my face. I saw shimmering spots and then everything went black.

After my fainting spell, my mother insisted that I spend the rest of the day in bed. Lying on my back gave me plenty of time to think and my irritation about the 'tea party' dominated my thoughts. The fact that Oliver had contacted my mother, without my knowledge, made me cringe. Was he trying to control me, by manipulating those closest to me? First, he'd involved Fiona. And now, my mother. Who did he think he was? His intensity was starting to annoy me. He seemed like such a nice guy, but maybe Angus was right, and Oliver's caring demeanor masked a more dark and devious side.

# Chapter 55

After a few days of rest, I was feeling much better – physically, at least – and my mother had taken me out shopping to cheer me up. I examined my image in the full-length mirror outside the dressing room. The heavy layers of the dark blue, double-breasted coat swamped my slender frame.

"I look like a soldier returning from the battlefield," I said, with a sullen face.

My mother laughed.

We were shopping for a new fall/winter coat at a store in *Copley Place.*

As I gazed at my reflection, I wished I could step through the glass and vanish into another world.

After rifling through the other jackets that hung like lifeless rag dolls from hooks inside the change room, my mother handed me a white wool parka with a fake fur-trimmed collar and three coal-black buttons down the front.

"Try this one, honey. You'll look adorable in it," she said, with a hopeful smile.

I removed the darker coat before it swallowed me alive and dropped it to the dressing room floor. Slipping my arms through the sleeves of the lighter-colored option, my spirits lifted for a brief moment. I stepped out of the small, enclosed space and swiveled around in front of a larger, three-sided mirror. As I gazed at my reflection from all angles, the rows and rows of clone-like versions of myself made me dizzy. I turned my back on the legion of likenesses and faced my mother.

"What do you think, sweetheart?" she asked.

I shook my head. "I'd get it dirty pretty fast."

"Maybe it comes in other colors. What about a warm burgundy?"

"I'm not sure." I shrugged.

"Let me get a salesgirl to help us."

"No, don't."

"Why not?"

I sighed. "Maybe I'm not in the mood for shopping, after all. Can we take a break for a while?" My vision blurred and my feet ached. I had thought a day out shopping with my mother might be just the distraction I needed, but it had frazzled my mind even more.

"Of course, dear." She helped me remove the ivory parka and placed it on a chair. "Let's get a cup of tea."

Back out in the light, open space of the central mall, my mood brightened. We descended the escalator to the café on the ground floor, which served overpriced gourmet sandwiches and soup to hungry patrons of the high-end retail complex.

We perched on stools at a tiny table and dangled our legs. We sipped loose leaf black tea from dainty china cups, with ornate floral designs, and nibbled on paper-thin, ginger snap cookies.

"What's going on with Oliver?" my mother asked. "Have you patched things up?"

My hand shook, almost spilling my tea. "I think he's interested in someone else."

"I find that hard to believe." Her eyes narrowed.

I bit into a cookie. Stalling for time, I brushed crumbs from my face with my hand and drank some of the hot tea.

My mother pursed her lips and held her tongue.

"I pushed him away, and someone else snatched him up."

She frowned. "Why did you push him away?"

"I don't know." I exhaled sharply. "He's a nice guy, but no one compares to Sean. And Dad." *Except Mark.* "Besides, I'm starting to have real misgivings about Oliver. He's coming on way too strong, going behind my back and involving Fiona and you. That makes me mistrust him. And it builds my walls up even higher."

"I understand what you're saying, sweetheart, but I wouldn't rush to judgement." My mother stared down into her teacup, then slowly lifted her eyes. "I didn't think I'd ever tell you this."

"What?

"This may not be the best time—"

"Just tell me."

"My husband, your dearly departed father," she said, settling her eyes on me, "was not as perfect as you believed him to be. His architecture firm was on the verge of bankruptcy."

"You're lying." I jumped off my seat.

"I'm afraid it's true." She twirled her teacup around in its saucer. "One of the buildings he'd designed was structurally unsound, and he was facing a massive lawsuit."

"Why didn't I know about this?"

"He wanted to keep it from you, to protect you. And he was too damn proud. It was about to hit the media—when he died. His lawyers ended up settling out of court and the story died too."

"Is that why you sold the house and moved into that tiny condo? You said the big place was too lonely without Dad."

"I lied."

I collapsed back down onto my chair.

My mother took a sip of tea. "And since I'm sharing secrets…"

I held my breath.

"I think he'd started seeing someone… just before he died."

"By seeing someone, do you mean, Dad was having an affair?"

She averted her eyes, but nodded her head.

My blood boiled. "Who was she?"

"I never found out. But I suspect she was someone much younger than me."

I gaped at my mother, in disbelief. I'd spent my whole life feeling bad about myself and the fact I couldn't live up to my father's high standards. But now, I'd learned that he was a fraud. A liar, a cheater, and a failure.

"Why didn't you leave him?"

"It wasn't completely his fault. We grew apart, after your baby brother died."

It was as if an ice-pic jabbed at my heart. "But why did you stay together?"

"We wanted you to have a proper family." My mother motioned for me to sit back down.

I shook my head and stayed standing. "It's all my f-fault," my voice quivered, and I struggled to catch my breath.

"What are you talking about, sweetheart?"

"The blanket." The word felt thick on my tongue. But all the walls I'd built up to bury my guilt, suddenly, crumbled. "I put it in his crib. It's my fault Gordie died. And it's my fault that you and Dad grew apart."

My mother looked horrified. "Oh no. Sweetheart. I'm so, so sorry. Little Gordie didn't die because of a blanket."

"But I heard you and Dad arguing…"

"At first, we blamed each other. But then, the medical examiner did an autopsy and that's when we found out that your poor baby brother had an undetected, congenital heart defect. It wasn't anyone's fault, least of all yours."

My face contorted; I couldn't breathe. "Why didn't you tell me?"

"We thought you were too young to understand. And we were too caught up in our own grief. I didn't realize how much you were suffering, too. I am so sorry."

I stood frozen on the spot.

My mother got up and wrapped her arms, tightly, around me.

When we separated, I slumped down on my seat and let out a long sigh. My mind was numb; it was all too much to take in. First, the news about my dad, my hero. My image of him was shattered. And then, learning the truth about my brother's death… The fact that my mother had been keeping so many secrets from me for so long was also upsetting. I thought we were as close as mother and daughter could be, but apparently, I was wrong. Wave after wave of emotion engulfed me.

"The truth is, I stayed with your father, because I was afraid to be alone." She stared down at her wedding ring. "And, in spite of everything, I still loved him."

"Since we're talking about Dad," I said, staring at my mother and straightening my shoulders, "I have something else to tell you."

"What is it, dear?" She sipped some tea.

"You know that Dad and I went out for dinner the night he died…"

My mother nodded, then put down her teacup and waited.

"After dinner, we dropped by his office—and we had a huge argument."

"What on earth did you argue about?"

"He started lecturing me about my career, or lack of one, and I said, 'You'd have been happier if Gordie had lived, and I was the one who died.' And he said, 'Maybe I would've.'"

My mother gasped.

"I told him I hated him."

"Oh, Erin." Her face fell.

"It's my fault that he died."

"What on earth are you saying?"

My face crumpled. "I read on the internet, that strong emotions, such as anger, can raise blood pressure and cause a stroke." The memory of my father keeling over and hitting his head on the desk played in my mind like a movie reel. I looked down at my hands and imagined them covered in his blood.

"Oh, you poor, poor baby." She sighed and shook her head. "Your father knew he had high blood pressure. The doctor had warned him to cut back on his work, his drinking, and his steaks, but your dad was so stubborn. And the impending lawsuit put him under a terrible amount of pressure…"

"It was still my fault. I pushed him too far."

"No, dear, no." She reached across the table and grasped my hand. "It was just a terrible coincidence."

My life was teeming with terrible coincidences. "I'm just a *terrible* person."

"Nonsense. You're a wonderful person." My mother picked up the Victorian-style teapot decorated with pink roses and strawberries. "You need to forgive yourself, let go of your guilty feelings, and move on with your life."

I dropped my eyes downward.

"Tsk. Tsk." She shook her head. "No wonder you've been hiding yourself away. Because of all this guilt you've been carrying around, you've convinced yourself that you don't deserve to be happy. My poor, beautiful daughter… you've built up a wall so high nobody can get in."

*Except Mark.*

"You just need to give it more time." My mother tipped the pot and refilled our cups. "Focus on the here and now. You can start by drinking more tea."

I did as I was told. The warm liquid felt soothing, as it slid down my throat. Talking to my mother had eased my burden of guilt about both my brother's and father's deaths. I stared down into the bottom of my teacup, searching for a pattern in the scattered, wet leaves that might hint at my future. I took the delicate teacup in my hands, its fine porcelain exterior warm against my fingertips. If I truly was worthy of happiness, I thought to myself, the universe would certainly send me a sign. I stared down into the tea, searching for meaning amidst the swirling patterns. With a mild turn, I revolved the cup, watching the mysterious contents from a new viewpoint. I searched fruitlessly for a heart-shaped image and the letter 'M' amongst the scattered tea leaves, but the sought-after symbols remained indefinite, buried within the hazy depths of the tea. Set on not giving up, I continued my mission for a glint of hope.

And then, as if by magic, it was revealed. A minute image progressively developed before my eyes, causing a tightening in my ribs. Steadily meandering its way along the side of the cup, a thin, ebony line appeared, matching the sinuous form of a snake. Its appearance sent a tremble down my spine, a portentous sense that left me breathless.

"Ah-ha." My mother's voice jolted me out of my head. "Now, I understand."

"Understand what, Mom?" I met her gaze.

"Why you pushed Oliver away."

*Because I'm in love with his brother.*

"To punish yourself."

"Punish myself? What do you mean?"

"If you blamed yourself for your brother's death and your dad's, you probably blame yourself for Sean's death, too."

I knocked my teacup to the floor, where it cracked into pieces.

# Chapter 56

I helped my mother hail a taxi, but I decided to walk. I needed time to think. It was early evening, and the light was fading. As I wandered on my way back to Beacon Hill, the definite ring of footsteps resounded consistently behind me, tapping like a timekeeper. A tingling feeling of fear slithered its way up my spine, sending quivers through my whole self. Thoughts of being followed, yet again, snuck into my mind, entangling with the notion that I might be slowly surrendering to madness. In a sudden rush of apprehension, I summoned the courage to steal a brief peep over my shoulder.

There it was, a shadowy frame, threatening ominously at the distance of half a block. Its silhouette bore a strange likeness to Oliver, mirroring his build and stature. With an assortment of faith and anxiety, I lifted my arm and waved, despairingly seeking any form of acknowledgement. To my disappointment, the figure stayed impassive, unaffected by my indication. My heart danced frantically within my chest, skipping a beat as my mind dashed to resolve the mystery behind me. Who was this obscure person, and what objectives lay hidden beneath their elusive presence?

Erring on the side of caution, I made a determined decision and instantly eased myself across the street, hoping to shake off any probable pursuer. Yet, to my amazement, the mysterious figure continued to pursue me, mirroring my every move. Persistence coursed through my veins, driven by a flood of adrenaline racing through my body. With a fresh burst of energy, I increased my pace, my feet rhythmically hammering against the pavement, desperate to create space between myself and this shadowy follower. Numerous blocks blurred past, each step taking me nearer to the security of a familiar environment. Finally, my zooming heart found relief as the figure, like a wisp of smoke dissolving into thin air, unexpectedly beelined off down a dimly lit side street. Solace washed over me, offering a brief pause from the haunting uncertainty that had bothered me moments ago. Who that person was and the purpose behind their steadfast chase remained concealed in an obscure fog, leaving me with a disturbing question mark hanging in my mind. *God, I'm really getting paranoid.*

Back at home that evening, I was physically and emotionally drained. After my mother's revelations – coupled with my own confessions – I needed a distraction. I got out my journal and my hypomania took over. I wrote and wrote, until my fingers ached and my eyes blurred.

*After the spa, Max drove us out of the city and headed east along the narrow, ring road that hugged the coastline. We seemed to be the only car on the highway.*

*"It's like we've landed on Mars," I said, as I stared out the window at the endless fields of moss-covered, lava rocks.*

*A few hours of driving through desolate landscape, led us to an Eden-like terrain.*

*We stopped at a tiny village nestled at the bottom of a mountain. At a quaint restaurant, we had a lunch that consisted of large bowls of lamb soup and a side of homemade bread. Once we had satisfied our hunger, Max noticed a wool factory across the street and insisted on buying me a beautiful gray-and-white sweater, despite my protests.*

*The road was lined with miles and miles of purple Arctic lupine that wound up and down mountain ranges like a black ribbon. Waterfalls tumbled from the mountain tops, like* Rapunzel's *hair.*

*"We'll stop at one of the waterfalls on the way back," Max said. "But we need to hurry to the lake or we'll miss the boat tour."*

*My new wool sweater was itchy. I slipped my fingers under the sleeves and scratched at my skin. And when we passed the ghoulish, gray-white tongues protruding from a monstrous glacier, I shuddered.*

*After endless hours of driving, we reached our final destination. Max had pre-bought two tickets for a tour on the lake, but I was surprised when I saw the boat. It had wheels and was parked on land. When it drove into the lagoon and splashed into the water, I closed my eyes and clutched Max's arm. I remembered reading news reports about boating disasters, with passengers trapped under water and dragged down to their deaths. Maybe this was my fate—to drown in the ice-cold waters of Iceland.*

*But when I dared to open my eyes, we were safely bobbing on the surface and surrounded by icebergs of all shapes, sizes, and colors—from azure to translucent white with black striations. "Look at that sky-blue one to the port side," I said, pointing and smiling at the seals basking on small bits of ice. But Max had turned away and was busy snapping photographs of the icebergs. I shivered and wrapped my arms around myself.*

*I became distracted by the young, Icelandic tour guide, who was leaning, nonchalantly, over the side of the boat. He scooped up a large chunk of ice out of the lagoon and held it in his hand. He chopped off some smaller pieces of ice from the larger chunk with a steel hunting knife, whose handle appeared to be carved from an antler or animal bone.*

*"Does anyone want to suck on a piece of thousand-years-old ice?" the guide asked.*

*Max removed a miniature bottle of whiskey from his pocket and two small, plastic cups from his backpack. The tour guide plunked some ice chips into the two cups, and Max poured the golden liquor over the ancient ice. He offered one of the cups to me.*

*Suddenly, cold lips pressed against my mouth. Max must have been sucking on an iceberg chip. I could feel his frosty tongue forcing its way between my lips. Startled, I pulled away.*

*"Is something wrong?" Max asked.*

*"Your lips are cold," I said, laughing. Like a powerful glacier, Max had carved a path into my soul. I pointed at a block of ice. "It looks like Moby Dick."*

*"You sound like Eva, with her literary allusions," he said, locking eyes with me.*

*I laughed, then looked away, pretending to admire another piece of old ice.*

*"We're only seeing a small part of the icebergs," Max said. "Ninety*

*percent of the ice is submerged."*

*"Just like people."*

*"What do you mean?" he asked.*

*"Hiding secrets below the surface." I peered up at him. "They're mysterious."*

*He met my gaze. "And dangerous. If an iceberg flips, it creates waves big enough to tip a boat."*

# Chapter 57

"Is something bothering you, Erin?" Maddie asked, during a break at work on Saturday afternoon. "You seem a bit down these days."

"Just men," I replied. "Can't live with them; can't live without them."

"Do you want to talk about it?"

"Not really."

We sipped our coffee.

"I know," Maddie said. "Let's cheer each other up by seeing who's had the 'best' customer question so far this week."

"Okay." I perked up. "You go first."

"Okay, you won't believe this, but a teenager asked me, 'Do you, like, have a book, like, that's signed by, like, Jane Austen?'"

"Oh my God. That's hilarious." I shook my head and smiled.

"Apparently, his mother loves *Pride and Prejudice,* and he wanted to 'like surprise her with, like, an autographed copy for her birthday.'"

"You're right. I don't believe it."

"Try and top that, if you can." Maddie folded her arms across her chest.

"I don't think I can top it, but I'll try. Yesterday, an older lady asked me, very politely, if we had 'that book,' the one they made 'that movie' about, you know, the one with 'that actress, the one who's won all those awards?'"

"OMG." Maddie snickered, and coffee snorted out of her nose.

I laughed so hard that tears streamed out of my eyes. I took two napkins, handing one to Maddie and using the other one myself.

"I'm glad you find coffee spurting out my nostrils so amusing. At least I cheered you up."

"Yes, you did. Thanks."

But the distraction was only temporary. As soon as we went back to work, I started to ruminate about Mark, again. I scrolled through the *Pemberley's* email account, replying to customer queries and complaints like an automaton, until I saw a message for Maddie—from Rowena George. My hand froze. The black-arrowed cursor hovered over the email. *I really shouldn't read it.* But my curiosity trumped my conscience, and I clicked it open.

*Dear Ms. Bain,*

*I hope this message reaches you—I seem to have misplaced your email address.*

*I am delighted to pass on some wonderful news. My publishing contact is interested in meeting with you. Please respond, as soon as possible.*

*Thank you, once again, for making my evening at Pemberley's such a success.*

*Yours truly,*

*Rowena George.*

"Oh God." I gasped.

"Erin? What is it?" Dave was, suddenly, standing behind me and peering over my shoulder. "Is something wrong?"

When had he come in? Without thinking, I pushed the delete button and swiveled around in my chair.

"It was nothing important," I replied and got up.

But he crossed his arms and blocked my path. "Remember, you're on probation. If it was a customer complaint, I have a right to know."

"No, no, it was nothing like that."

He frowned. "Are you sure? You sounded pretty upset."

"It was just another annoying piece of junk mail."

He looked unconvinced, but moved out of my way.

I strode over to a messy display table and started re-sorting the books.

"What was that all about?"

Maddie had appeared out of nowhere, and I almost jumped out of my skin.

"Are you okay?"

“Oh, you know Dave.” I rolled my eyes. “He peered, suspiciously, over my shoulder, and I told him to back off.”

“Good for you.”

“And then he got all huffy.”

“Men.” She shook her head. “I have a great idea. Why don’t we have a girls’ night out at *The Government,* the club near Fenway Park?”

My chest squeezed like a snake in the grass. I had deleted her email in a flash of jealousy that I now sorely regretted. But I forced a smile.

“You know what? I think a night out is just what the doctor ordered.”

# Chapter 58

Jeans, shirts, and dresses lay in a heap on my bed. Nothing seemed right. Each outfit was either too casual or too dressy. I didn't want to look like I was headed to the gym or the opera. Finally, I settled on black skinny jeans and a black blouse, trimmed with lace. A pair of comfortable, but feminine heels finished the look. After tossing my wallet, lipstick, and phone in a clutch, I was ready for a night of drinking and dancing. If it got my mind off the two brothers, the night would be a success.

As the Uber drove through the dark, downtown streets of Boston, my phone rang.

"Hello?"

I could hear someone breathing.

"Who is this?"

There was no response.

Frustrated, I hung up and checked the caller ID: Unknown. First, I felt like I was being followed. Now, I was getting weird calls. Maybe going out tonight was a mistake. I should have stayed at home and watched a movie. But it was too late now to change my mind. The cab had pulled up in front of a brown-bricked building with the sign, *The Drunken Duck.* After thanking the driver, I got out and stood on the street, nibbling on a nail. Maybe it wasn't too late to change my mind. I was about to hail a cab and go home, when Maddie ran out of the pub. She wore ripped jeans, an army-green hoodie, and blinged-out high-tops.

*Too late to leave now.*

"Erin, you made it." Maddie latched onto my arm and dragged me across the pavement to the entrance.

The British-style saloon, with its beamed ceiling, billiard table, and dartboard, bustled with the excited energy of people letting off steam on a Saturday night. Maddie pulled me towards the long, wooden bar.

I cast my eyes around the darkened interior, while Maddie ordered some drinks. The bartender lined up two tequila shots with lemon wedges and a saltshaker on the counter. Maddie scooped one up in her fingertips.

"Here's to a girls' night out." She grinned, then licked the 'V' between her thumb and forefinger and sprinkled it with salt. After licking off the salt, she lifted the shooter to her mouth and downed it in one gulp. "Nothing like the burn of a good, Mexican tequila." She sucked on a lemon wedge, then frowned at me. "You didn't have yours yet. Come on. Drink up."

I picked up a shot glass, tipped it back, and emptied it. Then I slammed it back down on the bar.

Maddie gestured to the bartender. "Two more of the same."

This time, I drank it down right away. My throat and belly were warm and my lips tingled. The shots had loosened up my body and my inhibitions. My mind was fuzzy and my body felt like it might float away.

"Let's head to *The Government.*" Maddie bopped up and down. "I want to dance."

I linked arms with her. "Let's go."

We walked down the block and stopped in front of a nondescript, red brick building that looked like a factory. There was a small, fluorescent, pink sign with the club's name and a long lineup.

"Follow me," Maddie said, winking.

I trailed behind her, as she marched up to the security guard, a tall man with buzzed hair and a black leather jacket. Maddie appeared to know him, and he lifted the rope for us.

Inside the club, it was dark and cavernous. Multi-colored lights flashed on the dance floor, where a sea of bodies writhed to the pounding music that flowed out of giant speakers. I glanced up at the DJ: she was an attractive woman with long, dark hair and huge, red headphones covering her ears. Hunched over the stack of equipment in her booth above the crowd, she was like a wizard casting a spell over the mesmerized masses below. My head spun like the records on the DJ's old-school turntable.

"Where's the bathroom?" I asked, yelling into Maddie's ear.

Maddie grabbed my hand and pulled me across the dance floor and down a dark corridor.

The bathroom was empty. I stood at the sink and pulled out my bottle of Prozac.

"Are those 'happy pills'?" Maddie asked, grabbing the bottle out of my hand. "Cool. Let's party." She shook out two capsules, snapped them apart, then spilt the powder onto the sink ledge. Leaning over, she snorted it up one nostril and then the other. "Your turn," she said, wiping the excess powder off her face. "Snorting it gives you a much stronger high."

I wavered. I had heard that snorting Prozac heightened one's senses. The idea was tempting, but the risk of overdose scared me. A picture of myself lying in the middle of the dirty, dance floor, my unconscious body punctured by pointy heels and bruised by heavy boots, flashed before my eyes. A pair of beefy paramedics would lift me onto a gurney and wheel me out to the waiting ambulance, as curious club patrons took photos on their phones and posted them all over social media. With the siren blaring, they would race through the downtown streets to *City Center Hospital. God. If Mark ever saw me like that, I'd die.* Besides, I was already buzzed on the tequila shots.

"YOLO—you only live once!" Maddie grinned at me.

She did have a point. My life had been such a mess lately, that it would be nice to escape all my worries for one night. My obsession with Mark was exhausting and trying to compete with the girl guide behavior of Fiona was impossible. And why did I care what Mark thought, anyway? And, if Oliver preferred Rachel, he could have her. Tonight was my time to let loose and shrug off all thoughts of the Rankin brothers and my mysterious stalker, if I even had one. It was probably just my imagination. But still. Snorting drugs was not my style, so I shook my head.

Maddie leaned over and snorted the remaining powder. Then she grabbed my hand and pulled me back out through the swaying swarm and onto the dance floor.

After a while, she pressed her mouth up to my ear, "I'm so glad you came out tonight. Your friendship means a lot to me."

A warm wave of shame crept through my veins like a viper, as I thought about the deleted email from Rowena George. I needed to tell Maddie what I'd done. She was a good friend and deserved better.

"I have to tell you something."

"What is it?" Maddie smiled at me, as she swayed to the music.

"Actually, it's more of a confession." My throat was as dry as a page from an old, dusty book. I stared straight at Maddie, whose eyes looked like two, black marbles, and said in a tight, flat voice, "You got an email from Rowena George."

"I did?" Maddie seized my hands with excitement. "But wait. That's good news. Why did you call it a confession?" Her forehead creased with confusion.

Fingers squeezed my neck. "Because I deleted it."

"You deleted my email?" Maddie's smile faded, and she dropped my hands. "I don't understand. Why would you do that?"

My head drooped like a dead tree. "I was jealous."

Maddie's eyes widened and she stared at me in disbelief. "I don't believe this. I thought you were my friend."

"We are friends. I'm so sorry."

But Maddie turned away and disappeared into the crowd.

I stood in the middle of the dance floor, alone and ashamed. My eyes darted, frantically, around. Where had Maddie gone? Suddenly, someone in a dark hoodie brushed past me, knocking me off balance. I swiveled around.

"Maddie? Wait up." I chased after her, but she ducked behind a loudspeaker and vanished like a shadow. Should I try and find her? Or give her some space? She probably hated me now… almost as much as I hated myself. My brain was a ticking bomb about to blow.

# Chapter 59

When I woke up the next morning, memories from the night before came crashing back and I cringed. How would I face Maddie at work? I pulled the covers over my head and groaned.

Around one o'clock, a ping jolted me awake. I sat up and snatched my phone. It was a text from Dave.

*Where r u? Your shift started an hour ago.*

"Shit!" I reached over and pulled open the curtain a tiny crack. Bright sunlight streamed in, making me wince and my head throb. I started to close the curtain, when something caught my eye. Was that a silver Tesla parked in front of my house? Was it Oliver? What was he doing here? I crawled out of bed and dragged myself down the hallway. Keeper bounded after me, barking and nipping at my heels.

"Shh, little one, Mommy's got a bad headache." I stopped to pick her up and calm her down.

But when I finally got to the front door and opened it, the car was gone. Had there even been a car? Maybe I was starting to have daylight hallucinations, too. I shut the door and headed to the bathroom. I needed a shower to wake myself up and clear my mind.

As I was heading out the door, I saw my elderly neighbor out on her front stoop.

"Excuse me, Helen, did you see a silver Tesla—"

"Tesla? What's a Tesla?"

"It's an electric-powered, sports car."

"Electric?" Helen's face crinkled into a smile.

"Anyway, did you see a silver car parked out here earlier?"

"I saw a silver car, but I don't know if it was a whatayamacallit—"

"A Tesla." My brow pinched. So, I hadn't imagined it.

"And there was a black one here the other day."

My ears pricked up. "A black one? Was it a car or a truck?"

"Car. Truck." Helen chuckled. "Gas. Electric. I'm afraid they all look the same to me, dear." She chuckled and went back to watering her flowers.

When I crept into the bookstore, I hoped I wouldn't run into Dave. I was almost two hours late for my Sunday shift.

"Not so fast, Fitzpatrick."

*Damn.*

"It's about time you showed up," Dave said, tapping a finger against the face of his watch.

"Sorry," I muttered, tucking my blouse into my pants.

"Now, if I could just track down Maddie," he growled.

"Maddie? She's not here?" *God, I hope she's okay. Maybe she's avoiding me. And I wouldn't blame her.* My face flared red at the memory of what I'd done.

"Nope." He tossed his arms up in the air, exposing his sweat-stained armpits.

Acid churned at the back of my throat, and I swallowed hard.

"I don't know what I'm paying you girls for." Dave's eyes bulged and his face reddened. "I've got customers lining up across the floor, their arms piled high with books, and no one to take their money."

I tugged a hand through my hair. "Did you try texting her? It's just so unlike her not to show up."

"I sent her a text, an email, and I called her phone. But it went straight to voicemail. I even looked up the emergency contact from her employee file – a roommate – but she said Maddie never came home last night."

"She never came home?" White spots flickered in front of my eyes.

"Anyway, you'll just have to work twice as hard to cover for her," Dave said, darting a hostile glance in my direction.

I went to the back of the bookstore and hid. My head ached, my legs were like wooden stilts, and I had a stabbing pain behind my eyes. My entire body was in agony. *Pull yourself together, Erin.* I dug my phone out of my purse and sent Maddie an urgent text.

*Where r u?*

Maddie usually responded to text messages right away. As the minutes ticked by, and she did not respond, I became more and more convinced that her absence from work was all my fault. Hopefully, she would show up, and we could talk it all out on our coffee break.

An hour before the store closed at five o'clock, Maddie was still missing in action.

"She'd better be in the hospital, lying at death's door," Dave said, pacing back and forth outside his office. "If I find out she slept through her alarm, or she's hungover, I'll have to put *her* on probation too."

A vice gripped my head. I got out my phone and sent another, more urgent text.

*Sorry about last night. But U have 2 call Dave. He's losing it!*

The previous night began to replay in my mind. The dancing and drinking. The so-called 'happy' pills. And then – *oh God* – and then I had told her about deleting the email from Rowena George. My chest screwed tight with shame. I sent another string of texts.

*I'm so, so sorry about what I did.*

*I'm a terrible friend.*

*Just please, please call Dave.*

My nerves were frazzled, as I stared, fixedly, at my phone.

*Where are you, Maddie? Why aren't you answering my texts?*

# Chapter 60

Each minute seemed like an hour. I processed customer purchases on automatic pilot, while my mind whizzed with worry. Where the hell was Maddie? Was this all my fault?

Twenty minutes later, Dave emerged from his office again.

I could just imagine Maddie joking, *"It's like seeing the abominable snowman twice in one day."* But Maddie was not there. And one look at Dave's ashen face, told me that he had terrible news.

"I just got off the phone with Maddie's mother," he said, in a softened tone.

"Her mother? What's going on, Dave?" My throat was as dry as chalk dust.

"Maddie's in the hospital."

"*City Center?*" I just couldn't help myself.

"No, *Boston Memorial.*"

"Oh my God." Guilt bulged in my brain. "Is she okay?"

He shook his head. "She had a seizure. A bad reaction to drugs. It doesn't sound good."

Gordie. Dad. Sean. And now, Maddie. It was too much. My sanity snapped like a twig. I turned away from Dave, strode towards a table full of discount books, and started rearranging them like an automaton.

"What a mess," I muttered to myself.

"Erin, did you hear what I said?"

"Tsk-tsk." I lifted a hardcover in my hands and rocked my head from side to side. "This doesn't belong here."

"Erin?" Dave moved towards me.

I heard the buzzing of fluorescent lights on the ceiling above me. Otherwise, it was as if my ears had been stuffed with cotton wool.

"What the hell's wrong with you?" Dave said, in a stentorian tone. "Didn't you hear what I said about Maddie?" He reached out and touched me on the shoulder.

"***Stay the fuck away from me!***" I lifted the hardcover book high in the air and slammed it straight down on the ground at his feet.

The book clipped the toes of Dave's shoes, stopping him in his tracks. His face turned bright red. "Who the hell do you think you are?"

But I looked right through him. *Oh Maddie, this is all my fault. I'm the one who gave you those damn pills and now, you could be dead.* The pages of my mind were being ripped from the spine, one by one. I shoved past Dave and started grabbing books from the shelves and tossing them across the store.

"What're you doing?" Dave said, spitting his words at me. "Have you lost your friggin' mind?"

Frightened customers stood and stared, as I moved to the magazine rack and flung them through the air, like I was freeing caged birds.

Dave approached me from behind and pinned my arms down at my sides.

"Let me go!" I thrashed my body, then went limp and collapsed to the ground. My eyes closed and I fell down a dark, bottomless tunnel. Down. Down. Down.

"Erin? Erin? Are you all right?"

I opened my eyes and saw a pinprick of white light.

*Am I dead?*

I squinted and saw a shadowy figure. "Maddie? Is that you?" I tried to sit up, but my body was a wet bag of sand.

"No, it's me, Suzy," the shadow said.

I blinked rapidly. "What happened?"

"You had some sort of psychotic fit and then, you fainted," Dave said, glaring down at me.

"Ignore him," Suzy said, whispering in my ear. She helped me up and handed me a bottle of water.

"Thanks," I said, gratefully gulping down the water.

A handful of customers lingered and stared.

"Is the young girl all right?" an elderly lady asked, her features folded into a frown. "Should we call an ambulance?"

"I'm fine," I replied, trying to smile. But something nibbled at the back of my brain, as I slowly lifted myself off the floor. And then I remembered: *Maddie might be dead.* My stomach plummeted and perspiration dampened my armpits. "I've got to get to the hospital and check on Maddie."

"No, I don't think that's a good idea," Dave said, crossing his arms. "You should go home. Suzy, you'd better go with her. I'll call an Uber."

"No, no, ***no!***" *This is all my fault.* I handed Suzy the bottle and stumbled towards the exit. "I have to find out if Maddie's okay."

# Chapter 61

The Uber ride to the hospital felt like it was taking forever. When it finally pulled up in front of the hospital, I leapt out before he'd even come to a full stop. I raced inside and accosted the first nurse I could find.

"Where is Maddie Bain? I need to see her right away."

"Let me check my computer," she said. "Ah yes, here she is: Madeleine Bain. She's in room 113."

"Yes, that's her," I replied, struggling to get my breathing under control. "How is she? Can I see her?"

"Are you a relative?"

"No, we work together."

"I'm sorry, but I'm afraid you can't see her," the nurse said, folding her arms across her chest. "She's in a lot of pain. It's family only, right now."

"Please," I begged. A chain winched around my head.

But the nurse had already moved away down the hall.

I waited until she had disappeared out of sight, then ran through the corridors searching for room 113. I was about to give up, when a dark-haired figure in a white coat appeared in the distance. My body became taut as a rope. Mark? What was he doing here? I tried to calm my breathing, as he got closer and closer. But when he was only a few yards away, my heart sank. It wasn't him. He had Mark's dark hair, but he was taller and slimmer. I bit my lower lip, as he brushed past me. *What was I thinking? This isn't even his hospital. I really am losing my mind.*

I scrunched my eyes shut and banged a palm against my forehead. When I opened my eyes, a middle-aged woman stood before me with a steaming cup of coffee clutched in her hand.

"Are you all right, dear?" she asked.

"I'm looking for my friend. She's in room 113."

"That's my daughter's room."

"You're Maddie's mother?"

The woman nodded.

"I'm Erin, a friend of Maddie's from work."

"Oh yes, I had a call from the owner of the bookstore," her mother said. "I've forgotten his name…"

"Dave."

"Dave, that's right," she said, sipping her coffee. "He sounded like such a nice young man."

I bit my tongue. "How is Maddie?"

"I'm afraid she had a terrible night." She shook her head. "Someone gave her pills, and she had a bad reaction. She suffered a seizure."

The chain tightened another notch. "But she's going to be okay, isn't she?" My voice was barely above a whisper. *Please let her be all right. I promise to be a better person, from now on.*

"I don't know, dear. They've got her hooked up to all sorts of machines." Her mother's tone was serious and subdued.

"Is there any chance I could sneak in and see her?"

"No, I think she's sleeping." She patted me on the wrist. "But I'll go and see."

A nurse rushed past, pushing an injured patient on a gurney. The rattling and squeaking of its wheels played havoc on my nerves, as I waited for Maddie's mother.

*This is all my fault. Why did I let her have those pills?*

A fluorescent light flickered above my head.

Finally, Maddie's mother re-emerged from the room.

I rushed over to her. "How is she? Can I see her?"

"She's awake."

I grinned. "Great. I'll go right in."

But her mother slowly shook her head.

My brow pinched. "I don't understand…"

"I'm afraid that my daughter doesn't want to see you." She stood in the doorway, arms crossed and legs splayed, blocking me from entering the room.

My stomach sank. “She doesn’t want to see me?”

Her eyes were hard as stone. “You heard me. Now, I think you’d better go, before I call the police.”

# Chapter 62

After a horrible night of no sleep, I got up and went into work. My life was a nightmare, but at least I still had my job. At least, I hoped I still did. I stood outside Dave's office and stared at the closed door. *God, I really don't want to do this right now.* I was about to turn and walk away when the door swung open.

"Erin? What're you standing there for?" Dave asked, furrowing his brows. "Come on in and take a seat."

I was a dead man walking, as I followed him over the threshold and crumpled down in a chair.

"Any word on Maddie?" he asked, settling into his leather throne.

I shook my head. I did not want to talk about it with him.

"Well, let's get straight to business." Dave laced his hands together and placed them on top of his mammoth desk.

I braced myself and stared at the wall behind him.

"I'm afraid this is the end of the line for you."

I tried to swallow, but I had a lump in my throat.

"Disappearing the night of the reading was bad enough…"

"I know, but—"

"But throwing merchandise and using profane language in front of customers is crossing the line." He unfurled his fingers and flipped open my personnel file.

"I'm so sorry, Dave." I hated to beg, but I loved my job at the bookstore.

"Can you give me one more chance? I was really upset about Maddie."

"We were all upset. That's no excuse for your behavior." He scribbled on a piece of paper and passed it to me.

"So that's it?" I fought back tears, when I saw the word 'termination' written in bold, black letters.

"That's it." Dave crossed his arms and rocked back in his chair. "I'll give you two week's severance, but I want you to pack up all your personal belongings and say your goodbyes."

"I can't believe you're doing this to me right now," I spat my words at him. "I could sue you for sexual harassment—"

"Go right ahead. It's your word against mine." He gave me a smarmy smile. "Do you honestly think anyone will believe you, after that psychotic – and very public – meltdown?"

I was about to say that Maddie would believe me, then my chest tightened and my chin drooped against my chest.

"Close the door behind you." He turned his attention to his computer.

*

That evening, my emotions deluged me in a thick fog, blocking my thoughts and leaving me floating. Pursuing comfort, I found myself standing before the medicine cabinet, its mirrored exterior reflecting my disturbed visage. With a heavy heart, I recovered my pill bottle, the vessel of short-lived suspension from pain. As I held it in my quivering hand, I stalled, my gaze absorbed by the small, white-and-green capsules snuggled within. In appearance, they looked like innocent candy, their colors fusing together like a tragicomic music. With a mix of anxiety and longing, I carefully grasped one pill between my fingertips, feeling its coldness against my skin. Setting it on my tongue, I swallowed, the act accompanied by a trace of bitterness.

But the charm of escape was a persistent voice, insisting that I seek further shelter. I continued the ritual, submitting to the urge to use. Pill after pill, they fell into my quivering palm, an agglomeration of relief and surrender. The bottle lay empty, its contents strewn across my hand, a heartbreaking testimony to the depths of my hopelessness. In this bleak act, I found both consolation and despondency integrated, a brittle balance between seeking comfort and succumbing to the vacancy.

The significance of those little capsules, once humble and harmless, now held an intolerable weight. They indicated a temporary pardon, a brief suspension from the constant currents of life. And as I stood there, absorbed by the gravity of my behavior, I became a mere spectator in my turmoil, drifting further into the void.

# Chapter 63

Someone was banging on my front door. Startled, I dropped the pills and the bottle into the sink. I scooped up as many capsules as I could and deposited them on the countertop. Who could it be? I was not in the mood for anyone's company right now.

But whoever it was continued to hammer on the door. Leaving the bathroom and the relinquished pills behind, I strode down the hallway. I peered through the peephole, but it was getting dark outside. I could see the shadowy outline of a male form and shrank back against the wall. Whoever it was, I hoped he would just give up and go away.

"Erin, I know you're in there. Open up."

Keeper barked and barked. "Shhh. Quiet girl," I said, pressing my finger against my lips.

"Erin? It's me. Oliver." He knocked again. "I have to see you."

I did not want to deal with him right now. Something about his recent behavior had made me uneasy. He had shown up at the bookstore, uninvited, and caused me problems with Dave. Now, he'd turned up at my house. I supposed I should be flattered, but instead, I just felt annoyed. He had even taken out my mother and gossiped about me behind my back. And I'd seen a car like his, parked in front of my house. It was creepy. My neighbor, Helen, had seen it too, so I knew I wasn't imagining things.

He was starting to scare me.

"Erin? Let me in. It's cold out here," Oliver said, shaking the door. It sounded like he was going to break it off its hinges, if I did not open it.

He was, obviously, not going to go away.

I blew out a sharp breath and opened the door. But only an inch. "Hi Oliver. I'm not feeling that well—"

But he pushed his way past me. "Brr. Winter's on its way."

Reluctantly, I closed the door behind him. Maybe this would be a good time to clarify my feelings to him and explain that I was only interested in being friends.

Keeper started circling his ankles. He picked her up and smothered her with kisses.

"How've you been, little girl? Digger misses you." Then he put the dog down, wrapped his arms around me and whispered in my ear, "I've missed you."

My stomach spasmed. *I need a drink. Desperately.* I pulled away from him and headed to the kitchen. Maddie had almost been at death's door. I had lost my job. And now, I had to deal with Oliver's unwanted advances. Could my day get any worse?

I got a bottle of wine out of the fridge.

Oliver stared at the label on the bottle and scratched his jawline. "A pinot noir from Central Otago, New Zealand? That's Mark's favorite wine."

I gave an embarrassed laugh. "Is it? What a coincidence. I think it was on special at the liquor store." I poured two glasses, then we headed into the living room. I was about to sit in the wingback chair, but Oliver pulled me towards the couch with him.

"So, how've you been?" He settled his eyes on me.

"Not bad." I swigged some wine.

"Go out last night?"

Blood drained from my face.

"Are you okay?" Oliver put his glass down on the coffee table and reached for my hand.

"I'm fine." I shrank away from him, perching on the edge of the couch.

"Are you sure?" He drew his brows together.

Keeper settled at his feet and began loudly licking her paws.

"What brings you here?"

Oliver scratched his jaw. "I've got news about my brother."

A nerve twitched under my eye. I swirled the wine in my glass and watched it wave up the sides like a whirlpool. I forced air in and out of my lungs.

"News about Mark?"

"He's taking Fiona out for dinner later tonight."

"Oh yeah?" I feigned only mild interest, but my fingers clenched the stem of my wine glass.

Oliver picked up his wine and took several small sips, staring at me over the edge of his glass. "I think he's going to propose."

My hands jerked, spilling my full glass of wine onto the floor. "Oh, shit!"

Oliver rushed out to the kitchen and returned with a dishcloth. He spread it over the red pool at my feet and soaked it all up.

"Thanks." I put down my glass and cupped my elbows in my hands.

"You seem upset about the news." Oliver's hazel eyes drilled into me, as if he was attempting to read my mind. "I thought you'd be thrilled."

"I'm just surprised, that's all. They haven't been seeing each other that long."

"When you know, you know."

"I suppose that's true." *I knew the second I laid eyes on your brother.*

"Anyway, I have my own confession to make."

My eyes narrowed. *No more. Please.*

"I went out to dinner with Rachel last night."

Was that all? My shoulders sagged.

"But that's not the important part."

I squeezed my hands together in my lap. I wished I could just close my eyes and make him disappear.

"The whole time I was with her," he said, scooching closer to me on the couch, "all I could think about was you."

I picked up my empty wine glass, to create a physical barrier between us.

"When we finished dinner," he said, trying to hold my gaze, "I dropped her off at home. I spent the rest of the night drinking, in different bars and dance clubs."

Dance clubs? The hooded figure from the night club flashed in my mind and I twisted my lips in thought.

"The thing is," he said, taking my wine glass and placing it on the table, "I've fallen in love with you." But his words barely made a dent in my thoughts. Instead, my mind was racing with questions. *Was Mark really going to propose to Fiona? What about me? What about us?*

Oliver stood up and took my hand and led me to the bedroom. I followed along like an automaton. He removed his shirt and guided me back onto the bed.

"I'm sorry Oliver. I can't do this. I have my period. And I'm exhausted."

His face fell, but he planted a kiss on my forehead, then he pulled his shirt back on. "Of course, I understand. I'll let you get some sleep and call you in the morning. I'll let myself out."

After he was gone, I lay wide awake, staring at the ceiling. My mind was swirling like a stormy sea. I slipped out of bed, careful not to wake Keeper, who was curled up beside me. Grabbing my phone and making sure it was on silent mode, I wrote a text to Mark.

*I suppose congrats are in order...*

But before I pressed send, I had second thoughts and deleted the text. Instead, I pulled out my journal and started to write.

*On the drive back to Reykjavik, Max turned off the highway and parked at a breathtakingly high waterfall that fell into a shallow pool. We got out of the car and stretched, and I noticed what appeared to be a path running behind the fall's curtain. He clasped my hand and led me toward it. He had a peculiar grin on his face.* What was he up to?

*As we climbed the path, we were sprayed by the waterfall. It was refreshing after the dry air in the car. A short time later, we were behind the waterfall's curtain. It was a secret space, a time capsule, hidden from the rest of the world. The thundering noise of the waterfall drowned out the noise in my mind. Sensing that Max was no longer by my side, I turned to see what had become of him.*

*"What're you doing?" I gasped.*

*He was down on one knee and looking up at me with a serious expression.*

*My heart stopped, and my jaw dropped.*

*He started to speak. But he had to compete with the pounding falls.*

*"I can't hear you." I looked out through the veil of water.*

*He reached into his pocket and pulled out a black box. He popped it open, and I stared, transfixed, at the sparkling stone.*

*He stood up and gripped my arms in his hands. "Marry me."*

*I would be Max's wife. We would be bound together forever in marriage.*

*"I love you, Faith."*

*My dead sister's name rang in my ears over the deafening roar of water.*

*"Faith?"*

*But the ground shifted beneath my feet, as a dark figure emerged out of the fog like a phantom. It was Faith. I clutched my fingers around the tour guide's bone-handled, steel hunting knife that had magically appeared in my pocket.*

*"What are you doing here?" I asked. "You're dead."*

*"Who are you talking to?" Max said.*

*"What're you doing here?" Faith echoed. "That's the real question. Isn't it, Eva?"*

*"Max asked me to marry him," I replied.*

*"I'm the one who should be marrying him," Faith said. "He loves* **me,** *not you."*

*I walked towards Faith, who stood on the edge of the waterfall. I pulled the knife out of my pocket and held it in front of me.*

*"What are you doing?" Max asked. "Are you crazy? Come back!"*

*I swiped the knife across Faith's astonished face, slashing it left and right. Like a vengeful troll, I raised it above my head and plunged it down into Faith's heart. Blood splattered into the mist-filled air, wrapping us in a translucent, red net. Then we fell over the edge of the falls, as if invisible hands had pushed us. Down. Down. Down into the pool far below.*

# Chapter 64

I clutched the arms of the chair to try and still my trembling hands. My chest fluttered from nerves and an excess of caffeine, as I waited for Dr. Pritchard to begin the session.

"It's been a while, since your last appointment."

My stomach clenched and unclenched like a fist.

The wind howled outside, rattling the windowpane.

Shuddering and shivering, I wrapped my arms around myself.

"I guess fall is finally here." The doctor gave me a closed-lip smile. "What's new, since the last time I saw you?"

"Where do I start?" *I found out my dad was a fraud and cheated on my mom. I betrayed my co-worker, who then overdosed on the drugs I gave her. And I got fired from my job. Last but not least, Mark proposed to Fiona.* I straightened my shoulders and cleared my throat.

"My mother and I went shopping together, recently." I hesitated. My heart thumped like a trapped bird against my rib cage. Could the doctor hear it? "Over a cup of tea, she proceeded to tell me that my father had ch-cheated…"

She waited.

The words caught in my throat.

"Take your time."

"…He was having an affair… just before he died."

"How did that make you feel?"

I took another deep lungful of air before continuing, "At first, I was shocked. But the more I've been thinking about it, the less surprised I am. I doubt it was the first time he'd strayed. He was never at home. He was always working late at the office or away on business trips. It was really just me and my mother at home most of the time. His absence was a constant reminder, that we weren't important enough for him to make time for us. And my brother's death just made it worse." I paused to try and calm my breathing, which kept hitching in my throat.

Dr. Pritchard gave me an encouraging smile.

I stared down at my hands, that were clasped, tightly together, in my lap.

"I've been thinking about what you said last time and I realized that you were right. My brother's death made me desperate for approval and more vulnerable to rejection. After Gordie died, I never felt good enough for my dad, yet I always seem to choose men just like him: ambitious, outgoing, charming, and successful. Maybe my subconscious is telling me that if I can make someone love me, like Sean or Mark—"

"Men who remind you of your father…"

"—It will prove my self-worth."

"Is your strategy working?"

I shook my head.

"You've spent years trying to please others and blaming yourself for things that weren't your fault. It's time to start over."

"How do I do that?"

"Surround yourself with people who love you unconditionally, avoid negative self-talk, and do things that make you feel good about yourself, like yoga and writing."

I raised my palms, in deference. "I'll give it a shot."

The doctor's lips curled up at the edges. "Is there anything else on your mind?"

"Actually, there is." I shifted in my seat. "I think that I've been experiencing some side effects from the Prozac."

"Such as?" The doctor's forehead creased.

"Anxiety. Mood swings."

Her face darkened.

"I had a nervous breakdown at work last week." *Should I tell her I got fired? But then, I'd have to explain about Maddie…* "And my insomnia's gotten even worse." I left out the hallucinations, my paranoia about being followed, and my manic writing—about murder. If I told the doctor everything, she might pull out a straitjacket.

"How long have you been experiencing these symptoms?"

I screwed up my face. "I'm not sure."

"We need to ween you off the medication over the next several months, to avoid withdrawal symptoms."

"I want to get off them, as soon as possible."

The doctor looked at me pointedly. "If you rush it, you risk getting headaches, dizziness, chills, aching muscles, nausea, or even electric shock sensations."

A nerve twitched in my forehead. I was starting to regret ever taking the damn pills. "I don't care. I need to get off them. Right away."

"I understand, but we need to be careful." She pinned me with her eyes. "Withdrawing too quickly is very dangerous."

# Chapter 65

The doctor was right. I needed to focus more on myself and my writing. Back at home that evening, relaxing by the fireplace, an idea struck me. I opened my laptop and googled literary agencies. What I needed was an agent. I started to compose a query letter, when my phone pinged. I cringed when I saw who it was. *Might as well get it over with.*

"Did I wake you up?" Fiona asked.

"No, it's okay. What's up?"

"I know it's late, but I have to come over."

My mind was swimming. She probably wanted to tell me all about her exciting engagement.

Keeper's snores filled the silence that lapsed between us.

"Please. Please. Please. I really need to talk to you."

"Give me half an hour." As soon as I hung up the phone, my jealousy rose to the surface like the Loch Ness monster. I snapped my laptop shut, strode to my bedroom and grabbed my journal. Back in the living room, I flopped on the couch and flipped through the pages, until I found the part I wanted.

*Faith sat down on the bed, and I pulled the knife out from under the covers.*

*"What're you doing?" Faith gasped.*

*But I answered her by slitting her throat. Faith fell backwards off the bed and her head hit the floor with a thud. Blood spurted out of her neck like water from a hose.*

Reading the part where Eva killed Faith helped dissipate my anger.

I heard a loud bang.

Keeper barked and leapt off my lap.

"What was that?" I sat up and listened.

There was another loud bang.

Keeper ran to the front door and barked and barked.

I slapped the journal shut, tossed it on the coffee table, and raced down the hall.

"Shush Keeper." I patted her on the head, then peered through the peep hole, but all I could see was darkness. My heart pounded in my head, as I cracked open the door and peeked outside.

A dark, shadowy figure was shifting around by the side of my house.

Fingers of fear gripped me in a chokehold.

"Who's there?" I said, calling out into the dark night.

"It's just little old me, dear."

My fear deflated. It was my neighbor, Helen.

"Sorry about all the racket." Helen giggled. "I'm just putting out the garbage bins for tomorrow's collection."

"Let me help you," I said.

"No, no, it's all done, but thank you for offering, dear."

Suddenly, Fiona appeared out of nowhere and climbed up the stairs. Her hand clutched at my sleeve, as soon as she reached the porch.

"Oh my God, I'm so desperate to talk to you," she said, stumbling through the door. Her face was flushed and her breath had the acrid smell of alcohol.

I was confused. Fiona wasn't acting like someone who had just become engaged. I shut the door and trailed her down the hall to the living room.

"I need a drink. If I try to speak, I'm afraid I'll cry." Fiona collapsed onto the couch. Her voice wavered as she spoke.

"I'll get us some wine." I grabbed a bottle from the kitchen, then filled two large glasses with red and watched as Fiona gulped hers down. I had never seen her behave like this. "Please tell me what's happened."

"It's over."

"What's over?"

"Mark and me. We're done. Finished. Kaput."

I could not believe what I was hearing. An avalanche of thoughts surged through my mind, as Fiona's words sank in. "I thought you were going to tell me you were engaged—"

"Nope." Fiona burst into tears. "He dumped me."

"I can't believe it." *It was about time.* "Did he say why?"

"He blamed it on his work." I handed her a tissue, and Fiona wiped her eyes. "He said being a doctor didn't leave any time for a relationship. But I think he was lying to spare my feelings."

"What do you mean? Why would he lie?"

"I think there was someone else."

A muscle twitched at the corner of my eye. *Oh God, she knows.*

"Can you believe that asshole?" Fiona sobbed.

I had never heard Fiona call anyone an 'asshole' before. I formed my face into a frown of disgust. "Did you confront him?"

"No, I was too shocked to speak or move. I just stood there, like an idiot."

Fiona scrunched up her face. "He must think I'm so naïve."

"No, no." I handed her another tissue.

"God, I'm so stupid." Fiona clenched her fists at her sides. "I really thought he was the one. Maybe he didn't even love me. But he made me feel so special. Erin, tell me the truth. Have I been a complete fool?"

"Of course not."

"What's that?" She sniffed and pointed at my journal.

Why had I left it on the coffee table?

"That's just a journal full of stupid scribbles."

"Can I look at it?" She reached over and picked it up.

"Definitely not." I tore it out of her hands and tossed it back down on the table, then poured more wine into both of our glasses. "Now, back to Mark. I'm sure he was telling the truth. His work at the hospital is all-consuming."

Part of me was sorry for Fiona. I knew how she felt, because I hurt the same way when Sean broke up with me. For a moment, I exuded the tenderness of a mother for a suffering child. Fiona and I had been friends for so long. It pained me to see her so hurt. But my feelings were bouncing around like a squash ball. I loved Fiona, but I also loved Mark.

Suddenly, a realization exploded in my brain like a bolt of lightning. Mark had broken up with Fiona, which meant—Mark was a free man.

# Chapter 66

The next night, I was on my way to Mark's. The noise inside my head was like the static between radio stations, as I sat in the back of an Uber that was taking me to his loft. I'd spent the entire day listing all the logical, left brain, reasons why this was a big mistake. But I'd invested so much emotional energy obsessing about Mark, that the right side of my brain had won out.

Now, it was nighttime, and I stood outside his steel door, my temples throbbing. *Am I really going to do this?* Dr. Pritchard's advice replayed in my head: *"Surround yourself with people who love you."* After the mess with Maddie, I had been determined to make a fresh start, but that was before Mark dumped Fiona and became a free man. Maybe Fiona wasn't the right woman for him. Maybe I was the one who could make him finally commit.

Suddenly, the door opened.

"Erin, this is a surprise." He was wearing light-green, hospital scrubs and holding a bag of garbage in his hand.

"Hi Mark." It was too late to change my mind now.

"Come on in." He waved me inside. "I'll drop this down the chute and be right back."

Doubts billowed through my head, as I walked down his hallway. *Why did I come? Should I make a run for it? This was a mistake. But what if Mark is my soulmate?*

"I'm back."

I almost jumped out of my skin.

"Can I get you a drink?" Mark moved to the kitchen and got out two tumblers. "When I finish a double shift, I like a scotch to unwind."

"None for me, thanks." I needed to keep a clear head.

"You can't let me drink alone."

On the other hand, a stiff drink might be just what the doctor ordered. Dr. Rankin, not Dr. Pritchard. "All right. Why not?"

He poured our drinks and headed to the living room.

I followed him, and he gave me one of the tumblers.

"Why don't you join me on the couch?" He patted a cushion with his free hand. "I need to relax and stretch out my legs."

I sat down next to him, then took a small sip of scotch.

"So, what brings you by tonight?" He took a long swallow of scotch, then fastened his eyes on me. "If this is about Fiona, you can save your breath. She's better off without me. I've come to realize that I just don't have the time for a relationship right now. At least, not the kind of relationship Fiona wants and deserves. I tried. I really did. But I feel like I'm burning the candle at both ends." He took another slug of scotch. "Besides, if she was really the one for me, I wouldn't have been fooling around with her best friend, would I?" He shook his head. "You both deserve better."

*Fooling around? Is that how he sees us?*

He didn't seem to have a clue as to why I was really there.

I'd waited so long for the chance to be alone with him again, so we could talk about our future – after we'd had sex at the hospital, he'd rushed right back to work, and the night he'd dropped by my house, he'd been too distraught about losing his patient to focus on anything else – but now, the moment had arrived and I couldn't find the words. Finally, I sat up, straightened my shoulders, and put my drink down on the coffee table.

Then I changed my mind. It tasted like old cardboard, but maybe it would give me the courage to confront him. I picked up the glass and knocked it back. It burned the back of my throat and tears welled in my eyes.

"If you're not going to talk, then I could use a good shag, as they say in Scotland."

I stiffened. *A good shag? Is that all I am to him?* How many other women had he *shagged* in that on-call room? Maybe I'd got him all wrong.

He put his empty glass on the table and turned towards me.

Dr. Pritchard's voice rang in my ears. *"You've spent years trying to please others and blaming yourself for things that weren't your fault. It's time to start over."*

He cupped my chin in his hand and kissed me, his tongue darting into my mouth.

My response was visceral. My brain shut down and my body took over. My heart fluttered, and my resolve melted like spring snow. As I kissed him back, words swirled like smoke in my mind. *He wants me. He needs me. He's my boyfriend now.*

But an image of Mark kissing a sexy, young nurse in pink scrubs, flashed against the back of my closed eyelids and my head snapped back. And Fiona's words echoed in my ears. She'd called him 'an asshole'. I jerked away from him.

"What're you doing?" Mark frowned. "We were just getting started."

"I'm sorry, Mark. I can't do this." *Why am I apologizing?*

I stood up and moved, robotically, to the bathroom without saying another word. I shut the door behind me and walked over to the sink. *What are you doing? Is this really what you want?* Bile bubbled in my throat. Turning on the tap, I splashed some cold water on my face and tidied myself up. Looking at my reflection in the mirror, I mouthed the questions I'd come there to ask.

"What do I mean to you? Do we have a future together?" Lifting my chin and pulling back my shoulders, I strode back into the living room.

"I think we'd better call it a night." He glanced at his watch and let out a loud yawn. "It's been a long day." He stood up, placed a hand on my back, and began to usher me down the hall.

My frustration flipped into anger. *He's trying to get rid of me.* Then the truth slapped me in the face. *I mean nothing to him.*

Rain pelted the floor-to-ceiling windows. A crack of lightning lit up the loft.

Fury flashed inside my skull, and my sanity fractured. My vision distorted, and I saw Dad's face, his eyes full of disdain. Then, Mark's face morphed into Sean's. *I won't let you do this to me, again. You men are all the same.* Balling my hands into tight fists, I flung myself at him and pounded his chest.

"You lying, cheating bastard! How could you do that to me?"

Mark grabbed hold of my wrists. "What the hell? Do what to you?"

Blood pulsed in my ears, and a fist squeezed my heart, tighter and tighter.

"I hate you!" I twisted my body and kneed him in the groin.

Mark collapsed to the floor and rocked back and forth, groaning in pain. "Bitch!"

"You. Arrogant. Asshole."

Each word on my lips held the mass of rage, as I released a swift kick into his back, highlighting my anger. The aggressive contact reverberated through the room, but I wasn't finished. My spiked heel found its place on his exposed neck, digging into his skin with a dogged revenge. His pain mirrored the misery that had immersed me. Yet, his retaliation was swift. He seized my leg with a pincer-like grip, forcefully tugging me off balance. Powerlessly, I crashed to the cruel floor, my head smashing against the uncompromising coffee table. The world rotated as stars danced behind my clamped eyelids, their exquisite glow a haunting backdrop to my pain.

Time seemed to stall in stasis, seconds lengthening into ages. Finally, I gathered the strength to shake off the perplexity. Crawling with intended purpose, I advanced through the room's space, my hands outstretching for the door that led to the haven of the balcony. There, a sparkle of freedom awaited. With shaking resolve, I rose to my feet and slid open the door, the pelting rain and cool breeze brushing against my thrashed frame. My gaze briefly remained on Mark, still sprawled on the floor, a throw pillow clutched to his neck in a weak attempt to curb the crimson tide. The sight steeled my resolve.

Outside, on the height of the balcony, I advanced toward the railing, inclining forward, resisting the void that invited me below. A melody of red and gold lights danced in the distant depth, their fine appeal captivating. The roaring clap of nature reflected the turmoil within me. Standing on the peak of submission, I rose on my tiptoes, stretching my arms outwards, desperate to bridge the cavity between grief and consolation. The darkness covered me, alluring me to take that final step. In that insightful moment, with eyes shut and heart heavy, I leaned forward, embracing the unknown. *It would be so easy. Climb over. Let go. Float away.*

A sudden grip tautened around my arm, causing me to thunderbolt to alertness. Shocked, my eyes soared open to face Mark.

"Leave me alone!" I jerked my arm away, desperate to get away from his grasp.

Frenziedly trying to reach me, Mark lunged forward. However, the slippery surface underneath his shoes double-crossed him, causing him to lose his footing. His body rocked backward, crashing vigorously against the glass obstruction of the balcony. The collision was so acute that the glass shattered with a loud crack, sending innumerable razor-sharp smithereens flying in all directions. Like an avalanche of fatal confetti, the glass smashed into countless pieces.

Captured in a dreadful moment stuck in time, Mark teetered alarmingly on the edge. Fear occupied his wide-open eyes as he flapped his arms in a pointless endeavor to reclaim balance. But immediately gravity claimed its success. Mark surrendered to the inescapable, disappearing, leaving behind a spooky void. The incident was an eerie demonstration of the consequences that developed before my eyes, leaving me breathless and filled with a mix of astonishment and despair. It was a moment where deeds carried greater weight than mere speech, where the outcome of one's behavior became an uncanny actuality.

# Chapter 67

My knees buckled. A strangled scream twisted in my throat. I peered over the edge, but all I could see was blackness.

"Oh my God! Mark!" I clapped my hands over my mouth.

Nausea shimmered in my stomach. Panicking, I ran back inside, grabbed the blood-soaked pillow and my whiskey glass and raced straight out the front door. After tossing the pillow and the glass down the garbage chute, I hurried to the elevator and pressed the down button over and over.

*Was this really happening? Was Mark really dead? Maybe it was all a nightmare and I'd wake up and he'd still be alive.* But when the elevator door pinged, and the doors slid open, I knew it was true.

Mark was dead.

As the elevator slowly descended, I stared at my ghost white face in the mirror. My body was trembling uncontrollably, and a drum was beating inside my chest. *Mark was dead. Mark was dead.* No matter how many times I repeated the words in my head, it still didn't seem real. I never should have come here tonight. It was a big mistake.

When the elevator jolted to a stop at the ground floor, I hurried out of the building and into the pouring rain. Soaking wet and sobbing, I ran as fast as my feet would take me, in the direction of Beacon Hill.

As soon as I got home, I raced to my spare bedroom and grabbed the fish hook. Raising it high above my head, I sliced into the printed painting that I'd bought to feel closer to Mark. I tore into the paper, ripping it into long jagged lines, until it was a shredded mess. Next, I looked around for my journal. I wanted to rip it to shreds too. But it wasn't in my bedside drawer, and I was too worked up to hunt for it, so I shoved the fish hook in my pocket and made my way to the bathroom.

Opening the medicine cabinet, I grabbed my bottle of pills. *Gordie. Dad. Sean. Mark. All dead. Maddie hated me. Fired from the bookstore. Betrayed Fiona. I'd lose Paige too.*

I stared at my reflection in the mirror, with weary eyes. The world would be better off without me. I turned on the tap and filled a glass with water. *My miserable life will soon be over.*

But my plan was interrupted by a loud banging. Keeper started barking. Someone was knocking on my front door. Not again. Whoever it was, I wanted him or her to leave me alone.

I dumped the pills into my hand, until the bottle was empty. Then, I raised them to my mouth and opened it wide.

"Erin? What are you doing?"

My heart skittered like a skipping stone on water. I swiveled around, spilling the pills onto the floor.

It was Oliver. He was the last person I wanted to see.

"What am ***I*** doing? What are ***you*** doing here and how did you get into my house?

"I saw the lights were on. I knocked and knocked. I heard Keeper barking. But when you didn't answer, I got worried. So, I grabbed the spare key from behind the shutter." His hair was soaked and matted to his head.

Lightning crackled, and thunder rumbled off in the distance.

I noticed his dark, hooded sweatshirt and frowned. Maybe I hadn't been paranoid and he had been stalking me all this time. But I was too upset about Mark to care any more.

Oliver bent over and when he stood up, a deep crease had formed between his brows. "Where'd you get this?"

My breath hitched. He held Mark's fish hook in his outstretched hand. *It must've fallen out of my pocket.*

"This belongs to my brother. Did he give it to you?" Before I could answer, he threw it against the wall, and it splintered into two jagged pieces.

A lasso tightened around my throat. He was scaring me.

Keeper was circling his ankles, desperate for attention.

Oliver hovered over me, with a threatening look on his face. "Where were you tonight?"

"That's none of your business." Anger had replaced my fear. Mark had possessed my mind for months, but now, he was dead and I was certainly not going to let his brother take charge of me. I picked up the broken pieces of fish hook, shoving them in my pocket before Keeper tried to eat them. "You need to leave." I pushed past him and strode to the kitchen. I poured myself a glass of red wine and took three big gulps.

"Tell me where you were." Oliver had followed right behind me, and his voice tremored with rage.

"I already told you, it's not your concern."

He gripped my shoulders and shook me. Red wine sloshed onto the floor. His fingernails dug into my flesh like talons.

"***Tell me.***" He spat the words at me.

I tried to get free. "Let go. You're hurting me." Why was he treating me like this?

He slid his hands down my arms and wrapped his fingers around both of my wrists. "Tell me where you were."

I tried to break loose. "Where do you think I was?"

He looked me dead in the eye. "I want to hear you say it."

I glared at him, adrenaline fizzing through my veins. "I was here the whole night."

"You're a liar." His face crumpled, then he released my wrists and collapsed onto a chair.

I rubbed my aching wrists. "What are you talking about?"

"Why don't you just admit it?" His fingers tapped the table, like a ticking time bomb. "You were at Mark's."

He must've been following me. Or tracking me with one of his cybersecurity apps. I remembered Angus warning me that Oliver had cyber-stalked another woman. *And all this time, I thought the pills were making me paranoid.*

Suddenly, it was as if the pin was pulled out of a grenade. No man was ever going to control, belittle, or use me again. Not my dad. Not Sean. Not Dave. Not Mark. And, definitely not Oliver.

"It's none of your business where I was. Now, I asked you to leave—"

Oliver slammed the heel of his hand down on the table.

I flinched.

"How many times have you been with my brother?" His eyes were like two shining daggers. "Tell me the truth."

I dropped my eyes. What did it matter now? He was dead.

The freezer hummed and clicked, as ice cubes dropped into the bucket.

He pounded his fist against his forehead, over and over, until it left a red welt. "You fucked him on the island in Cape Cod, didn't you?"

I shook my head and spilt some of my wine.

"***Liar.***"

"Oliver, you need to calm down. You're scaring me." I had never heard him shout before and his outbursts startled me.

"What is it with you women?" He rocked back and forth on the chair. "I offer you my heart and you stomp all over it."

I needed to calm him down and get him out of my house.

His eyes were glassy with rage. "Girls have always been drawn to my brother. I never understood it. But that's the way it's always been."

"Oliver—"

His voice cracked and spit shot out of his mouth. "I thought you were different, but you're just like all the others."

His eyes, brilliant orbs of blazing yellow, bright from the intense fluorescent light, expressed his extreme ferocity. Immediately, he leaped forward, launching himself toward me, the power of his motion flooring a chair in his path. Time seemed to idle as he rapidly closed the space between us, overwhelming me in a heartbeat. With a vice-like grip, his hands wrapped around my throat, squeezing like a constrictor's lethal embrace.

"Stop! I can't breathe," I gasped, my hopeless cry hardly exiting my withered lips. Urgency flowed through me as I fought back, clawing and scratching at his face, trying to break free from his powerful hold.

Keeper, my loyal comrade, growled and nipped at his heel, striving to protect me. But with a brutal kick, he sent her soaring, her helpless yowl fleeting into a corner where she retreated, injured and afraid. As the blood raced to my head, the world around me blurred, the strain growing to intolerable levels. Just as I feared my very eyes would burst from their sockets, he suddenly removed his hands. I staggered backward, puffing for air, coughing forcefully in a desperate try to repossess control of my ruined lungs.

My gaze dashed across the room, landing upon my lifeline—the phone lying like a silent witness on the kitchen counter. It lured me, encouragement in my gloomiest hour. I knew I had to call for help, to get away from this nightmare.

But as if Oliver held the ability to read my thoughts, he charged for the phone with brutal tenacity. A thunderous smash reverberated through the room as he cruelly shattered it against the callous surface of the fridge. Disintegrated pieces of my only means of reaching out for protection lay littered on the floor, taunting my desperate need. Time froze around us, the air dense with danger. Oliver prowled back and forth, his primitive roars resounding through the room, his mouth foaming with unmanageable rage. Suddenly, he stopped, fixing me with eyes laden with nothing but unmitigated hatred—a fierce stare that shot shivers down my spine, alerting me of the forthcoming danger that still loomed.

"You're nothing but a slut." He lunged at me. "And a whore. I saw you at that club, flaunting yourself on the dancefloor."

"Please, Oliver, please don't hurt me." I clasped my hands around my bruised neck. My throat burned, and it was hard to swallow.

He shoved me to the ground and sat on top of me. "This is all your fault." He sneered down at me.

I bucked my hips, but he was like a bag of cement. "Please, you're crushing me."

His fingers circled my throat and squeezed.

I thrashed and kicked my legs, until they felt like rubber and went limp. I lay without moving.

His thumbs pressed into my neck. "Look what you made me do." His voice had gone strangely quiet.

A sense of calm descended on me. *Maybe I deserve this. What goes around, comes around.* My eyelids flickered. The light faded.

And just as I thought my life was over, he let go.

I gagged and gasped for air.

But the nightmare was far from over.

He grabbed a knife from the wooden knife block.

"Do not move."

"Please, Oliver." I sobbed, shaking, then stiffening with rigor. "I don't want to die."

"Shut up." He pressed the chef knife against my throat. "***Shut up!***

***Shut up! Shut up!***"

# Chapter 68

"Erin? Where are you?" A voice called from down the hallway.

*I must be hearing things.*

"Erin? It's me, Fiona," she said, bounding into the kitchen. "Your front door was unlocked. Why're you lying on the floor?"

"Fiona?" *What's she doing here?* "Help me," I said, my voice weak and hoarse.

"What on earth's going on?" Fiona asked, crouching down beside me. And then she saw him.

He'd hidden the knife behind his back.

I coughed and clung onto my friend.

All of a sudden, he lunged at us both with the stainless steel blade.

"What're you doing?" Fiona tried to dodge out of his way, but he knocked her over, and her head hit the floor. She lay there, silent and motionless.

Oliver hovered over me, pinning me to the floor with his knee. I saw a flash of steel. A sharp pain pierced my side, followed by a warm, tingling sensation. Panicking, I flailed my arms out to my sides and tried to push myself up. But I was too weak. And then I remembered the broken fish hook. The pieces were still in my pocket. A last shot of adrenaline raced through me. *I'm not going to die without a fight.* I clasped part of the jagged hook in my fingers and lifted it up, up, and then down into Oliver's gleaming green eye.

"***Ahh! You bitch!***" He clutched his eye with one hand, but still kept hold of the knife with the other.

I tried to wrench it away from him, but the handle was slippery with my blood.

The blade cut through the air, spattering blood on our faces.

"I think you've blinded me. ***You. Crazy. Bitch!***" Oliver loosened his grip on the knife.

With a surge of adrenaline flowing through my veins, I mustered every particle of might within me. Resolve charged my actions as I acquired control of the scenario, overpowering Oliver's ruthless attack. The blade, a tool of defense, found its mark, penetrating his chest with a puncturing thump. The released pain pulsated through the air, his creepy shriek echoing like a harmed animal in suffering. The heaviness of his buckling body pressed down upon me, the blade digging deeper into his flesh. Gasping for beloved breath, I struggled against the stifling load, my lungs laboring below the hard force. My hands, motivated by desperation, established their grip on his shoulders, and with a final rush of energy, I pressed with all my force. Inch by aching inch, I managed to remove myself from under his lifeless figure.

In the fight, my elbow slammed into the handle of the knife, displacing it from Oliver's now motionless body. The metallic sound of the blade clanging against the merciless floor filled the room, representing an eerie reminder of the brutality that had unfolded. A crimson flood spurted forth, like an enraged geyser, from the huge wound in his chest. His shirt, soaked in a gruesome display, bore proof to the life force seeping away. The merging blood spread across the floor, making a threatening stain that mirrored the merciless battle that had occupied us both. Oliver, now without consciousness, lay stationary, his absence of movement like a lifeless mannequin, a bleak testament to the unchangeable outcomes of our dreadful encounter.

Meanwhile, Fiona had regained consciousness and called the police.

"Help…hurry… please," she said, panting into her cell phone.

I pushed myself up onto my elbows and took sharp, painful breaths. Gripping the countertop with my fingertips, I pulled myself up to a standing position. My heartbeat hammered my head like a fist; my breathing ragged. If only it was a dream – a horrible nightmare, but a dream all the same – and I could make it disappear by simply opening my eyes. I would wake up, and it would all be over.

But there would be no easy escape. A cold sweat prickled my skin, trickled down my back and pooled at the base of my spine. The room tilted. Reaching out a shaking hand to steady myself, I stained the surface of the milky-white, marble countertop with a bloody palm print. My throat constricted; I was drowning under icy water. I heard a strangled cry. It seemed to come from far away. But when the same voice began to mewl like a motherless baby, I realized, with a start, that it was coming from inside of me. My knees buckled. The walls closed in. My vision narrowed to a pinhole. I saw flashes of light, and then, my world went black.

# Chapter 69

I spent the following week recovering at *City Center Hospital,* with Fiona down the hall from me in the same ward. It was strange to be back in the same hospital where Mark had worked. Now both he – and Oliver – were dead.

Lying in bed all day gave me far too much time to think. I kept thinking back to when my mother was hospitalized, and how attentive Mark had been to her. And then, my mind would jump to having sex with Mark in the on-call room. How did we go from that to him falling off his balcony? The whole experience with the Rankin brothers made me swear off men for the foreseeable future. I didn't know if I'd ever be ready to open myself up to a relationship again. My heart was too broken.

When a detective came by and asked me a few questions about Oliver and Mark, I was terrified that the police would catch me coming and going from Mark's building and penthouse on CCTV. But apparently, the thunderstorm had caused a power outage and the security cameras were blank during the time I was there.

Meanwhile, the police had turned my house into a crime scene. I couldn't go home yet, even if I wanted to. My mother told me they'd put yellow crime scene tape across the front door. My life had turned into an episode of *Dateline*. I could picture the detectives scouring every inch of my house for clues, dusting for fingerprints and studying blood spatter patterns. How had it all come to this?

When my thoughts got too dark, I'd switch on the television and watch reality shows. And I had a few visitors, which helped to distract me.

Dr. Pritchard paid me a visit, to help me deal with my ongoing PTSD. And my mom came by every day. Fortunately, she didn't press me with her usual barrage of questions. Instead, she'd update me on Keeper, who was recuperating at the veterinary hospital. And she'd babble on about the future shopping trips that we could go on or the weather or the local news. Listening to her talk, kept my mind off my own troubles, for a while anyway. And Paige dropped by a couple of times, too. She brought home-baked blueberry muffins and a pile of trashy magazines. Fiona joined us and with the three of us together, it was almost like old times—except we all knew nothing would ever be the same again.

*

A few weeks later, I was headed home from *Jacked Up Coffee*, when I sensed someone behind me. I checked over my shoulder, and the hair stood up on the back of my neck. A hooded figure was running down the street after me. It couldn't be Oliver; he was dead. Was it a delusion from the post-traumatic stress disorder? Dr. Pritchard had warned me about flashbacks, nightmares, and anxiety attacks. Maybe if I closed my eyes, he'd disappear. I pressed my lids shut, then opened them and glanced back. No, he was still there. He was real. The figure got closer and closer. My heart rapped inside my chest. I wanted to run, but my legs had turned to jelly. Blood pulsed in my ears. He was only a few yards away. *Someone help me.* But there was no one else around. The figure was almost upon me. My insides were liquid. A gloved hand clutched my elbow, and I screamed.

"Erin? Are you all right? It's me, Fiona."

"Fiona?"

"You look like you've seen a ghost."

I tried to calm my breathing. "I thought you were… oh, never mind. What are you doing here?"

"I was in the neighborhood and thought I'd drop by and check on you."

There was a sudden susurration of wind.

I shuddered and wrapped my arms around myself.

"Winter's on its way." Fiona handed me the white disposable cup she'd been clutching in her hand. "Here, this coffee will warm you up."

I nodded my thanks, then took a sip of coffee, almost gagging on the sweetness. Why had Fiona put so much sugar in it?

"Let's head to my place, and I'll put on a fire."

When we reached my house, Fiona's eyes scanned the exterior. "I see the police removed the yellow crime scene tape."

"Yeah, the forensics team finished up a few days ago, but they left a real mess. Still, I'm glad to be home. I love my mom, but weeks of her hovering over me, first at the hospital and then, at her small condo, were starting to feel suffocating. Anyway, I'm just thankful to be alive. If you hadn't shown up when you did and called the police…"

A look slid between us.

Fiona shook her head. "Oliver seemed so into you. And I thought he was such a nice guy."

"I thought he was a nice guy, too. Who knew he'd turn out to be a murderous maniac."

"It's still so hard to believe they're both dead." Fiona's forehead furrowed. "I know Mark broke up with me, but I was in love with him. For a while there, I was envisioning him as my future husband and the father of my children."

I gave her a hug, and we stood there for a few moments, wallowing in our mutual misery. Then I let her go and opened the door, and Fiona followed me inside. Keeper – now fully recuperated from her injuries – circled our legs, and Fiona gave her a perfunctory pat on the head.

"I'll just take her out." I scooped my tenacious pug up in my arms. "Have a seat in the living room. I'll be right back."

As grateful as I was to be back home, I knew my house would never feel quite the same. My mother had hired professional cleaners to decontaminate the kitchen and remove the bloodstains out of the white, porcelain tiles—but they couldn't remove my memory of the violent assault or the image of Oliver's blood-soaked body lying dead on my kitchen floor.

Once I'd taken care of my precious Keeper, I shuffled down the hall to the living room and lit a fire to take the chill out of the wintry air.

"Let me help you with that." Fiona picked up the poker, that stood next to the fireplace. After repositioning a fallen log, she leaned the heavy, steel poker against the wall and stood in the doorway.

"How're you feeling?" she asked.

I eased myself down into my wingback chair. Keeper settled by my feet. "I've been spending most of my time in bed." I shrugged. "Although I don't get much sleep, thanks to this." I lifted my shirt and pulled back the bandage, exposing the ladder of black stitches down my side. It had been two weeks since I had been released from hospital, but the scar, where Oliver had stabbed me, still throbbed and burned.

Fiona cringed. "Jeez. That's an ugly mess."

My neck muscles stiffened, and I quickly covered the wound and yanked my shirt back down. Something seemed off with Fiona, but I couldn't put my finger on it.

"Why don't you sit down for a few minutes?" I waved an arm at the couch, then winced from the small stab of pain in my side. "You're making me nervous, standing over there in the doorway."

Fiona lingered on the edge of the room, with her hands behind her back. "I can't stay too long. I've got to catch up on all the student marking that piled up, while I was off work."

"At least take your jacket off and that hood. I can barely see your face." I frowned at her and narrowed my eyes. "Are you still cold? You're still wearing your mittens. I can toss another log on the fire—"

Fiona fiddled with the strings of her black hoodie, but didn't take it off. "No, I'm fine. I just want to ask you a couple of questions, then I've got to go."

I had a question for her, too. Grateful as I was for Fiona's serendipitous appearance on the night Oliver attacked me, I still wondered what she'd been doing in Beacon Hill. Looking at my friend, her face cocooned in the hooded sweatshirt, a suspicion slowly started to take shape in my mind. Was she hiding something from me? I studied Fiona from across the room—who was standing stone-faced and silent.

"I still can't believe Mark and Oliver are both gone," she said, her voice monotone. "Can you believe it, Erin?"

I shook my head. A man out walking his dog had found Mark's broken body lying in a crumpled heap at the bottom of his building. The coroner on the scene said he'd died on impact. Because of the level of alcohol in Mark's bloodstream and the structural failure of the balcony railing, police had treated Mark's fall as an unfortunate accident. To my immense relief, there had been no criminal investigation.

Fiona raised her eyebrows. “What do you think set Oliver off that night?”

Part of me wrestled with longing to tell the full truth to Fiona. The heaviness of Oliver’s allegation hung thick in the air, and deep down, I knew he had been right all along—I had certainly dishonored Fiona’s trust by sleeping with Mark. My conscience craved the deliverance of revealing, of unloading my shame in the hope of finding salvation in Fiona’s forgiveness. But the words stayed stuck within, suffocated by fear, uncertainty, and the irreversible damage they could cause to our friendship. The stillness between us grew pregnant with unspoken admissions, a cavity broadening with each passing minute. It was an excruciating dance of secrets and regret, where the truth stewed beneath the surface, threatening to spill over and reshape our lives forever.

I shifted in my seat, then delivered my answer. “I have no idea.” I gulped down more coffee, wincing at the syrupy aftertaste. My head was woozy. I blinked and tried to focus on Fiona. Why did her face look so fuzzy?

The fire sputtered and hissed.

My throat was dry as dirt, so I swallowed down the rest of the coffee.

Suddenly, Fiona stepped towards me and slammed something down on the coffee table.

My eyes widened, with surprise. “Where did you get that?”

It was my brown leather-bound journal.

# Chapter 70

"I took it the night I came here to tell you that Mark had broken up with me."

My chest constricted.

"Oliver told me that you'd started to write a new story, and curiosity got the better of me."

My eyes bulged. "You've read it?"

Fiona gave a sharp nod.

*Oh my God. She's read it.* My ears buzzed, and my vision blurred.

"Why don't I read some of it to you?" Fiona snatched up the journal.

I gasped for breath. "No. Please don't." I leapt at Fiona and tried to grab the book from her fingers, but I stumbled, and Fiona jerked it out of reach.

Removing a glove, Fiona flipped through the pages, skimming the lines, until she found what she was looking for. She began to read, her voice eerily neutral. *"I envisioned pressing a pillow over Faith's mouth as she slept."*

"Please stop." I covered my face with my hands.

*"The lack of air might wake her up, and I pictured my sister's arms flailing wildly, but I would hold firm until I felt my sister's body convulse and her legs jerk and stiffen. And then, all would be still. She would be dead."*

A car alarm went off outside, and Keeper let out a series of loud snorts.

"I'm Faith, aren't I? And you're Eva."

"N-no, of c-course not." My voice shook. I peered at Fiona through the gaps between my fingers. "It's just a s-stupid story."

It had started to rain outside, and drops pattered against the windowpanes.

"I think I deserve the truth, don't you?" Fiona's eyes were black, and her face flamed red. "That time on the sailboat? And the bus? Were you trying to kill me?"

"What? No." My head jerked up and my hands fell from my face into my lap. "Those were accidents." I looked at Fiona with pleading eyes, but was met by the ice-cold stare of the dear friend I had betrayed—the friend who'd saved my life. "My journal is pure fiction. Writing it helped me fill the hours when I couldn't sleep." *And it helped me cope with all my mixed-up feelings about Mark.* "But there's no truth to it."

Freezing rain pelleted the roof above our heads like rifle shots.

"Give me that journal," I said, my voice cracking. "So I can rip it up and throw it into the fire."

Fiona ignored me and flicked through more pages. "What about this 'Max' character? He's Mark, isn't he?"

I blanched, and guilt plucked at my throat.

Fiona glared at me, with eyes hard as stone. "The truth is, you wanted my boyfriend. And, according to what you wrote in these pages, you were willing to kill me to get him."

"No! It's one hundred percent fiction. I swear to you!"

"I don't believe you." She dropped the journal on the floor by my feet and pulled her mitten back on. "What an idiot I've been. Paige warned me to watch my back, but I wouldn't listen."

A frown contracted my brow. *Damn Paige and her big mouth.*

"She said you had a crush on Mark, but I refused to believe her. We've been friends for too long. I said you'd never betray me like that. I told her she must be confusing Mark with Oliver. But I was wrong, wasn't I?"

I bit my tongue.

"Let me tell you why Oliver was so angry that night." Fiona paced back and forth. "I told him that I suspected there was something going on between you and Mark. At first, he said that was impossible. But then, I showed him your journal."

"You showed him my journal?" A bolt of anger burst inside my brain.

"Why would you do that?"

Fiona's voice was as hard as flint. "So he'd know the truth. Why don't you just admit it? You fucked Mark."

I covered my face with a throw pillow.

"I knew it!" Fiona shrieked. "How could you do that to me?"

"I don't know."

"You don't know? You don't know? Is that all you can say? Look me in the eyes." Fiona ripped the pillow away from me. "The least you can do is give me a reason."

"I don't want to make excuses," I said, my chest heaving. "But I haven't been myself since I lost Sean." *And Dad. And even little Gordie.* "And being on Prozac – and then, trying to get off them – made me lose my mind for a while."

"You're blaming this on pills? Seriously?" Fiona's eyes were like daggers. "Pills didn't make you fuck my boyfriend."

My head slumped down into my hands.

The silence was thick between us.

"Mark was mine. And you took him from me," Fiona's face reddened and she spat the words at me. "Why, Erin? Why did you do it?"

I teetered on a knife edge. "If you want the truth, I fell for Mark, because he was so much like Sean. You must have seen the similarity—"

"Of course I did." Fiona put both hands on her hips.

"Wait. What?" I scrunched my face, confused. "You did?"

"When I met Mark at the art show, I couldn't believe my eyes. It was as if Sean had come back to life."

"But Sean was my boyfriend, so why—"

"No, Erin. You're dead wrong. Sean was ***my*** boyfriend."

# Chapter 71

A chill shot down my spine. "What are you talking about?"

"He didn't love you. He loved me." Fiona spat each word out like a bullet from a gun. "And when he got the job in New York, he asked me to go with him."

"I don't believe this." My face reddened. All the hurt and anger I'd tried to bury, bubbled back up to the surface. "The night of the car crash, I thought Sean was going to propose. But instead—he dumped me. When I asked him if there was someone else, he denied it. I knew he was lying, but I never dreamt the someone else was you."

The fire snapped and sizzled.

"What about me?" Fiona said. "I spent months holding your hand, while you grieved for Sean. I had to pretend to be the caring, supportive friend, while inside, I was dying."

I was too shocked to speak. What a hypocrite. She'd berated me for sleeping with Mark, but she went after Sean. Who was this person standing in front of me? I felt like I didn't know her at all.

Silence stretched between us, like a bungee cord about to snap.

Fiona gave me a dead-eyed stare. "What *really* happened in the car that night? Why did Sean swerve off the road and hit the pole?"

I blinked slowly at her. "I don't remember."

"How convenient. I think you know the truth," Fiona said, giving me a needle-like look. "But you're too much of a coward to admit it."

"What is the truth, Fiona? Why don't you tell me?"

"When Sean told you it was over, you decided that if you couldn't have him, then no one would. You undid his seatbelt and—"

"No, no, no. You're wrong. Sean was careless about his seatbelt, no matter how many times I told him to wear it." The room spun around my head.

A neighbor's dog barked, and Keeper started howling.

Fiona's cell phone pinged in her pocket, but she ignored it.

A memory dislodged in my mind. Suddenly, I was tumbling down a dark tunnel towards a tiny pinprick of light. I leaned forward, elbows on my knees.

"It was dark. Sean was driving me home. I was too angry to speak. And then…"

"And then, you grabbed the steering wheel and sent him straight into an electrical pole—and killed him."

I shook my head. "No, you're wrong. I remember now. His phone pinged. It was lying on the console between us. There was a text message. I didn't have time to see who it was from. But I saw what it said." The four words flashed to the forefront of my mind.

*Did you tell her?*

"Sean panicked. He reached for the phone and that's all it took. He lost control of the car and… oh my God… the text was from you. If you hadn't sent that message," I said, under my breath, "he might still be alive."

But Fiona didn't seem to be listening. "You've taken three men from me," she said, her face white with fury.

My mind clouded with confusion. "*Three* men? What are you talking about?"

The corner of Fiona's lip curled. "A few months before he died, I ran into your dad at a Starbucks downtown. He bought me a latte. We started chatting. He was always such a charmer. Since we're spilling all our secrets, I might as well admit it. I'd always had a crush on your father – the great Gordon Fitzpatrick – so I seized my chance and one thing led to another…"

It hit me like a slap in the face. The conversation with my mother scrolled through my mind.

*"I think he'd started seeing someone… just before he died."*

*"By seeing someone, do you mean, Dad was having an affair? Who was she?"*

*"I never found out. But I think she was younger."*

My face flamed red with anger. "How could you do that to my mom—and to me?"

"Why is everything always about you?" Fiona looked at me with eyes like two black holes. "This is about what ***you*** did to ***me.***"

"What are you talking about?"

"You told me that you argued with Gordon the night he died. You're the reason he had a heart attack."

I shook my head from side to side. "It wasn't my fault." *Dad. Sean. Mark.* "It feels like you've had a vendetta against me, and I have no idea why. What did I ever do to you?"

"If you want to know the truth, it all started with Professor Douglas."

"Our English prof? Back in college?"

"He said my writing showed real promise, but he chose you for the Farrington's Literary Award and forgot all about me. I faded into the background and off to teacher's college I went. Now, I'm stuck teaching hormonal teenagers, day in and day out. Sometimes, I just want to kill myself."

"I thought you loved teaching—"

"Nope. Never did. But I got my revenge. Winning your father's affection and then Sean's, made me feel superior to the great Erin Fitzpatrick."

*I don't believe this. I thought you were my best friend...*

"Finally, I was the special one."

*...But all along, you hated me.*

"If you felt this way, why did you stay friends with me?"

"That's a good question. At first, I chalked it up to a force of habit. We've known each other for so long. But later, I came to realize that watching you fail gave me a sense of pleasure. You were supposed to be this great writer, but you ended up working at a bookstore."

*Schadenfreude.* She saw me as a rival, a frenemy, not a friend.

"After Sean died, I felt hollow inside. His death nearly destroyed me. But then I met Mark, and he looked just like Sean. But he was even better than Sean. He was a doctor. And he thought I was wonderful, and I felt on top of the world, again." Fiona took a step towards me and jabbed a finger in the air. "But you can never let me be happy. You always have to wreck everything."

A heavy silence fell between us, like a lead curtain.

Fiona gave me a withering look, then angled away from me and stared out the window at the black sky.

Water gurgled down through the gutters outside. Thunder rumbled in the distance.

I clutched at the arms of my chair. Time slowed. A pain stabbed me behind my eyeballs. My thoughts spiraled. I heard a loud *thunk.* A log had tumbled to the edge of the fireplace, scattering embers dangerously close to the rug. I stood up and the room swayed. The pain in my side throbbed, as I tottered towards the fire, grabbed the poker, and pushed the log back inside the grate.

"Oliver really cocked things up," Fiona said, turning to face me.

I swiveled around, the steel rod clutched in my hand. *Cocked things up? What did she mean?*

Fiona gave me another withering look and curled her lips in disgust. "He couldn't get the job done and almost killed me in the process."

I gasped.

Fiona smirked and fixed me with an ice-cold stare. "Oh, and one more thing…"

The hair sprung up on the back of my neck.

"…You're a second-rate writer."

Fiona's school-teacher tone pierced my brain like a needle.

I held the poker firmly, my knuckles turning white as I raised it high above my head. The heaviness of the metal weapon filled my hands, its iciness sending shakes up my arms. The room fell silent except for Keeper's shocked yelp, a high-pitched sound that punctured the air. Her eyes enlarged with fear, her body automatically recoiling, observing the threatening danger.

In that split second, Fiona's face twisted with horror. A frightening shriek tore through her lips, ringing through the room. It was a sound that carried the mass of her fear, a primal cry born from the center of her soul. The poker came down with an impact fueled by anger and desperation. Time seemed to slow as it connected with Fiona's skull, the nauseating crack filling the room. Her body fell to the ground, a lifeless pile, the blow extinguishing any outstanding flicker of spirit.

There she lay, motionless, her pale face stained with blood oozing.

It bled slowly from the slash, forming a gruesome pool on the floor—a pure testament to the savagery of the act and the final consequences of my actions.

# Epilogue

I sat at my desk by the window and gazed out at the lake, through the gaps in the evergreen forest. The mountains loomed in the distance beyond, keeping a watchful God-like eye on the creatures below. The rays of the early morning sunrise painted the peaks a golden hue, and their mirrored twins were reflected in the water with perfect symmetry. But a moment later, a gentle breeze rippled the calm surface of the water, blurring the image.

I stretched my arms up above my head, towards the wooden beams in the cathedral ceilings of my log cabin.

"Time to head into town for groceries, old girl," I said to Keeper, my faithful companion.

A ray of sunlight filtered through the window, casting a ghostly shadow in the corner. Skittish in her old age, the portly pug let out a low growl, as she stood and stared into the empty space. I ruffled her head.

"There's nothing there but shadows, silly. Come on, let's go."

After driving into the town center, I decided to park and walk down the main street before getting groceries. I had my eye on a rocking chair at the antique store. It would be perfect for my mother to sit in on the porch, while sipping a glass of white wine and watching the sunset in the evening when she came to visit.

As I passed the district courthouse, the memory of my trial floated into my mind. Thank God my mother had hired a top-notch criminal defense attorney. His experience and skill, coupled with Dr. Pritchard's testimony, had saved me from a life in prison. Five years later, I could still hear the judge's words ringing in my ears: *"Not guilty, by reason of temporary insanity."*

I still suffered flashbacks, from time to time – Gordie, Dad, Sean, Mark, Oliver and Fiona – I had a lot of blood on my hands, so to speak. And the trauma was cumulative. The pain of each loss didn't just vanish overnight. One built upon the next, like blocks in a pyramid. Checking in with Dr. Pritchard by phone once a month was critical to my recovery. And so were the pills I continued to take. As the good doctor said, *"The healing process is a marathon, not a sprint."*

The main street of the small town was empty, except for two young women standing in front of the independent bookshop and examining the display in the window.

As I approached, they turned and one woman's face instantly gleamed with recognition.

"It's you, isn't it?"

I gave a slight nod.

"You're Erin Fitzpatrick. I love your books!" The young woman turned to her friend. "She's a famous author. She's had two books on the *New York Times* bestseller list. Her last one was number one for most of last year. I can't wait to see the movie. Would you mind if I took a selfie with you?"

A smile split my face and I complied with my fan's request.

But when Keeper and I moved away, I overheard the young woman whisper excitedly to her friend, "She's the one that killed her boyfriend and her best friend—remember, it was in all the papers a few years ago? I heard she got over a million bucks for her first book! But now, she hides away like a hermit – all alone – in a cabin in the woods."

My smile faded. And I felt a familiar tightening in my chest. Even though Fiona had turned out to be more frenemy than friend, I still missed her. I walked down the street, with Keeper in tow.

"Time for a shot of scotch, old girl."

With all the death in my life, I'd developed a taste for the hard stuff.

As Sinatra used to say, *"Alcohol may be man's worst enemy, but the Bible says, love thy enemy."*

# Acknowledgements

First, I'd like to thank the team at Kingsley Publishers for making my dream come true and publishing my debut thriller novel.

I'd also like to thank my family for all of their support. Karen McCarthy and Jack Fitton-McCarthy are my biggest champions. Cheers to my faithful writing companions, pug dogs Keeper (RIP), Digger and Pepper—I couldn't have done it without you. My parents, Richard and Meg Crabbe, my brother Geordie, as well as the McCarthy clan, have all given me lots of encouragement. In fond memory of my aunt, Maxine Goldberg, who gave me my first copy of Jane Eyre, which made me truly fall in love with reading. And in memory of my cousin, Dorothy Stannard, who also dreamed of being a writer.

Thanks also to my friends Mary Hewlett, Jill Strimas, and Robyn Fraser, a fellow author. Deepest gratitude to my friends and early readers: Leanne Dean, Kerry Sagar, and Diana Donato.

A special shout-out to life coach and fellow author Robin Blackburn McBride, who helped me believe that writing a novel and having it published was an achievable dream.

Especially grateful for the camaraderie of my Toronto writing group: Marsha Faubert, Catherine Fogarty, Margaret Lynch, and Katherine McCall.

Thank you to Margot Daley Photography for my author photo.

A key stage of the writing process is the editing phase, and I'm indebted to my editors over the years. Thank you to Emily Donaldson for reading my first and roughest draft. Thanks to author Ibi Kaslik, my novel writing instructor from the School of Continuing Studies at the University of Toronto, who edited a draft of my book and told me it deserved to be published. Thank you also to Emily Ohanjanians Editing. And finally, much gratitude to Jessica Cara Hallier, a meticulous copy editor.

Last but not least, I'd like to thank my high school English teacher, Mrs. Barbara Tangney, who first emboldened me to write.

# About The Author

C. Fitton, an avid reader of thrillers, lives in Toronto, Canada. She is a former high school English teacher, with a certificate in creative writing from the University of Toronto.

Currently, she is a PhD candidate in English Research at King's College London. Her personal essays have been published in Canada's national newspaper. She enjoys walking her pugs, kayaking on Lake Ontario, and traveling the world.

*Her Dead Boyfriend* is C. Fitton's first novel.

Connect with C. Fitton on social media.
**Instagram:** @pugsnpages
**Threads:** @pugsnpages
**Facebook:** Catharine Fitton Author
**Website:** www.cfitton.com

**Or her special readers group on Facebook:**
Official C. Fitton Reader Group